The Benevolent Society of Ill-Mannered Ladies

The Benevolent Society of Ill-Mannered Ladies

ALISON GOODMAN

BERKLEY PRIME CRIME
NEW YORK

BERKLEY PRIME CRIME
Published by Berkley
An imprint of Penguin Random House LLC
penguinrandomhouse.com

Copyright © 2023 by Alison Goodman
Readers Guide copyright © 2023 by Alison Goodman
Penguin Random House supports copyright. Copyright fuels creativity, encourages diverse voices, promotes free speech, and creates a vibrant culture. Thank you for buying an authorized edition of this book and for complying with copyright laws by not reproducing, scanning, or distributing any part of it in any form without permission. You are supporting writers and allowing Penguin Random House to continue to publish books for every reader.

BERKLEY and the BERKLEY & B colophon are registered trademarks and BERKLEY PRIME CRIME is a trademark of Penguin Random House LLC.

Library of Congress Cataloging-in-Publication Data

Names: Goodman, Alison, author.
Title: The Benevolent Society of Ill-Mannered Ladies / Alison Goodman.
Description: First Edition. | New York: Berkley Prime Crime, 2023. |
Series: The Ill-Mannered Ladies; 1
Identifiers: LCCN 2022050253 (print) | LCCN 2022050254 (ebook) |
ISBN 9780593440810 (trade paperback) | ISBN 9780593440827 (ebook)
Classification: LCC PR9619.3.G62 B46 2023 (print) |
LCC PR9619.3.G62 (ebook) | DDC 823/.914—dc23/eng/20221028
LC record available at https://lccn.loc.gov/2022050253
LC ebook record available at https://lccn.loc.gov/2022050254

First Edition: May 2023

Printed in the United States of America
6th Printing

Title page art: Roses © lisima / shutterstock.com; Dagger © omnimoney / shutterstock.com; Pistol © armi1961 / shutterstock.com

Book design by Elke Sigal

This is a work of fiction. Names, characters, places, and incidents either are the product of the author's imagination or are used fictitiously, and any resemblance to actual persons, living or dead, business establishments, events, or locales is entirely coincidental.

*This book is dedicated to all the women
out there who no longer have the patience or desire
to put up with any nonsense.*

Case 1

Till Death Us Do Part

1

SATURDAY, JUNE 6, 1812

We were to meet him at midnight in the Dark Walk. It was not an ideal arrangement: two unaccompanied women confronting a blackmailer in the most ill-lit, deserted part of Vauxhall Gardens. Still, I had come prepared—more or less. Now all we had to do was wait until the hour was upon us.

I angled my pendant watch at the oil lamps hanging high in the branch above my head but could not make out the dainty face. The famous light show was near its end; the thousand or so colored lamps, strung in festoons around the trees and pavilions, had all begun to gutter. Well, for once my unladylike height would be an advantage. Raising myself onto tiptoes, I lifted the timepiece to the dying glow of the nearest lamp. Finally, a glint of gold hands: a quarter to midnight.

I touched my sister's arm. She turned from watching the dancers silhouetted before the orchestra tower.

"Already?" she asked over Mr. Handel's soaring music.

"It is at least ten minutes to the Dark Walk."

She drew her lilac shawl tightly around her shoulders. "Are you sure we should do this, Gussie? We cannot trust this man to keep his word, especially in such a lonely place. He could attack us."

She was right. Mr. Harley had already proved himself dishonorable, and while the Dark Walk had a reputation as an illicit meeting place for lovers, it also had a grim history of assaults upon women, and sometimes even men. Nevertheless, I had promised Charlotte, Lady Davenport, that we would retrieve her letters as discreetly as possible. She had stood by us after the scandalous death of our father, so there had been no question that we would help her in return. Honor was not only the province of men, despite popular belief.

I hefted my reticule up between us, the rock within stretching the knitted purse out of its pineapple shape. All in all one of my less successful knitting efforts, but at least it made a substantial weapon.

My sister eyed it with misgiving. "We will end up transported to the colonies."

"Nonsense. I doubt I will have to use it. He wants his payment; we want the letters. It will be a straightforward exchange." More to the point, I *hoped* I would not have to use it. The idea for the makeshift weapon had come to me very late—less than an hour before we left for the gardens—so I had only managed twenty minutes of swinging practice in the stables. I hit my target two out of ten times: not an inspiring score.

Julia blew a resigned breath, the force of it fluttering the curl of purple feathers in her hair. Lilac shawl, purple feathers, gray gown; the shades of mourning. June and its sad anniversary of her betrothed's death was always a difficult month for my dear girl.

"Do you have the necklace?" I asked.

She held up her own reticule by its drawstring, the black beaded purse swinging between us like a pendulum. "I have checked it twenty times since we arrived. Will Lord Davenport not notice such beautiful diamonds gone?"

"Charlotte says he notices nothing but claret, cards, and horses." Which was to say, he was like every other married man in London.

"Lady Augusta! Is that Lady Julia with you?" a shrill voice called out. "But of course it is. How pleasant to see you both."

Julia squeezed her eyes shut and resolutely stayed facing the orchestra. "Oh Lud. We do not have time for her."

Indeed, we did not. But unlike Julia, I already faced the owner of the voice, and so had to smile our welcome as she advanced upon us.

"Lady Kellmore, how do you do?" I called back. I glanced at my sister. *We should run.*

Julia's mouth quirked. *I wish we could.* Sometimes we did not need to speak our thoughts to each other; we could read them within the other's face. Our father had called it our *langue de twin.*

Reluctantly, my sister turned to add her greeting and gave a soft groan, her pain no doubt due to the approaching burgundy-, orange-, and apple-green-striped gown.

"I am frozen to the marrow!" Lady Kellmore declared. "This summer may as well call itself winter and be done with it." She dipped a curtsy in answer to our own, her thin-lipped mouth pulled down into a grimace of sadness. "I am here with my brother's party but thought to offer my condolences to you, Lady Julia, since it is the second anniversary of Lord Robert's accident. I always said yours would have been the wedding of the year. We had all waited so long for one of you Colebrook twins to marry." She glanced my way, gathering me into the horror of our long spinsterhood. "Alas, it was not to be, was it? My own dear Kellmore is, of course, third cousin once removed to the Hays and it was such a blow to the family." She peered more closely at Julia's rictus smile. "And to you, of course. I see that you grieve still."

My sister managed to nod.

Holy star, if the woman kept this up she would drive Julia straight into an ocean of despair. This Vauxhall venture was meant to distract my sister from her sorrow, not exacerbate it. I took Julia's arm in preparation to leave, but Lady Kellmore was already wading into deeper waters.

"Such bad luck." Her green-gloved fingers momentarily circled the crepey folds of her throat. "To break one's neck during the hunt, and on such a low fence. Kellmore told me Lord Robert was always coming off—not the best of seats—but this time . . ." She brought her hands together in a muffled clap that made my sister flinch. "Snapped clean through. I blame that nasty Lord Brandale and his stupid course. It was all so sad."

"It was indeed a sad time," I said before Julia could engage. "Alas, we are on our way home, but it has been such a pleasure to see you again."

I gave a nod of farewell and tugged on my sister's arm, steering her down the small slope toward the orchestra tower. Her body was as tense as a harp string, the soft curve of her jaw clenched so hard that for once it matched my own angular lines.

"Put her out of your mind, dearest," I said over the opening bars of a finishing dance. "She means well but has all the delicacy of a draft horse."

"She is quite wrong about Robert's seat—it was admirable," Julia hissed as we skirted the dancers and stepped off the flattened grass onto the raked gravel of the Grand Walk.

I refrained from commenting—I had seen Lord Robert ride—but Julia's anger was heartening. Anything was better than the deep melancholy of the last two weeks.

Before us, festoons of blue and red lamps hung between the sycamore and elm trees that lined the wide path, their illumination still reassuringly steady. The Grand Walk was the heart of the pleasure gardens, but the company was scant here too. Most of the supper boxes that fronted the walkway had been vacated, only a few parties still drinking sack and picking at the dishes before them. We passed the box we had hired, decorated with Mr. Hayman's Maypole dancers painted upon the back wall, its beauty obscured by two waiters deftly stacking our abandoned dishes. The smell of roasted chicken and ham lingered in the air, reminding me I had been too distracted to eat the supper we had ordered. It was clear the evening's entertainment was almost at its end: the gardens would be closing soon. The Dark Walk would most likely be deserted by now. An ominous prospect. Then again, we did not want any witnesses to our sordid exchange.

I linked my arm through Julia's, for warmth as much as solidarity, and we crunched along the wide boulevard.

"We should have worn half boots," I said. "I can feel every pebble through my slippers."

"One cannot wear half boots with full dress," Julia said firmly. "Even in circumstances of duress."

I stifled a smile. My sister's sense of style and occasion was always impeccable, and rather too easy to poke.

Julia glanced sideways at me. "Oh, very funny. Next you'll be suggesting we wear unmentionables."

"If only we could," I said. "Breeches would be far more convenient than silk gowns."

"How would you know?" Julia demanded. "Heavens, Gus, you haven't actually donned Father's clothing, have you?"

She knew I had kept some of our father's clothes after his death; he and I had been much the same height and wiry build. By all rights, the clothes belonged to our brother on his succession to the title—as all our father's property did—but I had taken them anyway. A connection to him and a memento mori of sorts.

"Of course not. I am only surmising."

Julia settled back against my arm. "To even try them would be ghoulish." She nudged me gently and angled her sweet smile up at me. "Even so, you would look rather dashing in, say, a hussar's uniform. You have the commanding height for it, and the gold trim would match your hair."

I snorted. Julia was, as ever, being too loyal. My brown hair did not even approach gold—in fact, it now had streaks of silver—and my five foot nine inches had so far in my life proved to be more awkward than commanding. She, on the other hand, had been blessed with the Colebrook chestnut hair, as yet untouched by age, and stood at a more dainty five foot two inches.

When we were children I had once cried because we were not identical. Our father had taken me aside and told me that he found such duplications unsettling and he was well satisfied with his two mismatched girls. He had been a good father and a better man. Yet in the eyes of society, his sordid death atop a rookery whore five years ago had become the sum of him.

It had nearly tainted my sister and me, too, for I had recklessly gone to the hovel to retrieve my father—I could not bear to think of his body gawped at by the masses, or as a source of their sport. As fate would have it, I was seen at the brothel. An unmarried woman of breeding should not even know about such places, let alone debase herself by entering one and speaking to the inhabitants. I became the latest on-dit and it was only the staunch support of our most influential friends that silenced the scandalmongers and returned us to the invitation lists.

A small group of middlings—the women with shawls clasped over dimity gowns and the men in belcher neckerchiefs and sober wools—clustered around a singer at the side of the path. The woman's plaintive ballad turned Julia's head as we passed.

"'The Fairy Song,'" she said. "One of Robert's favorites."

I quickened our pace past the memory; fate seemed to be conspiring against me.

We attracted a few glances as we walked toward the gloomy entrance to the Dark Walk, mainly from women on the arms of their spouses, their thoughts in the tight pinch of their mouths.

"Maybe we should have brought Samuel and Albert," Julia whispered. She had seen the matronly judgment too.

"Charlotte does not want our footmen knowing her business," I said. "Besides, we are not quivering girls in our first season. We do not need to be chaperoned all the time."

"Do you remember the code we girls made up to warn each other about the men in our circle?" Julia asked. "The code based on these gardens."

"Vaguely." I searched my memory. "Let me see: a Grand Walk was a pompous bore, a Supper Box was a fortune hunter . . ."

"And a Dark Walk was the reddest of red flags," Julia said. "Totally untrustworthy, never be alone with him. It was based on all those awful attacks that happened in the Dark Walk at the time. Do you recall?"

I did—respectable young girls pulled off the path and assaulted in the worst way.

"That was more than twenty years ago, my dear. We are women of forty-two now, well able to look after ourselves."

"That is not what Duffy would say."

Indeed, our brother, the Earl of Duffield, would be horrified to know we had gone to Vauxhall Gardens on our own, let alone braved the lewd reputation of the Dark Walk.

"Duffy would have us forever hunched over embroidery or taking tea with every mama who saw her daughter as the new Lady Duffield."

"True," Julia said, "but you are so vehement only because you know this is beyond the pale. Not to mention dangerous."

I did not meet her eye. My sister knew me too well.

"Well, we are here, anyway," I said, indicating the Dark Walk to our right.

Huge gnarly oaks lined either side of the path, their overhanging branches almost meeting in the middle to make a shadowy tunnel of foliage. One lamp lit the entrance but I could see no other light farther along the path. Nor any other person.

"It lives up to its name," Julia said.

We both considered its impenetrable depths.

"Should we do as Duffy would want and turn back?" I asked.

"I'd rather wear dimity to the opera," Julia said and pulled me onward.

I knew my sister just as well as she knew me.

Above us, the leafy canopy made the air seem even colder, and only the glimpses of the half-moon between the branches provided light. The bright sounds of the pleasure gardens—music and voices and the distant clash of crockery—grew more and more muffled as we trod the path.

"Charlotte said we were to head in the direction of the mural of the artist, and Mr. Harley will hail us at some point," I whispered. The mural was, apparently, a painted joke: the canvas depicting an artist with ladder and pots and brushes who was painting the very mural upon which he stood. I peered into the gloom, finding the faint outline of a very large rectangle at the far end of the long path, the moonlight falling upon it in a strange, flat manner. "I think that may be it up ahead."

"Why is Charlotte not doing this herself?" Julia asked. "Why did you say we would do it?"

"Because she invited us to all her routs and dinners after Father died and did not allow anyone to turn their back on us."

Charlotte had been one of those friends who had used all her position and influence on my behalf without any expectation of return. In fact, she had not even asked for this favor to reclaim her letters from her blackmailing lover. Rather, I had offered our services when she told me the sorry tale. It had seemed the perfect way to repay her generosity and at the same time distract my sister.

"You are exaggerating again," Julia protested. "I remember no one turning their back."

I tucked in my chin. My sister had a tendency to rewrite history. No, that was too harsh. She saw a kinder, godlier world than I did; a happy outlook that I was determined she should keep. I knew, from experience, that the alternative was far too bleak.

Julia allowed me to quicken our pace. "We should have brought a lamp."

"From where? The convenient lamp shop beside the orchestra?" My voice held too much edge.

"Don't be such a Miss Snippety-snup," Julia said.

I pressed her arm in apology. Uncertainty and ill-conceived plans always made me sharp.

"Ah." She pointed. "Do you see?"

Indeed, I did: a dim glow, set beyond the edge of the path. A lamp. The light moved forward as we approached, and the figure of a man in a tall beaver hat and greatcoat stepped onto the path.

"Mr. Harley?" I inquired.

The man bowed. From what I could see in the light from his lamp, he was well-made, with a neat waist and wide shoulders made even more impressive by the extravagance of capes upon his greatcoat. He failed a little, perhaps, in his height: an inch or so shorter than myself, although he definitely had the weight and reach advantage. I could smell Price and Gosnell's lavender water, the same scent our brother wore. The choice of the fashionable man, or, more likely in this case, the man aping his betters. His face was handsome, too, in an expected kind of way: nothing overly individual but everything well modeled. A broad brow, a bold chin, and a wide mouth currently sporting a charming smile. The truth of Mr. Harley, however, was in his eyes: pale blue and narrowed into an expression of irritated calculation. Why on earth had Charlotte risked so much for him?

"She has sent you?" he demanded. "Of course she did. Not one for facing consequences."

"If you refer to the Countess of Davenport then, yes, we are her emissaries." His obnoxious manner prompted me to voice my thought. "I cannot see what she saw in you, though."

His smiled widened. "The countess was quite satisfied with our liaison. Why, she was so satisfied she could barely move from the bed."

My cheeks heated. Beside me, Julia gasped and gripped my arm to steady herself in the face of such vulgarity.

"Now to the matter at hand," Harley added, his voice shifting from sly innuendo into brisk business. "Follow me."

He turned and stepped farther into the bushes, the light illuminating a rough track. From the fresh snap of branches and trampled grass, it had been recently forced.

Julia tugged my sleeve. "Gus, we cannot go off the path."

"Mr. Harley, we will deal here," I said loudly to his retreating back.

He stopped and turned, the yellow lamplight catching his frown. "No, Lady Augusta, we will deal where I say we deal."

So he knew who we were. I should have expected it. A man with such a calling would, of course, be in possession of a well-thumbed *Debrett's*.

"I think not," I said, keeping my voice measured. "We deal here or we do not deal at all."

He stood for a moment—at least five of my hard heartbeats—then slowly retraced his steps. Beside me, Julia gave a shallow sigh of relief.

I glanced at her and tilted my head: *Stand behind me, dearest.*

Her mouth tightened: *I stay at your side.*

Brave girl, but I knew she was not built for confrontation. I widened my eyes: *Please!*

Reluctantly, she stepped back. I was, after all, fifteen minutes the elder and seven inches taller. Besides, I had the rock. I shifted my reticule, feeling the reassuring swing of it.

He stopped before me and looked both ways along the path. In the distance, the shadowy figure of a man stood before the mural, apparently studying it with intensity. Otherwise the Dark Walk was empty, the leaves of the moon-silvered trees around us whispering in the cool night breeze.

"Show me the necklace," he said.

"Show me the letters," I said, matching his curt tone.

We gauged each other—both standing our ground—and he gave a slight nod. I turned to collect Julia's reticule as Mr. Harley reached inside his greatcoat.

"I believe we can make a—" I stopped, for I was staring into the barrel of a pistol. A sixteen-bore, if I was not mistaken. The cur had actually drawn a gun upon us.

"Give it to me, Lady Augusta," Mr. Harley said.

Rage as much as fear wound my hand back. I swung my reticule at him with all my strength, the silk-clad rock slamming upward into his nether regions. He gave a piercing shriek and, for an instant, I saw the shock upon his face. I had found my mark! He crumpled to his knees, lamp and gun dropping from his hands into the undergrowth. I lunged and scooped up the gun. Harley was already rising from his pain, his face red and his expression murderous. He had to stay down. I tapped him sharply across the temple with the gun butt, just enough to knock him free of his senses. At least I hoped it was just enough; there was always a margin for error.

He toppled heavily onto his side.

For a moment, Julia and I stared at his prone body.

"Oh, Gus, what have you done?" Julia finally said, her voice soft with horror.

"He is not dead." My words were more hope than certainty.

"He could have shot you! He could have shot me!"

"No. It was not cocked."

If there was one thing I did know, it was whether a gun was cocked or not: the advantage of having a hunting-mad father and a very careful gamekeeper who had not balked at teaching a young lady how to shoot. Whether or not I had known it before I struck the man was another matter altogether—one best left unpicked.

"Here, hold this." I passed Julia the pistol—only a small tremble in my hand—and retrieved the fallen lamp, still alight. I peered into Harley's face. Alarmingly pale. I pulled my glove off and gingerly cupped my bare fingers near his nose and mouth. Ah, a soft expulsion of air upon my skin. I had not killed him. For that, I was thankful. I set the lamp down and edged my hand into his greatcoat pocket. Empty.

"Hurry," Julia urged, holding the pistol as if it were a dead rat. "Someone is coming!"

By the sound of his footsteps, the man who had been viewing the mural was heading our way at some speed. I wrenched the other side of Mr. Harley's greatcoat out from under the weight of his body and thrust my hand into the freed pocket. My fingers closed around a wad of paper tied with ribbon.

"I say, are you all right down there?" the man called.

Julia slid the gun into her reticule as I pulled the wad free. A stack of letters, with an address scrawled in Charlotte's hand upon the top packet.

Mr. Harley stirred, his eyelids fluttering open.

I leaned in, only inches from his bemused expression. "Leave London, Mr. Harley," I said slowly and clearly, "or we will expose you for the blackguard you are. Do you understand?"

The sense of my words locked into his eyes. He nodded.

"Is that you, Lady Julia? Is Lady Augusta with you?" I recognized the voice: Bertie Helden. Not the sharpest needle in the case, but a gentleman to the core. "Are you all right? I must say, I don't think Duffield would want to see you here."

I rose from my crouch and wrapped my glove around the letters, hiding the package in the folds of my muslin skirts.

"Lord Cholton, well met," Julia said brightly as Bertie peered in upon our scene, his round face flushed from exertion. "We are well, but we were passing and saw this poor man. He seems to have collapsed."

Bertie considered the figure of Harley and shook his head. "I'll wager the fool is just foxed. I am sorry you had to see such a display. Do not worry, I shall inform the garden constables."

"Thank you, Lord Cholton," I said and curtsied.

Taking the cue, my sister curtsied, too, and we retreated along the path as Bertie bent to the aid of the detestable and dazed Mr. Harley.

2

ST. GEORGE'S HANOVER SQUARE CHURCH, LONDON

Holy Communion used to give me comfort, but now it was a hollow act. I crossed myself and pressed my lips over the sour-cherry taste of the wine. Reverend Cartwright made the holy sign, wiped the chalice rim with its white cloth, and stepped across to the next supplicant kneeling at the altar rail.

He had not yet recognized the goat among his flock of lambs: a somewhat oblivious shepherd.

I rose from my knees, gathered my hem from the danger of my bootheels, and followed Julia back along the aisle to our box. A few months ago, that short journey would not even have registered upon me. Now it felt as if all eyes seared through my chest, finding the black stain of doubt upon my heart. A foolish notion, and yet the thought of being discovered was insupportable. To be an apostate was worse than being Catholic.

More to the point, if Julia found out I no longer believed, her fear for my eternal soul would be more painful than the doubt itself. It would be too cruel to rock her faith when she needed it most.

Six months ago our doctor had diagnosed a small thickening within her breast. He had said it was likely to be cancer, but he could not be sure. On that slim uncertainty, Julia had made me promise not to dwell upon it in either thought or conversation. It was God's will, she had said, and so she could bear whatever was to come. Even then, something within me balked at such a statement. What kind of god allowed such suffering—the untimely demise of a beloved betrothed and father and now a breast canker—to fall upon one of his most devoted worshippers? Certainly not one that I wished to exalt.

I swung open the oak door of our box and sat back down on the cushioned pew next to my sister. Our father had purchased the family box in St. George's years ago, partly because the church was convenient to his two London addresses, but mainly because it was the most fashionable church in London. Perhaps the god whose existence I now questioned would smite me for sitting in his house. A philosophical absurdity—if he did not exist then he could not smite me. In the last month or so I had found it took a great deal more philosophy to doubt than it did to believe.

Charlotte sat in the opposite box, eyes downcast as if in prayer, but I could see her expression: set somewhere between boredom and impatience. I had her letters and diamond necklace wrapped discreetly in a linen handkerchief in my reticule, ready for their triumphant return. She must have felt my attention, for she looked up and smiled. I glanced at the doors of the church and tilted my head: *Meet me after the service?* She nodded.

I still could not reconcile the idea of her with Mr. Harley. I suppose there was no accounting for the draw of carnal desire. I had not truly felt that kind of yearning for some time and so perhaps I had forgotten the power of it. What made one person ache for the touch of another, especially if there was little love in the equation? The question occupied my mind until we were finally released into the unusually humid morning.

"That was a rather long sermon," Charlotte commented as I

joined her on the portico. She stood beside the last stone column, fanning herself and keeping her other acquaintances at bay with a haughty tilt of her head.

"Perhaps he is hoping to bore the sin out of us," I said.

Charlotte waved her fan down her elegant length. "Then, behold, I am sinless."

"I doubt it, my dear," I said dryly, winning an earthy laugh from my friend. "Still, you are now at least safe from the sins of others." I drew out the letters and necklace, wrapped discreetly in linen, from my reticule. A glance at the open church door reassured me we were unobserved by the departing congregation. "We not only retrieved your letters but, as it transpired, kept the necklace as well."

Charlotte closed her fan and took the packet. "Thank you, Augusta." She clasped my hand for a second, a gesture that spoke volumes, for she was not one for casual intimacies. She tucked the packet into her own reticule. "But how did you manage to keep the diamonds? The Edward Harley I know would not give up such a prize easily."

I gave a quick summary of the previous night's adventure.

"Good God, he drew a gun upon you? I knew he was a touch smoky, but I did not expect him to be an out-and-out scoundrel. I am glad he is leaving London, but I am sorry to have put you both in such danger."

I waved away the apology. "It certainly distracted Julia from her melancholy."

Charlotte looked across the portico where my sister stood in conversation with the vicar. "Are you sure? Forgive me, but she still looks rather wan to me."

"It is just this sudden heat," I said. "I assure you Vauxhall did her a world of good."

Charlotte blinked at the false note in my voice, but I could not air my true concern. Julia had not only forbidden me to dwell upon her diagnosis; she had also sworn me to complete secrecy. The knowledge of it sat within me like a flinty stone, always grating upon my spirit but occasionally shifting into this sharp jab of fear.

Old Mr. Pontworth walked past on his cane, nodding his farewell to us. We returned the salute with smiles. Charlotte waited until he was out of earshot, then said, "If you truly think it helped, I may have another venture that will divert Julia."

I stared at her, aghast. Had she learned nothing?

She snorted, covering the inelegance with her kid-gloved hand. "Do give me some credit, my dear. No, this is another matter entirely and not my own. I will understand, however, if you do not wish to be involved, especially after Mr. Harley's violence."

"Mr. Harley did not frighten me in the least. What is the venture?"

She nodded toward a small group of people waiting for their carriage to move up in the queue of equipages. "Do you see that girl in the blue pelisse?"

I did. Her face was turned away from me, but she held herself in the same manner that Charlotte did, with the easy grace of the natural beauty. Unlike Charlotte, however, she also had a fragility about her, emphasized perhaps by the severe line of her military-inspired pelisse and the tall shako hat set upon her blond curls.

"That is Millicent Defray," Charlotte added.

Defray. I knew the name but could not place the connection. I needed Julia's memory.

Charlotte saw my struggle. "Millicent married Henry Defray three years past and is one of Georgina Randall's daughters."

"Ah yes." Georgina Randall was an old seminary friend of Charlotte's and, if I recalled correctly, her three daughters had all made good matches in their first seasons. A maternal triumph. "Is Millicent in some kind of trouble?"

"No. It is her older sister Caroline. I stand as godmother to both girls, and dear Millicent has applied for my help, but I cannot see a way forward. Perhaps you and Julia could speak to her?"

"If you cannot help her, I do not see what we can offer."

Charlotte raised her brows, fixing her eyes upon mine. "Do you not, my friend? I see a great deal of courage and cleverness and, frankly, a desperate need to commit to a purpose bigger than just this." She gestured to the polite society gathered at the church door.

"I have a purpose," I said, waving away her double meaning and sweet concern. "To distract my sister from her melancholy. But you are right, inasmuch as Julia does seem happier when aimed at a purpose. So, tell me Caroline's problem."

"I think it would be best if Millicent told you the story herself. Will you speak to her, Augusta? If you wish to distract Julia, then this would certainly do it. And you would be helping a very sweet girl. Two, in fact."

"Charlotte, you are being excessively coy. What is their difficulty?"

My friend, however, merely shook her head. "I will tell Millicent to call upon you tomorrow."

3

HANOVER SQUARE, LONDON

The drawing room door opened. A deep, polite clearing of a throat brought my eyes up from *The Times* and its report that Lord Liverpool had been appointed our replacement prime minister after the shocking assassination of Perceval a month ago.

Our butler stood at the doorway, his eyes slightly narrowed.

At the table, Julia stopped sorting her embroidery cottons. "Oh no, what is it, Weatherly?"

A casual observer would have seen only the impassive face of a well-trained butler, but Julia and I both knew he brought unwelcome news. Weatherly had been with our family since we were eighteen, and over the past twenty-four years we had come to understand his every expression. As, indeed, he had come to understand ours. He had arrived at our father's house as a newly freed man and worked his way from third footman to underbutler. Then, ten years ago, when Father allowed Julia and me to set up our own household in his second London residence, Weatherly came with us as our butler. Hence, he considered himself the main guardian of our well-being and managed us all, from kitchen maid to earl's daughters, with grave efficiency leavened by the occasional touch of dry humor.

"Lord Duffield is on his way from the mews, my ladies. He is reported to be in some"—he paused for emphasis—"agitation."

Julia glanced at me. *Vauxhall.*

I nodded. Our brother only visited to either scold us or ask us to act as hostess for some concert or theater party he had arranged. Someone must have reported back to him that we had gone to Vauxhall on our own. Perhaps dear Bertie had mentioned it. He could never keep anything to himself.

I released a resigned breath. "Tea, then, Weatherly."

"Yes, my lady. Cook has just made a batch of her almond praline biscuits. May I suggest a plate? I believe they are Lord Duffield's favorite."

"Good idea. Thank you."

Weatherly bowed and retreated.

"I wonder just how much of the story Duffy has," Julia said.

"Hopefully only our presence at the gardens and nothing else."

I placed my newspaper on the side table and rose from the armchair, feeling the need to walk out some of my irritation. These missions of brotherly correction always raised my hackles; he was, after all, our junior by five years. I had to admit, too, that the events at Vauxhall had left me somewhat uneasy with myself: hitting Mr. Harley may have been justified self-defense, but it was not civilized behavior. And without civility there could only be chaos.

At the window, I lifted my watch to the light and noted the time: near eleven o'clock. Early for Duffy to be out. I let the watch drop back upon its neck chain. The small gold timepiece—a prime example of Prior's artistry—had been a present from my father. A gift given to me would usually be replicated for my twin, but not in this case. On presenting the watch to me, my father had said that my mind was one that sought order, like a man's, and that he felt I would appreciate the new instruments that could measure time with precision. He was right: I did find some strange solace in the accurate circling of its hands, and a sense of control by knowing how time passed. Although, right now, that knowledge was adding to my ill humor.

I looked down into Hanover Square, seeking diversion. The world outside was abuzz. A bun man called his wares, stopping his raucous song as one of the undercooks from next door ran out to meet him. Across the fenced green, the Kempseys' maid swept their front steps, and an oysterman hauled a small barrel from his cart and hoisted it onto his meaty shoulder. Lord Alvaney's curricle passed with his matched pair of bays—such sweet steppers—and a lady in a truly hideous blue bonnet trimmed with squirrel traipsed the footpath toward Bond Street, a drab companion in her wake.

None of it diverted me from my resentment.

"I am not in the mood for one of Duffy's lectures," I said.

"I know." Julia abandoned her cottons and joined me at the window, placing a sympathetic hand upon my shoulder. "He does it because he thinks you do not respect him, just as Father did not. Besides, he has the right to lecture us now, as head of our family."

I squinted malevolently at the last comment, prompting a soft snort of laughter from my sister.

"So, we stay with the story that we visited the gardens to hear Mr. Handel's new music?" she asked.

"It will have to do."

Julia picked a curled yellow petal from one of the roses arranged upon the side table. "I wonder, is there enough time to change the flowers?"

"I doubt Duffy will notice."

"That is not the point. Fresh flowers are very calming and always brighten up a room."

Since my sister was ten times more interested in the style of our home than I was, I said no more. Besides, the decoration of the house had been her project from the start, and the last thing I wished to do—especially now—was divert her from any enjoyment or distraction. She shook her head, clearly abandoning the idea. "I fear he will arrive midarrangement and that will not do."

Her prophecy proved correct. Less than a minute later, Duffy walked at uncharacteristic speed around the corner and ascended the steps to our front door. I returned to my chair and paper and Julia to her embroidery cottons. A tableau of domestic bliss.

The door opened again to admit Weatherly, who announced, "The Earl of Duffield."

Duffy strode into the room as we rose to curtsy.

"Sisters," he said, bowing.

As was his custom, our brother wore an elegant Weston coat with his cravat tied in the difficult mathematical style and his Colebrook chestnut hair pomaded into a passable Brutus. All in all, the very picture of a fashionable London gentleman. Although, like the ghastly Mr. Harley, he did lack somewhat in height. Duffy stood at least two inches shorter than me, which had enraged him as a boy and still infuriated him as a man.

"Brother," I said with too much edge. Julia shot me a glance. "How pleasant to see you," I added for her peace of mind.

"Do take a seat," Julia said. Her manners were always exemplary, even amid familial discord. "We have just this minute ordered tea."

"Excellent." Duffy sat on the sofa as Julia took the other armchair beside me. He looked around the room, foot tapping upon the carpet. Not his usual manifestation of anger; he was more a pace-the-room type of man.

"We were not expecting a visit today," I prompted.

"No. I was in the area."

That, it appeared, was the end of that conversation. After another few moments of his foot tapping, room inspection, and silence, I decided to wade in again. "Did you read about Liverpool? He cannot be pleased about being the Regent's fifth choice, but at least he should be able to form a government and hold the cabinet together."

Duffy shook his head. "Really, Augusta, you only embarrass yourself with these unwomanly opinions."

"What news do *you* bring, brother?" Julia asked quickly, intercepting my indignation. She glanced at me again, another plea for harmony. I bit back my comment.

He sat up slightly. "What do you mean my news? What have you heard?"

"Nothing. Should we have heard something?" Julia asked.

He settled back in his seat. "No. That is, I do have some news—"

The door opened to admit Samuel, our footman, with the tea tray and, I noted, a generous plateful of almond biscuits. He placed the tray on the side table between Julia and me.

"Thank you, Samuel. You may go," I said.

"Is the tea already in the pot?" Duffy asked, plainly appalled. "Do you trust your servants to measure it?"

"We do," Julia said mildly. She picked up the pot and began to pour.

"They'll steal from you, mark my words."

"They have not done so yet," I said, which I thought was remarkably restrained.

"What is your news?" Julia asked. She passed a cup to Duffy, who accepted it with a nod of thanks. "Praline biscuit?"

"No, thank you." He took a sip of the tea, eyeing us over the brim.

It seemed a scolding for Vauxhall was not the purpose of his visit after all. It was a relief to know our brother had not heard of our adventure in the Dark Walk, particularly since Charlotte's goddaughter—Mrs. Defray—had arranged to call on us this afternoon to discuss her sister's situation. Another possible adventure. Even so, Duffy's odd reticence was unsettling. I received my cup and took a biscuit; I no longer restrained myself for the sake of elegance, especially in my own home.

Duffy placed his cup down upon the side table. "Are you acquainted with Sir Henry Woolcroft and his daughter, Miss Harriet Woolcroft?"

I had not heard of them. I turned to Julia; she knew everyone's connections, often as far back as three generations. She could also remember what everyone wore—at least the garb of the ladies and gentlemen she had met—at every rout and ball we had attended, down to their jewels. An entirely useless accomplishment, she admitted, but, like her knowledge of the peerage, completely reliable.

She stirred her tea pensively. "We are not acquainted, but I believe Sir Henry is a baronet with a good lineage and a large estate in Yorkshire." She stopped stirring, a small frown creasing her brow for a second. "Ah yes, Sir Henry's only son recently died of illness. Miss Woolcroft is now his only heir."

"Quite correct, Julia, as ever," Duffy said. "I have decided it is time I wed, and I have decided that Miss Woolcroft will be my wife."

"Good God." I stared at my brother. He was thirty-seven and we had all quite given up on him abandoning his bachelor life. "Have you offered? Has she accepted?"

"Not yet, but I have every belief she will."

"Of course she will," Julia said loyally. "Is she nice?"

"An heiress," I said, trying to understand this sudden decision. "Are you in need of money, Duffy?" It came out more abruptly than I had anticipated.

"Gussie!" Julia protested.

"I am not in need of funds, Augusta. However, it is time I did my duty. Miss Woolcroft is a pleasant girl known for her piety whom I believe has every chance of continuing the line."

"So, a love match, then," I said.

My brother pursed his lips. "Love? Really, Augusta, this is an important decision. If you think love is essential to a good match it is no wonder you are still unmarried."

"Duffy, that is unkind," Julia said.

He shook his head, realizing he had also insulted his favorite. "I beg your pardon, Julia, I did not mean to offend you."

"No, you meant to offend me." I gave Duffy my best false smile. "A pious girl? I did not think that was one of your prerequisites."

"Women are the vessels of piety," Duffy pronounced. "The keepers of morality. When a woman fails in piety, she fails in her essential femininity."

"Oh, for goodness' sake," I said, feeling heat rise through me. Had Duffy somehow guessed my secret? I searched his face for malice, but it held only the certainty of his own words. "Women are not just—"

"When do you offer, Duffy?" Julia intercepted again. She was far too careful with his dignity and feelings.

"I will be visiting Yorkshire this week and hope to have the happy announcement by Friday."

"We shall look forward to the news and meeting Miss Woolcroft, won't we, Gussie?"

I picked up my biscuit and bit into its crisp sweetness. There was no better gag than almond praline.

4

Two hours later, Duffy had gone and Mrs. Millicent Defray sat upon our drawing room sofa with her green-gloved hands clasped in her lap and a bruised look in her large blue eyes. A cup of tea stood cooling beside her on the side table, the replenished plate of pralines untouched. I had taken up a position by the mantel—I always thought best on my feet—while Julia sat opposite the girl.

"I thank you for seeing me," she said. "I have tried every other avenue I could think of, even the law, and no one will help me." Her voice was so soft and gentle that I felt compelled to take a step closer to hear her words.

"What is the problem?" I asked. "Lady Davenport did not go into detail other than it involves your sister."

"I see." Millicent paused, as if weighing up her godmother's reticence. "I believe Caroline is being held prisoner by her husband, Sir Reginald Thorne."

I shot Julia a glance. *Husband.* No wonder Charlotte had refused to go into any detail. One could not interfere between a husband and wife.

"Mrs. Defray, I am afraid it is her husband's right, by law, to do so, if that is what he wishes," I said.

"But it is not his right to murder her, is it?" Millicent said with some asperity.

She looked from me to Julia, her pretty child's mouth compressing into a straight line. The show of spirit suited her, bringing some harder edges to an excess of softness in both face and fashion. Her peach silk pelisse was trimmed with a cluster of green chiffon roses along the collar and her fashionable chip hat was adorned with more billows of sheer olive silk and a sweeping cascade of yellow and brown ostrich feathers. I could see Julia's critical appreciation. She herself was in a new morning gown of apple-green-and-pink-striped silk, and she had chivvied me to wear my teal round gown. Apparently, it brought out the blue in my eyes.

"As far as I know, British law does not yet condone the murder of wives," I said. Julia frowned at my tone. She was right, of course; this was not the time for flippancy. "What makes you think your sister's husband wishes to murder her?"

"It seems poor Caroline is barren," Millicent said. "She and Sir Reginald have been married five years, and there has been no issue. No sign of any issue. Sir Reginald is desperate to have an heir."

"He is the last of the Thornes," Julia explained. She knew I would have no idea of the man's connections. "His younger brother died three years ago in the Spanish campaign and there are no cousins with the name."

"How do you know that?" Millicent fixed wide eyes upon Julia.

"My sister knows everyone's connections," I said. "Please, continue."

"Ever since his brother died, Sir Reginald has been obsessed by the need for an heir. And now I believe he wants to—" She dabbed at her mouth with a silk square.

"Have done with Caroline and move on?" I supplied. I was not overstating the danger to Caroline's well-being. The way of the law meant that divorce was a lengthy, expensive business that required a rare Act of Parliament that inevitably ruined both parties, socially and financially. Only the most desperate and most wealthy could consider it. The unfortunate demise of a spouse through accident or illness was far more economical and socially safe.

She nodded. "The last letter I received from Caroline said as much. She fears for her life." She rummaged in her reticule and pulled out a crumpled and messily crossed letter, handing it to me. "Read it. You will see."

It was indeed a desperate missive, recounting acts of cruelty: a beloved little dog shot dead, friends turned away, medications prescribed by a dubious physician, and a bald statement of imprisonment. I already hated Sir Reginald.

"How did she get the letter to you?" I asked, passing it to Julia.

Millicent locked her fingers together. "A sympathetic maid carried it to town and posted it."

Julia made a soft sound of horror as she read the page. "He sounds like a monster," she said, passing the letter back to Millicent, "but in what way do you think we can help?"

"I am hoping you could extract Caroline. Sir Reginald will not let me or my husband or any of our relations into the house. We plan to send Caroline to my husband's people in Ireland."

"Extract her?" I echoed.

How could we even get into Sir Reginald's house, let alone extract the girl? I crossed my arms over my bodice. What on earth was Charlotte thinking? Yes, I was looking to distract Julia from her worry and grief, but not by putting her—or myself, for that matter—outside the law.

"My godmother said you were most enterprising and made it your business to help others," Millicent said, her blue eyes widening even more with entreaty.

Made it our business? Charlotte had led her goddaughter to believe we were some kind of benevolent society.

"I fear Lady Davenport is exaggerating our experience and our abilities," I said.

In all truth, our defeat of Mr. Harley had been more luck than skill. I was not inclined to stretch that luck any further.

"Lady Augusta, I have nowhere else to turn and I fear time is running out." Millicent shook the letter, the paper crackling with urgency. "This was sent a week ago."

I looked across at Julia: *We must say no; it is impossible.*

She lifted her brows: *But the poor girl in that house—can we really refuse?*

I frowned: *It is quite illegal. Besides, your health.*

She tilted her chin: *I am well enough. Could we live with ourselves if Caroline ends up dead?*

I ducked my head: *Of course not. It would be too awful.*

Julia nodded: *I think we must try.*

I released a long breath: *I suppose so.*

"Mrs. Defray, my sister and I will help you," I said. "We cannot promise anything, but we will attempt to remove Caroline from her husband's house."

"We will try this week," Julia added. She glanced at me: *We must act now, Gussie—we may already be too late.* She touched the gold cross at her throat. A quick prayer for the girl's safety.

At least one of us still had faith. Perhaps that would be enough.

Later that night, I sat alone in the drawing room, watching the embers in the fire glow their last. Julia had already gone up, claiming she wanted to be fresh for the adventure ahead, but the weariness in her eyes seemed far greater than usual. She had picked at her dinner, too, much to the despair of Cook, who had made her a particularly delicious cheese tart. Was I right to take her on this mad endeavor tomorrow? We had discussed our plan—such as it was—and Julia had, quite rightly, raised the number of unknowns ahead. We would have to improvise, I had said, which was another way of saying I would make it up as we went along. Yet, I wondered if my sister's strength was up to such a task.

A knock upon the door drew me from my thoughts. My hand was a fist, full of paisley silk shawl; I must have gathered it into a ball. Three quick strokes smoothed the soft, damp edge out. "Yes? Come."

Weatherly entered. "My lady, may I speak with you?"

His expression held an unusual mix of determination and discomfort.

"What is it? Is Cook threatening to abandon us again?"

No answering smile. Instead, he closed the door and stood before it with hands neatly behind his back. It was to be a solemn interview, then.

"My lady, I am aware of your plans for tomorrow," he said.

Of course he was; he knew everything that occurred in our house. "Do I detect an objection?"

"Would it sway you if I did object?" he asked, with only a modicum of his dryness. "But no, I do not oppose the plan in general. I understand why you are embarking on such a course of action. I am here to suggest you do not take Samuel."

"Why not? He is our footman and it would be somewhat odd for us to be traveling without him." I searched for a reason why Weatherly would take such issue. "Do you think we place him in danger without his knowledge? I assure you he knows what we intend to do and has agreed to it."

"You misunderstand me, my lady. I think you should take me in his stead."

I stared at him, nonplussed.

"Not as your butler, my lady, but as your footman," he added.

"Samuel is a good man, but he is young and has very little experience of the world." He paused, as if debating what to say next. "I know, only too well, the brutality of men when they have power over another, my lady. I have seen women and children whipped to death on a man's whim. And . . . much worse. I would not be able to live with myself if I did not do everything in my power to help Lady Thorne and to keep you and Lady Julia safe."

I sat for a moment, silenced by such a declaration of his past and his loyalty. I knew his story only in the broadest terms: a child taken, enslaved, and finally freed upon English soil as a young man. My father had known it in full, and had once told me that I should never hear it, or any other of its ilk, if I wished to retain my faith in humanity. Of course I ignored his advice and sought out reports of the foul trafficking in pamphlets and books including Equiano's hugely popular autobiography. Suffice to say my father was right. I joined Mr. Wilberforce's abolitionist ranks immediately, despite the man's view that women were unsuited to political thought. And so it was that five years ago I raised a glass of wine with Weatherly to mark the passing of the Slave Trade Act. Although, frankly, it had not gone as far as either of us had hoped toward eradicating the vile practice.

"You want to come as a footman? Are you sure?" I finally said.

Could he even pass as a footman? He was only a few years younger than Julia and me, and a footman was usually in his twenties. Still, Weatherly did stand at near six foot—the required height for a fashionable footman—and had kept a youthful figure. Nor was it unusual to see an older man of color still in a footman's position; unjust as it was, not many freedmen were promoted into a household's senior staff. It might work. And I had to admit, the idea of Weatherly's efficiency alongside us appealed to my burgeoning apprehension.

"I am sure, my lady."

"Samuel will be disappointed. He was looking forward to the day out. You had best give him a half day in compensation."

"As you wish, my lady."

"But, Weatherly, you do realize we will have to call you by your first name again."

His rare smile appeared. "I am sure my consequence will survive the ordeal, my lady."

"I am not sure we will," I returned, only half joking. "Well then, tomorrow you return to a footman's livery."

He bowed and turned to go.

"Weatherly," I called.

He turned back, a slight frown upon his face: he had heard the lilt of urgency in my voice.

"Have you noticed . . . Do you think Lady Julia is her usual bright self?"

Weatherly's eyes met mine, the worry within them mirroring my own. "I could not say, my lady."

Of course not. He would never comment upon one of us to the other.

"However," he said slowly, "I believe Miss Leonard intends to visit the apothecary tomorrow to fulfill a new prescription from the doctor. Do you wish to add anything to Lady Julia's order?"

A doctor's prescription? When had Julia seen the doctor again? The only time she had not been in my company was the day before yesterday, when she had taken a walk accompanied by Leonard, her maid. That must have been it.

"No . . . but *thank you*," I said.

Weatherly bowed and departed, closing the door softly behind him.

The room suddenly felt too quiet. I smoothed the edge of my

shawl again, finding a small comfort in the feel of the soft silk against my fingertips. Julia had, to my knowledge, never seen a doctor without me before. Why did she not tell me? The answer clawed itself into my heart. Something must have changed and she did not wish me to worry.

5

THE ROAD TO BRIGHTON

"Really, Gus, must we have guns in the carriage?" Julia asked from the carriage seat opposite.

Oddly, she preferred to travel with her back to the driver, in the bodkin seat. I, on the other hand, became nauseous if I did not face the way we were moving. "It is the middle of the day," she added. "I hardly think a highwayman is going to assault us in broad daylight."

I patted the pair of pistols in their mahogany box, set prudently open next to me. "If you recall, Mr. and Mrs. James Barrett were stopped near here only a month ago by a gang of desperadoes. They lost all their jewels and their driver was shot. The man lost his arm."

Julia peered out the window as if expecting to see a highwayman pop up beside the carriage. She was wearing a new silver silk poke bonnet and its edges projected so far past her face that the exercise required her to turn in her seat. "I thought that happened on the Bath Road."

"No. It was this road."

The carriage lurched over a rut, rocking us both to the left. I steadied myself with a hand against the silk-lined wall.

"But the Barretts were stopped at night, were they not?"

I inclined my head, forced to concede the point.

Satisfied, she settled back against the cushions, smoothing the lavender skirt of her carriage gown. "Have you thought of a way for us to see Caroline yet?"

"Nothing that holds any water. Have you?"

"I can only think of a broken wheel, which is not without foundation on this road. We could arrive at the doorstep and claim shelter whilst our carriage is being fixed at the closest village."

I wrinkled my nose, an expression that always irritated Julia. "I've already thought of that and discarded it. We would not have ready access to the carriage."

Julia's mouth tightened. "Well, my apologies for lagging two steps behind you, as usual."

She pointedly turned to look out the window. The poke bonnet hid her face, but from the hitch of her shoulders I knew it was not only anger that had made her snap at me. She was anxious, and rightly so; Sir Reginald was going to be a nasty obstacle.

"Still, it is probably our best option," I said.

Her shoulder twitched in acknowledgment, but she did not look around or answer.

We continued in silence, the moment of disunity slowly mellowing into our usual companionable quiet. The road behind us was quiet too; the coach carrying Mrs. Millicent Defray and her worthy husband no longer followed us. They had taken up their position at the posting house in Hickstead to await our return with Caroline. The plan was for them to whisk her away in a different equipage in case Sir Reginald pursued us. That is, if we managed to extract Caroline.

I pushed the mohair carriage rug over my lap onto the seat beside me; far too warm for that now. Settling back again, I watched the passing hazel hedgerows with their thick untrimmed summer brush alive with darting birds. The quiet warmth and the rocking of the carriage had lulled Julia into sleep, her chin sunk upon the pink silk of her high-buttoned spencer and her mouth open and emitting the occasional soft snore. She had already moved away from the purple crapes of mourning into the softer colors of her sorrow. Charlotte had been right about organizing another diversion for Julia, and also about her appearance; my sister did look wan, with a smudge of darkness beneath each eye. She had still not told me about her visit to the doctor. It was so unusual for her to keep such a thing from me that I felt I could not press her upon it. If she wished to tell me, she would. I just hoped it was not more bad news.

Our mother had died of a breast canker when we were thirteen. Her sister—dear Aunt Eliza, who had presented us in our mother's absence—had suffered the same fate. Was it perhaps within the humors of our family? The Colebrooks, it was said, were prone to melancholy and its disorders, although my father had often joked I was made more of bile than sadness. Even so, was I destined to follow Julia? Would I, too, find a hard mass of malignancy within my breast? I laid my hand upon my chest, my heartbeat strong and steady beneath the warm flat of my palm. If I did, I doubted I could face it with the same brave equanimity as my sister.

Heat from a shaft of sunlight, made even hotter through the thick glass window, was beginning to penetrate the silk of my gown's skirt. I slid a few inches across the seat, drawing the pistol box with me. The carriage jolted and swayed, and I let myself wander into the realms of what could have been, an alternative story where Julia was not ill and Robert had not fallen from his horse and died in a ditch. A story in which he had stayed home from that doomed hunting party, married my sister, and set up house in Hanover Square to host dinner parties and make morning calls. Would they have had a family? I smiled at the idea of being an aunt. Two children perhaps: a boy for duty and a girl for company. No more than that; I would not want to risk my sister, even in a fantasy. We would all go to the Exeter 'Change and see the animals and Bullock's Museum for the Egyptian treasures.

Opposite, Julia gave a deep sigh in her sleep. Most likely a dream about Robert—they were still quite regular. She had a memory that could, quite literally, recall everything she had experienced in exact detail. Yet such a phenomenal memory also had a drawback: every conversation, every moment with Robert, was indelibly inscribed upon Julia's mind. For her, there could be no softening or blurring by time. She had loved him fervently and still did after two years of loss.

I had not yet experienced such a deep attachment to a man and felt as if I stood on the other side of a pane of glass, unable to really understand her pain. It was one of the few things we could not share. Although I'd had the usual schoolroom and dancing-master infatuations—and even a few passionate kisses with a young man bound for the army who had been entirely unsuitable—it sometimes worried me that, in all my adult years, I had never felt a strong attachment. Perhaps I was incapable of it, a cold fish. Julia said it was only because I had never met a man who could match my wit or adventurous spirit. That was quite possibly true; all the men of our acquaintance were as dull as Fordyce's sermons and had all the adventurous spirit of bread-and-butter pudding. It was also true that after I learned about coverture from my reading, I became less and less inclined to hand over my half of our inherited fortune and all my legal and property rights—including the rights of my own body—to a husband. It would have to be a grand love, indeed, for me to willingly merge so completely with a man that I was all but legally obliterated. Most women did not have the choice to say no, but I did.

Julia awoke with a jerk as we bounced over another rut. She surreptitiously wiped the side of her mouth with the tip of her gloved finger. "Where are we?"

"I believe we are less than half an hour from Sir Reginald's estate."

She blinked, then shifted in her seat to focus, past her bonnet, upon the woodland we were passing, now thick with upright hazel, beeches, and low lush grasses.

"My apologies for falling asleep."

"It is no wonder. It is so hot in here." I knew I was beginning to harp upon the subject, yet I felt compelled to ask, "Are you sure you are up to this, my dear?"

"Do not fuss," she said from behind the curve of her bonnet. "Besides, Dr. Thorgood has measured it twice now and does not think me in imminent danger."

Ah, finally it was out. "You saw him again?"

She turned so that I could see her reassuring smile. "I did, two days ago. Do not be vexed with me, Gussie. I had a little pain and did not want to trouble you with it."

Pain? It was the first time she had ever mentioned pain. "Perhaps it would be worthwhile to gain another opinion. Dr. Thorgood has treated us with great skill since we were girls, but he is near ending his tenure in his profession."

"I could not bear to think of another doctor poking and prodding me in such places. No, I have a new tincture to take alongside the blue mass pills, and all is as well as it can be. It is this heat that makes me weary. So draining."

The air in the carriage had, indeed, warmed into an uncomfortable stuffiness. I was tempted to unhook the gold-braid frogs on my velvet pelisse and let it hang open. Instead, I unlatched the window and pushed it down, closing my eyes as the cool rush of air brought a moment of relief. Dr. Thorgood did not think her in imminent danger; good news indeed. Even so, this was the first time she had admitted to pain and the first time she had decided not to trouble me with something so important.

"Look at all the dust you are letting in!" my sister protested.

The carriage pace suddenly slowed and I heard a shout outside. I opened my eyes. The entire road billowed with dust, too much for just our carriage. I poked my head out the window just as we came to a shuddering standstill, the horses shrilling their distress as they were pulled up. Among the swirl of dust, I saw the shapes of two horsemen. One of them had a blunderbuss trained on our driver and footman; the other urged his mount toward our window.

"Put the gun down or I'll blow yer head off!" Blunderbuss Man yelled.

I pulled back inside and grabbed one of the pistols from the box, covering it with the corner of the carriage rug.

Julia gasped. "Gus, no!"

"Be quiet, dear. Do not make a move."

I wrapped my hand around the butt of the pistol, the quick beat of my heart pulsing to the end of my fingertips. What on earth was I planning to do?

A man with a blue kerchief tied across the bottom of his face drew alongside the open window, his horse blowing irritably at the close quarters. Gray, intelligent eyes considered us. For a second I thought I saw recognition flash through them.

He had not raised his gun.

"Ladies, your valuables, please." A pleasant baritone, polite and without any local accent.

I rotated the pistol's cock from half to full and hooked my finger around the trigger.

"We have no valuables that could possibly interest you, sir," I said. "You should leave now before you come to harm."

The gray eyes crinkled into surprised amusement. "Harm?"

I flicked off the rug and raised the pistol, no more than ten inches from his forehead.

"I see." His eyes fixed upon the barrel. "You have a steady hand, my lady."

"I do, and a steady nerve. Call your companion from my driver and let us continue on our way."

Thick eyebrows lifted. "I do not believe you will fire that gun, so let us move past this show of bravado."

On that instant, a blunderbuss shot exploded outside. The cabin lurched, throwing me backward, my finger tightening upon the trigger in reflex. The pistol's discharge boomed in my ears, the recoil slamming its butt into my chest and punching all the air from my lungs. The man at the window jerked and twisted, then dropped from sight. His horse screamed and reared, a blur of bulging eyes and straining neck, its front hooves slamming against the carriage door. I heard shouts—our driver and footman—and then another shot.

I gulped for air, the cabin hazing into gray. All I could draw into my lungs was the acrid stink of spent gunpowder.

"Gussie, are you hurt?"

I felt the soft kid of my sister's gloved hands around my face. Finally, I pulled in a full breath, the blessed air easing my burning chest and clearing my sight.

"Winded," I managed and pushed away her frantic ministrations. I rubbed my chest. The bruised flesh ached, but there was no other damage as far as I could tell. My corset must have shielded some of the blow.

Weatherly wrenched open the door. "My ladies, are you safe?"

Julia sank back into her seat. "We are whole. Are you and John Driver unhurt?"

"Yes, my lady. The blackguard fired upon us but missed." Weatherly ran his hand through his hair. He had lost his hat. "John Driver tried to hold the horses, but one reared in the traces and the man bolted. I shot after him, but it missed too. He is gone." He looked back at the ground outside, mouth twisting. "I see you found your mark, my lady. I think he is dead."

Oh no, had I really killed the man? I sat up. "It was not intentional." I placed the spent pistol back in the box and slid across the seat. "Quick, let me see."

I climbed down the carriage step, leaning upon Weatherly's arm a little more than usual. Dust still hung in the air, the motes swirling in the dappled sunlight. Trampled hazel bushes showed the path of the fallen highwayman's horse into the woodland. The man himself lay facing us on his side upon the road, blood oozing in a bright wash across his forehead, matting his dark brown hair and dripping into the dirt. The neckerchief had dislodged, showing more of his face: tanned skin now overlaid with a sickly pallor, and a high-bridged nose that could only be called Roman.

"Is he dead?" Julia whispered beside me. Weatherly had helped her down and she stood clutching the side of the carriage.

I took a careful step toward the body with a sick sense of déjà vu. Shades of Mr. Harley, but this time with a lot more blood. Was he breathing? I took another step.

His chest moved.

"Ah, he is alive!"

"Dear God, thank you," Julia said and crossed herself.

As far as I could see, the ball had only grazed his forehead. A nasty gash ran from his eyebrow to his ear and still streamed with blood, but there was no hole in his head so the ball had not entered his brain.

Julia clutched my arm. "Gus, I know that man."

"What?"

Her face was intent as she searched that phenomenal memory. "Heaven forfend, it is Lord Evan Belford."

I was finding it hard to look away from the gory wound I had inflicted; if the ball had been half an inch inward, the man would have been very dead indeed. I forced myself to look beyond the blood at his profile. Now that Julia had mentioned it, he did look familiar. Yet it did not make sense.

"It can't be Lord Evan. He was transported to the colonies over twenty years ago."

It had been a huge scandal at the time. Lord Evan, the first of two wild sons sired by the Marquess of Deele, had been challenged to a duel and killed his man. In such cases, the survivor would have relied upon the laxness of the courts to overlook the crime or been smuggled to the Continent: at the time we were not at war with France. However, Lord Evan had been apprehended, cast into jail, and tried. If I recalled correctly, he had maintained he had merely pinked his opponent across the chest. The opponent, however, had died at the scene, and the eyewitness accounts claimed Lord Evan had thrust with fatal intent, sealing his guilt. He was sentenced to be hanged, but that sentence was commuted to transportation to the new penal colony at New South Wales. The family had disowned him, of course, but had never fully recovered.

"Look at his ring, Gus."

I turned my attention to his hand, sprawled in the dirt. One long finger sported a heavy gold ring set with a large ruby. For a highwayman, he had remarkably clean and well-manicured nails.

"That is Lord Evan's family signet," Julia said. "I remember remarking upon it when we danced at the Nashes' rout in our first season. Do you remember? I wore the pale green muslin from

Paris and you wore that rather handsome cream silk with the bugle beads."

I shook my head. That was more than twenty years ago; I could not even remember what I wore two days past. "This man could have stolen it. He is a highwayman."

"True," Julia said. "But you cannot deny he has the Belford nose. Gussie, I am sure it is Lord Evan."

If my sister was certain, then the man was indeed Lord Evan Belford. Lud, I had just shot a marquess's son. Even worse, I had shot an acquaintance.

"Well then, we must attend him." I looked around for something to staunch the wound, my eye fixing upon our hovering butler. "Weatherly, give me your neckcloth."

I pulled off my gloves and passed them to Julia as Weatherly unwound the length of livery muslin from his throat and handed it to me.

"Do you have any alcohol in your medicine supplies?" I asked my sister.

"Just some brandy for shock."

"That will do. Weatherly, would you please bring Lady Julia's medicine box."

He ducked back into the carriage and returned with the large brass-bound casket that held all the preparations Julia used to doctor our household, and a velvet cushion. He placed both beside the fallen man. "You cannot kneel upon the road, my lady."

I stifled a wild laugh. No doubt a reaction to the shock, although some of it might have been the sight of the velvet cushion upon the blood-spattered dirt. Pushing aside the inappropriate mirth, I knelt and peered at Lord Evan's pale face. The closer inspection confirmed my earlier opinion. "It is just a graze, and the powder has burned him a little too."

"How can you be so calm?" Julia demanded.

"Focusing upon the facts is the only thing keeping me from screaming, dearheart." She placed her hand on my shoulder as I opened the box and found a silver flask of brandy. Our gamekeeper had impressed upon me that a gunshot wound should always be doused in alcohol. He had fought on the Continent and learned the practice from a battlefield surgeon who had saved his leg from amputation. I uncorked the flask and poured the brandy over the long gash, blood and spirit pooling upon the road. It was a good thing Lord Evan was senseless, for I could only imagine the pain of such a procedure. I pressed the muslin against the wound. The white cloth blossomed red. So much blood. The metallic smell of it beneath the fruity stink of brandy made me queasy. "Weatherly, get John Driver's neckcloth too, please. We must bind Lord Evan's wound."

Weatherly headed off to the front of the carriage.

"We cannot leave him on the road," Julia said. "For all his sins, he is the Marquess of Deele's older brother, and Deele is one of *our* brother's cronies." She clutched me a little more tightly. "Gussie, if Lord Evan had not been convicted, he would now be the marquess instead of his younger brother."

"But he *was* convicted, so he cannot claim his title. Still, for the sake of his connections, we must take him with us and find a nearby house to provide help."

A very inappropriate thought suddenly came to mind, straightening me upon my knees. No, it was too mercenary to voice. And yet . . .

"I'm sure the closest house is Sir Reginald's." I glanced up at Julia.

As ever, she caught my meaning in an instant. "Gussie, you cannot think it would work! What would we say?"

"Sir Reginald has never met us, nor, I wager, any of our family. The story could be that our brother was escorting us to"—I waved my free hand—"Brighton or wherever, when suddenly we were set upon by ruffians. Our poor brother was shot and we are in dire need of assistance. Sir Reginald will not deny us—it would be an affront to civility. After all, he is only a baronet."

She did not look convinced. "What about his clothes? He is filthy."

I considered Lord Evan's prone form. "His jacket and breeches are a bit dusty, granted, but they seem well-made enough." In fact, on closer inspection it was clear that Lord Evan had chosen to spend some of his ill-gotten gains on a good tailor; not Weston, of course, but probably one of the better military suppliers. "I think it will answer well, my dear. We will be able to secure medical help for Lord Evan *and* find a way to remove Caroline."

"What if he wakes up?"

"I doubt he would want his true identity known. I think he will play along for the promise of his freedom and a good pouch of money."

If he survives, I thought. It was almost a prayer, but the hypocrisy of calling upon a god I doubted pulled me up. Still, some part of me craved the intercession of something other than my own inadequate self.

"I am not sure, Gussie," Julia said. "It does not seem right. I have hartshorn salts in the box too. We could attempt to wake him."

"I am not sure hartshorn and a head wound would deal well together. Besides, he is far more useful to us senseless than awake. What do you say? Do we adopt Lord Evan as our brother?"

"You are mad, you know," Julia said.

"You come from the same stock, my dear."

She smiled. "True."

6

THORNECREST

The country home of Sir Reginald Thorne was at the end of a long beech-lined driveway that announced to the world that here dwelled *a family of consequence*. The winding approach and the canopy of lush spring trees allowed only glimpses of the house until, voilà, one's carriage was upon a gravel courtyard set before a handsome honey-stone house.

To my eye, Thornecrest had clearly started life as a hunting lodge—the bones of the smaller building were still apparent—but generous wings had been added. No doubt in concert with the Thorne fortunes. As our carriage came to a stop, I noted only two bricked-up windows; Sir Reginald was not a man to allow the window tax to darken his life. One window on the second story had ornate iron bars set across it and heavy curtains, tightly closed. A nursery perhaps; bars were not unusual for such rooms. Or was it something more sinister? Thornecrest did not look like a prison, but how many handsome houses throughout England incarcerated the women within?

"Are you ready?" I whispered to Julia, who now sat next to me.

She patted the set of her bonnet. "I believe so. At least Lord Evan has not woken up."

We both contemplated the man propped in the corner of the cabin across from us. It had taken us twenty minutes to reach Thornecrest, and in that time Lord Evan's wound had stopped bleeding and his color had improved, but he had shown no flicker of consciousness. In repose, the signs of old suffering were evident upon his face: deep lines from nose to mouth, a knit of pain between thick brows, and the line of a scar that followed the path of his cheekbone. I had finally remembered the one time I had danced with him more than twenty years ago, and could almost transpose the memory of his younger face upon these older, more harshly drawn features. That was a time when men wore embroidered coats and powdered wigs and we women wore huge silk gowns made heavy with side panniers and stiff stomachers. As I recall, Lord Evan had looked rather fine in embroidered silk and had been vying for the hand of Charlotte, the beauty of our season. He had failed to secure the dance and ended up with me, not that his manner had indicated his disappointment. On the contrary, he had been the perfect partner: witty, graceful, and attentive. And, most importantly, a good six inches taller than myself. It had been a pleasant half hour amid a rather dire night of reels and country dances.

It was plain that Lord Evan was no longer that man, reduced now to common theft and violence. Even so, if he woke I hoped enough of his former self remained to carry us through our rescue. Mainly, however, I was banking on his thief's desire for money. Lud, what a mess.

"He is much changed," Julia said, echoing my thoughts. "Disfigured and so aged. A rather stark gauge of the passing years. For all of us."

She lifted her shoulders and let them drop, as if shaking off the reminder of our mortality. Or, more to the point for me, her mortality. From birth, we had walked together through our lives, hand in hand. Now it was possible she was forging ahead, her faith promising her everlasting life. That promise, however, was no longer mine. If I eschewed God and everlasting life, I also eschewed heaven. There was no place for us to reunite beyond the grave. From the moment she had told me the doctor's diagnosis, I had conceived that brutal separation—without God and the hope of heaven—over and over again, always amazed to find myself still standing, still breathing, when the thoughts receded. Doubt, I think, took as much courage as belief.

"Having second thoughts?" she asked.

"And third," I said.

"Too late now." A jerk of her head directed my attention to a rotund butler descending the stone steps with magnificent stateliness. Two footmen in drab livery flanked him on either side. Julia raised her parasol as if it were a battle standard. "Here I go."

She drew in a long breath, then let out a sobbing howl that would have rivaled the best opera singer's. It was so loud that even Lord Evan's eyelids fluttered. I leaned forward, heart thumping, eyes fixed upon his lean face, but his head lolled back and he seemed to sink further into oblivion. Lucky Lord Evan.

Weatherly opened the carriage door, even his impassivity twitching a little under Julia's piercing wail. I took his offered hand and stood for a moment on the carriage step to survey the lay of the battleground, then alighted with my face set into what I hoped looked like a sister's frantic concern for a beloved brother.

"You there," I said to the approaching butler. "Whose house is this?"

His shoulders hunched slightly as Julia's keen rose to a crescendo. "You are at Thornecrest, madam, the home of Sir Reginald Thorne." He bowed. "Who may I say is calling?"

I raised my voice over Julia's din and commenced attack. "I am Lady Augusta Colebrook. My brother, the Earl of Duffield, is within and has been shot by a highwayman. We need sanctuary and a physician. Now!" I took a few determined steps toward the house. "Is your master at home?"

"I am," a voice boomed from the front doorway.

Sir Reginald Thorne emerged from the gloom of his house. Just the physicality of the man made my hackles rise. He was all bully-threat: chest thrust out, meaty shoulders held back, and a thick corded neck that gave the impression of rammish intransigency. As he strode to the portico steps, it crossed my mind that a willowy girl-bride would have little effect upon such dimensions.

He stopped upon the top step—high-ground tactical advantage—and gave a stiff bow, regarding me through narrowed eyes. "Your brother would be better served if you went on to the village, Lady Augusta." His rather wet lips pursed in irritation. "There is a physician there."

Holy star, the man was going to refuse us.

I drew myself up. "The villains who shot him are still at large, Sir Reginald. Besides, as you can hear, my sister, Lady Julia, is quite overcome."

He allowed a dismissive glance toward Julia's noise. "Quite. However, you would find the physician for both your brother and your sister more quickly if you continued on your way. My wife is, at present, unwell, and I am sure you do not wish to expose yourself or your family to such danger."

Damn, the illness-in-the-house feint—he really did intend to stop our entry. I waved to Weatherly to hand Julia down. The more of us out of the cabin and on our way indoors, the better.

"I understand, Sir Reginald." I took a few steps closer to the house and countered with the imminent-death block. "Even so, my brother is bleeding from a head wound and there can be no doubt he will be placed in far greater risk by more travel. I insist that you send one of your men to the village for the physician."

Julia stepped down to the gravel, still clutching her parasol like a standard. Her sobbing rose into another shrill wail and she managed a vaporish stagger that was neatly caught by Weatherly. Sir Reginald tucked his chin to his chest—the ram standing firm. As Weatherly delivered Julia into my arms, I saw the dismay in my sister's eyes before she buried her face in my shoulder. *We are losing the battle.*

Not while I had breath in my body.

"We must bring my brother inside," I said over her sobs, then pointed to one of the footmen beside Thorne's butler. "You there, help my man carry Lord Duffield into the house." I steered Julia toward the steps and made my final attack. "Or would you prefer that the Earl of Duffield died in your driveway, Sir Reginald?"

Ah, that gave him pause: a dead earl on one's property was sure to garner attention from a magistrate. Not to mention the scandal papers. The kind of scrutiny a potential wife killer would wish to avoid.

Sir Reginald rocked back upon his heels. "Bryden will show you and your sister to the drawing room, Lady Augusta." He turned and retreated indoors.

Bryden, the butler, issued soft commands to the two footmen. One young man immediately headed to an archway that presumably led to the stables. The other joined Weatherly at the carriage.

Bryden bowed, his jowly face set into forced welcome. "My ladies."

We followed him up the stone steps, Julia still huddled close to me. I fleetingly squeezed her arm: *A close run.* Her eyes widened in agreement as she drew breath for another penetrating howl. Bryden hitched one plump shoulder against the din. She really was doing an excellent job.

We entered the house, pausing for a moment as Bryden divested Julia of her parasol and laid it upon an ebony hall table. To my surprise the large entrance hall was light and well-appointed, with a graceful ironwork staircase that wound sinuously up to the first floor.

What had I expected: a dingy, damp prison of a house? I rather think I did; the perils of education and a lively imagination. Still, I would much rather a mind given to such color than one caught in the dull drab of womanly ignorance.

Bryden opened a double door to our left and stood back. "If you will wait here, my ladies," he said over Julia's softer sobs.

We entered the Thorne drawing room. Bryden bowed and closed the doors behind him with a click that firmly announced this was where we were to stay.

We waited in our tableau of distress as his footsteps receded, then Julia peeped up from my shoulder. Seeing we were alone, she sighed and stepped away from my sisterly comfort. "So, Bryden did not take our bonnets."

"Sir Reginald intends our stay to be very short indeed." I pulled my gloves from my hands, then untied my bonnet ribbons and lifted the hat from my head. "There, we are here to stay now."

"If only it were that easy," Julia said. She looked around. "This is a better room than I expected."

Crimson damask silk lined the walls, the opulent color interspersed with large gilt mirrors and portraits of men upon the wall, all with the same high color and thuggish brow as Sir Reginald. It was a little unusual for the family portraits to be in the drawing room and not on the staircase, but maybe Sir Reginald's taste did not run to the traditional drawing room fare of landscapes and pastorals. There were no portraits of the Thorne women, either; unworthy of paint, perhaps, or did abject fear not translate well onto canvas? A very pretty pianoforte had been placed in the corner in good view of an apple-green velvet sofa and matching chairs. I counted three Egyptian-inspired side tables, one set with a Wedgwood urn in blue porcelain. Julia had nearly bought the same design from the London showroom a year ago but had decided its dimensions were too large for the hallway table.

Either Sir Reginald kept up with fashion or, more likely, this was the stylish hand of Caroline before she fell out of favor.

Outside the row of tall windows, Weatherly and the other footman had finally pulled the senseless Lord Evan from the carriage and were dragging him upright between them toward the house, his head lolling to one side and his boot toes digging ruts into the gravel drive. Our carriage, however, did not move toward the stables. I placed my gloves and bonnet upon a side table and watched a wiry groom approach John Driver, their exchange bringing our coachman scrambling down from his seat. Although I could not hear the argument through the glass, it was heated, with much accompanying gesticulation. John finally turned upon his heel and went to the heads of the lead horses, a scowl upon his sweat- and dust-smeared face.

"It seems Sir Reginald has ordered our carriage to stay out front," I said.

Julia turned from her study of the room and took in our stationary equipage. "It will be ten times harder to smuggle Caroline out in full sight of the house. That is, if she is even here. Do we stay with the plan?"

I bit back my own chagrin. "Yes. We will just have to deal with the carriage when the time comes."

"Then I had best start my fit." Julia sat down upon one of the green velvet armchairs, pressed her face into her hands, and drew a deep preparatory breath. I tensed, ready for her howl, but she dropped her hands and looked up again. "I have no doubt they'll take me to a room to rest, just to stop the noise, but what if the maid stays, Gussie, or takes up station outside the door? How will I manage to look for Caroline?"

"Improvise, my dear."

She eyed me, clearly unimpressed with the suggestion, then drew breath again and set up a shrill rising keen. Just in time, for the door suddenly opened to admit Bryden, followed by a maid with her arms full of linen. Behind them, Weatherly and the other footman dragged their limp, senseless burden into the room. The maid bobbed a curtsy—eyes wide with curiosity at the sight of Weatherly—then bustled over to the sofa and, with an expert flick and snap, unfolded a sheet and let it settle over the cushioned seat and arms.

Of course, no use getting blood upon the velvet.

"Put him down there," Bryden ordered the footmen.

It was not the most gentle of undertakings, but Weatherly and his counterpart eventually positioned Lord Evan on the sofa with his head propped on one sheet-protected sofa arm and his booted feet hanging over the other. The movement had done him no favors; his pale complexion now also held an ominous gray cast, and fresh red blood showed through his makeshift bandages. Thank goodness a footman had been dispatched to find the physician. Lord Evan might be at his most useful unconscious, but I did not want the man to die.

In the chair beside me, Julia continued her cacophony. All eyes settled upon me. Ah yes, I was the steady sister. I hurried over to Lord Evan's side and sank into the chair beside the sofa, taking his slack hand. It was warm; at least that was a good sign.

"The physician will be here soon, Lady Augusta," Sir Reginald said, coming a little way into the room, his body still half-turned to the door. He plainly had no intention of staying with us, a lucky turn of events.

"Thank you," I said over Julia's sobbing. "Would you be so kind as to allow my sister to rest in a darkened room? If she lies down, it will quiet her nerves." I added some emphasis on the word *quiet*.

Sir Reginald nodded curtly to his butler. "Show Lady Julia to the Cornflower Room."

"I hope my sister's distress does not disturb Lady Thorne," I added as Julia rose from her seat.

"The Cornflower Room is not close to my wife's chambers. She will not be disturbed."

"Thank you so much for your kindness, Sir Reginald," Julia managed through her sobs. From the tilt of her head I knew that she, too, had noted the clue to Caroline's whereabouts, but I did not dare catch her eye. She followed Bryden from the room, her whimpers receding farther into the house.

Sir Reginald watched her leave with a frown—did he already regret offering her a room or was he just glad to be out of earshot?—and then turned back to me. "If you require anything else, Lady Augusta, my servants will assist you." He bowed and retreated, leaving a release of tension in his wake. Not only from me; both his maid and footman breathed small sighs of relief.

I turned to Weatherly. "Please retrieve Lady Julia's medicine box from the carriage and take it to her." I gathered the maid and footman into the command. "You will show my man the way?"

They both bobbed their assent. Weatherly made his own bow, his eyes meeting mine for a second in acknowledgment of his true objective: to question Sir Reginald's staff about their mistress. The three of them left the room, Thorne's footman softly closing the door behind them.

Our plan was in motion.

7

I waited, listening for any sounds of new approach, but all stood silent. I was alone. Well, more or less. I looked down at Lord Evan. The curve of black lashes upon his cheek and the beginning of dark stubble across his jaw accentuated his pallor.

"It is just you and me now." I placed his warm hand back upon his chest and patted it lightly. "Try not to die, sir."

The hand closed around mine. "Always my intent." I stared into a pair of gray quizzical eyes. I recoiled. To no avail; his hand tightly enclosed my own. "What the devil is your intent, Lady Augusta?"

"You are awake!" A stupidly obvious thing to say. I pulled against his impertinent clasp again. "Let me go!"

He immediately released my hand, but the strength of his hold stayed imprinted upon bone and flesh.

"How long have you been awake?" I demanded, trying to cover my shock.

"Since sometime in the carriage." He tentatively touched the makeshift bandage and winced. "Thank you for binding the wound." He sniffed experimentally. "Brandy?"

"Our gamekeeper advised me to always clean a wound with liquor," I said.

He nodded, clearly endorsing the measure.

"I'm glad you approve," I added with as much iciness as I could muster. "You say you woke in the carriage?" I searched my memory. Julia and I had discussed our plans at length on the short journey here. "Then I think you must already know our intent, Lord Evan."

He closed one eye in a judgmental squint. "Yes, but I cannot credit it. You intend to snatch a woman from her husband. That is kidnapping, Lady Augusta. Not the usual behavior of Lord Duffield's sensible twin sisters, as I recall."

Ah, he remembered us; I had, indeed, seen a flash of recognition on the roadside.

"Then you must also recall that, as sensible women, we are not inclined to overstating a situation, Lord Evan," I said, softening my voice into a heated whisper. "Lady Thorne is in imminent danger of being murdered by her husband."

"Imminent?"

I nodded. "We cannot be certain if she is still alive or even in this house, but I think she must be from Sir Reginald's reaction to our arrival. As you no doubt heard, he was not keen on allowing us inside and he is very keen for us to leave."

"Why on earth are you attempting this?"

"Her sister Millicent received a letter, a plea for help, that had been smuggled out by a sympathetic maid. The family cannot gain access, so Millicent asked us to intervene."

"A rather extraordinary request." Lord Evan dug his elbows into the couch seat and tried to sit up. "God's blood!" He collapsed back against the arm cushion.

I overlooked the profanity—the man was in extremis, after all—and grabbed a velvet cushion from behind me. "Here, lie back upon this. You must raise your head slowly. You have lost a great deal of blood."

He took the offering and positioned it behind his head with a baleful look. "If I recall, it is your fault I have lost a great deal of blood."

Undeniable, but then again, I had not started the encounter. "If I recall, you attempted to rob us."

His mouth twitched upward. "Touché."

"And your companion tried to shoot my coachman."

He nodded soberly. "Yes, not well done. My apologies. I told him there was to be no shooting, on any account." The edges of his mouth quirked up again. "I must point out, however, that you commandeered my senseless body to play your brother."

"True." I sat back. He was very quick. "Perhaps we could call it even."

The quirk broadened into a smile. "I like your idea of fair play, Lady Augusta."

"But now we have arrived at the matter at hand," I said. "You are awake, Lord Evan."

He looked away, all trace of amusement gone. "You must stop calling me Lord Evan. I have taken the name of Hargate. Jonathan Hargate."

"You are Lord Evan to me." I did not want him to forget his noblesse oblige, whatever he called himself. "Besides, you are wearing the Belford signet ring," I added, nodding to the ruby upon his finger. "That must mean something."

He shifted his hand as if to shield the ring. "How on earth do you know it is my family ring?"

"My sister recognized it. She remembers everything, even from twenty years ago."

He eyed me disbelievingly but said, "It means nothing. I left it here in England with a friend for safekeeping in case I returned and required money."

Yet here he was stealing for a living with the ring on his finger, clearly unsold.

"Then why—"

"You know I could expose you to Thorne and end this dangerous masquerade," he said, a rather abrupt forestalling of my question that brought us back to the delicate situation at hand.

I inclined my head. "True. And I could have you detained and taken to the local magistrate. I think you have more to lose than we do; we have not yet committed a crime, but you will hang if you are caught. However . . ." I paused for effect, fixing my gaze squarely upon his own. "I could offer you payment to continue this pretense." My voice sounded calm but my heart was thumping. What if he refused? What if he got up and left?

Something flickered within his eyes. Avarice? Offense? I could not tell.

"A guinea," I added. "And medical attention. All you have to do is act senseless, and once we have escaped with Lady Thorne, you go on your way."

He dug his elbows into the sofa again and this time managed to push himself more upright. "I do not keep good company, Lady Augusta, but even among my criminal society, Sir Reginald is known as a brutal man. Do you think I would lie on this sofa while you and your sister court such danger? I may no longer be Lord Evan, but I am not brought so low as to ignore females in distress or take payment to protect them."

Yet he would take money from females by force?

He obviously saw the thought upon my face, for he lifted his hand in acknowledgment. "Well, yes, I did attempt to rob you, but that is in the past and now we must face this predicament that you have placed us *all* in. I insist on offering you and your sister protection and helping you secure Lady Thorne's freedom."

"You cannot even stand, let alone provide protection."

"I have been in far worse states than this and hauled rock all day. I assure you I am quite capable."

Hauled rock; the work of a convict. I had heard about the conditions in the new colony, and my mind flitted across the idea of "worse states." Had he been flogged? A ghastly thought.

"Do your family know you have returned to England?"

He frowned at the change of subject, the movement in his wound making him wince. "I am no longer considered a Belford, so there is no reason for them to be apprised of my return. As I said, I am Hargate now."

Why then had he returned to England? But I did not ask the question, for there was something closed within his face that warned me from the subject.

He tilted his head at my silence. "What do you say? Are we in league together?"

He wanted to help and he did not want to be paid; the deal seemed all in my favor. Was it the noblesse oblige I had hoped for, or something more suspicious?

"We are in league, as long as you understand that my sister and I are rescuing Lady Thorne and you are only here to help. If needed."

"Of course. I am well aware of my position in the world, Lady Augusta," he said dryly. He looked around the room, locating something beyond my shoulder. "Ah, excellent, Thorne has provided wine. Shall we toast our agreement? I am parched."

I rose to see a full decanter set upon a nearby bureau. In truth, I felt the need for a glassful myself.

"If you find Lady Thorne, how do you propose to get her out of the house?" Lord Evan asked as I lifted the silver top and sniffed the wine's bouquet. A rather figgy burgundy.

"Julia was to smuggle her out the back to our carriage in the stables while I distracted Sir Reginald. We would then take our leave with her hidden inside our cabin and deliver her to her sister and brother-in-law in Hickstead." I poured.

Lord Evan looked pointedly at our carriage standing outside the windows. "The plan is going well, then."

"Like clockwork," I said with a wry smile. I handed him a glass and returned to my armchair.

"*Salute*," he said.

I raised my own glass and sipped as he finished his in one long gulp. All in all, the liquor was smooth, but a little heavy for my taste.

He considered his empty glass dispassionately. "I feel I must say that your rescue is simple to the point of naïve. Do you have a plan in case Thorne offers resistance? From what you say, he has already demonstrated his violent lack of respect for your sex, and your rank may not be enough protection."

He transferred his attention from the glass to me. If there was one person who knew about the failure of rank, it was Lord Evan. To be honest, I had barely imagined resistance. In my mind, we would rescue Caroline covertly and without violence. And now, I had to admit, with a great deal of blind reliance upon our rank.

"Clearly you have not," he added. "What on earth were you thinking?"

The fact that I had, indeed, not fully considered our venture stung me just as much as his tone. "I admit I do not have the benefit of your criminal experience. Perhaps you can suggest a more violent plan." The words were out before I had time to reconsider. Heat rose to my cheeks. "I am sorry, that was not well said."

He watched me for a moment, then shrugged. "I do have more experience, but I do not suggest violence." He passed me back the glass, a wistful smile requesting a refill. "Well, not unless it is visited upon me," he amended.

I placed his glass and my own down firmly upon the side table. "Too much wine can incite a fever after a bullet wound." More wise words from our gamekeeper. Besides, Lord Evan had annoyed me by being right. An unfair reaction, to be sure, but he had shaken me out of my complacency, an uncomfortable place to land. Ignoring his crestfallen expression, I asked, "What, then, do you suggest we do?"

"The problem is how to get Lady Thorne to the carriage."

"Agreed. I have thought about how we could get the carriage moved around to the stables, but Thorne has ordered it to stay out front."

He tilted his head to one side, considering me. "I have another idea, but it is a little mad and would require a great deal of nerve."

I bristled. "I assure you I have more than enough nerve."

"Indeed, you seem to be a woman of great resource."

I glanced at him, seeking the barb in his statement, but his eyes and that mobile mouth held only sincerity. I felt my cheeks heat. During my life, my nerve had only ever been celebrated by my sister, my father, and dear Charlotte. For the most part, it had been condemned as unfeminine, particularly by my brother.

"What is your idea, then?" I asked.

"Since you seem to have a talent for substituting one person for another," he said with only a touch of drollery in his voice, "what if Lady Thorne switched places with you or Lady Julia? Do you know if her build is similar to your own or your sister's?"

It was a good idea, which annoyed me again. However, I had to move past my own resentment for the sake of Caroline. "I met her years ago, before she was married." I shut my eyes for a second, trying to place myself back into the past. "I believe I stood over her, so she could be a similar height to my sister." The idea gathered momentum. "Julia brought a gown for Caroline in case . . . Well, we do not know what state she is in. Julia could wear it instead and Caroline could dress in Julia's clothes and walk out with me as my sister. Of course, Julia would have to get to the carriage too. That will be difficult but, yes, it could work."

He nodded. "I have seen someone escape from a prison by the same method. But it's not only your gumption that is needed. What of Lady Thorne and your sister?"

I knew I could count on Julia, but would Lady Thorne be able to enact such a masquerade? Was she even awake?

A commotion outside drew my attention. A gig driven by a slim man in sober black pulled up beside our carriage. As Thorne's groom ran to the horse's head, the man picked up a black case from the seat beside him and alighted with an apprehensive glance at the house from under the broad brim of his Clericus hat.

"I believe the doctor has arrived," I said. "You must still pretend to be senseless. You are our reason for staying here."

"Don't let the damn man bleed me," Lord Evan said, settling back down upon the cushions. "Losing more blood is the last thing I need."

"I could not agree more," I said fervently, for I had not found many in this world who shared my suspicion of the practice. What earthly good could come from cutting another wound into an already ailing body or removing precious blood? Surely the fact that people died from loss of blood undermined the activity. "Do not worry. I will not allow it."

With a nod, Lord Evan closed his eyes. I stared down at his pain-worn face, a little taken aback by his trust and my own avowal of protection. My father used to say, *Odd circumstances make for odd allies*, mainly in response to the never-ending war on the Continent. What would he have thought of this alliance with an ex-convict? I rather think he would have enjoyed it. Lud, how I missed him.

8

It seemed to take an age for the doctor to come to the drawing room, yet it was only a short distance from gig to door. Perhaps Sir Reginald or Bryden had delayed him with instructions to be rid of us. I sat forward in my chair, then dropped back again, trying to simulate an anxious attitude, but in all truth I did not need to simulate it; my anxiety was real enough. If this was the doctor who attended Caroline, maybe I could discover more about her situation. Or more to the point, her state of existence. But could I get the man to talk?

Finally, the knock came upon the doors and they opened to admit Bryden and the man from the gig, carrying his case.

"Dr. Haymer," Bryden announced.

The doctor bowed and hurried to the sofa, trailing a whiff of medicinal herb and sweat. His face was not without intelligence, but it also had an unfortunate weaselly cast to both nose and chin that matched a nervous manner. "Your brother has been shot, I hear, my lady."

"Luckily a glancing wound," I said as the doctor placed his case upon the side table. From the corner of my eye, I saw Bryden take his leave and close the doors behind him. No attempt to stay and keep watch upon our interaction. Our ruse seemed to be holding.

Dr. Haymer studied me with a darting professional eye, clearly suspicious that I might at any moment fall into a fit of womanly hysterics. Evidently I was deemed calm enough, for his attention turned to Lord Evan.

"The wound has been dressed, I see."

"Only temporarily. I had to use the neckcloths of my servants."

"Yes, well, that is most . . . very practical." He studied me again, this time aghast that a lady would have the stomach for such activities. "I shall redress it and bleed him to prevent a fever. Perhaps you would like to step out, my lady?"

"No. I cannot allow you to bleed him," I said. "He would not wish it."

"I understand your delicate sensibilities, my lady, but this is the appropriate course."

"No. He does not wish to be bled. I assure you."

The doctor drew himself up. "My lady, you must step aside. Otherwise you place your brother in further danger!"

I sat forward. "I said no."

"You are not thinking rationally, my lady. It is completely understandable, but—"

"Enough, man! Lady Augusta is as rational as they come," Lord Evan said, opening his eyes.

The doctor rocked back upon his heels, startled. "Ah, you are conscious, my lord. That is indeed a welcome sign. Do you have pain?"

"I have a cracking headache. Even so, I will not be bled." Lord Evan sat up and swung his feet to the floor, the movement strong and assured. At least it looked strong and assured, but he dug his fingers into the cushioning for support. He shot me an apologetic glance; so much for maintaining the pretense.

"But, my lord, bleeding is necessary to rebalance the—"

"Dress it. That is all."

The doctor's mouth bunched into a small circle of disapproval.

"As you wish, my lord." He opened his case, casting me a peevish glance; I might not be hysterical but I was plainly unmanageable.

I stood, feeling the need to call upon all my height for what came next. "I have a question of another order for you, Dr. Haymer."

He began to rummage through his collection of instruments and medicines. "I will answer if I can, my lady," he said without looking up. I bit back my irritation; Dr. Haymer was one of those who showed a woman her worth by focusing upon something else while she spoke.

"Do you attend Lady Thorne?"

Ah, that stopped him. He straightened, a wary look coming upon his narrow features. "It is not my practice to talk about patients except to family members, my lady."

"Yet I think you will answer Lady Augusta's question," Lord Evan said, and although he was seated and wore a makeshift bandage askew upon his head, he still managed to bring menace to the command.

"I am under no obligation to do so, my lord," Haymer said.

He was proving more staunch than I had anticipated.

"If you wish to continue practicing medicine, you will answer me," I said and caught Lord Evan's eye, trying to warn him of what was to come. "My brother here is a magistrate and he does not look kindly upon those who stand in the way of his inquiries." It was not exactly a lie; my real brother was indeed a magistrate.

The newly invested official rallied magnificently to his duties. "Indeed, I do not. In fact, I would say that any obstruction of my inquiries would result in a new inquiry as to why I was being obstructed." He kept a stern gaze upon the doctor, but I saw a flash of amusement in his eyes. "Answer my sister, sir!"

The doctor wet his lips. "I do so under protest, Lord Duffield. Yes, I have attended Lady Thorne."

So here was the dubious physician in Caroline's letter. "She is in this house? Where?" I demanded.

"Upstairs, on the second floor."

Involuntarily we all looked up at the ceiling, as if we could see the poor woman.

"What is her ailment?" Lord Evan asked.

"A nervous disposition. Delusions. She often descends into violence."

The skepticism in Lord Evan's face mirrored my own.

"What is the treatment? What do you prescribe?" he asked.

"Laudanum."

I knew the drug, an opiate of great strength. My own doctor had prescribed some for a cough a year ago and only one dose had sent me into a stupor. I had heard that just three spoons of the stuff could kill a man.

"How much do you prescribe?" I asked.

He cleared his throat. "I send a bottle a week."

"A week!" Lord Evan echoed. "Good God, man, surely you realize what Thorne is doing."

The doctor's thin jaw shifted. "I do not know what you mean, my lord."

"How much is he paying you?"

"I'm sure I do not understand you," the doctor said firmly.

"How long have you been supplying that much laudanum?" I asked, trying to keep the outrage from my voice.

"Only a few weeks."

I could see Thorne's ruthless plan unfolding before me: first, a few weeks of forcing his wife to take the drug until she had a dependence upon it, and then one day very soon she would take far too much. A tragic and fatal accident.

"When did you last see Lady Thorne?"

"Two days ago."

I clenched my fists by my sides. "And how was she?"

"Insensible," the doctor admitted. "But Sir Reginald told me she'd had another episode of violence and they had administered a dose of the laudanum for her own safety. I had no reason to disbelieve Sir Reginald. I have seen her attack her husband and Bryden with my own eyes."

No doubt fighting for her life.

"Doctor, please dress his lordship's injury. Then leave and never return or send any medications again," I ordered in my most implacable voice.

Haymer frowned. "I will not be commanded in such a manner, even by you, Lady Augusta. This is not your house."

"Do not imagine my words to be empty, Dr. Haymer. If we hear that you are treating Lady Thorne again, my brother will arrange for your license to be revoked. He has friends in the Royal College, you know."

It was ignoble intimidation on my part, but then the man had contributed to the imprisonment and drugging of a woman, potentially to death.

"You cannot do that. I have done nothing wrong," the doctor protested.

"You have done nothing that could be considered right, though, have you?" I replied.

The man had the grace to lower his eyes.

"Do your work, Haymer, then leave," Lord Evan ordered. "Speak to no one of our conversation, especially Sir Reginald or Bryden, or I will bring the law down upon you in every conceivable way. Do you understand?"

The doctor gave a tight nod and quickly dressed the wound in silence. I watched him closely in case he thought to take some revenge, but it was a reasonable job considering his hands were not entirely steady. At the end he packed up his case and with a stiff bow hurried out to his gig.

"I am convinced now," Lord Evan said as we watched Dr. Haymer through the window. The little man stared back at us for a rancorous moment, then climbed into his gig and steered it around our own carriage, urging his pony into a smart trot down the driveway. "We have to find Lady Thorne and see what state she is in."

"If she is insensible, we will not be able to walk her out disguised as my sister."

"Our sister," Lord Evan said, flashing me a grim smile.

"I will go to Julia. Perhaps she has discovered more."

"I cannot allow you to wander a potential murderer's house on your own. I will come too." He gathered himself to rise from the sofa.

I placed my hand upon his shoulder, a gross breach of decorum. "No. Stay here. If you are seen creeping around the house, then you are clearly well enough to leave and we lose our reason for being here."

His body tensed under my untoward touch, but he merely nodded his acquiescence and settled back onto the sofa. Why on earth had I taken such a liberty? He was more or less a complete stranger, and yet here I was manhandling him and trusting his sense of honor.

"I will tell Sir Reginald that you must rest here until the evening," I added. "That will give us time to find her and see what we can do. If you can engage him at all, please do so. The less he wanders his own home, the better."

I headed to the door, collecting my bonnet and gloves on the way.

"If you need me, just yell," he said.

"Ladies do not yell," I replied over my shoulder.

"But renegades do."

I caught a glimpse of myself in one of the mirrors as I passed; my color was high and I had the remnant of a smile upon my face. There was no getting around the shameful truth: for all the danger we were in, I was enjoying myself.

9

Bryden must have been watching the drawing room door, for as soon as I entered the hallway, he emerged from his butler's pantry.

"I see Dr. Haymer has left, my lady," he said.

"Yes." I did not offer any more, although I could see his disquiet at the doctor's abrupt exit. "Where is your master? I would speak to him."

"I am here, Lady Augusta." Sir Reginald stepped out from the room opposite, arms folded. Had he been watching and waiting too? "I trust that Haymer was able to assist your brother. He did not stay long enough for me to speak to him." He glanced at Bryden from under his brow, a reprimand if ever I saw one. Then again, perhaps I was too keen to see sinister collusion.

"No, I believe he had another urgent medical matter to attend," I said blithely. "The good news is my brother has regained his senses. Haymer said he must rest until this evening before we can move him again. I trust that is not too inconvenient."

"Yes, well, what must be, must be," Sir Reginald said with his customary lack of grace.

"I am now more concerned for my sister." I looked up the staircase, arranging my expression into a worried frown. I considered my next words; best to sow the seeds of our plan if it were to go ahead.

"Once she has worked herself into one of these vaporish fits, they can last for days."

"Days?" Sir Reginald echoed.

"It might be best if I send her to Brighton first in our carriage, so that her own doctor can be called and she can rest in her own bed, and then it can return for us." I could not help adding, "It is a good thing it is still standing out front."

He did not react to the jibe. "Bryden, show Lady Augusta to her sister."

"Your bonnet and gloves, my lady?" Bryden said, holding out his hand to collect my outerwear.

I did not wish to be parted from my belongings in this house—who knew when a hasty retreat would be required—but I handed them to him; to do otherwise would have been odd. He placed them upon the side table beside Julia's parasol and then led the way up the staircase. I could feel Sir Reginald's eyes upon me as I climbed. Were his suspicions aroused? I could not see how; Lord Evan's wound was plainly real, and I had not shown any more interest in his wife. He had no reason to think I had any connection to Lady Thorne's family. Besides, there would be few men in this world who would believe that two women could even conceive of such a daring plan, let alone two women well past their prime. To be constantly underestimated sometimes worked in one's favor.

As I followed Bryden along the first-floor corridor, I caught up my fob watch and noted the time: almost three o'clock. By my reckoning, we had only thirty minutes of polite solitude, at most, before my sister would be expected to descend the stairs and depart. Any longer than that and suspicions would be aroused. Thirty minutes to find Lady Thorne, enact a risky masquerade, and spirit her away in the carriage. Was it even feasible? I let my watch fall back upon its chain, its small weight tapping against my bodice as I walked. A reminder of the seconds already ticking away.

Unlike the portraits in the drawing room, the paintings in this less visible part of the house were definitely second-rate, mainly studies of dead game or bowls of fruit. The rooms on the floor above—where Lady Thorne was being kept, according to the doctor—had been beyond my view as we ascended the staircase, and so I was no wiser as to her position. Nor did I wish to ask Bryden for information. From the doctor's report, it seemed likely that Bryden was in collusion with his master, or at the very least following orders without moral protest.

I had to admit, Lord Evan's warning about the risk of our venture had taken root in my mind. By law, our attempt to extract Lady Thorne would be considered kidnapping or abduction and very much outside the law. However, the fact that Sir Reginald was mistreating his wife was not against the law and would not be so until she was dead by his hand or design. According to the laws of England, and indeed God, she was his chattel and he could do with her as he pleased up to the point of murder. Was it any wonder that I could not reconcile this God with my own moral sense? Or indeed, with my own sense of existence as a human being in my own right and not merely an adjunct to my father, brother, or husband? But without the guidance of God or sensible law, how did one know if one's actions were right? Were Julia and I in the wrong?

Halfway along the corridor, Bryden stopped in front of a door.

"The Cornflower Room, my lady."

"Thank you. You may go."

He bowed and set out the way we had come. I waited a few moments—enough time for him to move away in case Julia was not within—then rapped upon the door.

"Come."

Blue velvet curtains were drawn across the window, but a candelabra set upon the white fireplace mantel lit a nicely managed scene of suffering: Julia reclining upon a blue chaise longue near the window, her hand to her forehead and softly moaning.

"It is me, dearheart." I closed the door.

She immediately sat up. "Lud, I thought you would never come."

We met halfway, at the end of the large bed plump with covers and pillows. I clasped Julia's hands, her touch bringing its customary comfort.

I searched her face. "You have found her!"

"I believe so. At least, I have found a locked room on the floor above. Bolted on the outside!" She eyed me shrewdly. "What has happened?"

"Lord Evan is awake."

A knock on the door swung us both around to face it. Julia flung herself back down upon the chaise longue, hand raised to forehead again.

"Who is it?" I called.

"William, my lady. I have brought Lady Julia's medicine casket."

Ah, Weatherly.

"Good thought," Julia said to me.

"Come," I called again. Weatherly entered, carrying Julia's supplies. "Is there anyone else out there?" I whispered.

He poked his head out again, then closed the door. "No one, my lady."

"Good." I waved him and the casket over to the bed.

Julia was on her feet again. "What did Lord Evan say? He must be willing to keep quiet, since you are up here."

"Lord Evan is awake, my lady?" Weatherly asked.

"Yes, but he is not going to give us away. In fact . . . he wants to help."

"Help? Beyond keeping quiet?" Julia looked up from unfastening the casket. "No! We cannot trust him."

"Forgive me, Lady Augusta, but I must agree," Weatherly said. "He tried to rob you."

"I know, but you have not spoken with him," I said. "He is still a gentleman at heart. A little ragged around the edges, perhaps, but his noblesse oblige is still there. I'm sure of it. Moreover, he had a good idea about how to get Caroline out of the house and he is very quick; he played along beautifully when the doctor came."

Julia's eyes narrowed in speculation. "Lord help us, you like him."

"Why do you say that?"

"I can hear it in your voice, Gussie, and you are defending him as if I have him on the dock." She tilted her head. "What makes you think he is trustworthy?"

"He has a sense of humor," I said, and then added the final proof. "And he found my observations funny too."

"Ah." Julia nodded.

It was a fact that many men of our acquaintance did not think a woman capable of a genuine sense of humor, or if she did exhibit something of the kind, that it was a singular and unfeminine trait. Consequently, my sister and I believed that if a man did accept and enjoy a woman's humor, it was a sign of both intelligence and worth. Perhaps a singular belief in itself, but so far it had proved infallible. Julia's own Robert had found her gentle wit vastly amusing, and he had been one of the cleverest and most honorable men I had ever met. Conversely, Duffy had always thought my humor to be the very reason I was unmarried; in his opinion, no man would put up with such a sharp tongue.

"Now that he is awake, I am not sure we can really reject his offer of help," I added. "Besides, I feel somewhat responsible for him. After all, I did shoot him and bring him here."

Julia opened the casket lid and peered inside. "I hardly think you need take responsibility for him, but I do think you are right—we will have to accept his help since we cannot send him back to an unconscious state. Did you discover anything from the doctor?"

I apprised her of the interview with Dr. Haymer.

"What a cur! So much laudanum. I am glad Lord Evan threatened him," Julia said vehemently.

"It also means that when we find Caroline, it is possible she may not be awake."

"I was thinking the same." Julia rummaged inside her casket and withdrew a small bottle. "Hartshorn," she said, shaking it in triumph. "It will rouse her if she is not too far gone, poor girl."

She turned to Weatherly, standing guard near the door. "Did you find out anything from belowstairs?"

"Most of them will not talk, my lady. I'd say they're scared of Bryden. One of the senior maids, Agatha, was friends with Lady Thorne's abigail, Curran, and she opened up a little. Told me Curran walked to the town a few weeks back and never came back. Her box is gone, too, so she meant to go."

"The sympathetic maid, perhaps, who posted the letter?" I suggested to Julia. "We must look for her after this is all settled. She has sacrificed her position to help her mistress. Anything else, Weatherly?"

"William, my lady," he gently corrected. I nodded, waving for him to continue. "Agatha also said that all the servants have been told that their mistress is mad and if they see her out of her room, to get Sir Reginald or Bryden. For her own good."

"Did Agatha say which room? Is it the locked one upstairs?" Julia asked quickly.

"She didn't say so directly, my lady, but she looked upward when she said it, so I think it might be."

"Excellent work, Weather . . . William," I said.

"So, what is this new plan that the amusing, and amused, Lord Evan has suggested?" Julia asked me.

Ignoring the gentle taunt, I apprised her of the masquerade Lord Evan and I had concocted. Well, most of the masquerade; as I explained it to her, I came to the realization that we had not addressed a rather large problem. Almost immediately, an obvious solution offered itself to me, but I fancied neither my sister nor Lord Evan was going to be pleased with the risk it entailed. Let alone Weatherly.

"Such a masquerade could work, I suppose," Julia said slowly. "If Caroline is to wear my ensemble, then I will need to change into that day gown I brought for her. We must hope that Caroline is near enough to my size to be convincing." She spoke to Weatherly. "William, go to the carriage. You will find a blue-striped dimity gown and a pair of kid slippers wrapped in cloth."

"And when you retrieve them, inform John Driver of the change of plan," I added.

Weatherly bowed, carefully opened the door, and peered out. With a conspiratorial nod, he exited, closing the door with an exaggeratedly soft click. It seemed he was rather enjoying himself too.

"It feels disrespectful calling him William again," Julia said. She closed the casket lid and stared at it for a moment, then looked up with a frown. "My dear, if you and Lord Evan are distracting Sir Reginald as we get into the carriage, how are you going to then make your way to the carriage for our escape?"

Ah, she had seen the problem. I modulated my voice into my best big-sister tone.

"As I see it, you will need as much time as possible to get Caroline away, so Lord Evan and I will not depart with you. We will stay back and keep Sir Reginald from following you."

"Are you insane?" Julia crossed her arms. "Nothing in this world will make me leave you in the company of an enraged husband and a highwayman whom you imagine is some kind of lapsed gentleman."

Put like that, it did sound rather insane. "Do you have a better idea?"

"Yes, you get in the carriage with us and leave Lord Evan to deal with Sir Reginald!"

That was indeed possible, but something within me resisted such an exit. Firstly, for good strategic reasons, but also, I had to admit, because it seemed rather poor form to abandon Lord Evan to take the brunt of Sir Reginald's wrath. I suspect he would have agreed with Julia's plan, but since he was not present, his vote was mine.

"That is all very well, but as you have more or less intimated, we cannot rely upon Lord Evan's sense of duty. What if he does not try to stop Sir Reginald from following us?" I was plunging Lord Evan further down in my sister's estimation, but it was a reasonable argument if one had not actually met the man. "If Sir Reginald came after us and dragged Caroline back, we would have no legal recourse, and we would be open to charges of kidnap. No, I must be there to extend the masquerade and ensure you have enough time to get to Hickstead."

Julia lifted a mulish chin. "And then what? Just how do you think you are going to depart? By magic?"

"Sir Reginald expects our carriage to return, so let it return. Send Weatherly back for us. Lord Evan and I can take our leave and make sure that Sir Reginald thinks we are still heading to Brighton. We will pick you up in Hickstead and continue home."

After a moment of hard consideration, Julia's chin lowered. "I suppose so."

"It is a good plan, Julia, with every prospect of success," I said firmly.

"It is about as mad as it can get," she said just as firmly. "But we are in the thick of it now and I can see no other way to proceed except to abandon Caroline, and we cannot do that. We must trust in God."

And a great deal of luck, I thought, but I did not voice it.

She sat down on the chaise longue. "Promise me one thing, though, Gussie. Do not trust Lord Evan as if he is a friend."

"Of course not. I am not a fool for a handsome face," I said.

She eyed me gravely. "And when did Lord Evan become handsome?" she asked.

I had no answer for that, so I returned to the door and busied myself looking for Weatherly's return.

10

Ten minutes later Julia and I cautiously emerged from the Cornflower Room. Julia, hastily clad in the retrieved dimity gown, closed the door behind us with a quiet click. Weatherly had returned with the gown and shoes in mere minutes—he must have sprinted there and back—and then stood guard outside the door while the costume change was in progress. Julia's original clothes lay on the bed, ready for their new inhabitant. Now we were ready for the heart of the matter: retrieving Lady Thorne.

I pointed Weatherly to the staircase that led to the second floor: a far more prosaic wooden example than the sinuous iron-and-gilt showpiece that dominated the entrance hall.

"Keep watch," I whispered.

He nodded and trod softly to his position.

"You have the hartshorn?" I asked Julia.

She held up the small brown bottle. "I pray she is awake. How will we get her back here and into my carriage gown if she is senseless?"

"One thing at a time, my dear."

She nodded, chewing on her lip: a nervous habit from childhood. I led the way past Weatherly and up the staircase, keeping close to the wall and almost upon my tiptoes. Halfway up, a floorboard creaked under my foot, the sound immense in our silence. I stopped, holding my breath. Julia froze behind me. Both of us looked back at Weatherly. He leaned over the banister, peering down to the ground floor. Finally, he glanced up and shook his head. I released my breath and we continued upward, coming to a cautious halt upon the uncarpeted second-floor landing.

Julia pointed to a door on our right. "There."

I did not need the direction; the stout oak door was held fast by three heavy barrel bolts and a keyhole with a large iron key protruding from it. A lot of locks for one young infirm woman.

I pressed my ear to the wood and listened.

Julia raised her brows: *Anything?*

I shook my head. Perhaps she was not in there, or worse, already dead. I reached up and eased the top bolt out of its catch plate, its progress accompanied by a grating rasp. Julia closed her eyes. The second bolt slid back too easily, the snib coming to rest with a tiny clunk. Julia's eyes flew open, her apprehension mirroring my own. We both looked down the stairs, but nothing stirred. I took a deep breath and worked the third back, gritting my teeth as it scraped along its full course. Finally, I turned the key counterclockwise in its lock.

"There," I breathed.

I turned the handle. The door opened into heavy gloom and an assault of odor: vomit and dank feces underlaid by a sharp medicinal punch. I recoiled, gagging against the stink.

"Dear God," Julia said, pressing her hand to her nose.

I forced down another gag and stepped in. The heavily curtained window allowed a crack of sun into the room, my sight adjusting to the minimal light. Gray shadows coalesced into furniture: a narrow bed set against the far wall with a faded red damask cover and a small human-sized mound in its center. A mound that did not move at the sound of our entrance. A table stood beside the bed, a collection of brown glass bottles upon it.

"Look at all the laudanum," I whispered to Julia, more to release my shock than from any real need to alert her to the fact. This was no invalid lady's bedchamber. It was a prison. "Close the door."

With the door shut against any casual discovery, we approached Caroline, for it could be no other in the bed. She lay on her side, the cover over her head so that only a small wedge of profile was visible: badly bruised lips and the tip of a nose. One pale hand was curled upon the stained pillow. Were her lips bruised from being forced to swallow the drug, or from ill treatment? Either option curled my hands into fists. How I wished I could force a pint of laudanum down Sir Reginald's throat, preferably still encased in the bottle.

"Lady Thorne," I called softly.

No movement. No sound.

Beside me, Julia's hand clutched the gold cross at her throat. "Are we too late?"

I leaned over, trying to discern if the girl breathed, but the light was too dim. I reached across and held my finger under her nose. Nothing. Then, soft warm air against my skin.

"She is alive."

"Dear God, thank you!" Julia kissed her cross.

I touched Caroline's shoulder, or at least where I guessed her shoulder to be under the covers. Perhaps she would respond to a more intimate approach. "Caroline, wake up. We are here to help you."

Still no response.

"Does she hear us?" Julia raised her voice slightly. "Caroline."

I glanced at the door, but it remained motionless and there was no sound beyond. "Lower your voice, my dear."

"We cannot carry her down the staircase," Julia whispered.

"I know. Time to try your hartshorn."

Julia flipped open the hinged lid upon the small vial, both of us turning our heads from the waft of its ammoniac contents.

"Good God, that is strong," I said.

"I buy the best; Dr. Palmers." Julia leaned over and held it beneath Caroline's nose.

It took but a second. Caroline drew in a deep, violent breath, her eyes opening wide. She hauled herself up amidst the foul tangle of nightdress and bedclothes. Julia recoiled as Caroline lunged at us, her bony hands locking around my wrists. I wrenched my arms back, dragging the girl with me.

"It is all right, we are here to help you," Julia hissed.

I stumbled back, trying to pull myself from Caroline's grasp, but she used my momentum to launch herself from the bed, slamming her slight weight into my body. I staggered and hit the wall, pulling her with me.

I gasped from the impact, then managed, "Stop! We are here to help you!"

Julia launched herself back into the fray and hauled upon Caroline's shoulders, loosening the girl's grip. They lurched away from me as if in a drunken dance until Julia spun her around again. I caught her arms, wrenching her from my sister's grasp.

"Millicent sent us!" I said, hissing the words an inch from Caroline's terrified face. "Do you understand? Millicent sent us. We are here to rescue you."

"Millicent?" Caroline strained to look over her shoulder at the door. "Millicent? Where is she?" The words rose into a sob.

Julia grasped the girl's narrow shoulders. "She is not here. Your husband will not let your family come, so we are here to take you home."

Caroline fought her way through the haze of laudanum to focus upon us. "Home? But who are you?"

"I am Lady Augusta Colebrook and this is my sister, Lady Julia Colebrook."

Georgina Randall had clearly instilled exquisite manners in her offspring, for Caroline, half-dead and covered in her own excrement, inclined her head. "How do you do. I am Lady Thorne." She hesitated. "I am Caroline."

"Are you able to stand on your own?" I asked.

She nodded, so I cautiously released her arms, ready to catch her again. She swayed but remained upright, jaw set with effort. Such courage.

"My husband?"

"Downstairs, so we must move swiftly."

"He has made me out to be mad, you know, but I am not mad," she said, her voice a soft rasp. "For five years I ran this house for him—I ran it well. But I could not get with child. I wanted to, so much, but I could not. I would have gone mad, you know, except for Curran. She knew what was happening. Whenever she could, she watered down the laudanum. She got out, didn't she? She sent my letter?" The words spilled out of her, a lancing of the horror.

"Yes, she sent it."

She caught my arm. "Is she safe? I could not bear it if she were harmed."

"She is not here and as far as we know, she is safe." I could give no further reassurance, but Caroline nodded, clearly relieved that her maid had at least escaped the house. I looked across at my sister, crouched by the bed. "What are you doing, Julia? We must go."

She ran her fingers across the carpet in a large arc. "I dropped the . . . Ah, found it!" She rose, clutching the vial of hartshorn and peered at its contents. "Still half left."

"Come, now," I said, guiding Caroline to the door with a hand to her damp back. I could feel her resisting, still unsure. Or perhaps just terrified. "The longer we stay, my dear, the higher the risk your husband will think something is amiss."

"If he finds me out of the room—" A shiver hitched her shoulders high. "Why are you doing this for me? You don't even know me."

"Your godmother is my good friend," I said.

"Aunt Charlotte? She sent you too?"

"Indeed, the countess and your whole family wish you to be free."

"They are sending you to your connections in Ireland," Julia added. "Your family is going to protect you."

At such declarations of support, Caroline moved more determinedly toward the door. Another thought stopped her short again. She looked up at me, the whites of her eyes stark in the dim light. "How are we to get out? How are we to get past him and the servants?"

"It is not going to be easy," I admitted.

I began to lay out our plan. As I spoke of switching clothes, masquerading as my sister, a calm walk to our carriage, I heard the sheer insanity of the endeavor. I could feel it, too, in the growing tension across Caroline's shoulders beneath my supporting arm.

"But is it only you two ladies and a footman and driver?" she asked, her voice hollow. "There is no one else?"

"We are up to the task," I said. She did not need to know the complication of Lord Evan.

She grasped my forearm, her grip weak but her nails digging

in her desperation. "This cannot fail. If I am returned to this room, I will not survive it."

"We will not fail," I said firmly.

Ahead of us in the gloom, I saw Julia's pale hand lift to her forehead to make the cross.

11

Julia opened the prison door a crack and peered through it.

"Clear," she whispered and opened the door wider.

We edged out onto the empty landing, our weight sending a creak through the floorboards. Caroline could walk with Julia's help, but every footfall wobbled with effort. I closed the door and inched the locks back into position—a gratifyingly silent process now that I knew their idiosyncrasies—then led the way to the top of the staircase.

Slowly we started to descend the steps, me at the front, Julia at the rear, and Caroline in between us in case she pitched forward or back.

On the floor below, Weatherly stood stalwartly at his post. He glanced up, relief in his eyes. Then, suddenly, his attention shifted downstairs. A noise. We heard it too. The sound of approach. Weatherly lifted his hand: *Stop.* I held my arm across the staircase to halt the progress of Julia and Caroline.

And then, voices. Two young women, giggling and whispering in the entrance hall.

Maids.

Weatherly glanced up, a warning in his eyes.

There was no possible way that Caroline could get back up the stairs in time. I waved Weatherly toward the approaching girls. *Stop them*, I mouthed. He gave a tiny nod and, with admirable swagger, descended the steps whistling a jaunty tune.

"Aren't you full of yourself," one of the maids said, her sharp voice amplified in the empty entrance hall. "Mr. Bryden will 'ave your guts for garters if he hears you goin' on like that."

"But he's not here, so I'll whistle as I like."

A clear message: Bryden was not in his pantry. Was he someplace on the floor below? I peered along as much of the corridor as I could see from my perch. No sign of anyone.

"You be careful of him. He don't like your kind," a second voice said, but there was some sympathy in her tone.

"Well, in that case, why don't you show me where I can get some warm water for my lady. So's I can avoid him," Weatherly said.

"Sure, I'll show you." The second voice punctuated her boldness with a giggle.

"We'll both show you," the sharp voice added firmly.

"Where you from?" the second voice asked as the sound of their footsteps receded. Weatherly's reply was faint, muffled by walls and distance, until finally the stairway settled back into silence.

Thank heavens for Weatherly; he was proving most adept at subterfuge. I hoped he truly meant to fetch the water too; Caroline needed a good wash or her stink would give us away. I waited a moment longer, listening, but all remained quiet.

I waved Julia and Caroline forward. It seemed to take us forever to reach the bottom of the steps, and even longer to make our slow way along the corridor with Julia on one side of Caroline and me on the other, each supporting an arm. I barely breathed the whole way along it, my hearing stretched to listen for footsteps.

Finally, we made our way into the Cornflower Room. I closed the door and leaned against it.

Safe, for the moment.

I gathered up my watch. We had no more than ten minutes left, at most.

"Gussie dear, I believe Caroline has fainted," Julia said behind me. She stood with her arms wrapped around the limp girl, straining to hold her up. Alarmingly, she looked just as pale as Caroline.

"My dear, let me take her!" I jumped forward and took hold of Caroline's arm, shouldering most of her weight. We half dragged, half carried the girl to the chaise longue and dropped her a little untidily onto its seat, her head lolling back against the blue velvet cushions. Julia set the hartshorn bottle upon the side table.

"Julia, are you quite well? You look worse than Caroline."

"I doubt that," Julia said. Her voice held a note of *do not fuss* and she did not look my way, sure signs that she was hiding something. She bent to study the girl's pale, bruised face. "Poor child. I wonder when she last ate? Perhaps that is part of her weakness."

"Good thought. Do you have anything in your casket?"

Julia turned to the box, considering her supplies. "The brandy will help, and I believe I have some Bath Biscuits. Not an enticing meal, but she must eat something to give her the strength to stand." She suddenly pressed her hands to her face. "Oh, Gus, how could Thorne do such a thing? He must be a madman."

Not mad and not alone in his brutal sanity, but I did not voice my thought. I took Julia's hands from her face and held them in my own. "Are you sure you can go on? I fear you are not as well as you say."

She pulled her hands from mine and turned back to the casket. "We are running out of time. Wake Caroline with the hartshorn and I'll find the brandy and biscuits."

The subject of her own health, it seemed, was closed. For now, at least.

Weatherly did indeed bring the warm water. He had seen Caroline's state as she came down the stairs and anticipated the need, bless his keen butler's eye. It was clear, however, that the small pitcher he had been able to acquire was not adequate for the task ahead. She really needed a full bath, perhaps two. Nevertheless, with him in the hallway standing guard, we roused Caroline, stripped her of her rancid nightgown, gave her a Bath Biscuit, and began to wash away the weeks of misuse.

I had never before considered how difficult it was to bathe and dress another person. As I wiped Caroline's face and arms, I gained a new respect for my maid Tully's daily efforts on my behalf. Alongside the reticence that must come with touching another in such an intimate way, it was hard to manage the placement of limbs or judge how hard to press, especially when I could not always distinguish what was grime and what was bruised flesh. But it was when I moved to wash Caroline's back that a rather obvious and disturbing problem presented itself: every bone in the girl's spine and rib cage was visible. Although she was the same height as Julia, my sister's carriage gown would hang upon her as if a child wore her mother's clothes.

"Padding," I said out loud at the end of this realization.

"What?" Julia asked.

I looked around the room, focusing upon the large bed. "We must pad your body with the bedclothes, Caroline."

The girl laboriously swallowed a mouthful of dry biscuit and nodded. "I did not dare eat what they gave me," she whispered. Her voice had still not recovered any volume.

"No, padding will take too long," Julia said.

"She is half your size. Thorne or Bryden will note it."

"Lady Augusta is right," Caroline added. "Bryden notices everything and he is my husband's creature."

It took Julia only a minute or so to wrangle a sheet from the layers of bedclothes, but it took us a great deal longer to cut and wrap the cloth around Caroline to create a semblance of Julia's figure and button the carriage gown over it. Precious minutes ticking away. She had no undergarments, no corset, so the modeling was far from perfect, as was the method of securing it; we had to use a series of knots and sacrifice a few of our own dress pins. By the time I tied the poke bonnet ribbons around Caroline's chin, I feared she would faint again from the exertion of standing. Would she even be able to walk out of the house as we planned?

Outside the door, Weatherly said, "I believe Lady Julia is still indisposed, Mr. Bryden."

Damn, we were out of time. Julia looked wildly at me. I waved her behind the bed and pressed Caroline down onto the chaise longue, motioning her to lie upon it and stay still.

The inevitable knock sounded. I waited until Julia ducked out of sight behind the bed, then walked to the door, my heart thumping. "Who is it?"

"It is Bryden, Lady Augusta. Do you or Lady Julia require anything?"

If he noticed anything awry here, we were finished. I took a deep breath and opened the door.

Thorne's butler stood squarely in the doorway. Weatherly had taken the suitably subordinate position behind him, yet he loomed over the smaller man. In the periphery of my sight, I could see his jaw clamped shut. He was not as calm as he appeared either.

Bryden's eyes met mine for an impassive second and then he turned his attention to the wedge of dimly lit room behind me. If

Caroline did not move, all he would see over my shoulder was a reclining figure in a poke bonnet upon the chaise longue. At least that was the desperate hope. I fought the urge to turn and check.

"Lady Julia is minutes from departing," I said. His gaze swung back to me, his jowly face giving nothing away. "Please inform our coachman to ready the carriage."

He bowed his head. "Of course, my lady."

"William, pack up Lady Julia's medicine casket and take it down."

"Yes, my lady." With a deferential incline of his head, Weatherly inserted himself between Bryden and the door, forcing the butler to step back. A neat move that enabled him to close the door between us and Bryden. I moved to the chaise longue as Weatherly listened for the other man's retreat downstairs. I would wager my left arm that Bryden still stood outside.

"Julia, are you ready?" I asked, raising my voice a little.

Julia rose from behind the bed. "I am, my dear," she said, matching my volume but adding an invalid's quaver. "I am sure I can walk to the carriage now."

We all heard the creak of floorboards outside. Bryden finally moving downstairs. Weatherly held up a restraining hand: *Wait.* All of us remained frozen in our places: a tableau of strained listening. Finally, he opened the door a crack.

He nodded. "Gone."

I offered my hands to Caroline and pulled her up from the chaise longue.

Her grip trembled within mine. "I can't do it," she whispered. "He will know it is me."

"Caroline, you are just minutes away from freedom and safety." I squeezed her hands. "You have been so brave. Do not fail now. You know what to do. Let Lady Julia and me manage the rest."

She drew a deep, quivering breath. "Yes. Of course. Of course."

Julia eyed Caroline's blanched face then passed me the bottle of hartshorn. "Just in case," she murmured.

Indeed. I closed my gloved hand round the vial and gathered Caroline into a close hold. "Remember, keep your head turned into my shoulder and the handkerchief up to your mouth. We are just going to walk out of the house and I will put you into the carriage. And then you and Julia will be away."

"But how will you get to the carriage?" Caroline asked Julia. "Surely you will be seen."

"I am going to make my way out the back of the house and then around to the carriage."

"You should take the staircase at the other end of the corridor," Caroline said. "On the ground floor you will find the conservatory. There is a door there that will take you into the garden and from there a way to the front of the house."

Julia pressed her gloved hand over Caroline's trembling fingers. "That is a better plan than I had. Thank you."

"Are you ready, Caroline?" I asked.

"Yes." The word was all but breath.

"Julia?"

"As ready as I will ever be," my sister said.

I nodded to Weatherly. He opened the door. Beyond it stood the landing, the staircase, and the entrance hall. Quiet, unremarkable, and probably no more than fifty yards in total, yet one of the most frightening terrains I had ever faced.

12

I led Caroline out onto the landing, her head tucked into my shoulder, the extravagant edge of my sister's poke bonnet and the linen handkerchief obscuring her face. We shuffled a little, trying to find a rhythm that allowed the close embrace. Finally, I tightened my grip around her right arm and padded waist and steadied our gait. Even through the heavy layers of cloth, my hands felt the trembling strain in her body. At the corner of my eye, I saw Julia carefully close the Cornflower Room door, then head toward the staircase at the other end of the corridor. She was on her own now. Nothing I could do except trust that she would find her way through the house and to the carriage without being seen.

Caroline and I began our slow descent down the main stairs. Weatherly followed, two steps behind, with the medicine casket clutched to his chest: a silent, tense procession.

Too silent. Too tense.

"You will be in Brighton soon, sister," I said, forcing my voice into the soothing tone reserved for peevish invalids.

No sign of Bryden in the entrance hall yet, but it would not be long.

"Be sure to send William for the doctor as soon as you arrive," I continued. "Not Dr. Henry. I do not think he understands your nerves. Send for Dr. Garden. Lady Melbourne recommends him most highly. Duffield and I will follow as soon as he is able. I am sure it will be soon, for he is well awake and Dr. Haymer thought that a very good sign, so you must not worry."

My wittering had taken us down to the bottom of the steps and the inevitable appearance of Bryden. He emerged from his pantry, the exemplar of an efficient butler, bowing and collecting Julia's parasol from the side table.

Damn. I had forgotten the parasol. I did not have a spare hand to take hold of it, and if he tried to pass it to Caroline, she would look at him. A reflex. If she somehow managed to control the impulse, then that would be suspicious in itself: a lady did not blindly grope for an accessory. Or worse, such an interaction with one of her jailers might overthrow Caroline's slender control. As it was she trembled against me, her fingers digging into my waist with the pressure of panic.

I watched Bryden approach, every sedate step bringing catastrophe closer. What to do? My father's advice would be *When in doubt, attack*. It did not always serve him well, but in this case—

"For goodness' sake, Bryden!" I said sharply. "Are you blind? Lady Julia is in no fit state to carry such a weight. Give it to William."

"Of course, my lady." He bowed and stepped aside as we passed him. From the corner of my eye, I saw him hand the parasol to Weatherly.

Thorne's footman opened the front door. So close now. No more than ten yards to the portico, and then the stone staircase and into the carriage. John Driver had circled it around to stand at the bottom of the steps.

To my right, the drawing room door was closed; no chance to see Lord Evan. Was he still well enough to play his part? Still willing?

"Nearly there, my dear," I said to Caroline. She was leaning upon me heavily now, her breathing fast and shallow. *Dear God, do not faint, girl.* I dug my thumbnail under the lid of the hartshorn bottle and eased it off, suppressing the ammoniac rise with the pad of my thumb.

Out the front door, my eyes fixed upon the footman. Would he see anything amiss? But no, his eyes remained suitably fixed upon the wall opposite. We stepped into the warmer outside air, leaving Bryden and the house behind.

"I see you are set to leave, Lady Julia," Sir Reginald called up from the driveway. "I shall hand you up."

Dear God! Involuntarily, I clutched Caroline closer to me and felt her draw a quivering breath. He had been standing behind the stone balustrade, unseen. Did this new hospitality come from suspicion or from relief that he would be soon rid of at least one of us?

"How kind, Sir Reginald," I called back as calmly as I could.

A flash of white at Caroline's feet caught my eye. Oh no, some of the sheet padding had come loose and dragged upon the ground behind. Would he see it? Nothing I could do about it now.

"Courage," I murmured into Caroline's ear. "All is in hand."

It was plainly not, but I steered Caroline down the steps. I was all but carrying the girl, her body slumped against mine, her limbs heavy and her breathing so shallow she must surely faint. If she buckled, I would have to use the hartshorn. A problem in itself—it would throw her head back and all would be discovered.

I met the worried gaze of our coachman, stiffly upright in his high seat. Had he seen Julia enter the carriage as planned? He gave the barest shake of his head. Damn, Caroline could not leave without Julia in the carriage. The poor girl would not manage without my sister's clear head and support.

On the pretext of a small cough, I searched the courtyard for any sign of Julia. Was she still in the house? Perhaps she had come to some mishap. No sign of my sister.

Another two steps brought us to the gravel courtyard and Sir Reginald.

"I trust that your sister is well enough to travel," Thorne said, eyeing Caroline's trembling form, her head still tucked within my shoulder.

"I think the sooner she is home, the better," I said as Weatherly made his way to the carriage to open the door. Thorne was still watching Caroline. Desperate to divert his attention, I added, "Is this road the quickest through to Brighton? Should I direct my coachman to take another route?"

"It is the quickest," Thorne said.

At the edge of my sight, I caught a flash of blue dimity at the far corner of the house. Julia, stranded, no doubt, by Sir Reginald's appearance, and half the courtyard to cross before she made the carriage. All in plain sight.

"No, William, put the casket within," I called impatiently; more shrill commotion to distract Thorne. "Lady Julia will wish to access it during the drive."

Weatherly bowed and placed the casket and parasol within the carriage, then pulled down the step and took his position beside the open door. To all other eyes, he was the picture of service, but I saw the tension in his body and the readiness of his fists.

Under my hands, Caroline trembled convulsively, every panting breath breaking into a soft gasp of terror. Her reaction was too severe to be ignored, even by a man like Sir Reginald. He stepped closer, his attention momentarily caught upon the bright white sheeting that fanned out from beneath Caroline's hem. He frowned; it did not make sense to him. But he was not a fool; any moment, it would.

When in doubt, attack.

I flung the hartshorn in his face, the liquid soaking his mouth, chin, and cravat. His head jerked and he staggered back, his yelp cut short as he fought for a full breath amidst the ammonia.

I thrust Caroline into Weatherly's arms. "Get her in the carriage!"

I spun on my heel, ready to shout for my sister, but she was already running toward us, gown held up and a grimace of pain as the pebbles bit through the soles of her slippers.

Thorne dropped to his knees, still fighting for breath, his face purple from lack of air or rage. Probably both. I readied myself to kick him, but in that instant he toppled onto his side, either out cold or dead; I did not care which, as long as he stayed down. Weatherly bundled Caroline into the carriage, her limp form collapsing across the bodkin seat. Through the open carriage door I saw Julia wrench open its opposite and clamber in, chest heaving and eyes wide.

"Get in, Gus," she begged. "Come with us now! Please."

"Go!" I slammed the door shut and pushed Weatherly toward the coachman. "Get them to safety."

He clambered up beside the coachman. "My lady—"

"Stay with the plan." I waved my arms at John Driver. "Go, now!"

Our coachman cracked the whip over the lead. The horses gathered their haunches and launched forward, the gravel crunching under hoof and wheel. The carriage rumbled down the driveway, lurching upon a dip in the gravel, streaming a trail of dust. I looked over my shoulder. Framed in the far drawing room window, Lord Evan stared down at the fiasco. His face was a pale blur and then he disappeared. Was he coming to my aid or did he just know when to run?

I took a deep breath and shrieked, "Help! Help!"

Bryden came out of the front door at an unseemly trot, trailed by a footman. Lord Evan followed, a little unsteady on his feet but lean face set with determination. In all truth he should have stayed inside for the sake of our story, but I had never been so glad to see my authority flouted.

The butler stared down at Thorne. "What is wrong, my lady? What happened?"

"He has had some kind of seizure," I said. "He dropped after the carriage pulled away."

"Yes, I observed it from the window," Lord Evan said, joining our dramatic tableau. His chest rose and fell too quickly from such a short distance; not a good sign.

Bryden crouched down and held a finger beneath his master's nostrils, bright red from the burn of the salts. "He is breathing," Bryden announced. "What is wrong with his nose?" His own nose crinkled. "And that smell?"

"It must be an apoplexy," Lord Evan said. "I have seen it before. Quickly, now, get him into the house."

Burned nostrils and the stink of ammonia from an apoplexy? I met my confederate's gaze over the balding pate of the butler. He gave a small shrug, but the customary amusement in his face was gone. For all the absurdity of the situation, we both knew it had just become a great deal more dangerous.

13

Sir Reginald lay sprawled senseless upon the sofa, the protective white sheet bunched up around his haunches. I had removed his cravat, still wet from the hartshorn, and with it most of its eye-watering stink and the hard evidence of what I had done. It now resided inside the Wedgwood urn. Bryden had gone to organize the return of Dr. Haymer, hopefully a futile mission if the man had truly heeded our warning.

Lord Evan sat in the armchair next to me sipping a glass of claret. "If he remembers what happened when he wakes, he will be livid."

"Indeed." I turned my watch over and checked the time. "It has only been fifteen minutes. We must give Julia and Caroline at least thirty minutes. More if possible." I leaned forward to check Sir Reginald's breathing. Regular and strong. "Perhaps we should bind him."

"In his own home, with witnesses?"

"He had no difficulty overdosing his wife in her home. I feel no compunction about binding him."

Lord Evan tilted his head, conceding the point. "Even so, we should play this as an apoplexy as long as we can. So far, you are still within the law." He stood—a pained unfolding of his long body—then splayed his fingers and bunched them into tight fists.

He repeated the exercise a few times, then added, "Besides, it would be a rum thing to do when the man is unconscious."

"Those are the words of a gentleman," I said.

Ignoring my observation, he picked up the Wedgwood urn and tested its weight. "Heavy," he remarked. He placed it back upon the table and walked to the mantel. The gilt carriage clock at its center received the same attention. "Even heavier."

"Are you thinking of weapons? Do you expect him to be violent?" I asked.

"Best be prepared." He strolled over to some silver candlesticks on a side bureau but rejected them in favor of a small bronze statue of Diana and her hounds. "If he does wake with full knowledge, then you should leave the house, my dear. Walk down the driveway as fast as you can and wait for your man to come back. I can delay Thorne." A quick lift and bounce assessed Diana's usefulness.

Ridiculously, all I could focus upon was his use of *my dear*. Entirely inappropriate. I frowned, pushing away the absurd sense of warmth and safety the man engendered. "I will do no such thing. It is clear that the gunshot and fall from your horse have brought you lower than you will admit."

"Perhaps, but he will not be at his best, either." He placed the statue back onto the bureau and returned to the chair but did not sit. Instead he stood looking down upon me, the smile in his eyes gone, his demeanor grave. "Lady Augusta, please leave the house. I am not sure I can delay Thorne and keep you safe at the same time. I could not bear it if you were harmed."

Bear it? Strong words, and perhaps merely his gentlemanly concern showing itself. Yet, if I were honest with myself, those words suited my thoughts too. Lord Evan's safety had, without my realizing it, become rather more important beyond the mere convenience of his help.

Of course I could not utter such an irrational and forward response, so I said, "I am not leaving. And if it comes to it, do not think I will stand idly by while you deal with Thorne. I can heft a clock just as well as you."

"I believe it," he said. "You are entirely admirable."

I folded my hands on my lap, trying to calm the hard beat of my heart. "That is settled, then."

He made a small bow.

We resumed our watch of Sir Reginald, the silence between us as much a conversation as our spoken words. *I am not leaving. You are entirely admirable.*

Finally, Sir Reginald stirred.

"The fun begins," Lord Evan murmured. He took a position beside my chair, our forces marshaled.

Sir Reginald's body jerked as if he had been touched by an electrician's rod. He opened his eyes, his bleary gaze wandering across the room to rest upon us. "Good God, my head aches." He scrunched his eyes shut again, then opened them wide to find some focus.

"What you need is some wine," Lord Evan said heartily.

The volume of his voice shut Sir Reginald's eyes again. "No. No wine."

"You have had some kind of seizure," I said. "Bryden has gone to fetch Dr. Haymer. I have ordered broth."

"Broth?" Sir Reginald struggled upright, propping himself on his elbows against the cushions. "I don't want any cursed broth." He drew in a huge wet sniff, wincing at the abuse of his red, burned nostrils. "Salts!"

I tried a concerned smile. "Yes, we used hartshorn to bring you around. Alas, it did not work."

He shook his head, I think as much to clear it as a rejection of my words. "That's not it." He stared at me, his bleariness slowly sharpening into recollection.

"You swooned, man," Lord Evan said firmly. "Sit back until the quack can physick you."

But no, Sir Reginald had remembered. His pale face puffed into a furious puce, his eyes bulging with the truth. "You damn well threw the stuff in my face!"

He launched himself from the sofa. I was up and out of my chair in a second, my reflexes honed in childhood by a younger brother. Lord Evan stepped forward, fists clenched, but we were not Sir Reginald's target. Instead, he staggered into the side table, kicked it across the carpet, gripped the back of the sofa for a second of stability, then pushed off toward the door.

"Bryden!" he yelled. "Is she in her room?" He wrenched open the door, the handle slamming against the opposite wall with such force that it dug out a chunk of wallpaper and plaster in an explosion of dust. "Bryden, goddamn it, get up there!"

I caught a glimpse of Bryden running up the stairs. Sir Reginald lurched unsteadily across the foyer and hauled himself up after him, hand over hand on the balustrade. The maid who had brought the sheet peered around the corner of the drawing room doorway, then disappeared.

"It seems Thorne has realized the truth," Lord Evan said. "I don't suppose you have another pistol nearby?"

"Alas it is in the carriage." I allowed a moment of regret—still, could I have really shot a man in cold blood?—then looked at my watch again. "They should be near Hickstead now, but we should give them more time. To be certain."

"So, we delay him," Lord Evan said. He leaned a hand casually on the back of the armchair, but he was patently near the end of his stamina.

"Yes. I think his fury will bring him back to us. Besides, he does not have their direction. We must confound him as long as possible."

We heard a crash above—the prison door flung open—and then a roar of fury and footsteps thumping down the staircase.

"Get my damn horse ready!" The volume of Sir Reginald's order placed him in the foyer.

Lord Evan cast me a quick, reassuring smile. "Stand back." It was said with quiet resolve, yet he swayed upon his feet. I caught his arm, bracing his weight for a second. Our eyes met in acknowledgment: it would have to be a very short battle indeed. He gently drew his arm away.

Sir Reginald ran into the drawing room, all unsteadiness gone and face even more purple. "Where the hell is she? Where are you taking her?"

I struck an attitude of bewilderment, yet everything had coiled inside me, ready. "What are you talking about, Sir Reginald?"

"Don't gammon me, woman. You've taken my wife. Where is your coach heading? Tell me, now." He stalked toward us.

"I suggest you stay where you are, Thorne," Lord Evan said, drawing himself to his full height and breadth. Lud, what did that cost him?

"Are you saying that Lady Thorne has stowed away in our carriage?" I asked, glad that the sofa stood between his spitting fury and me.

"Stowed away? Ha! You have abducted my wife and, by God, you are going to tell me which way they are heading."

He ran toward us, a blue vein pulsing across his florid forehead and meaty fists up.

Lord Evan leaped upon the sofa and over its back before I had even moved. He landed in front of Sir Reginald, using the momentum to cannon into the heavier man. The impact forced Sir Reginald back a step, but he was ready for Lord Evan's grapple. They collided and swayed, fighting for balance and a handhold of tailored coat, but it was not an even match. Sir Reginald outweighed Lord Evan by at least one class and had recovered a great deal more strength.

He punched Lord Evan in the ribs, a hammer blow that drew a gasp from Lord Evan. He quickly rallied and elbowed the side of Sir Reginald's head, enough to break the heavier man's hold. They drew apart—an instant of ragged gulps and quick assessment—then clashed again in a bone-crunching effort to bring the other down. Stalemate.

They met in another grapple, but this time Sir Reginald wrenched his arm free and slammed his knuckles into Lord Evan's head injury, ripping away the bandage. A cur's blow that reopened the wound. Lord Evan grabbed at the back of the sofa to steady himself, dashing away the flow of blood in his eyes. Sir Reginald, seeing the advantage, lunged and locked an arm around his throat. A choke hold. Lord Evan clawed at the strangling forearm and rammed his body against Sir Reginald, once, twice, to no effect.

The time to intervene was upon me. I spun around, looking for a weapon. Diana? Too heavy; I did not want to kill the man. Ah. Three steps and I had the Wedgwood urn in hand. I gathered my skirts in my other hand and clambered onto the sofa. The soft seat sank under my feet. I lurched to one side, dropping onto one knee, my hands full of urn and gown. Hauling myself upright again, I dug my toes into the soft cushions and pressed my knees against the back.

"Turn him," I yelled, raising the urn in both hands.

Lord Evan gave a low roar of effort and spun Sir Reginald in a semicircle that brought him up against the sofa back. I positioned the urn over our opponent's head, but before I could bring it down, he hauled Lord Evan around again. The two men faced me, staggering as they fought for a break in the other's hold.

"Back!" I ordered.

"I'm trying!" Lord Evan rasped. He elbowed Sir Reginald in the gut. Sir Reginald buckled slightly, enough for Lord Evan to heave the man around again, positioning him under the urn.

With all my strength, I slammed the Wedgwood down. It smashed across Sir Reginald's crown in a blue explosion of very fine porcelain and wet cravat. Lord Evan jumped back as Sir Reginald collapsed onto his knees, clawed at the back of the sofa, then toppled onto his side.

14

I peered down at Sir Reginald's inert body. His face held no animation, but his chest rose and fell in a strong rhythm.

"Good shot," Lord Evan said. He picked up the remains of his bandage and pressed it over his reopened wound, staunching the flow of blood.

"Is he truly senseless? Can we be sure?" It occurred to me that I had been checking people's vitals far too often in the past few hours.

Lord Evan steadied himself with a hand upon the sofa and bent to study the sprawled man. "He's knocked out, but for how long is anyone's guess."

I gathered my gown again and stepped off my precarious perch, legs trembling from the excess of excitement. "It is time to go."

"I believe I see our means." A nod directed my attention through the window. Sir Reginald's groom stood in the driveway holding the bridle of the horse his master had ordered. Lord Evan tossed the bloody bandage onto the sofa and offered his arm. "I may as well be hanged for a horse thief as a highwayman."

"I would prefer you did not hang at all, sir," I said, placing my hand upon his forearm.

A soft curse turned us both toward the doorway. The smash of porcelain had brought an audience: Bryden, one of the footmen, and the curious maid stood staring at their prostrate master.

"What has happened here?" Bryden demanded. He stepped into the doorway, blocking our exit.

"I think you know what has happened," Lord Evan said evenly.

"You have been party to a crime, Bryden," I added as we walked toward the door. "My brother is a magistrate. It is in your own best interest to let us pass."

We approached at a steady pace—our demeanor demanding compliance—but I held my breath; was Bryden so loyal to his master that he would attempt to stop us? I clenched my fists. If he did, I would not hesitate to punch him. Indeed, even if he did not, the scoundrel deserved a facer for what he had done to Caroline.

He still stood in the doorway, jowly face set into a belligerent scowl.

"Stand back," Lord Evan said. "Otherwise, I will—"

Enough was enough. I stepped forward and swung. My knuckles slammed into Bryden's teeth and jaw, sending spikes of pain through my bones. I gasped and shook my hand as the man staggered back clutching his face, colliding with the poor maid.

Lord Evan grabbed my arm and steered me across the foyer. The footman—clearly not an admirer of Bryden—abandoned his cursing superior and hurried ahead of us to open the front door, handing me my bonnet and gloves. I caught a glimpse of his face as we passed onto the portico, chin tucked in and lips pressed together in a vain attempt to stifle a grin.

We descended the steps at a dignified pace, although every part of me wanted to run to the horse, wrench the bridle away from the wiry individual who held it, and ride at speed from the house.

"A well-executed facer," Lord Evan remarked as we emerged into the sun. "Is your hand injured?"

"No, but it hurts like hell," I said, allowing myself the vulgarity. One knuckle had split and was seeping blood, and I could already feel the other knuckles swelling. "I should have tucked my fingers more tightly."

"True, but you put good weight behind it."

He smiled, but it was with sympathy. A fly circled his face, drawn to the new blood. What an elegant pair we made. I waved the persistent insect away as we approached the big roan hunter, at least eighteen hands and deep-chested to take Sir Reginald's weight. The horse watched us with a flick of his ears.

Lord Evan held out his hand and allowed the horse to snuffle his palm. Introduction made, he stroked its muzzle. "I see Sir Reginald has ridden him ill, but you've kept him well. What's his name?"

The young man, half-wary, half-pleased by the praise, laid a grubby hand upon the horse's shoulder. "Plato."

"And your name?" Lord Evan inquired.

"I'm called Jack, my lord."

"Jack, I will be straight with you. Lady Augusta and I are going to take Plato."

After a moment's silence Jack said, "Aye." He squinted at me, clearly weighing up whether he should make his next comment. "Beg pardon, my lady, but I saw through the window. The vase. Me and Plato had a right laugh."

With that understanding achieved, Lord Evan took Plato's reins and held up a coin. A crown: easily a week's wage for the man. "If you are asked, pass on the intelligence that we are headed to Brighton. I will leave Plato at the Hickstead Castle Inn by sundown. You know it?" Jack nodded. "Ask for the landlord. He'll hand the horse over to you and no one else. You have my word on it."

Jack took the crown, sliding it into a pocket. "He's got a big heart, does Plato. He'll take the two of you, but no more than five miles at a trot. Perhaps ten at a walk."

"Understood," Lord Evan said. "You go up first, Lady Augusta, and I will ride behind."

With a nod, I donned my bonnet and tucked my gloves into my pelisse bodice. Jack bent and interlaced his fingers. "My lady?"

Gathering my hems, I stepped up into Jack's hands. One hoist and I landed rather inelegantly in the saddle, which of course was for a man and so had no sidesaddle pommel for my leg. The short pommel would have to do. Achieving some stability, I rearranged my velvet pelisse, muslin, and petticoats into some semblance of respectability and took the reins. Lord Evan swung up behind me, the horse sidestepping at the doubled weight.

"I shall need to hold you, Lady Augusta," he said.

I nodded, ignoring the hiss of society in my ear: *such a compromising position*. His arms circled my waist and the warm solidity of his body pressed against my back. My instinct was to stiffen against such unfamiliar intimacy, but that would make riding even more awkward. I took a breath and relaxed into his embrace. At such close quarters he smelled of claret and gunpowder and another unnameable scent that seemed to strike me in my core. I felt a sudden compulsion to lean and press my nose against his neck and breathe that earthiness into me. Good God, such a base reaction. I am sure I did not have such a violent response to my army boy, so long ago. I jerked away from the absurd impulse and felt myself tip forward; I was going to bring us both off the horse. I grabbed at the pommel as Lord Evan caught the back of my pelisse, halting my descent.

"You will have to lean into me," he said abruptly.

Very much the last thing I should do. If anyone I knew saw me in such a position, I would be totally ruined. Even so, practicality must override impropriety. Not daring to look at him, I settled back against his chest, his arms once more encircling my waist. I coughed—an excuse to continue avoiding his eye—and hoped my cheeks did not reflect the heat that had risen through my body.

Jack retreated a few steps and we were away at a sedate trot. Riding double was difficult for both horse and riders, only to be attempted in an emergency, and not at speed. We made our way along the driveway, painfully and precariously in my instance. I could only imagine it was the same for Lord Evan, astride the back of the horse and desperately depleted.

We passed between the evenly spaced beeches that lined each side of the driveway, the sunlight catching the swirl of dust rising from Plato's hooves. An afternoon breeze rustled the thick foliage overhead into a soft murmur and provided some relief from the sticky discomfort of the ride. A velvet pelisse and lawn gown would not have been my choice of equestrian ensemble in such warm weather.

"You took a great deal of care with the groom," I said into the tense silence. "A full crown and the careful return of the horse."

I finally had enough composure to look at him: pale and weary, but still with that gleam of humor. "I have looked after the livestock of a villain too," he said. "I was once Jack."

"Ah." An inadequate response to the story that lay within that statement. A story for another time, perhaps, when his voice did not crack with fatigue. "What of your own horse? Will you be able to retrieve it?" To lose a mount was a disaster, not only for the lost monetary investment and convenience, but also for the connection one has with one's animal. I would be devastated if I lost Leonardo, the hunter my father gave me a few years before he died.

"I suspect my so-called partner will find him," Lord Evan replied. "If not, Holbrook will not have gone far."

"Holbrook?"

Lord Evan smiled. "Where I acquired him."

I decided not to delve too far into the word *acquired*. "Do you think Sir Reginald will survive? He is indeed a villain, but I do not want his life upon my conscience."

"He is still breathing and it was only a porcelain urn. I have had worse hits to the head." He touched his congealed wound, a side-glance taking the sting out of the jibe. "Besides, if he does die, the blame will be with me. I am already a convicted murderer."

"So, another would not make any difference?" I had, of course, conveniently forgotten his conviction. Even so, I found it hard to tally that crime with the man clasping my waist. Julia would be horrified at such a reckless surrender to his dubious charm.

"Another would make no difference at all."

"A bargain lot, in fact?"

"A positive boon to my reputation." His bobbing weight slid a little to the right and it occurred to me that I was holding him up as much as he was holding me. He clasped my arm fleetingly, righting himself. "All joking aside, Lady Augusta, when he does recover he may make a great deal of trouble for you and your sister. He knows who you are."

"True, but right now my brother is riding with the Four-in-Hand Club and Countess Davenport is sitting in our house taking tea and ready to swear before God that my sister and I were at home the whole afternoon. As are my servants."

We had made the gates, still open, with the road beyond them empty. Only the thud of our horse's hooves and the calls of birds could be heard. No commotion behind us. Not yet, anyway. I turned Plato toward London, urging him to maintain his highly uncomfortable trot along the dusty road.

"How did you manage to enlist the countess?" Lord Evan asked.

"We completed a small service on her behalf, and she is most grateful."

"So, this escapade is not an isolated incident?"

I did not answer; I had not thought of it in such a way before, but he was right. This was our second enterprise on behalf of a woman in trouble. And despite all the violence and chaos and current predicament, I did not regret it at all.

We rounded the curve of the road, much to my relief. If Sir Reginald recovered enough to give chase, then he would no longer see us the moment he came out of his gates. I eased Plato back into a walk, the smoother gait eliciting a sigh from Lord Evan. He would not be able to ride behind the saddle much longer, for the horse's sake as much as his own.

"There is a place up ahead that will give us a good view of the road, but also conceal us," he said. "We can wait for the return of your carriage there."

Our thoughts were once again in union.

15

It took us a good ten minutes to reach his vantage point, and most of it passed in silence. Not from an unwillingness to converse, but more from my focus upon searching for any sound or sight of pursuit and his exhaustion. Twice I had to rouse him in order for both of us to stay upon the horse, and for the last half mile I clasped his grip around my waist with my free hand to lock his hold into position.

Finally, he pointed to an opening in the tangle of trees and undergrowth beside the road. "There. We can wait in there."

I urged Plato into the gap within the roadside growth of hazel bushes, cow parsley blooming with its tiny white flowers and a concealing clump of silver birch trees. Lord Evan the highwayman clearly knew the area well: it was an excellent place to watch for vehicles coming from London. On his order, I led Plato into the midst of the trees, the snap of twigs under his hooves sending a flight of tiny dun wrens into the air.

"We cannot be seen from the road here," Lord Evan said.

He dismounted, somewhat untidily, more of a controlled fall from the horse. Before I could manage my own dismount, he grasped my waist and swung me to the ground. A foolish move in his condition, yet I did not protest or pull away from his grip. I should have, of course, but we had just spent twenty minutes or so clinging to each another on the horse, and such missishness would have been disingenuous.

He looked down at me and smiled, the sheer enjoyment of the adventure alight in his eyes and echoing my own exhilaration. We had defeated Sir Reginald! We were victorious! It was a mad moment of affinity, and within its rush I impulsively touched his cheek: a rasp of stubble, a rough edge of scar, and his vital warmth under my palm. He drew a sharp breath, and the light in his eyes flared into something quite different.

His response was so unaccustomed, so long gone from the pristine days of my life, that I snatched my hand away. Yet my own body burned with the same heat, a blaze compared to the innocent fire of my youthful dalliance.

He stepped back.

"By my reckoning, your carriage should be on its return journey." He turned and looked through the foliage, leaning a hand upon the trunk of a stout birch. "You should not have long to wait."

I caught the horse's reins. "I do not mind waiting."

He nodded, his profile set into stern lines. He was, quite patently, avoiding my gaze.

"I am concerned that you are not recovered enough to return to your life," I ventured. "I am to blame, after all. Perhaps you should accompany us back to London. You could stay with us until your wound is healed."

That made him face me, but not with any easing of his stern expression. "I thank you for your concern, but you are not to blame, and I cannot accompany you to London. I am no longer part of your world, Lady Augusta. I am not Lord Evan Belford."

"But—"

"No, dear lady. Perhaps I am wrong, but it is my guess that you are thinking to rehabilitate me in the eyes of society. That cannot be. I have fallen too far and I will not drag you and your sister down with me."

He was not wrong; I had, indeed, thought that maybe Julia and I could bring him back to bon ton. Nor was he wrong about the probable outcome of such an ambition. Yet, I could not reconcile the man before me with the crime of such a dishonorable murder. It did not tally.

We both heard the rumbling sound of an approaching equipage coming at speed. Lord Evan crouched behind a thick clump of hazel. From my vantage, I glimpsed a rise of dust from the London direction. Could it be Weatherly already?

"It is your coach," Lord Evan called back and covered the short distance to the road at a run, his arms held wide to flag them down.

Part of me sighed my relief; another, smaller part felt a moment's regret.

The drum of hooves slowed and with it came billows of dust, clanking of tack, and groaning of springs and leather straps; John Driver had seen Lord Evan and pulled up the horses. I led Plato out of the undergrowth, the horse grabbing a mouthful of cow parsley on the way to the roadside.

"My lady!" Weatherly peered down at me from the driver's box, as dusty as John Driver beside him. "We thought you would still be at Thornecrest. Is all well?"

"Yes, of course," I said.

"Gussie!" Julia's voice, full of relief. Lord Evan took Plato's reins from my grip as the coach door slammed open and my sister, dimity skirts hitched around her ankles and without bonnet or spencer jacket, climbed down. "Oh, thank God you are safe and whole."

She ran to me, her momentum rocking me onto my heels as she enclosed me in a hug. From the strangling wrap of her arms, she had been very worried indeed. I returned the embrace, smelling the mix of dust and worry and rose balm in her hair.

"Has Caroline gone with Mr. and Mrs. Defray?"

"Yes. All went as planned."

I hugged her more tightly. We had done it! We had saved Caroline. "But what are you doing in the carriage?" I demanded. "You should be safe at Hickstead."

She pulled away to look me in the face, her own expression exasperated. "Did you truly think I would not come back for you? I take it you had to flee Thornecrest? Are we to expect pursuit?"

Lord Evan cleared his throat. "Lady Julia, such a pleasure for me to finally meet you when conscious." He bowed, sending me a gleam. I managed not to snort. "There is, indeed, a possibility of pursuit. You and Lady Augusta should get into the carriage and be on your way. We do not want Sir Reginald to find us conversing on the highway."

Julia inclined her head at the bow, but she had seen the gleam. From the tightening of her mouth, I knew it did not sit with her sense of propriety. "You are quite right, sir. Thank you for your assistance, but we no longer need the help of a highwayman. It is time you went back to your *business* too."

"Julia!" I protested.

Lord Evan—ever the gentleman—did not acknowledge her dismissal. Instead he addressed John Driver. "Can you turn here? There is no ditch on either side."

Our driver assessed the terrain and gave a terse nod. With a gruff "walk on" to the horses, he started to move the carriage into the tricky maneuver. From experience, I knew it would take a few minutes to manage the change of direction. A few minutes to say good-bye to Lord Evan. It already felt too abrupt.

He bowed to me. "Thank you for such an interesting afternoon, Lady Augusta. I have enjoyed our adventure."

Was that it? I could not leave it at a mere thank-you and good-bye. Not after what we had been through. "How do I correspond with you, Lord Evan? Do you have an address?"

"We both know it would be better if you did not," he said, yet I saw the regret in his eyes.

"Lord Evan is right, Gussie," Julia said. "Let him go on his way."

I ignored my sister. "What if we need your help again?" Admittedly, a disingenuous appeal to his gentlemanly impulses. "We may take on another escapade."

"Indomitable," he murmured. He glanced at Julia, almost as if in apology, then gave me the direction. "If you send a letter addressed to Jonathan Hargate at the White Hart in Reading, it will reach me."

"Hargate. White Hart, Reading," I said, committing it to memory. I was not about to lose my only way of contacting him.

John Driver and Weatherly had managed to turn the carriage around, although the roadside hazels and grasses had not survived the exercise. Weatherly left his position at the lead horse's head and hurried to open the carriage door for us. From his stiff demeanor, he, too, did not approve of this leave-taking.

"Come, Gussie, we must go," Julia said, taking my hand. "Good-bye, Lord Evan."

He bowed.

"Tend to that wound," I said. "Do not take any foolish chances!" Could he see the promise to write in my eyes?

"Try not to hit anyone else with an urn." He smiled, but it felt like a final good-bye.

Julia pulled on my arm and I allowed her to lead me to the carriage door. Lord Evan gathered Plato's reins, stepped into the stirrup, and swung deftly up into the saddle. He raised his hand in salute, then turned the horse and urged it into the roadside woodland.

Julia ascended the carriage steps and sat down in her usual bodkin seat, but I turned and watched Lord Evan until I could no longer see his figure or the horse moving amid the foliage and low dappled sunlight.

"Gussie, get in. Please! We must leave now!" Julia implored.

I gathered my gown, climbed into the coach, and slumped back into the seat. Through the open window, I searched the roadside, but it was now just a quiet vista, the flit of birds the only movement among the trees.

Lord Evan was gone. Perhaps forever. Yet, as I shut the window, it was as if a thread still connected us, spinning out further and further, as strong as silk. Did he feel it too? Perhaps I was deluding myself, victim to some newly awakened part of me that was spinning a hopeful lie made of loneliness, affinity, and—to my shame—the call of his body to mine.

16

HANOVER SQUARE, LONDON

TWO WEEKS LATER

Julia stood in the drawing room doorway and considered her preparations with a critical eye.

"Do you think we should seat Miss Woolcroft on the sofa or in a chair? The prospect from the sofa is a great deal more agreeable, since one can see the church spire, but the chair is more comfortable."

For my sister's sake, I abandoned the window and my vigil for the postman and tried to focus upon the task at hand. Duffy, his bride-to-be, and her father were about to call; our brother wished to introduce Miss Woolcroft to us. Or perhaps we were to be introduced to Miss Woolcroft, since she would soon be the ranking female in our family.

"The chair," I said.

"No, I think the sofa," Julia said.

I refrained from asking her why, then, had she asked for my opinion? I cupped my watch in my hand: twenty past two. The second delivery never came before three.

"It has been weeks now since you wrote to him," Julia said. She crossed to me, and her gray silk gown—commissioned for the occasion—shimmered in the slant of sunlight from the window. Gray again; she was slipping back into melancholy. She patted my arm. "I do not like to see you so dejected."

The irony almost made me smile. Almost. "Perhaps he has not picked it up yet from the inn," I said. Or maybe it had never arrived, or he had been arrested, or his wound had putrefied and he had died. I closed my hand around my watch, trying to stop the useless run of catastrophe.

"It is also possible that he may choose not to reply," Julia added, her tone careful.

"Is that what *you* wish?" I asked. Unfair, but disappointment made me sharp.

Julia withdrew her hand. "You say he is a gentleman, and a gentleman would know that corresponding with an unmarried woman is inappropriate, and that in this case it is entirely futile. He said so himself on the roadside."

"It is not that," I said, which was not entirely true, since, to some degree, it *was* that. Still, I knew such an alliance was impossible. "I just do not believe he is a murderer. I think there is more to it."

"He was convicted and served his sentence, my dear, and now he lives by theft. If he has the sensibilities of a gentleman, as you keep telling me, he would not wish to pull you down to his sordid level. I applaud him for that."

She did not understand at all. There had to be something amiss with that conviction and I was determined to find out what it was. "But—"

"No, Gus dear. You must leave it be. He has nothing to offer you but degradation and he knows it. I think you are mistaking the high emotions of our adventure to be something else. You must come to your senses for your sake as well as Lord Evan's." Julia did not often put her foot down in such a way. She gave my arm another pat—half sympathy, half reinforcement that this was, indeed, the end of the conversation—then bent and twitched a sofa cushion into a more acceptable shape. "Duffy and the Woolcrofts will be upon us soon. Why don't you go up and change that cameo for your amber beads."

I peered down at the cameo half-hidden by the lace of my chemisette. "What is wrong with this?"

"The beads will set off the russet of your gown better. Besides, they make a far more handsome showing."

I eyed my sister. "Heavens, you are nervous!"

"We are about to meet our sister-in-law," Julia said. "What if she does not like us?"

More to the point, what if we did not like her? But I did not voice my contrariness. I had been all prickle for the last week and my sister did not deserve such ill humor.

"You are too sweet." I dropped a kiss upon her forehead, ending our disunity. "She will love you as everyone else does."

"But you promise to be on your best behavior? No spats with Duffy?"

"I promise," I said, making my way to the door. As long as Duffy did not start a spat with me.

Tully, my abigail, was of the firm opinion that my cameos worked perfectly well with the gold tones of my gown—she had suggested the set, after all—but since I rarely gainsaid Julia's authority on dress, she unclipped the necklace and matching earbobs and stalked into my dressing room to retrieve the required beads.

Was Julia right? Had I mistaken the excitement of rescuing Caroline for an affinity with Lord Evan that did not really exist? It was possible—she had more experience in matters of attraction and love than I did—and Lord Evan and I had only been in each other's company for a few hours. Yet that sense of trust and connection between him and myself had seemed real. I feared I might have already stepped beyond the point of sense and was running headlong into a rather frightening new world of sentiment.

I crossed to my writing desk and picked up the letter I had received from Caroline two days ago. Absurdly, holding it seemed to bring me closer to the possibility of receiving a letter from Lord Evan. A blatantly idiotic feeling since there could be no link between the circumstances, but the heart was, I was learning, often idiotic.

I unfolded the packet and reread the core of Caroline's news:

> *I am in Ireland now and recovering well with dear Curran as my maid/companion. I have instigated a divorce from my husband, which of course will take a few years and be of great cost, but our family feels it will be the best outcome, despite the social ramifications. As you are no doubt aware from my sister's correspondence, Sir Reginald attempted to drag us all into an abduction scandal but was dissuaded by his solicitors once it had been established that you, your sister, and your brother had all been in London during the time in question. I do not know how you managed such a marvelous sleight of hand, but I thank you for it. And, since I know Lord Duffield was not part of the plan, I trust that you will pass on my thanks to the mystery man who also helped me. Although my future is uncertain and I can never be a wife again, I have a loving family who will not allow me to languish in body or spirit. And indeed, perhaps it can be said that the future, by nature, is uncertain and thus holds the possibility of happiness for us all. I send you my best wishes and hope that one day I may be able to repay your kindness.*

I folded the letter. *The future is uncertain and thus holds the possibility of happiness for us all*; I longed to believe such staunch optimism. Yet by her own admission Caroline faced a life alone—a divorced man or woman could not marry again—or, if she did find a man who would flout the law for her, it would be a life outside society. That, indeed, would be a brave love.

I placed the letter back on the desk. Why did Lord Evan not write? He had given me his alias and the direction to the White Hart, so that surely meant something, didn't it? Perhaps he had never intended to write. Perhaps I should stop waiting and let that be the end of it.

I touched the small split upon my knuckle—all but healed. Of course, one letter could easily go astray. Especially one sent to an inn. Another letter would seal the matter, and I could add Caroline's thanks. If it also went without reply, well then, I would have *my* answer.

"Do you want the amber drops, my lady, or the bobs?" Tully asked from the dressing room doorway. She held up an earring in each hand.

I pointed to the earbobs. As soon as Duffy's afternoon call was over, I would write again.

17

I had just returned to the drawing room when we heard the clatter of a coach pulling up outside our door. Julia waved me to the chair that had been designated mine and took her own seat. She passed me my work and picked up her own.

"Really?" I said, the half-stitched embroidery draped limply in my hands. "It is not like they are surprising us with a visit."

"You are right. I am being ridiculous." She returned her piece to the basket and took mine back, tucking it on top with fluttering hands. Her anxiety had finally communicated itself to me, and I rearranged the position of my amber beads, snatching the chance to glance at my watch upon its chain. Two thirty.

We both sat silently, listening to the sounds of entrance, hat and coat removal, and the creak of weight upon the stairs. Julia kneaded her hands together, then folded them tightly in her lap. A knock and the door opened. Weatherly led Duffy, his bride-to-be, and her father into the room. "The Earl of Duffield, Sir Henry Woolcroft, and Miss Woolcroft," he announced, his tone seemingly unremarkable, but Julia sent me a glance; she had also heard Weatherly's *judgment reserved until a later date*. I wondered what had happened downstairs to occasion such censure.

My sister and I rose from our chairs. My first impression of

Miss Woolcroft was of a short, trim figure in green pin-tucked silk, a longish pale face, and fair hair arranged in the currently fashionable side knot of curls. Her father, a squat man with the same fair hair, wore reasonably well-fitting garb but seemed ill at ease in such townwear. He bowed, his daughter bobbing into a curtsy at his side.

"How do you do, Sir Henry, Miss Woolcroft," I said, curtsying alongside my sister. "Lady Julia and I are enchanted to finally meet you."

Miss Harriet Woolcroft's eyes were good, large and brilliant, but too close together to be declared fine. Her nose had clearly been inherited from her father and matched the length of her face, while her mouth, plump with youth, seemed to hold the habit of being pursed. She was no beauty—we at least had that in common—but dressed as one, and she certainly had a firm sense of herself. Her gaze had not once come in our direction. Instead, she looked around the drawing room, her focus pausing upon the handsome mantel and the view from the windows, then gave a bright nod to Duffy that clearly communicated approbation.

"As am I," she said, her attention finally falling upon us. "Delighted."

"Indeed," Sir Henry said.

Like his daughter, he was short, but his skin was ruddy—the color I always associated with the hunt and dealing with tenants—and he had an air of solidity in both body and spirit.

"Please do take a seat." Julia waved a hand toward the sofa. "We have arranged tea."

Father and daughter sat on the sofa while Duffy took a rather posed position by the mantel.

At first our conversation was confined to the details of the wedding, which was to be held at my brother's country seat, Duffield House. Wedding trip plans were then discussed—Cornwall followed by the Lake District—and the disappointment of no continental travel expressed and reexpressed. Bonaparte had much to answer for, including a disruption to Miss Woolcroft's pleasure.

Tea came at that point, and I poured, sensing Miss Woolcroft's silent disapproval that the tea was already in the pot. Duffy's influence, or was it the other way around?

With refreshment in hand, a long silence ensued. I glanced at Julia. My sister's brows lifted; she had also noticed the change in atmosphere.

"There is something I wish to discuss with you both," Duffy said, placing his cup and saucer upon the mantel.

Ah. So, there was another reason for this visit.

"Miss Woolcroft and I, upon our marriage, wish to move into this house rather than the Henrietta Street house."

I sat very still. He wanted our home?

"This address is far more fashionable now," he continued, "and you two have more or less retired from fashionable life, so it seems more fitting that we have Hanover Square. You can, of course, have Henrietta Street."

Retired? We had an invitation for almost every night during the season, sometimes even two or three. I did not need to look at Julia to know her distress. It vibrated through her like a struck harp string.

Before I could refute Duffy's statement, he moved to stand behind his betrothed and said, "Most importantly, Miss Woolcroft attends service every morning, and with St. George's on the corner, this house is far more amenable to her devotions."

"Indeed," Miss Woolcroft said, bright smile in place. She

daintily placed her teacup and saucer upon the table at her side. "I was so happy when Duffield assured me you would exchange the houses as our bridal present."

I looked at Duffy. He had the grace to look away. It was, of course, his house. As male heir, he had inherited all the property in our family and so he had every legal right to insist upon the exchange. And yet, I could barely focus for my rage.

"I propose we start the move straight after the wedding; that way all will be managed before we return from Cornwall," he said to Julia in his overriding hearty voice, still not daring to look my way.

Julia put down her own cup and saucer on the table, her hand shaking so much that the two porcelain pieces rattled against each other.

"Well," Mr. Woolcroft said, standing up abruptly. "I think it is time for us to make our way back to the hotel, daughter."

"We are but just come, Father. And we are still discussing—"

"It is time to take our leave, Harriet."

"No, I wish to stay."

Mr. Woolcroft all but pulled his daughter up from the sofa and bowed to us. "Lady Augusta, Lady Julia, it has been a pleasure. Duffield, we shall meet you later at the hotel for dinner."

With a hurried curtsy from Miss Woolcroft, they departed the room, our footman closing the door behind them.

"Samuel, you may go," I said, every word clipped with the effort of holding back my bile.

As soon as the door closed, I rose to my feet, hands clenched in the effort to not slap our brother. "You coward. Making it a fait accompli, then telling us in front of strangers. Do you have any idea how this will affect Julia now that—"

Julia stood abruptly and grabbed my arm. "Augusta, no," she

said, stopping my momentum. I had never seen her eyes so fierce. "We must discuss this amicably."

I swallowed my words, although I could see no benefit from shielding our brother from the truth. Especially now.

"Yes, listen to your sister," Duffy said. "Besides, the Woolcrofts are not strangers. They are more or less family now. I cannot see how it is such a great thing, Augusta. It is not like I am turning you out onto the street."

"But it is our home, Duffy," Julia said.

He pushed away her quiet statement with an irritated hand. "You two can make another home—you have always only needed one another. This house has a far better outlook and the green will be excellent for children when they arrive. Surely you would not begrudge your nephews or nieces the boon of nature."

"For God's sake, Duffy, do not use the welfare of children who do not exist to justify your selfishness," I said.

"I will not allow you to take the Lord's name in vain, Augusta," Duffy said primly.

"Is that Miss Woolcroft speaking?" I asked. My fury and disgust added, "She is already bringing out the worst in you, Duffield; your meanness of spirit."

"Augusta, enough!" Julia said, shocked. "Let us all calm down. Please! In truth, Duffy, you could have told us privately. Allowed us to become accustomed to the idea. This was unnecessarily cruel."

"He is too much a coward," I said, ignoring her pleading hand upon my arm.

"And you are rapidly becoming a bitter old woman," Duffy returned. "Is it any wonder I took this route? Is it any wonder that no man has sought your company? Always insisting too much upon your own importance. You have made your choice in life and chosen to ignore the duties and graces of womanhood." He glanced at Julia, a small incline of his head acknowledging that she, at least, had tried to become a proper woman. "I have offered you Henrietta Street. It is more than many others would have done. For once, be grateful and content."

With that he made a sketchy bow and left the room.

18

Julia and I stood for at least a minute in silence after our brother's exit. I was struggling for breath, my rage like a rock in my throat. From below came the sounds of Duffy descending the stairs, demanding his hat and coat, then departing the house.

His house.

Julia sank down upon her chair again. "I am sure he did not mean those things." She curled her fingers into mine, like she used to when we were chastised as children.

"Ha. I am just as sure he did." I patted her hand but broke away to pace the length of the mantel. "This, I am afraid, is just the beginning of our insignificance. Or perhaps I am fooling myself and we are already irrelevant."

"You are too dramatic," Julia said. "After all, we can take Henrietta Street, and then all will be well."

"Henrietta Street is too small and too dark. Besides, you love it here. You put so much effort into decorating it."

"And I will love Henrietta Street, eventually. As you will. Duffy is right in one thing; if we are together, then we are at home."

"True, dearheart, but it is not the point." I turned and paced the length again. "Do you not see? It is the attitude behind his high-handedness. We are now just a burden. Not wives, or mothers, or grandmothers. Our one purpose unfulfilled. We can be swept aside."

Julia pressed her lips together, refusing my words. "We are not a burden. We have our own income."

"I do not mean in that way. We are not seen to have any value in the world. Not anymore."

"We saved Caroline. That has value, does it not?" Julia said stoutly.

I stopped pacing. "You are quite right, my love." A thought dawned upon me; not completely new, for the nub of it had occurred to me in Sir Reginald's house. "In truth, we were able to save Caroline because Sir Reginald marked us as ape-leaders. Old maids with no juice left."

Julia grimaced. "I wish you would not use that expression."

I was about to ask which expression when a knock sounded upon the door. "Yes?" I called.

Weatherly entered carrying the silver salver. "The afternoon post, my ladies." He carried the silver salver directly to me, his expression at its most butlerish. Was it Duffy's exit or the mail that had earned his disapproval? A packet lay upon the salver, the direction written in a bold hand with minimal flourish. A hand I did not recognize. I snatched it up.

"Is it from him?" Julia rose from her chair.

"Thank you, Weatherly." I waited, teeth clenched with impatience, as he bowed. Like Julia, he did not approve of my attempt to contact Lord Evan and made it clear by the rigidity of his expression. As soon as the door closed behind him, I dug my thumbnail under the wax seal, snapped it apart, and unfolded the packet.

The note was short.

The White Hart, Reading

Monday 22nd June 1812

Dear Lady Augusta,

Thank you for your letter. It makes my heart lighter to know that you do not believe I committed the crime for which I was convicted and that you wish to clear my name. However, I insist that you do not delve into the events of twenty years ago. My past cannot be changed nor, alas, my future. Any investigation would be dangerous and it would be insupportable if you were to suffer on my account. If you wish to do something for me, dear indomitable, then forget that we ever met and live a happy and long life.

Your fellow renegade,
Evan Belford

He had used his real name although I had written to Jonathan Hargate. I touched the scrawled signature as if it could somehow translate my belief back to him.

"So, it is from him," Julia said. "I can tell by the mooncalf look upon your face. What does he say?"

I looked up, squinting at her description of my face. Mooncalf? "He says I should not only forget what happened twenty years ago, but also forget him." I scanned the letter again. Why would an investigation be dangerous? Surely that would only be the case if there was something dubious to be discovered.

"He is right." Julia eyed me soberly. "But I gather you are not going to do so."

I folded the letter and tucked it inside my chemisette, close to my idiotic heart. "How did you feel when we were saving Caroline?"

"Most of the time I felt frightened," Julia said, but her mouth quirked up; a touch of devilment that I had not seen since Robert's death. "But, I have to admit, at the same time I felt exhilarated, and capable and clever. Does that sound conceited?"

"No, I felt the same. And frankly, I do not wish to go back to sewing and taking tea and shopping my life away. What do you say?"

"What are you asking me? To help you save Lord Evan?"

"Not only him. Anyone who needs our help." I grabbed her hands, hoping to bring her with me on this mad idea. "In particular women like Caroline, who have no other recourse. No one need know we are doing it. In fact, I doubt anyone would ever believe two old maids could even take on such a venture."

"Old maids. I really do hate that expression," Julia said.

"Then let us be something else."

"Useful," Julia said. "I would like to have some purpose. Our Heavenly Father may take me unto him soon, but I do not want to sit here just waiting for the inevitable."

I squeezed her hands. I could not be so phlegmatic about the inevitable, nor did I want her to step back into that gray silk world of mourning and memory. For myself, I no longer believed that this world was mere preparation for the next. This was all the life I would have, and I had to do as much with it as possible.

"Then it is settled. We shall be useful. But just as importantly we shall be defiant, occasionally ill-mannered, and completely indomitable."

"Surely not ill-mannered," Julia said.

I smiled. "That, dear sister, remains to be seen."

Case 2

An Unseemly Cure

19

DAVENPORT HOUSE, LONDON

I had come to the ball to dance with a murderer.

Admittedly, I did not have any particulars of the man or the actual murder, but I had a feasible theory: twenty years ago, Lord Evan's younger brother, the current Marquess of Deele, arranged the death of Lord Evan's duel opponent in order to incriminate his brother. As far as I could determine, Deele was the only person who had benefited from Lord Evan's removal from society and the family's line of succession. Of course, Lord Evan would be appalled if he knew I was approaching his brother, but he was currently somewhere in Sussex robbing people, so he had no say in the matter.

"Augusta, I am so glad you and Julia were able to come," Charlotte said as we moved up in the receiving line. The queue of guests snaked through the marble hallway and curled around to the dining room, which had been transformed into the ladies' retiring chamber. My dear friend always hosted a ball at the very end of the London season and it was one of the most sought-after annual invitations. This year I had asked her the favor of inviting Deele.

Her greeting was odd, though. *Able to come.* Perhaps she had noticed that Julia had recently made her apologies for a number of routs and balls.

"You are looking exceptionally well," I said. It was no lip service; her lightness of spirit had returned.

She leaned a little closer, the lily scent she used sweetening the air between us. "It is the relief that Caroline is safe and a certain someone has well and truly gone from London. I hear he is now in Bath."

So, Mr. Harley had taken my warning to heart and removed himself from London and Charlotte's life. A good outcome, although I hoped the women of Bath were able to resist his dubious charms.

Charlotte eyed my hair, dressed with pearls instead of its normal lace cap. "So, you are dancing tonight?"

"If I have any say in it. Is Deele here yet?"

She shook her head, the diamond drops in her ears shimmering in the candlelight. "Not yet. I will introduce you when he has arrived. What do you hope to do?"

A good question. "I want to see him. Size him up."

It was a pity I could not tell the marquess that his brother had returned to England. It would be interesting to see his reaction. But that would be a step too far; Lord Evan had made it clear that his presence must not be made known to any of his family.

Julia, beside me, clicked her tongue in sisterly condemnation. "You-know-who expressly asked you not to pursue this, Gus."

My twin was reading my thoughts again. Or perhaps it was more that she herself did not want me to pursue the matter. I caught her eye; she had chosen to wear a dove-gray gown with silver lace at the décolletage and a matching cap. I could not help but think the color emphasized the shadows of fatigue upon her face. She had woken up with one of her bilious headaches but had claimed she was recovered enough to come to the ball.

"Even so, you know it is right to help him," I said.

Charlotte, who knew the story of how we had met Lord Evan,

covered a knowing look with her fan. "She has the bit between her teeth, Julia. There is nothing we can do."

Julia shook her head in resignation. "I try, to no avail."

At the corner of my eye, I saw the impatience of those waiting in the line behind us. "You will find me?"

With a flick of her wrist, Charlotte shut her fan. "When I am finished here. There is someone else I wish you to meet. A surprise."

For a mad, heart-leaping second I thought she might have invited Lord Evan. But that was impossible. "A pleasant surprise, I hope?"

She did not return my smile. "Perhaps, but more informative, I think."

On that mysterious pronouncement, Julia and I curtsied and made our way up the crowded grand central staircase of Davenport House.

The entrance to the ballroom was another queue, moving slowly forward as the Davenports' butler announced each guest. I could hear the musicians already at work: a folk tune that was just discernible beneath the bass rumble and soprano shriek of conversation. I looked around for acquaintances: Lady Jersey returned my nod, and I exchanged a smile with William Lamb, who was alone and clearly facing down the whispers about his wife, Caroline, and Lord Byron. Then I spotted George Brummell and nodded a greeting. George was, as usual, impeccably dressed in his sober uniform of plain cream waistcoat and superbly fitted black evening jacket. Since we were old friends, he awarded me a rare sincere smile and strolled over to where Julia and I stood waiting our turn to be announced.

"Lady Augusta and Lady Julia, how pleasant to see you. Will the fashionable world be enjoying your literary soirees in Brighton this year?"

"Alas no, we go to Duffield House for our brother's wedding and then return to London to relocate to our new address," I said.

Julia, knowing George and I shared a friendship based on political views and confidential matters, politely withdrew to greet Lady Beecroft behind us.

"A new address?" George inquired.

"Our brother desires to move into our family's Hanover Square house after his wedding and so my sister and I have purchased our own home. In Grosvenor Square."

George smiled. "Do I detect a note of triumph?"

I compressed my lips over my own smile—Grosvenor Square was even more fashionable than Hanover—and said gravely, "You must visit once you are in town again."

George leaned closer and said, for my ears only, "As it happens, we stay in London—the whole summer, God help us."

I matched his soft tone. "His Highness is not going to Brighton at all?" It was the Prince Regent's favorite summer destination, and he rarely missed a chance to visit in the company of his closest cronies and latest paramour.

George gave the barest shake of his head. "Matters of state."

I pulled back slightly, searching his shrewd eyes. Without a doubt, the situation with the United States. They had declared war, although the interim government had been in the process of offering appeasement. Or perhaps it was news from Spain; Wellington had been advancing upon the French in Madrid.

"Continent or colony?"

George, however, was giving nothing else away. Understandable since there were so many people around. He surveyed the crowded ballroom ahead. "I am yet to meet your brother's betrothed."

Although a statement, for all intents and purposes it was a question, and a rather dangerous one at that. As the most important leader of fashion, George "Beau" Brummell could ruin a woman's social standing with just one quizzical lift of his arched eyebrow, and right now he was asking me if Miss Woolcroft was to suffer that fate. I had not warmed to the girl, but that did not mean she should be cast out into the social wilderness. "I believe she and Duffield will be here tonight. Do be kind, George. You will be granting me a favor if you acknowledge her."

"I am rarely kind, Augusta. Besides, I hear she is from the North."

"True. But you do like to have favors hidden up your sleeve."

He smiled and offered his perfectly tailored sleeve for admiration. "Quite full of them."

"Room for one more?"

He bowed. "Always, for you."

I watched him stroll away.

Julia returned to my side. "Is he going to approve?"

"It would seem so."

"Duffy should kiss your feet. Miss Woolcroft is now assured of success."

"I doubt it would ever cross Duffy's mind that I could influence anything in his world."

At that point we were greeted by the butler and announced.

Charlotte had surpassed herself this year. The ballroom was decked out in white summer roses, their perfume almost covering the beeswax burn of hundreds of candles set in gilt chandeliers, candelabra, and sconces. The soft light bounced off the huge line of mirrors along the far wall, which reflected the ebb and flow of white muslin gowns, shimmering jewel silks, diamonds, black jackets, red uniforms, and the vigorous flutter of fans.

"It is already so hot," Julia said in my ear. She flicked open her own fan as we moved into the milling assembly.

"A drink may help." I took two glasses of champagne from a tray held by a footman and handed one to my sister. Since the diagnosis of the tumor, she did not do well in overcrowded, hot spaces. We both sipped, silent for a moment in appreciation.

"Look, there is Duffy and Miss Woolcroft." Julia angled her fan toward the far end of the ballroom, near the blue-velvet-swagged windows, but I could not see our brother or his betrothed through the crowd. "We should—"

"Lud, not yet. We just got here."

Julia pursed her lips. "Well, I shall go and make my greetings and say you are on your way."

"Certainly, if you wish to lie."

"Are you going to hold a grudge forever?"

"He is throwing us out of our home, Julia. I feel quite within my rights to hold a grudge."

"You are not usually so resentful, Gussie."

With that, my sister departed. I watched her weave her way through the throng, acknowledging the warm greetings she received with a sweet smile and elegant incline of her head. She was right; I was not normally of a resentful nature, but Duffy's high-handedness had triggered the worst in me. Still, my fury had prompted Julia to finally agree to invest in our own London house and be done with relying upon the benevolence of our brother. Granted, an unusual venture for two unmarried women, but we had the funds and it guaranteed us a home forever. It also relieved us of the obligation to explain anything about our comings and goings to our brother, especially about our new even more unusual venture: helping women escape dangerous situations.

I heard Charlotte give the call for the first dance set—the popular "Butter'd Peas" and "Juliana"—and quickly moved off the chalked dance floor to avoid the surge of people creating their sets.

Across the room, Bertie Helden fixed his myopic eyes upon me with intent. Bertie was a dear man, but in the hierarchy of dancers in the room, he did not even make the bottom rung. I ducked behind two turban-bedecked matrons and headed off in search of Charlotte.

I found her beneath the musicians' gallery, urging a flushed young man to request a dance from a hopeful muslin miss attended by her mother. As I waited for the awkward drama to unfold, I finished my champagne—it was indeed very good—and returned the glass to a passing footman. With the introduction between swain and damsel finally achieved, Charlotte took leave of the pleased mama and held out her hands to me.

"I am glad you decided to find me instead. So many people." She smiled her satisfaction at such a crush and linked her arm through mine. "Now, we must to the supper room." She paused for effect. "Madame d'Arblay is here."

Ah, so this was the surprise guest: Madame Frances d'Arblay, otherwise known as Fanny Burney, the famous and esteemed author of *Evelina*.

"Is she truly back in London?" Madame and her émigré husband had returned to France during the '02 truce but were caught in Paris on the resumption of hostilities. They had been unable to return to England for ten years.

"Arrived in London yesterday, with her son. I did not know if she would come—she has been inundated with invitations, of course—but here she is. I know you enjoy her writing, but there is another reason I wish to introduce you."

At that moment, the musicians struck up the music. "Butter'd Peas" was a longwise dance—the men down the left side of the ballroom, the women down the right—which left us a relatively clear path along the wall to the doors. We emerged onto the landing, empty apart from a couple in deep discussion and a gentleman leaning upon the banister and watching the front door, presumably for a late arrival.

"There, that is better," Charlotte said. She steered me past the intent gentleman and said softly, "Did you know that Madame d'Arblay had her breast removed by surgery last year?"

Good God, a breast removed. Who could even conceive of such a thing?

"I had heard she was unwell, but not that."

"She wrote of the experience to her sister, who allowed me to read the letter." Charlotte's elegant shoulders lifted for a minute as if the memory crawled across her skin. "It was a most harrowing read. The surgery was a last resort, but it appears to have been a success."

"Why are you telling me this?"

"My dear Augusta, it has been obvious to me for some time that Julia is not well, in a serious way, and it would seem the problem lies in the same area." I pulled back from her hold, but she laid her hand upon my forearm. "Have I overstepped?"

In truth, it was no surprise that Charlotte had noticed Julia's illness. She noticed everything, a required skill for a society hostess. Yet Julia had made me promise to keep her illness a secret. Now that Charlotte had deduced the fact of it, did I admit she was right, or try to keep my sister's confidence? It seemed too late to deny it. Besides, the idea of speaking out my terror to my friend brought such a sense of relief that I could not withstand its pull.

"Do you think anyone else has observed the same?"

Charlotte sighed at my tacit acknowledgment. "Perhaps a few may have noticed, but not the cause. Madame d'Arblay's letter detailed her symptoms and they seem to correspond with Julia's, so I made the connection."

"Julia does not want it known."

"You have my word." She paused for a moment, the silence between us full of my dread and her sympathy. "I thought an introduction to Madame d'Arblay might be useful."

Another of Charlotte's skills: bringing the right people together. I had, of course, not even considered surgery. Such a barbaric, brutal solution and only ever done in extremis since the outcome was more often death than cure. We were not even close to that yet, were we?

"Does Madame d'Arblay know why we are being introduced?"

"No. But if you agree, I shall hint at it. She is most astute."

I nodded my assent and, arm in arm, we walked to the supper room.

Charlotte had repurposed her morning room to serve supper and had thoughtfully positioned groups of chairs around small tables for dining and conversation. A number of them were already inhabited, mainly by older guests seeking refuge from the crowded heat of the ballroom. The serving table ran the entire length of the room and was already fully stocked with both sweet and savory delicacies. I drew in the smell of freshly brewed coffee, cooked ham, poached salmon, and the new fad, pungent Parmesan ice cream. A few guests picked at the displays, one gentleman pausing to admire the large pineapple that rose above all in the silver gilt epergne.

Charlotte leaned in close to my ear. "There she is." A nod directed my attention across the room.

In my mind, Fanny Burney had remained the same as she was depicted in the charming portrait that appeared on the frontispiece of her works: a youthful, pixieish woman with an amused mouth, a large bonnet, and the tall, gray, powdered hair of fashion past. The woman who sat with a bowl of tea among a small circle of admirers was in her sixth decade at least. Still, the air of gentle mischievousness had survived. And, while the beauty borrowed from youth was gone, the weight of years had added to her charm, filling out her face to advantage and erasing most of the marks of age from its intelligent expression. At our approach, Madame placed her cup upon the table and rose from her seat, her admirers politely withdrawing in favor of their hostess.

"Countess Davenport, my thanks for your invitation." Madame's voice had a fascinating burr, no doubt created by Paris.

"It was my pleasure. We are all so delighted to have you back." Charlotte turned to me. "Lady Augusta Colebrook, may I introduce Madame d'Arblay."

The novelist curtsied, as did I.

"I hope I do not embarrass you by saying I am a great admirer of your work," I said.

"Thank you. It is most kind." Even now, after so many years of laudation, she flushed at the praise.

I knew from my readings that she had served as a Keeper of the Robes in Queen Charlotte's court and survived French society during the long years of this war. Both dangerous battlegrounds. Perhaps it was whimsy on my part, but I sensed a solidity within her, as if she had learned the secret of how to stand strong against the crashing waves of life.

"Lady Augusta is particularly interested in the letter you wrote to your sister about the events of a year ago, Madame," Charlotte said, her voice inflected with meaning. On that, she graciously nodded to us both and departed.

Madame fixed her attention upon me, her head tilted in sympathy. "Are you interested in my letter on your own behalf, Lady Augusta?"

I hesitated—should I lie?—then shook my head, suddenly and absurdly overcome. "My twin sister," I managed through a rise of tears.

"Ah, *c'est terrible*. In what way can I help?"

I looked around the supper room. More guests had arrived, probably seeking relief from the robust energies of the dance. This was no place to discuss such writings. "Would you be willing to speak to my sister about your experience?"

Madame laid her palm upon her bodice, over her heart. Or perhaps over the site of her surgery. "It is a recollection that is still distressing, and not for the fainthearted listener, Lady Augusta. Not for the easily alarmed." She pressed her fingers to her forehead, as if just talking of it caused her pain. "Still, if your sister is in need of my experience, then I must do what I can to assist. We women must be vigilant upon our own behalf."

From the tone of her voice, the ordeal had been one of great torment. Perhaps I should not subject Julia to such a retelling. Yet Madame had already acceded to my request and I could not back away from such kindness or gracious concession now.

"Perhaps you would do us the honor of calling upon us in the next few days?"

"Indeed. That would be most *convenable*. I am in London only for a short time." She hesitated, clearly considering her schedule. "It is not a conventional time for a call, I know, but would Sunday suit?"

"We will be delighted to receive you."

That was without doubt a lie; Julia was not going to be delighted in any way. Here I was telling Charlotte and a famous novelist I had met moments ago about her illness. Yet surely she would agree we had to explore every avenue of cure, including Madame's last resort.

I bowed a farewell and made my way to the landing, blinking away the unexpected rise of grief.

"Lady Augusta!"

A man stepped out from an alcove, bringing me up short. Bertie Helden. Lud, had he been lying in wait?

He bowed, his pale pate visible through the thinning hair on his head. "Would you honor me with the next set?"

Since I was determined to dance with Lord Deele, I could not refuse Bertie—if I did, I would have to sit out the rest of the ball. I mustered as much graciousness as I could. "I would be delighted, Lord Cholton."

It was a painful half hour: he stepped on my foot twice and missed at least three of the figures. Nevertheless, he did make amiable if unexciting conversation and laughed at my witticisms, albeit a little uncertainly. At the end of the set, I curtsied to his bow and we departed the floor more or less intact.

"May I obtain refreshment for you, Lady Augusta?" he asked.

"Lord Cholton," Charlotte said, arriving just in time to cover my hesitation. "I must away with Lady Augusta. Will you excuse us?"

Bertie bowed. "Of course." He looked almost as relieved as I did.

Charlotte took my arm and steered me through the overheated dancers milling around the refreshment trays. "Bertie's sisters are trying to get him married again," she whispered.

"Ah, that explains his attentions. Surely they know by now the poor man does not wish to be married." It was obvious to everyone but Bertie's sisters that his taste lay in the Greek way.

Charlotte, however, had moved on from Bertie's travails. "Prepare yourself, my dear." She pointed her fan to a tall figure standing near the doors. "Deele has arrived!"

My breath stopped in my throat. He looked so much like his older brother: the same lean countenance, thick brows, and high-bridged nose. He smiled at a passing acquaintance, and the expression was so similar to Lord Evan's that I found myself smiling too. Damn, I had to stand firm against such borrowed affinity. Deele had most likely destroyed his brother's life.

As we crossed the floor to him, I tried to focus upon the differences; the marquess was shorter and broader in build, his face smooth, without the scars and wear from twenty years of hard labor in a hostile land. His eyes, too, did not have the lurking humor of Lord Evan's, nor did they give the sense of a keen mind always in motion.

"Lady Davenport." Deele bowed his greeting; he did, however, have his brother's elegance and athleticism. "I hope you can forgive my wife's absence. She sends her regards."

"But of course. A ball is not the place for a lady in such imminent condition," Charlotte said. So, Deele's wife was enceinte. Did Lord Evan know he was to be an uncle? Charlotte indicated me with a graceful wave of her hand. "May I introduce Lady Augusta Colebrook."

"Lady Augusta, I am well acquainted with your brother. He has mentioned you often."

I let that pass. "I understand you both belong to the Four-in-Hand Club. I have never driven four horses, but the challenge appeals."

At that moment, Miss Claremont, the reigning blond beauty, took the center of the dance floor and called the next set. A quadrille and a waltz.

"Do you dance, Lord Deele?" Charlotte asked. "Lady Augusta does not join us often on the dance floor, but tonight she has made an exception."

"In that case, would you honor me, Lady Augusta?" Deele said, taking the hint.

"I would be delighted." I took Deele's offered arm and sent a quick glance of thanks to Charlotte.

We joined another three couples in a set of eight and I insisted—with a gracious smile against the customs of rank—upon taking the fours position at the right of our square. More time to talk to Deele while the lead and third couples danced the first figure. But how best to initiate a conversation about Lord Evan? Deele would most likely not engage in such an exchange, but even the manner of that refusal could give me some information.

The music signaled the honors. Our set bowed and curtsied to one another, and the quadrille began.

"I remember dancing with your brother when my sister and I were first presented. It must be at least twenty years past," I said as the lead lady and third gentleman launched into their chassé.

Not a particularly adroit method of introducing the subject, but it would have to do. We stood at almost the same height, so he stared straight into my eyes, nonplussed. Since raising the specter of a disgraced relative was not the usual conversational fare at a ball, it was a fair response.

"You knew my brother? What do you remember of him? Were you well acquainted?" It was eagerly and sincerely said, the opposite of my expectations. Seeing my return astonishment, he drew back. "Forgive me. It is not often his name is spoken in polite company. Indeed, it is not spoken at all in my family."

"I imagine it was a most distressing situation," I said, scrabbling over my bemusement. I found some purchase on the truth. "He was most congenial company. Resourceful and honorable. It is hard to reconcile the man with the act." I bit my lip; exactly how had I determined his resourcefulness during a dance? Deele did not seem to notice the slip.

"Indeed," he said. "It is what I have said all along. My brother was playing cards with a man by the name of Sanderson at White's. He caught Sanderson marking his cards and accused him, but the scoundrel countered by accusing Lord Evan of cheating and challenged him to a duel. A ridiculous accusation. Lord Evan was—is still, I hope—one of the most honorable men I have ever met."

"I take it you do not believe he killed his opponent?"

He straightened as if I had him on the stand. "I do not and I have never believed it."

"Do you have any idea how the death occurred?"

An odd question from a lady, but Deele had clearly marked me as an ally. "I do not. From the court testimonies, Sanderson was dead when the doctor in attendance and the seconds checked on him. Maybe he died of fright or another natural cause." He shook his head. "My brother maintained he only pinked him and he was as good a swordsman as ever held a rapier, so he would know what injury he had inflicted."

"Who was his second?"

"It was his friend, Lord Cholton."

Bertie Helden? We both looked across the dance floor at the short, stout man under discussion, currently struggling through the first part of the figure with the willowy Miss Dancourt.

"A most unwholesome creature," Lord Deele said, vehement disgust in his voice. "He will surely burn in hell."

I stared at him. "Whatever do you mean?"

Deele patently recollected to whom he was speaking. "I beg your pardon, Lady Augusta. That was not meant for gentle ears. Please ignore what I said."

I realized he was not referring to the duel but to Bertie's preference for the fair youth rather than the blushing maid. My estimation of Deele plummeted: to wish such ill upon a man because of his nature was abhorrent. Deele might look like his older brother, but Lord Evan was ten times the man.

I had come to this ball with the theory that Deele had arranged the duel to incriminate his brother. Or if not him then maybe Lord Evan's second. But Deele did not seem to shield his thoughts or emotions, whether it was concern for his brother or distaste for Bertie. He seemed an unlikely candidate for such subterfuge, although I could not wholly discount him. And what of Bertie, Lord Evan's second? I did not believe he could hurt anyone, nor had he ever exhibited the kind of devious mind that could arrange such a crime. Indeed, why would he wish harm upon his friend? I now had more information and even less idea of what could have happened.

"Lady Augusta?"

Deele was holding out his hand to me. It was time to dance.

20

HANOVER SQUARE, LONDON

Why did we stay so long at the ball?" Julia said. "I feel terrible."

I looked up from *The Times*. Across the breakfast table, she picked at the brioche on her plate, rolling the soft bread between her fingertips. She did indeed look drained. But then my reflection in the wall mirror above her showed the same pale complexion.

"Do you need your medicine box?"

She waved away the question. "I have already taken my pill and elixir."

"Charlotte expects us for dinner tonight. Are you sure you will be well enough for it?" My friend's follow-up dinner was almost as much fun as her ball itself. An exchange of keen observances and current news gleaned from the cream of fashionable society.

"Of course," Julia said. "It is only a lack of sleep."

I was not so sure of that but let the subject go and peered into my cup: empty. "Where is Weatherly? We could do with some fresh coffee." Another cup or two might shift the ache behind my eyes.

"I asked him to oversee the packing of the hallway paintings."

The art in our home was Julia's special project. Every year at the Royal Academy Summer Show she bought a piece from an up-and-coming artist. Her contribution to the arts, she said, since her own drawing talents had stalled at the age of six, along with mine, much to the despair of our governesses. The collection, now, was greatly lauded and Julia's pride and joy.

"Should they pack the Lawrence as well?" I ventured.

We both looked at the large portrait of us hanging on the far wall. Father had commissioned it from the famous man upon our royal presentation. It showed us in our glory days: a sweet-faced Julia seated upon a gilt chair with me standing behind her, my hand upon her shoulder. Both of us with our hair elaborately curled and powdered, and huge panniers upon our cream gowns. Lud, I did not miss hauling those metal frames around.

"No, I thought the room would be too bare without it," she said. "It can stay until we make the final move."

Earlier in the week, we had decided the morning room would be the last boxed up for our imminent move to Grosvenor Square, and so it had become our haven amidst the turmoil. Mrs. Sutton, our indomitable housekeeper, had rearranged the furniture and somehow fitted in two armchairs, the Italian marble occasional table, and a chaise longue to create a petite drawing room near the window. Somewhat cramped, but quite cozy.

We returned to the quiet rhythms of our breakfast—Julia drinking coffee and leafing through *La Belle Assemblée* while I read the morning paper and made inroads into the caraway cake. The household disruption beyond the walls, however, was ever present; in this instance, some kind of agitation in the hallway that was exacerbating the ache in my head.

I read a sentence about the campaign in Spain, then found myself reading it again. I could not seem to focus upon the words. I wanted to put my seediness down to our three o'clock departure from Davenport House, but it was more likely Charlotte's excellent wine. After Deele's disclosure that Bertie had been Lord Evan's second, I had resolved to talk to Bertie immediately, but it was not to be. He left immediately after the set and I lost my chance. I spent the rest of the night dancing; it was rare that I forwent my lace cap these days, and so I took the opportunity in both hands along with frequent cups of wine punch. Clearly, by the pain in my head, rather too frequent. My plan now was to write to Bertie after breakfast to request a meeting at Promenade today. The invitation would no doubt surprise him, but I hoped he would agree to it.

Another invitation also played upon my mind. I laid down the paper. "Did you meet Madame d'Arblay last night? She was the surprise guest that Charlotte mentioned."

Julia, in the process of realigning the bodice pleats of her white morning gown, looked up with a smile. "I did, briefly. A very amiable woman. Older than I expected, but then one has a frozen image of a person and they never age from it, do they?"

"I had the same experience. I took the liberty of inviting her to call upon us on Sunday."

Now was the time to tell my sister the true purpose of Madame's visit: to hear the particulars of her surgery. But if I did, I was almost certain Julia would refuse to sit with us. She did not believe in the idea of surgery and would be appalled that I had betrayed her trust. Yet I needed her to hear the truth: if it came to it, the same kind of procedure could save her life. Should I walk the path of honesty and tell her, or the path of cowardice?

"Really? That will be most interesting," Julia said. "She must have such stories to tell. I will ask Cook to make those little iced fancy cakes."

"Indeed, a good thought."

So, the path of cowardice, then. At least for now.

The noise outside the door cohered into someone crying—a woman—and Weatherly's voice.

"What on earth is going on?" Julia asked.

I rose from my chair and crossed to the door. The crying had become pleading and I caught the name William, used with some urgency. Whoever this was, she was on terms of intimacy with our butler.

I opened the door and peered out. Weatherly stood in the hallway holding both hands of a young Black woman who looked to be in great distress. She stood obliquely to me, so I could not see her face, but her dress was neat, if somewhat old: a blue gown with a striped chemisette beneath and well-worn half boots made of jean. The ribbons upon her straw bonnet were untied, and she wore no gloves. A hasty departure from someplace, perhaps? Whatever the case, it was plain that something serious had happened.

"Weatherly, is this a friend of yours?"

Our butler quickly stepped away from the young woman and bowed. I had never seen him so discomposed. "My lady, forgive the disruption. Allow me to introduce Miss Sarah Finchley, an acquaintance. She went to the back door but one of the cook's girls sent her away."

Miss Finchley curtsied. She had a lively face and a direct gaze that was, at this moment, full of urgency. "I beg your pardon, my lady. I should not have come to the front door, but I had to see Mr. Weatherly."

"On what matter?" I glimpsed Betty and Eliza, our maids, peeping around the dining room doorway.

"To save a child's life, my lady," Miss Finchley said. "In fact, her very soul."

There could be only one response to such a dire utterance. Besides, I admired her determination in the face of social transgression.

"You must come into the morning room, Miss Finchley. Tell us what has happened."

"No, my lady, that is not necessary," Weatherly said.

"I think it would be best, Weatherly, just for the fact of removing your friend from the curiosity of our household." I waved Betty and Eliza back to their duties and ushered Miss Finchley into the morning room.

"My lady, I am sorry for the disturbance," Weatherly murmured, following us and closing the door.

Julia observed our arrival with some astonishment.

"This is Miss Finchley," I said. "She is an acquaintance of Weatherly's and has come to report that a child's life and soul are in danger."

Miss Finchley curtsied. "Mr. Weatherly is our benefactor and I thought he would know what to do."

"Benefactor?" I echoed, glancing at our butler. He had never mentioned supporting a cause; not that he was obliged to do so. We all had our secrets.

"Miss Finchley and her sister run a home for orphaned and abandoned girls," Weatherly said.

"Girls of all nationalities and faiths, my lady, and some who are infirm or illegitimate," Miss Finchley added, a searching glance assessing our response to the statement. Clearly, our lack of shock or disapproval reassured her, for she continued. "I teach them their letters and a skill to earn a living. It is only a few rooms in a house, but Mr. Weatherly generously gives us money for food and to pay the rent."

"A noble cause, Weatherly," Julia said, nodding her approval. "But I thought female orphans were the responsibility of the parish. There is the Asylum for Orphan Females in Lambeth."

"They do not take girls who are infirm, or considered deformed, or of color, my lady," Weatherly said.

"I did not know that," Julia said, turning to me in consternation. "It is not right. They are children of the parish too."

I nodded. Certainly an injustice that needed to be addressed, but we were drifting from the urgent matter at hand. "Tell us what has happened to the child, Miss Finchley," I said. "One of your girls, I presume?"

"Yes, her name is Marie-Jean. She is but twelve years old and not one to run away. I have looked everywhere and asked everyone who may have seen her, but I think she has been taken."

"By whom?" Julia asked.

Weatherly stepped forward. "It is most likely the work of a bawdy-house owner, my lady."

Julia stared at him, aghast. "A child of twelve? Surely not."

I had no trouble believing the likelihood of such a kidnap. When I was twelve myself, I had gone into my father's study alone—a forbidden enterprise—and found a *Harris's List of Covent Garden Ladies* hidden in a drawer. The slim book had been rather instructional in its description of what the prostitutes offered their clients in London, but what had stayed with me most were the ages of some of the girls described: barely a year or two older than myself.

Weatherly cleared his throat. "There is a heinous practice, my lady, that requires a girl child." He looked to me for permission to continue. I nodded. We must hear it all. "Please forgive the plain speaking, but some believe that the pox can be cured by congress with an unstained child. It is called the Virgin Cure."

"Dear God." Julia clasped the gold cross at her throat. "That is despicable. Revolting."

I crossed to the mantel, needing to take some kind of action—even if it was just walking—to alleviate the cold horror in my innards. "Do you have a plan in mind, Weatherly?"

"I fear those that offer such a practice keep it hidden. If you allow, I will go to Covent Garden and the rookeries today to find out as much as I can."

"Of course. I am sorry to say it, but by fact of rank and gender, we can be of little use at this point in the search." I paused: that was not quite true. "Wait, there is some aid I can offer. I will send word to Mr. Hargate. You will need help to navigate the criminal world, Weatherly, and he is part of that world. He may be able to extract more information from his criminal associates."

Weatherly—like my sister—did not approve of my association with Lord Evan. Not that it was much of an association, given he had only answered one of my letters with the request to forget I had ever met him. Still, I had no doubt he would rally to my request for help. A certainty that was based on his demonstrated sense of honor and, admittedly, my own desire to see him again.

"It is a good thought, sister," Julia said. She saw my surprise and tilted her head: *We must retrieve the child by any means.*

Grudgingly, Weatherly nodded. "I may not be able to enter some of the establishments. His company would solve that."

"It is settled, then," I said. "I will send word immediately."

Even in the best of circumstances, Lord Evan could not reach us until the early hours of tomorrow. It was at least forty miles to Reading and it would take our groom most of the day to carry my letter to the White Hart. And that supposed that Lord Evan was even close to the inn he used as his address. Would one night's delay be too late to save the child?

"My ladies, if you allow, I will go now with Miss Finchley to continue the search," Weatherly said. "I am not sure I will be back before you return from dining with Lady Davenport tonight."

"Take as long as you need, Weatherly. Samuel will be able to manage the house for a night," I said.

"I will pray for you," Julia added. "Our Father will surely help such an endeavor."

Miss Finchley curtsied again. "Thank you. I cannot express the depth of my gratitude for your interest."

They departed, our haven suddenly filled with a new coldness. My sister rose from the breakfast table and crossed to the window. Her attention, however, was not upon the bustling square outside but had turned inward.

"I know evil exists, but this is beyond what I could have imagined," she said, her voice so subdued it was almost lost within the clamor of life beyond our walls. "I am going to church. Will you come?"

I turned away in case she could see the godlessness in my eyes. "I will stay and write to Lord Evan."

She nodded and, without another word, left the room.

I no longer had the right to ask her god for anything, but if I did I would be on my knees too. As it was, I gathered paper and pen from my writing box and started to compose a prayer of a different sort.

21

HYDE PARK, LONDON

Julia and I stood by the gates at Hyde Park Corner, watching the beau monde and lower orders of London stroll along the wide gravel footpaths. A rainbow of pastel parasols ducked and twirled in the wind while gentlemen in linen jackets clung to straw beavers. The thud of hooves on the tan drummed a beat beneath the wind-snatched calls of greeting and conversation. Yet, by this time next week, most of fashionable London would be gone, fleeing the stinking city for the seaside or a country estate. Lucky devils.

A woman in a blue riding habit frogged with gold braid rode past on a chestnut; she had a good seat and light hands. As good as my own. I had not ridden for far too long—my dear old mare Lily had died a year back and I had not yet found another London mount. How I missed the exhilaration of riding, and the sweet bond between horse and rider. Perhaps I could bring Leonardo, my hunter, back from Duffield House. Father had given him to me—his last gift before he died and doubly precious because of it—and, although a hunter was not really a horse for the tan, I longed to ride him again.

I cleared my throat to free it of a nose-wrinkling clash of sun-baked road dung and briny whelks from a nearby vendor's barrel. I had chosen to wear a heavier cotton promenade gown to counter the warm, gusty conditions, but my shift already adhered to the small of my back and my palms itched within their kid gloves.

Even a violent twitch of my shoulders failed to loosen the damp cling of cloth.

Where was Bertie?

On receipt of my note this morning he had sent back an immediate acceptance to meet at half past four. *Absolutely delighted*, he had written, although I suspected he was as far from delighted as could be imagined. At least he had agreed to come.

I gathered my watch upon its chain and checked the time. It was near the end of Promenade. Surely Bertie would not fail me. And what of Thomas, our groom? Had he reached the White Hart yet? I squinted up past the peak of my bonnet at the rain-ominous clouds, trying to calculate where the boy might be on the road. I had given him carte blanche to change horses as often as he needed, so if he had made good use of that expedience, he should be near Reading and Lord Evan by now. Closer to home, we had not yet heard anything from Weatherly about his search of the brothels and low taverns. Frustrating, but expected.

"I wish we could do more to help search for the girl," I said. "It feels obscene to be strolling around the park when that poor child is facing such a hideous fate."

Julia looked at me with sympathy but said nothing. We had already had this debate twice over and both times she had been right: I could not go near Covent Garden or the rookeries ever again. We could not afford another scandal like the one I had caused by entering a brothel to retrieve Father's dead body. Moreover, women of our rank just did not go around rookeries inquiring about children for sale. No one in that world—or, indeed, ours—would ever believe that an unmarried lady could seek or even understand such sordid information. Not to mention the physical dangers of such action. Yet that logic and caution did nothing to alleviate my desire to burst through every bawdy-house door and search for the child.

"Bertie is late." I let my watch fall back upon its chain.

I inadvertently caught the eye of a middling man of about forty standing near the whelk vendor. He seemed very intent upon us. A pickpocket or just rude? He wore fashionable long pantaloons and a handsome waistcoat worked in a sunburst pattern of blue and gold: very stylish for one of his station. His burly height, too, was unusual, and although his nose had clearly been broken at some point and was a little crooked, his face held a firm confidence that was oddly attractive. Still, such a fixed stare was impertinent.

"Bertie is always late," Julia said. "It is an immutable fact of the man, as is his good humor." She had also noted the middling man's gaze and dipped the edge of her parasol to shield us from his insolence. "I do not see how questioning him about the duel will help Lord Evan in any way. Bertie must have given his testimony at the court case, and it did not change the verdict then, did it?" She observed me with a small furrow between her brows. "Surely you do not seriously think Bertie Helden could have been part of some shady plot."

It did seem unlikely that Bertie could have killed one man, ruined another, and hidden it all this time. Still, he had been Lord Evan's second and one of the first people to reach the fallen Sanderson, so he had to be under suspicion.

Julia saw my hesitation and shook her head. "You are grasping at straws."

"Maybe. But you will help me, won't you?"

Julia did not answer, for her attention had become diverted upon the crowd. "Oh no, Mrs. Ellis-Brant is heading this way. I was cornered into conversing with her at the ball last night. I do believe she now thinks we are friends."

"Lady Julia," Mrs. Ellis-Brant called, marching toward us. She gave a small wave of a pink-gloved hand. "Lady Augusta, how do you do? Last night was such a sad crush, wasn't it? A triumph for our dear Lady Davenport."

Emelia Ellis-Brant was extremely aware of her own consequence—her husband was a cousin to the Earl of Davenport and therefore Charlotte's cousin by marriage—and a rumormonger of the worst sort; petty, malicious, and not above fabricating a good story. Although I had found no hard evidence, I was certain she had spread the worst stories about our father upon his death. I always fancied she looked like that little pet ermine in the Da Vinci painting: blond haired, sleek, and fiercely dissatisfied. Her fussy pin-tucked yellow gown and chartreuse summer spencer did nothing for her sallow complexion. I could only suppose her mantua-maker disliked her as much as I did.

Even so, civility forced me to return her salute with a nod.

"How do you do," my sister added politely.

Right at that moment, Bertie decided to appear with what looked like flecks of straw upon his tan linen coat and his round face damp and flushed. "My apologies for being delayed, Lady Augusta. There is an overturned hay cart on Piccadilly." He bowed to us all, clamping down the wind-lift of his hat with a practiced hand. "Lady Julia, Mrs. Ellis-Brant, well met."

"Lord Cholton, it is not often we see you at Promenade," Mrs. Ellis-Brant said.

"Not one for walking, but Lady Augusta has invited me," Bertie said.

"Ah, a rendezvous at the gates," Mrs. Ellis-Brant said brightly. I could almost hear her rodent mind scratching up the story.

"We are old friends," I said quickly, but it was too late; Bertie's sisters would, no doubt, be apprised that Bertie and I were courting. "Good day, Mrs. Ellis-Brant."

Bertie bowed his farewell and offered me his arm, Julia taking up the rear guard. I steered him rapidly along the wide promenade that ran alongside the riding tan, making for the side path that led to the Serpentine. It was nearing time to dress for dinner, so the fashionable crowd had already started to thin, but we were all still forced to weave around a large family spread out three deep, a strolling couple oblivious to all but themselves, and a phalanx of young men keeping pace with a blond and bountiful member of the demimonde riding along the tan to bouncing advantage.

As I had hoped, the side path was less populated, the gravel way sheltered from the uncomfortable wind by a line of trees. I cast a look over my shoulder. Julia walked behind us within discreet earshot.

"Thank you for meeting me, Lord Cholton," I said as we slowed our pace.

"I must admit I am surprised by the invitation," Bertie said. He angled an anxious glance at me. "It will set tongues wagging."

"As we just saw," I said dryly.

Bertie allowed a polite smile, but his expression was still that of a trapped man. Best to relieve his mind. "I am not here to discuss our unmarried states, Lord Cholton. We are both, I think, happy as we are." For a second, Lord Evan's face flashed into my mind.

Bertie blew out a relieved breath. "Good Lord, yes. Marrying is the last thing I want to do." He frowned, realizing the gross insult he had just delivered. "I mean, if I was to ever consider it, then you would—"

"Yes, yes, of course." I waved away the attempted retrieval. "I asked you here because I want to discuss something that happened twenty years ago. The tragic duel between Lord Evan Belford and a man named Sanderson."

Bertie stopped walking, his face draining into an alarming shade of gray. "I beg your pardon?" He visibly collected himself and resumed walking. "Why are you interested in such ancient history?"

Ah, I had not thought of a plausible answer to that question. It was his turn to observe my discomfort.

"I cannot say." A lame answer that hung between us.

We walked in awkward silence for a few seconds, and then Bertie said, "Are you acquainted with Lord Evan?"

I noted his use of *are*, not *were*. Did he know that Lord Evan had returned to England or was it just a hopeful usage for a long-absent friend?

"I met him in our first season, before he was convicted," I said, then added carefully, "He is a most charming man."

Bertie kept his eyes upon the gravel path. "Indeed. A good friend. Always."

Uncharacteristically reticent. I glanced back at Julia, glad to see that her interest had been piqued too. I raised my brows: *Does he know?*

Julia gave a small shrug: *Maybe.* She lifted her chin toward Bertie: *Ask him.*

It would be a risk, but a small one.

"My sister and I have recently made a new friend. Perhaps a mutual acquaintance," I said. "Mr. Jonathan Hargate."

It was as if I had touched Bertie with an electric rod. "You know!"

"We do."

Bertie wet his lips. "What do you propose to do with that knowledge?" He glanced over his shoulder, gathering Julia into the question.

"Nothing. We have only his best interests at heart," I said.

"It is true. Rest assured we will not expose him," Julia added.

"Thank God." Bertie pressed his hand to his chest, his whole body seeming to lift and slump into a relieved huff. "I have sat upon the news of his return for months. I am not built for this kind of subterfuge."

"You seem to have done very well so far," I said encouragingly.

He flushed at the praise. "I did not even know if he would come, or even if he was alive. I sent the letter to him two years ago, hoping it would reach him in the colonies. It's a bad business, but I knew Belford would want to help if he was able. The letter took a year to get to him, and another for him to come back. But now he is here. Not that we can do much, yet." He spoke so quickly his words ran into one another; keeping quiet had, indeed, been difficult for him.

"A letter about what? The duel?"

"Good Lord no, about his sister and—" He stopped walking, halting us all. "He did not tell you?"

"Tell us what?"

Bertie shook his head. "If Belford has not told you, I cannot do so. It is not my problem to share, Lady Augusta." He theatrically pressed his lips together, sealing his silence.

"You are speaking of Lady Hester Belford?" Julia asked. Knowing my ignorance on such matters, she directed the next to me. "Lady Hester is Lord Evan's younger sister by a good ten years and not seen within society for over two years. The story is that she is very ill."

"I cannot elaborate, Lady Julia," Bertie said. "If you are a friend of Belford's, then it is up to him to apprise you of the circumstances."

I had to admit my curiosity about Lady Hester had been piqued, but harping upon the matter would achieve nothing; a gentleman like Bertie would not be budged upon a matter of honor, especially that of a friend's. "We understand, Lord Cholton," I said. "But are you certain he has returned because of his sister and not the duel?"

"I am sure of it." He cocked his head. "I suppose there is no harm talking of the duel. What is it you wish to know?"

"All the particulars."

He scratched his chin, clearly trying to recall those long-past particulars. "Well, they met here in the park at dawn, as it was always done. Is that the kind of thing you wish to know?"

"Yes. Everything you can remember." It stood to reason that they had dueled here in Hyde Park—it had been notorious for such meetings twenty years ago. Suddenly, it felt vital to see the place where the duel had been fought, as if by walking the exact ground I might gain some insight into what had truly happened. "Could you show us the site?"

Bertie squinted across the fields to our right. "I have not been there for some time, but if that is Park Lane"—he pointed in the direction of the thoroughfare, hidden from view by a dense line of oaks—"the dueling site would be that way." He turned to our left. "We will have to leave the path and head toward The Ring."

Julia closed her parasol—more for strolling than traversing pasture—and we followed Bertie off the path, his robust pace taking me by surprise. The summer had left the grass with a tinge of brown upon it and a straw-like bounce underfoot. I loosened my own stride a little, drawing in air that was blessedly free from the stink of warm sewage and smoke.

A robin sang—a rising glissando that found a fervent high note, then stopped, the silence filled by the answer of another hidden bird. Beside me, Julia carefully stepped over the scatterings of yellow daisies and purple-blue cornflowers. Even as a child, she would never tread upon a flower. One of our governesses had told her fairies lived upon the petals and to this day she felt obliged to avoid them. In the distance, a small herd of the summer park cattle turned their heads at our progress, then returned to their grazing.

The broad expanse of cloudy sky fired me with a desire to peel off my gloves, shrug off my spencer, and run helter-skelter across the field. Not that I ever would, particularly in such a public place. It must be thirty years since I had run with that kind of abandon across the fields of our father's estate, Julia and Duffy trailing behind me. I was always the fastest. Always in front. That was, until I had to step back behind my brother.

I shared a smile with Julia as we both clamped our hands upon the brims of our wind-buckled bonnets; it had been a while since we had walked together with such vigor. Yet, despite the exercise and uncomfortable warmth, my sister's cheeks and lips remained pale. I glanced at Julia again, noting the slight labor of her breath; she was too reserved in Bertie's company to request an easier pace. I took her hand and slowed our momentum. Among the letters I had written and sent this morning was one to Madame d'Arblay, a reiteration of my invitation and our address. Would Julia receive Madame when I finally told her the truth of the lady's visit?

The Ring, or the remains of it, stood near the center of the park and had been the site of all fashionable activity fifty years ago. I remembered my father talking of it: a large fenced ring bordered by trees around which all the bon ton circled in carriages, on horses, or on foot, viewing the newest fashions and exchanging the latest gossip. Now only the ring of trees and a few weathered railing posts marked its old glory. Releasing my sister's hand, I shaded my eyes and studied the landscape. The trees were sycamores and old, their branches spreading into one another to form a dense canopy. Aside from the view of people upon distant paths, we could have been standing in a field in the middle of the English countryside.

"So, you were one of the first to go to Sanderson upon his wounding?" I asked Bertie.

He mopped his damp brow with a lawn kerchief. "Yes, as well as Sanderson's second—a Colonel Dyson, as I recall—and the doctor, a man by the name of Lawrence. We all attended him. He was alive when we arrived, even alert. The doctor examined him, but I could see he was concerned."

"Sanderson was alive?" I asked. Yet Deele had told me he had died by the time the two seconds and the doctor arrived. A faulty memory, or a lie?

"He was, but perished swiftly."

"Did you see him pass?"

"Not directly. I had gone to meet Belford and Jollie, who were approaching at a run with a few other onlookers. Belford was concerned, which, I hasten to add, is not the behavior of a man who had thrust to kill. I said that in the trial."

"Who is Jollie?"

"That would have been Rupert Jollie, my dear," Julia said, who must have calculated the genealogy as soon as his name was mentioned. "The fourth Earl of Dansford, now deceased."

Bertie nodded. "That's right. Jollie had come as an unofficial second to Belford since he'd been at the card game too. He was far more in the know about duels than I was, so he organized the doctor and helped me run the proceedings."

"So, both Dyson and the doctor were with Sanderson when he died?"

"Yes, both saw him pass." He looked around and pointed to a pair of sycamores to the west. "Over there, that is where Sanderson staggered and died. I remember because you could see the Guard House through those two trees."

The Guard House was indeed still visible: a distant gray stone edifice. A man stood upon the path that led to it. I squinted at the small lone figure facing us. Was that a blue sunburst waistcoat and a pale length of pantaloon, like the man at the gate? I could not be sure. Whoever it was, he turned on his heel and, with a slight limp, continued to walk along the path until he disappeared beyond the Guard House.

I turned my attention back to the matter at hand. "I think it would help if we staged the deadly moment. Lord Cholton, would you show Julia where Lord Evan stood, then show me exactly where Sanderson died?"

We were soon in position. Bertie obligingly took the part of Sanderson and propped himself against the appropriate tree. I crouched beside him, both doctor and colonel, and looked to where Julia stood, more than fifty yards away, beside the remains of the fence. Except I could not see her at all. The land rose a little in a small bank and we were facing outward toward the Guard House. I stood, Julia immediately coming into view. She waved her parasol. I waved back and crouched again.

"Was this small bank here at the time of the duel?" I asked Bertie.

His brow furrowed. "I cannot be sure, but I think so."

I repeated my experiment, achieving the same result: no line of sight. I waved Julia over to us.

"When you were crouched, I could see only the tops of your heads, not the whole," she offered, at the edge of the gentle decline. "Is that of help?"

"Indeed," I said. "If this bank was here twenty years ago, then Sanderson, the doctor, and Colonel Dyson were not in view from the dueling ground at the time of his death." I turned to Bertie. "And you, I presume had your back to them, since you were on your way to meet Lord Evan."

Bertie eyed me. "You are thinking that perhaps the colonel or the doctor had time to visit some mischief upon Sanderson? It seems unlikely. They would have to be colluding, being in such proximity, and it was clear before the duel that they did not know each other. Besides, both swore under oath that the man died without further interference."

I pushed myself back upright and dusted off my gloved hands. "Do you know where either of them is now?"

Bertie gathered himself, too, and stiffly rose to his feet. "I do not even know if they are still alive." He looked at me quizzically. "After the trial and Belford's conviction, I always thought that someone ought to have looked more closely into Sanderson. He was the one who was killed, after all. But it was all aimed at Belford and Sanderson's quarrel, and since all of us at the duel had seen Belford pink the man across the chest, that is where the inquiries ended."

I stared at him. "Good God, you are right." I had unthinkingly taken the same well-trodden path, my focus upon Lord Evan, the convicted, not on Sanderson, the victim. Somehow, I had to find more information about the duel itself and the man who had died.

Bertie knocked his knuckles against his head. "Not a total wooden-top, hey? Does Belford know you are hunting around this old history?"

I hesitated.

"He does and he has asked Lady Augusta not to proceed," my sister said crisply. Her announcement of my stubbornness was beginning to feel like a refrain.

"You will agree, I expect," I said to Bertie truculently.

He adjusted the fit of his hat and dusted down his linen coat. "This is all public knowledge, Lady Augusta, and if anyone can find something that helps Belford, then it will be you. I've always said you were as smart as a whip." He offered me his arm.

Of course! The duel and its repercussions were all public knowledge. The court case would have been detailed in the papers and magazines of the day. Perhaps something could be found within one of them. I had my next step. I took Bertie's arm with renewed determination.

"I would like my friend back in his rightful place and his rightful life," Bertie said wistfully, then smiled up at me, his expression gently astute. "And something tells me you would too."

22

HENRIETTA STREET, LONDON

After Julia and I parted from Bertie, I dropped her back at Hanover Square to rest before our dinner engagement with Charlotte, then ordered John Driver to take me to my brother's residence in Henrietta Street. I was galvanized by the idea of finding something about the duel within the periodicals of the time. My father had subscribed to the *Gentleman's Magazine* for years and bound them into annuals for his town library. Surely I could find the one for 1792.

I rapped the brass knocker on the front door of my brother's house, hoping he was not at home. Pullam, the butler, opened the door, allowing the hint of a warm smile to lighten his craggy face.

He bowed. "Lady Augusta."

"Pullam, how good to see you." I walked past him into the hallway. Duffy had inherited him along with the house, and we were old friends. "Is my brother here? I am not expected."

"Lord Duffield is at home, my lady."

Unfortunate. Still, it would be unlikely my brother would be interested in why I wished to borrow a book.

"It is but a flying visit," I said, waving Pullam away from taking my bonnet.

"Lord Duffield is in the drawing room. If you will follow me."

He led the way up the staircase, although, of course, I could have found it blindfolded. Julia and I had lived here with Father for years before we set up our own household. The parting had been mainly at his behest; I suspect our spinsterish presence had been interfering with his exuberant love of life. I was glad Julia and I had chosen to buy the house in Grosvenor Square and not take up residence here again. It was the center terrace house in a row of three and so quite dark inside, especially at night. Even now it was gloomy although it was not yet a summer six o'clock and Duffy had candles in every sconce. Moreover, it did feel as if Father's ghost walked up the stairs beside me. An unsettling sensation.

Pullam knocked on the double drawing room doors and, hearing my brother's consent, opened them.

"Lady Augusta, my lord," he announced.

My brother, not yet dressed for dinner, put down a glass of whiskey and rose from his armchair to sketch a bow to my curtsy. "Augusta, this is unexpected." And, it seemed, not entirely welcome. Even so, he motioned to the chair opposite. "Will you sit?"

"No, thank you, I do not intend to stay long. I have come to borrow a periodical from Father's collection."

"Oh." He shrugged. "As you wish."

"Thank you."

I prepared to take my leave, but Duffy held up his hand to halt my departure.

"Before you go, Augusta, why did you not greet Miss Woolcroft last night at the Davenports' ball?" His tone was accusatory. "Julia came to us, but you did not."

"You know how it is at one of Charlotte's balls. Always a crush."

"Yet Julia managed it, and you are usually joined at the hip." He wet his lips. "I do not like this resentful streak in you, sister. And I warn you, I will not allow you to take one of your dislikes to Harriet. I expect you to welcome her into the family with the proper deference.

She will be your senior in rank and I will insist you respect it. From now on."

I lifted my chin. This was exactly why Duffy and I should never be in the same room without the diplomatic presence of Julia. It was upon my lips to tell him of the favor from George Brummell, but no, I would not pander to his self-importance.

"You can be assured I will show Miss Woolcroft the proper deference when she is countess, brother. And I have not taken, as you say, 'one of my dislikes' to her. Yet, even if I did, you cannot govern such things."

He drew himself up to his full, inferior, height. "I am your brother and the head of this family. It is my duty to govern you and rein in your impulsiveness."

"My *impulsiveness*? What on earth do you mean by that?" Good God, had he heard about our Vauxhall adventure?

"Grosvenor Square. I cannot believe you have bought a house without consultation with me. I am sure it was your idea and not Julia's. And Jackson tells me you did not use his services to buy it."

So, not Vauxhall. A relief, but still, the purchase of the Grosvenor house was none of his business.

"We used our own agent. It was *our* decision and *our* money, Duffy."

"You no doubt made a bad deal upon it. You think you are so clever, Augusta, but women do not have a head for these things. Besides, you are making me look miserly, as if I cannot house my own sisters. You should have taken this house."

"Ejecting us from Hanover Square does not make you look miserly, brother, it makes you look cruel and selfish. Perhaps you should think on that."

I turned and departed the room, fists clenched in an effort to hold back my anger. No head for business? It was not I who had sunk money into that ridiculous risky land speculation in the new America. He had lost thousands.

I paused upon the landing, stopped by a sudden notion. While Duffy had claimed he was not marrying Miss Woolcroft for her inheritance, had that American speculation taken more of a toll than he admitted?

Still, even if he felt forced into a mariage de convenance, it did not pardon his insufferable condescension. I could almost hear Father's laughter—it had been a private joke between us that Duffy would turn into a pompous ass by the time he was forty. We had been three years too generous.

I had, on occasion, felt sorry for Duffy when we were children. He had never had the sporting prowess or sharp cleverness that our father admired, and his nature had a grudging aspect to it that often showed as truculence and inflexibility: two traits Father had disliked. To make matters worse, Father had often bemoaned the fact that I had been born a girl—not his heir—in front of Duffy. It cannot have been easy to hear such a dismissal. Still, he *was* Father's heir—with all the title, land, and power that came with it—and so my compassion for his early sufferings was limited, as was my patience with his brotherly "corrections."

By the time I descended the stairs and reached the study at the back of the house, I had regained some measure of calm.

Pullam, upon hearing my mission, sent one of the housemaids in before me to light the candelabra. I entered the room with mixed feelings; it had been my father's retreat and if any place in this house held his spirit, then this would be it.

Everything seemed to be as he had left it: the large mahogany desk still set with his inkwells and sands, three walls lined with his books, and a worn leather wingback armchair set beside the mantel. All the surfaces were dust-free, of course, for the maids would have been cleaning it along with the rest of the house, but it did not feel inhabited. Except, perhaps, by my memory of Father's presence. I walked over to the armchair. How many evenings had I been allowed to curl up in it with a book while my father worked upon his papers? Hundreds. How I missed the comfortable silence of those times.

I twitched my shoulders, shaking off the nostalgia, and headed to the shelves along the back wall. If my memory was correct, Father had kept all the periodical annuals together upon the third and fourth shelves. I drew off a glove, then gathered my hem and crouched to read the gold lettering upon the uniform series of red leather-bound books. The *Monthly Review.* Mainly nonconformist book reviews. I ran my fingertip along the smooth spines. Next came its opposition, the *Critical Review*, a staunch upholder of the Tory and church line. My father did always like to be balanced. Aha, the *Gentleman's Magazine.* My fingertip skipped along the years in reverse until I reached 1792. I pulled the book from its position and flipped open to the title page for June, the month of the duel.

Too dark to make out the print. I stood and held the annual to the candlelight. No mention in the June edition. I did, however, see a short article about poor Penelope Wardrup. I read the headline: BARONET'S DAUGHTER STABS BROTHER. Both Lord Evan's duel and Penelope's attack upon her brother, Mr. Oliver Wardrup, had been the social scandals of that year. Penelope had been presented with Julia and me; a quiet girl with the largest blue eyes I had ever seen. We had been quite friendly, sharing an enthusiasm for books and horse riding. It had been a shock to us all when we heard that she had seriously wounded her brother. And then she disappeared from society. The whispers had it that she was sent to India to marry a Company man before the law stepped in. I hoped she found some happiness there.

I returned to my search for report of the duel, flipping over the pages to July. Ah, there it was: AN ACCOUNT OF THE TRIAL OF LORD EVAN BELFORD.

It was a fascinating read, the details of the duel more or less matching Bertie's account except for two things: the colonel's name was recorded as Drysan, not Dyson—a mistake by Bertie?—of Albany House, Piccadilly, and it was not Dr. Lawrence who had testified about Sanderson's injuries. A Dr. Robie, who apparently had performed the post-death examination upon Sanderson, had taken the stand and pronounced the wound made by Lord Evan to have nicked the man's heart, thus sealing the defendant's fate. Yet Lord Evan and Bertie had been adamant the wound had been shallow.

I closed the annual and tucked it under my arm. A lot could have happened in twenty years, but maybe Colonel Drysan and Dr. Lawrence were still alive and in London. And maybe, if we were lucky, they would be willing to give their account of the duel one more time.

When I returned home, I would send one of our footmen to Albany House to make some discreet inquiries.

23

DAVENPORT HOUSE, LONDON

Charlotte placed her napkin upon the dining table and signaled to the footmen to pull out our chairs.

"Ladies, shall we?" she said.

It was time to withdraw and leave the men to their port so that we could get down to the real meat of the evening: discussing the previous night's ball over coffee.

We departed in line of precedence: Charlotte first, followed by Julia and me, then Lady Donelly, an old mutual friend, and finally Mrs. Ellis-Brant, her face set in its usual expression of ermine dissatisfaction. It had been an unhappy surprise to find Mrs. Ellis-Brant and her husband in the drawing room prior to dinner. A hurried, whispered conversation with Charlotte had explained all: she had been forced to invite the couple due to their family connection. Lord Davenport, it transpired, rather liked his cousin Mr. Ellis-Brant.

I followed Julia toward the stairs that led up to Charlotte's drawing room, noticing a slight unsteadiness in her gait.

"Are you quite well, my dear?" I murmured to my sister, taking her elbow as we ascended. "You hardly ate anything at dinner. Do you wish to go?"

I had to admit I was not against leaving early. It still felt wrong to be going about our usual business while Weatherly scoured Covent Garden for news about little Marie-Jean and Thomas rode to the home counties to bring Lord Evan to our aid. I had left instructions for a footman to fetch us if Weatherly returned, and the distances to and from Reading demanded that Thomas and Lord Evan could not arrive before the early hours of the morning. My enforced lack of action wore upon me, as did the wait to see Lord Evan again. Still, Samuel had discovered that Colonel Drysan still resided at Albany House, and I had managed to pen a quick letter of inquiry to the gentleman before we had come to Charlotte. That was some action, at least, even if it was not toward saving Marie-Jean.

"Do not worry. I am just a little dizzy," Julia said softly.

I peered more closely at my sister's wan face. The hollow shadows under her eyes seemed darker. "I think we should go home."

"Absolutely not," Julia said firmly. "It is just the aftereffect of my headache. It will pass soon." She squeezed my arm reassuringly. "Besides, I do not wish you to miss your favorite part of the evening."

I tilted my head at Mrs. Ellis-Brant turning the landing below us and raised my brows: *It will not be the same with her here.*

Julia gave a small shake of her head: *It would be rude to leave now.*

"Charlotte will understand if we go," I said aloud.

"I said no," Julia said, a sudden flare of anger in her voice.

By then we were in the drawing room. I watched her make her way to the sofa, her steps still holding an odd trepidation. She must feel wretched to show such irritability.

Before I could sit beside her, Mrs. Ellis-Brant planted herself on the seat with a conspiratorial smile at my sister and a rustle of turquoise-and-pink-striped silk.

"How lovely to have a chance to converse again, Lady Julia," she said, leaning a little too close.

Julia drew back and smiled politely. My poor girl—I should have insisted we go.

"Come, sit," Charlotte said to me, patting the blue-silk sofa seat at her side. "Lady Donelly, you take the armchair. I know you feel the cold and it is closer to the fireplace."

The drawing room fire was lit, its heat thoughtfully shielded by a screen painted with a beautiful pastoral scene: one of Charlotte's own endeavors. We made our way to our designated seats. As I sat beside Charlotte, Mrs. Ellis-Brant turned to me, her little rodent face alight with arch teasing.

"Lady Augusta, are we to expect an announcement soon about you and Lord Cholton?" she asked silkily. "You were such a handsome couple at Promenade."

"Indeed not," I said as pleasantly as I could manage. "As I said, Lord Cholton and I are old friends. That is all."

"Good God, Lord Cholton and you, Augusta?" Rosalie, Lady Donelly said. Her much lauded limpid blue eyes and sweet face hid an acerbic wit and surprisingly earthy sense of humor: two of the many reasons why Charlotte, Julia, and I liked her so much. "I want to see that wedding. And that wedding night!"

"Well, you will not," I said, casting her a mock-quelling look. "Mrs. Ellis-Brant is conjuring an attachment where there is none." And yet she had nosed out a connection, just not the one that she imagined.

The footmen arrived with coffee, tea, and tiny iced cakes—Julia's favorite, but she did not take one. Had she eaten anything at all this evening?

I took a coffee and sipped at the rich flavor. I had heard recently that there were those who thought coffee disturbed a woman's mind. I always found it rather sharpened mine. Perhaps that was the real objection to it.

"I was not expecting to see Deele at the ball," Rosalie said, returning her cup to its saucer. "He courted me, you know, once upon a time in my first season. Alas, he did not appreciate my sense of humor nor I his moral super . . . I mean certainty." She glanced sideways, across at me and Charlotte, laughter in her eyes.

I smiled back. "Now, I would like to have seen that."

Rosalie laughed. "A lucky escape for both of us. And I am sure he is happy with Lady Deele. I believe she is imminent, is she not? Her first, I believe."

"She is rather old to be having her first," Mrs. Ellis-Brant said, nibbling at a cake: little ermine, scratch, scratch, scratching up gossip. "Twenty-six years of age, or is it twenty-seven?"

"I was the same age when I had Lord Albeware," Charlotte said crisply.

"But he is your second son, is he not, my lady?" Mrs. Ellis-Brant said sweetly. "To be of that age for your first . . ." She shook her sleek blond head, taking a sip from her own cup. "But then Lord Deele had to take what he could get, didn't he? The best families would hardly want to ally themselves with the Belfords after what happened to the older brother, Lord Evan."

"Really, Emelia," Charlotte said repressively. I could feel my friend pointedly stopping her gaze from shifting to me.

Julia also made a small sound of demur, leaning a little farther away from the ermine. My sister, like myself and dear Charlotte, did not want Mrs. Ellis-Brant bringing Lord Evan or his family into the conversation.

Or did I?

I stared at Mrs. Ellis-Brant, the opportunity unfolding before me. The woman made it her business to know other people's business. Would she know the story behind Lady Hester's disappearance from society? Or at least some version of what might have happened beyond the catchall explanation of illness? I would be allying myself with the worst kind of gossip—a rather opportunistic and hypocritical alliance—but it could be a step further to discovering what might have happened to Lady Hester. And a step closer to helping Lord Evan in the undertaking that had brought him back to England.

"Or his sister," I said into the awkward silence. "I hear she is not really ill, as reported."

Mrs. Ellis-Brant returned my stare, then drew in a breath, seizing upon the unlikely support.

"Indeed," she said. "I heard otherwise too."

I ignored the surprised glances from Charlotte and Julia and leaned closer, inviting the story.

Mrs. Ellis-Brant put down her cup, eyes wide with collusion. "My maid heard from Mrs. Lanniard's maid—the Lanniards live next door to the Deeles in town, you know—that Lady Hester Belford is not confined by illness but ran off with someone!"

"Really?" I said, returning my own cup to its saucer. "Who did she run off with?"

"Ah, now, here is the thing," Mrs. Ellis-Brant said, pausing for dramatic effect. "It was not a man, but a woman. She ran off with a woman!"

"Nonsense," Charlotte said. "You make it sound sordid. If she did venture away with a woman, it would most likely be her companion."

Mrs. Ellis-Brant sat back, a triumphant smile upon her face. "Not just a companion, Countess. The maid saw them . . . well, let us just say the kiss was well beyond friendship, and the placement of hands. . . ." She trailed off, brows raised. "It was all very Ladies of Llangollen and Miss Lister."

She referred to three of the most famous, or perhaps infamous, women who were said to live a sapphic life. The Ladies of Llangollen were Lady Eleanor Butler and Miss Sarah Ponsonby, who lived together in Wales at their house called Llangollen, although they denied their cohabitation was anything more than friendship. Miss Lister of Shibden Hall, however, was far more open about her nature. I met her a few years back on a visit to York—a young woman of extraordinary confidence whose manly interpretations of dress and preference for female company left scandalized whispers and arch admiration in her wake. Before then I had, naively, never considered that the Greek love could be felt by women as it could be by men. For a few hours after I had met Miss Lister—and enjoyed a strange, exhilarating flirtation—I wondered if perhaps my own unmarried state pointed to such a dangerous preference. But no, those unsettling feelings I sometimes felt were always directed toward men, and my unmarried state was my own inclination, and the product of receiving offers from pompous fools, dull intellectuals, and the occasional fortune hunter.

"That is why Lady Hester has not been in society for two years," Mrs. Ellis Brant said. "She is off somewhere living an unnatural life."

It was an even chance that the story was false. Or at least a hodgepodge of half-truths. Even so, something about his sister had made Lord Evan return to England and put himself in great danger. Was this part of the reason? I had seen Lord Deele's nasty response to dear Bertie at the ball. If his own sister was, indeed, sapphic, it would be unlikely he would help her out of any difficulty. In fact, he would probably disown Lady Hester. Perhaps Lord Evan knew of his brother's beliefs and had come to the same conclusion, resulting in his illicit return to help his sister. It was too bad I had not heard about Lady Hester prior to the ball. I could have questioned Lord Deele. As it stood, I could perhaps ask Lord Evan—

"Julia!" Rosalie's urgent call startled me out of my musings. "Augusta, Julia has fainted."

Across, on the sofa, my sister had collapsed against the cushions, eyes closed, face bleached of color.

"Julia!" I jumped to my feet, Charlotte a moment behind me.

Mrs. Ellis-Brant gaped at my unconscious sister, then rose from the sofa, away from her inert figure.

"Good God!" I skirted the coffee table and knelt on the seat beside her. Even her lips were without color. I shook her shoulder, her collarbone a stark ridge under my hand. No response. "Julia, can you hear me?"

"Try this," Lady Donelly said, pushing past Mrs. Ellis-Brant to offer a small silver vinaigrette. "It has fresh salts in it."

I grabbed the tiny silver box, flipped open the lid with my thumbnail, and held it under my sister's nose. Her chest rose as she inhaled.

Nothing. Not even a flicker of her eyelids. Dear God, what was wrong? I realized I was panting. I drew in a steadying breath. I had to remain calm.

"Hold it closer," Rosalie said. "She needs to fully take in the vapors."

I thrust the tiny box up until the silver filigree grate within it almost touched Julia's nostrils. Her chest rose and then she gasped, her head jerking back, eyes opening wide.

"What?" She batted away the vinaigrette with a limp hand and took another gasping breath.

"You fainted, my dear," I said.

"Should I call a physician?" Charlotte asked behind me.

"No need for a doctor," Julia said. She squeezed her eyes shut and opened them again. Finally, her gaze locked onto me. Fully lucid, thank heavens. She reached for my hand, her skin cold but her grip reassuringly firm. "I am quite well, sister. Just a little woolly. I am sorry to alarm you." Her gaze found Charlotte and Rosalie and finally Mrs. Ellis-Brant, standing well back from the sofa. "I am sorry to alarm everybody. The aftereffects of a migraine."

"Are you sure you do not need the physician?" Charlotte asked again.

"Not at all." Julia struggled upright.

"I think it is time we went home," I said. No protest, this time, from my sister.

Charlotte nodded. "Of course. I will call for your carriage." She gave a nod to one of the footmen at the door, who immediately exited on the errand.

I looked across at Mrs. Ellis-Brant. Scratch, scratch, scratch: my sister's faint was already being turned into the latest gossip. But not if I could help it.

"I am so glad we are among friends," I said. "It would be regrettable if the aftereffects of a migraine became the latest on-dit."

"Indeed, it would," Charlotte said firmly. She stared at Mrs. Ellis-Brant with the full weight of her rank and society standing. "No one here will speak of it. You can be assured of that."

Mrs. Ellis-Brant's little ermine eyes darted away from Charlotte's gaze. She would be silent, if only to ensure her advantageous connection to the Countess Davenport.

24

HANOVER SQUARE, LONDON

A touch upon my shoulder dragged me from the soft cocoon of sleep. I opened my eyes and blinked, trying to adjust to the close glow of a candle. My maid's tired, sleep-puffed face filled my vision.

"My lady, are you awake?"

I managed a murmur of acknowledgment. I had not thought I would sleep at all, considering Julia's fainting fit and what was at stake with the girl, but the exertions of the ball, Promenade, and dinner had knocked me hollow.

"Is it Lady Julia?" I asked, fighting my way through my fatigue. She had seemed quite recovered by the time we retired to bed. Still, one could not discount a faint.

"No, my lady. You said to wake you the very moment Thomas arrived," Tully said, lighting the candle beside the bed with her own. "John Driver has sent up word the boy is waiting in the stables."

If Thomas had arrived, then so had Lord Evan. I pushed myself upright, all sleepiness gone. "Get my red silk robe. And a cap. Then tell Weatherly to take Thomas and whoever is with him to the morning room."

Tully lowered her voice. "Mr. Weatherly does not seem to have returned yet, my lady."

"Ah." I digested that unexpected news. Still, the best time to question the occupants of a brothel would be when they were awake, so I had to assume the best. "Never mind. When we are finished here, show Thomas and his companion to the morning room."

Tully curtsied and crossed to the sconces upon the wall, deftly lighting the candles within them before heading into my adjoining dressing room. The carriage clock on the mantel showed a half hour past midnight; Lord Evan must have been in the saddle the minute after Thomas delivered my note to make such good time. A pleasing thought.

I entered the dressing room to find Tully before the open clothes press, shaking out the folds from my robe. "Shall I pin your hair, my lady?"

"Yes." I sat on the dressing table stool, then stood up again. "No, my plait will do."

Time was of the essence, and I could hide the worst of the night escapes under the cap. With a nod, Tully held out the robe. Obediently, I turned, my arms quickly encased in the wide sleeves and the rest of the silk deftly wrapped around my body. She half crouched—her own topknot of light brown hair somewhat sleep askew—and tied the belt firmly, then was up again, reaching for the cap. It was one I had recently bought at the urging of Julia.

"I thought this might be the occasion for it, my lady," Tully said in her blandest of maid voices.

"Did you now?" I said matching her tone. Tully had discreetly posted my first letter to *Mr. Hargate at the White Hart in Reading*. She had then witnessed my increasing despair as weeks passed without reply, and my delight when that reply finally arrived. She also knew that I had sent Thomas on a mad ride to Reading. Clearly, she had put two and two together and come up with an entire Gothic romance. The sentimentality of her youth, perhaps, and an addiction to Mrs. Radcliffe.

She positioned the cap upon my head, the tip of her tongue

between her teeth as she worked. "There." She gave one last adjustment to the jaunty side ribbon. "The blouson style suits you, my lady. Lady Julia was right."

"In matters of caps and clothes, Lady Julia is always right," I intoned.

With a quick smile and a curtsy, Tully took her candle and departed.

I considered the effect in the dressing room mirror. It was a pretty cap, but Lud, I looked tired; at least I would not shock anyone with undressed hair.

Equipped with my own night candle, I quietly opened my bedchamber door and stepped into the dark hallway. My sister's room stood at the other end of the shadowy corridor. Hopefully we had not disturbed her sleep. She needed rest and Lord Evan did not need both of us to explain the situation.

I made my way to the staircase, my candlelight bringing a momentary glow to the porcelain vase upon the side bureau and the wild, white eyes of a painted horse. As I rounded the first-floor landing, it occurred to me that I would, in a few moments, be alone with Lord Evan in my nightclothes in the wee hours of the morning. Scandalous behavior. If Duffy ever found out, he would have an apoplectic fit. I snorted, quickly pressing my hand over it; such schoolgirl nonsense was unbecoming in a woman my age. Besides, the reason for the breach of propriety was entirely too serious.

Tully had lit the way with a candelabra in the front hallway and, from the soft glow that emanated through the open doorway, the sconces in the dining room too. I crossed the hallway quickly, my letter to Colonel Drysan a flash of white in the silver salver, ready to be sent. I forced myself into a more sedate pace. It would not do to run in like a hoyden, however much I wished to do so.

I saw Thomas first, standing near the mantel, his cap in his hands and his short jacket and breeches spattered with mud. I looked around the bare room, emptied of all its furniture for the move.

No Lord Evan.

"Where is he, Thomas?"

"He did not come, milady." Thomas ducked his head. "He asked me to give you this." He offered a wax-sealed packet.

He did not come; it was as if the words stripped all the air from my lungs. I could not even step forward, every muscle locked. Why had he not come? There must be a reason. Drawing a shaky breath, I took the packet—my name written upon it in Lord Evan's hand—and broke the seal with my thumbnail. I held the note up to the light of the candelabra.

Evening, Friday, 21st August

The White Hart, Reading

My dear Lady Augusta,

Forgive me for not coming to you as you have asked, but it is not in your best interest for me to arrive upon your doorstep. Nor is it in mine. It is clear you entertain the idea that by drawing me into your life, you will be able to help my situation. You cannot do so, and I ask that you do not try again. For my part, there are too many old acquaintances and newer associates in London and I am wanted by the law. If I am recognized and arrested, there is more at stake than just my own life.

Believe me when I say any connection between us will be harmful to you and your sister. Although it means I must forgo your company, I will not contribute to your social denigration or indeed, your safety.

Your friend, always,

Lord Evan Belford

The words blurred. I had thought he would come. I had been sure of it. I pressed my knuckles under my eye, trying to stop the welling disappointment.

"I'm sorry, milady." Thomas had retreated to the shuttered window.

"It is not your fault." I collected myself—no use distressing the boy. The flickering light accentuated the hollows of exhaustion at his temples and eyes. "You did an excellent job. Go now, get some food and rest. You are freed from your duties for the day. I will tell John Driver."

Thomas bobbed into a bow. "Thank you, milady."

"Wait." I could not leave it at that. "Was Mr. Hargate well? Did he look well?"

"Aye, milady."

"Did he say anything else?"

Thomas shook his head. "Just to give you the packet."

"I see. Thank you."

Thomas bowed again and departed, keen, no doubt for his bed.

I ask that you do not try again: how many times did I need to see his request to stop writing to him? Well, now I had seen it. Now it was done. Apparently, the connection I had felt—that I thought we had both felt—was all in my imagination. Good God, for all his kindness was he laughing, even now, at my presumption? Or worse, feeling pity. I pressed my palm against my flushed cheek; the heat of mortification.

I folded the letter. A child was still in peril. My own disappointment, my own foolish sense of disillusion, were beside the point.

I had just returned to my bedchamber when I heard a soft knock upon the door.

Weatherly stood outside, still clad in his greatcoat, hat in hand. The search had plainly exhausted him; his eyes seemed deeper in their sockets, his normally genial expression drawn into clenched jaw and tight mouth.

"We think we have found where she is, my lady," he whispered, sliding the brim of his hat between his fingers over and over again, a sure sign of great consternation. "It is not good news. A bawd who knows about the trade in children told me that Marie-Jean and some other girls were being taken to Cheltenham tonight. Apparently, they are bound for one of the bawdy houses that caters to the quality."

"Good God," I said, trying to get past the revolting thought of children supplied for gentlemen during the summer season. Cheltenham was the most fashionable spa town at present, superseding even Bath, and would be thronging with the ton. I had heard that even Lord Byron intended to take up residence.

Weatherly passed his hand down his face. "Is Lord Evan on his way?"

"Lord Evan is not coming," I said, my voice suddenly too loud in the corridor.

"Then I must go to Cheltenham now." Weatherly prepared to turn, but I grabbed his arm, ignoring the breach of etiquette.

"And will you be able to find the house? Will they admit you?"

He stared at me mulishly, then his shoulders slumped. "Probably not. But I cannot leave her there."

"We will not leave her there. You are done to a cow's thumb, Weatherly. Get some rest. I will think of a gentleman who will help us and we will go to Cheltenham tomorrow. Early."

He swayed upon his feet. "But what if . . ."

The same terrible thought had occurred to me. "They are traveling tonight and it will take at least eight hours to get there. More likely ten. Nothing can happen to them when they are traveling," I said firmly.

There was no such guarantee, of course, but Weatherly was so exhausted that he nodded his agreement.

"Tomorrow," he said, and with a bow headed back along the corridor, his steps uncharacteristically heavy.

I had made a bold promise—a gentleman to help us in our quest—but who would be willing to take on such a sordid rescue?

I returned to bed, but not to sleep, my mind too busy turning over the gentlemen of our acquaintance.

First, I ruled out our brother. Although he was a magistrate, Duffy would never risk his reputation for a child from the rookery or condone our enterprise. Moreover, he would try to stop us. George Brummell, for all his frippery, had the trust and ear of royalty—no small recommendation—but my friendship with him did not stretch to this kind of favor. And, although Bertie Helden had proved he could keep a secret, I was not convinced I could trust him or that he would be up to the task. All the other men in our life were either husbands of friends or assembly room acquaintances: none suitable to be trusted with our secret activities or even imagine us capable of them. It was beginning to look hopeless.

I tried not to think about Lord Evan, but my thoughts landed on him over and over again. Although I had no claim upon the man, his refusal still felt like a betrayal, and the pain of it and my own foolishness curled me into my sheets. Did he think me just a stupid, interfering woman?

My father once told me that three o'clock in the morning was the hour of sneaking death and mad inspiration. As I heard the clock downstairs strike for the third time, I sat up in bed and stared into the darkness, every nerve ablaze with a dangerous, perfect idea.

If the bawdy house admitted only men of rank, then that was what I must become.

25

Julia looked up from Lord Evan's letter and leaned back against her white linen pillows. Her color had improved greatly, the ghastly grayness of last night gone from her complexion and the brightness back in her eyes. She slowly refolded the sheet of paper. I watched her from the end of the bed, daring her to say "I told you so."

"I am sorry, my dear," she said softly and passed the letter back to me.

Of course, she would never be so mean-spirited. The chastisement was all my own.

"He implies that someone else's life relies upon his freedom," she added. "Do you think it is his sister?"

"I don't know. Possibly. But more to the point, he has left us high and dry," I said, perhaps a little too harshly. I apprised her of Weatherly's Cheltenham discovery, finishing with the immediate problem. "Since the brothel is for men of the ton, Weatherly would be refused entry, although, frankly, he is more of a gentleman than many of those who hold the epithet. Even if he could push his way in, I gather these places have ruffians who enforce order—violently."

"Violently?" Julia echoed.

"Perhaps. But do not worry, I will take a gun."

She lurched upright. "No, Gus, you must not! Apart from the danger, do you seriously think you could shoot another person in cold blood? If, God forbid, you killed someone, you would put your mortal soul in danger. And you could be imprisoned or worse. What would I do without you?"

Indeed, the same question had been haunting me since she had told me about her illness. And after last night's faint, it had been preying even more so upon my mind.

"I am not going with the intention of killing someone, Julia," I said.

"Look what happened with Lord Evan—you nearly killed him."

"That was an accident."

"Exactly. Guns are too dangerous, too unpredictable. Promise me you will not take one." She grabbed my arm. "Promise me!"

"All right, I promise," I said, extricating myself from her tight hold. "We will do this with guile, not guns."

She sat back, satisfied. "Good. But you are right, we need help. Duffy will not do it."

"I agree." I crossed my arms. "I have considered all our acquaintances and I cannot see any of them bestirring themselves for the sake of an orphan girl."

Not even Lord Evan.

I pushed the thought away.

Julia drew her legs up under the covers and eyed me suspiciously. "Yet you have something in mind. Something mad, I presume."

"Not mad. Bold. I intend to go with Weatherly to Cheltenham disguised as a man." She gathered herself for protest, so I hurried on. "It is the best solution—we will not have to involve anyone else and I can ask for the girl and smuggle her out. I might even be able to get Weatherly inside to help as my valet or footman."

Julia stared at me. "What if you are recognized or unmasked?

If you are found in another brothel, I doubt even Charlotte's and Mr. Brummell's influence combined could protect you."

"It is certainly a risk," I said. "But I can see no other way."

"How will you manage such a masquerade? You may shine in our Shakespeare readings, but this is an entirely different situation altogether."

"I assume these places are not built upon an excess of inquiry. I will do everything in my power to avoid the other patrons. My plan is to go in, find the child, and rescue her with as little interaction with anyone else as possible. Besides, if I am not totally convincing as a man, I am sure it will not mean instant unmasking. There are many men who tend toward the feminine. Do you remember the Chevalier d'Éon?"

"Of course. He was charming and wore gowns better than most of us. But that was his nature. You will be trying to pass as a man with only a few hours to perfect the act."

I had to concede the point. "Even so, I have already sent word to Monsieur Pierre to cut my hair at eight this morning, and Tully is retrieving Father's clothes. They have already been packed but I'm sure she will find them."

"Father's clothes?" Her mouth pursed into a moue of distaste—she had always been uneasy about wearing a dead person's clothes. "Do you think cutting your hair is necessary? The short style is really for young women, not someone our age. Besides, what will people think?"

"They will think I am aping Caroline Lamb. Everyone is following her lead and having their hair cropped."

Julia shook her head. "Even with cropped hair, you will still look like a woman. What about side-whiskers? Most men are wearing them now and—"

I held up a hand, stopping her objection. "I have thought of that. I will tell Monsieur Pierre to take some of the hair he cuts to a wigmaker to make a pair of side-whiskers this morning and send them over. I will say it is for an amateur dramatic performance."

Julia touched her own chestnut hair, still in its night plait. "You should have ringlets and a braided knot made, too, just in case."

"Certainly, I can ask for those as well," I said, keeping the impatience out of my voice. She was clearly worried about more than my hair. "It will work, Julia."

She sat back. "It sounds like madness to me, but I see you are decided."

"I am."

"So be it. But if you are going to do this, then I will come with you to Cheltenham. This is as much a risk to me as it is to you. Besides, you must have a bolt-hole and someone outside the masquerade in case things go awry."

"You cannot be serious, my dear. You fainted last night. You are not well enough for such exertions."

"You really must stop telling me what I am able to do," she said, tapping my hand in gentle admonition. "Besides, I know why I felt so ill. I believe I took two of the blue mass pills by mistake, instead of one."

"Two? How did that happen? Does not Leonard manage your medicines?" Then I remembered. "Ah, she was on her half day."

Julia nodded. "It was my mistake. I have done it once before, too, and I felt exactly the same on that occasion—a sick headache and faint. But I have recovered now, as I did then, and so I will be coming to Cheltenham."

"I really do not think you should—"

It was Julia's turn to hold up her hand. "I am going. That is final."

Each of us, it seemed, was decided.

Monsieur Pierre stood behind me with scissors in hand studying his work. He bent quickly, snipped one last errant piece of hair, then returned to his watchful posture.

"Voilà! It is done," he said, his émigré accent and his own exuberance giving the announcement an upward flourish.

It was indeed done. Although I had seen the entire haircut unfold in the reflection of my dressing room mirror, I still sat forward to scrutinize the result. Did I dare think the style suited me? Even to my eye, the close layers highlighted my cheekbones and brought my angular face into balance. I turned my head to the left. In terms of our immediate goal, my jawline was still firm and had enough angle to pass as male, albeit a soft-faced, older male. Then again, I was not trying to pass as a Johnny Raw.

I glanced at Julia, who sat on the chaise longue beneath the window. She gave a tight smile.

Monsieur hovered behind me, mobile mouth pursed. "If your maid brushes it forward, you will achieve more of the Titus effect for your dramatics." He demonstrated with a few deft strokes of his soft hand through my layered hair. The flattened style immediately made the angles of my face more pronounced. "Then your maid can brush it back again for the more feminine style." He raked his long fingers back across my scalp, the style softening into a more feminine shape. "Use some pomade for both styles," he added, directing this to Tully. My maid nodded. She had avidly watched the entire cut; a lady's maid who could cut hair as well as style it was a treasure beyond price.

"You are an artist, Monsieur," I said.

He smiled—with some relief in the expression—and gave a small bow. "I thank you, my lady." He waved to his young assistant, a slim boy with beautifully coiffed black hair, who had also been observing his master's work. "Pick up the hair for Lady Augusta's wigs."

The boy scooped up my shorn brown plait from the dressing table, then crouched and retrieved the larger hanks of hair that had fallen onto the sheet that Tully had spread over the rug.

"You can have the side-whiskers to me by eleven o'clock?" I asked.

"Of course, my lady. Bernard here will deliver them along with some theatrical gum and my own patented pomade."

Bernard, in the process of placing my hair into a silk bag, gave a charming smile and bobbed into a bow. He would go far with that smile and head of hair. And, of course, the requisite French pronunciation of his very south-country name.

"The bun and ringlets will take longer," Monsieur added. "I shall send them . . . with my account?"

I nodded my assent, which sent Monsieur into another elegant bow. After a few final instructions to Tully regarding the placement of said bun and ringlets, he waved his hand for Bernard to open the door and they swept out for their next appointment.

"Tully, bring up my father's clothes," I said. They were currently being aired and pressed downstairs in readiness for my grand transformation. As Tully curtsied and departed, I turned to my sister, who still sat silently upon the chaise longue.

"So, you are quiet. Do you hate it that much?"

"It is a dramatic change." Julia tilted her head. "At first I thought it too short. But now I like it. Even beyond its initial purpose."

I smiled, absurdly glad of her approbation. "I do too." In my mind, I saw a flash of Lord Evan's face. What would he think? A foolish question—it no longer mattered what he thought. Still, I could not help asking, "You do not think it *too* masculine, do you?"

"No. And with the hairpieces you will have more choice."

"And just think, it will not take a day to dry," I said, cheered by the thought.

Before long, Tully returned with my father's clothes laid across her arms. Although none of us had much experience in the intricacies of male apparel, I was soon dressed. First a strip of calico to bind down my small bust. Then a linen shirt—the bulky tails tied around my nethers and almost as uncomfortable as the pads of cloth tied for our courses. Over this, moleskin breeches held up by firm suspenders that held my shoulders back in an entirely unaccustomed way. Then one of my father's favorite cream embroidered waistcoats, a navy superfine jacket, and, after a few abandoned attempts, a reasonably well-tied starched cravat in the simpler Napoleon style. Hussar boots finished the ensemble, the toes stuffed with cloth to make up the extra room. For once, my lack of abundant womanly curves was an advantage; the fit of the breeches over my thighs was confrontingly tight. If I had been Rubenesque, it would have been an immediate giveaway.

Julia stepped back from our efforts and considered the effect. "You will need to pad the shoulders a little. Otherwise, it is rather good. What do you think, Tully?"

My maid walked around me, considering. "I can sew in some shoulder padding in a trice, my lady. With the addition of the side-whiskers, you will look quite the gentleman." She stopped before me. "Except . . ."

"Except what?"

She pressed her hand over her mouth, suppressing a giggle. "I think I need to stuff a stocking." She pointed at the problem.

I looked down. "Ah, I am unmanned." I shot a glance at Julia. Unlike Tully, she was not amused.

"This is not a joking matter," she said.

That was, indeed, the solemn truth. "You are right, sister. Tully, make that necessity and sew the pads into the shoulders. As soon as Monsieur Pierre's boy delivers the whiskers, we will be on our way."

26

As planned, Weatherly and I arrived in Cheltenham before Julia. The summer evening had softened into dusk as we drove along High Street, its intersection with the wide tree-lined Promenade serving as the center of fashionable life in the spa town. An empty sedan chair carried by two hefty men passed us as I let down the window of our hired chaise and breathed in the smell of town smoke, horse dung, and roasting meats, all underpinned by the tang of fresh country verdure. I caught snatches of soaring violins through the grind of our carriage wheels, probably a summer concert at the Assembly Rooms.

The rush of air and music brought a moment of optimism. Weatherly had spent most of the long journey instructing me in the ways of manliness and, for one solid hour, describing the commendable work done by Miss Finchley and her sister in the poorest areas of London. I now felt more secure in my masculine role and outraged by the plight of children in the rookeries.

Weatherly peered out his window. "Is that not Lord and Lady Melbourne over there?" he asked.

I spotted the couple, in full dress, standing on the corner of the Colonnade, the shop-lined continuation of the Promenade. They were in conversation with Mrs. Roberts, one of our literary salon friends. So many acquaintances in town. I drew back from the window although it was unlikely they would have seen me.

"You cannot avoid everybody. Cheltenham is too small and too crowded for that," Weatherly said. "You must be bold."

As Weatherly had pressed home during our journey, confidence was the key to this venture. Besides, I had to test my disguise sometime. I leaned forward again to watch the passing pedestrians.

"If there is a room at the Plow, I will register and then you should start the search for the brothel," I said. "If the Plow is full—" I stopped. He already knew the plan. It was nerves compelling me to go over it again and again. If the Plow was full, we would find a room at another inn and await Julia's arrival, which could be hours depending upon the change horses John Driver secured and their rate of travel. When she arrived, her part was to wait in our carriage outside the York Inn a little farther down High Street. Once we knew the location of the brothel, she would move the carriage near it, ready for us to flee with the rescued child.

Weatherly nodded his agreement. "May I suggest you take that opportunity to eat? It is going to be a long night, my lady"—he shook his head at his slip—"I mean, Mr. Anderson."

I returned to the view of High Street. Our carriage had become one in a slow-moving line of equipages behind a farmer's cart heading out of town with only one horse and no sense of urgency. By happenstance, I caught the eye of a shabby young woman in an astonishingly low-cut gown standing within the shadows of a doorway. She smiled and mimed something obscene with her hand. I drew back, shocked. Yet, she had clearly thought me a man, albeit at a distance and traveling past. I would take that as a good omen.

We finally reached the Plow Inn. The four-story building—its classic frontage painted a fresh white—stretched almost the entire town block. Our coach pulled up a little way beyond the entrance, the commodious courtyard already housing two other carriages: one discharging a family, the other in the midst of changing horses.

Weatherly offered a tight smile. "And the curtain parts to reveal two men, seated in a carriage."

"Act one, scene one," I returned, but I could not manage a smile.

As if on cue, the post chaise door opened. A young footman, dressed in neat drab, bowed and placed a set of wooden steps against the carriage for our descent. Behind him, another footman headed to the back, where my luggage had been strapped. I rose, picked up my hat from the seat beside me, and climbed down the steps, flexing my fingers against the impulse to take the footman's arm: so many feminine habits to overcome. I stood, contemplating the inn as Weatherly descended the steps behind me, without the careful attentions of the footman, and received my bag from the second footman. The exemplar of an efficient valet. I nodded my dismissal to the coachman, then walked—in what I hoped was a striding, manly way—into the inn.

The reception hall was abuzz with activity: the father of the newly arrived family was loudly organizing their traveling trunks to be taken up, small groups of gentlemen made their way to what looked like an expansive coffee room, and footmen hurried hither and thither. Even so, a man with an easy air of authority and a magnificent set of side-whiskers noted my entrance and approached with a nicely judged bow. "May I help you, sir? I am Mr. Bickham, the proprietor."

"Bickham, I am Mr. Anderson. I have not reserved a room but I am seeking one for the night. Is it possible?"

Was my voice too high? I had lowered the register, but perhaps it sounded false?

Apparently not, for Mr. Bickham said, "We do have one chamber that has become available, sir." He eyed Weatherly, standing a little behind me. "Alas, it does not have an adjacent dressing room for your man. My apologies, but it is the summer season, you see.

We can provide bedding for the floor if you like, or he can go in with the grooms."

I waved a dismissive hand. "Bedding will be sufficient."

We planned to be returning to London with the child before midnight, so bedding was a moot point. Even so, we had to maintain the ruse.

"Did you wish to dine too, sir? All of our private rooms are currently in use, but we make excellent offerings in our Coffee Room. It is the best in the area."

I rocked back on my heels at the idea. I had assumed I would dine in my room; respectable women did not take their meals in the public eating rooms of inns. Yet, here I was, not a respectable woman, but a respectable man. And, although eating in the public room could compound the peril of discovery, the idea was too tantalizing to resist. It might be my only chance to ever do so. Besides, I needed to practice my male persona.

"I believe I will." Too tentative. I steeled myself and added, "Yes, within the hour."

Had he noted my diffidence? But he merely bowed and ushered us toward the staircase. Mr. Anderson had made his debut.

We were shown up a narrow, dim staircase to the room, a small but pleasant enough chamber with whitewashed walls, a reasonably sized bed with crisply ironed linen, and a window that looked out upon a rear courtyard and a ramshackle cluster of outbuildings and stables. I peered out but saw no horses or grooms.

"This room looks out upon the *old* set of stables, Mr. Anderson," Bickham said. "Now that we have our new stables, we only use these for the occasional overflow and storage, so your rest will not be disturbed."

With that reassurance and a bow, Mr. Bickham retreated and closed the door.

"A good situation," Weatherly said, taking his own survey from the window.

I crossed to the mirror to check the condition of my side-whiskers; the gum was beginning to itch beneath the false hair. Still, they seemed to be holding up well. I pressed upon both sides of my face to make sure of their adhesion, then smoothed down the crown hair of my Titus. I peered a little closer at my eyes: bloodshot and ringed with blue circles. I might have looked weary last night, but tonight I looked fagged to death. I sighed, my breath misting the glass and blurring my face into a moment of smooth vigor.

Beside me, Weatherly stowed my bag—packed with my gentleman's evening clothes—upon a small table.

"Will you be able to dress yourself?" he asked, laying out the silk evening breeches on the bed.

I turned from the scrutiny of my reflection. "Of course. Mr. Anderson does not need to be levered into his jacket like a fop," I said, trying to lighten his mood.

He gave a distracted nod. "Then if you allow, I'll start the search. Lady Julia should arrive and send word of her whereabouts soon."

His voice cracked with fatigue. Like myself, he had barely slept an hour in the carriage, and I suspected he, too, had managed little slumber the night before. Both of us were drawing upon reserves made of dogged resolve.

"Once you have found the place, Weatherly, come back and get some food. As you said, it is going to be a long night."

"No need to be concerned on my behalf, my lady. I will not let you or Miss Finchley down," he said with some vehemence.

A mention of Miss Finchley again. A thought dawned upon me, and the obviousness of it made me shake my head at my own slow wit.

"You hold Miss Finchley in a great deal of esteem," I said.

Weatherly eyed me from under his brow. "I do, my lady. She is an admirable young woman."

Perhaps I was about to overstep the bounds of our relationship, but if anyone deserved the regard of an admirable young woman, then it was the man standing before me.

"I do hope you know that if ever you wish to marry, Weatherly, you can be assured that Lady Julia and I would welcome your wife into our household. If that is what you wished."

He shook his head. "I have no plans to marry, my lady, but I thank you for the consideration."

I could not glean anything from his tone. Was it love unrequited, or undeclared, or perhaps I was entirely wrong and it was only platonic admiration? Whatever the case, by the awkward silence now upon us I had been horribly de trop.

He bowed. "If you allow, I will take my leave."

With Weatherly gone upon his part of the plan, I surveyed the clothes laid out on the bed. The only sticking point I could see was the cravat. Tully had packed half a dozen to cover the inevitable failures, yet I still did not feel confident enough to tie another that would sufficiently hide my lack of Adam's apple. The one I already wore would have to do, even though it no longer held its pristine folds.

I exchanged my moleskins for silk breeches, stockings, and buckled shoes. The soft clinging breeches revealed even more than the day breeches, and it took a few moments to accustom myself to the sight of my thighs so tightly swathed in white silk.

I ran my hand down one flank; still fairly well muscled from walking and riding, but definitely more softness through my flesh than a few years back. Julia often said age was turning her into a blancmange. I was perhaps more of a well-set flummery. Still, it did not show through the silk.

It had been years since I had taken such notice of my body. It had never been fashionable. I had not had the rounded bounty required at our heyday, and I had lost any bloom of youth by the time the current Grecian style, which suited my long body, became the mode. Although never pronounced beautiful, my body had always been adequate for my needs. And, for many years now, unbothered by base longings, first by sheer will and then by years of habit. Yet, I had to admit that ever since I had ridden double with Lord Evan, I felt every inch of my body to the very core of my womanhood. It was both a revelation and an uncomfortable frustration to have such yearnings again. Especially when there was no likelihood of them ever being fulfilled, particularly by the man who had prompted them. It had also been many years since I had felt the hollow despair of being only adequate in face and body. I did not like the return of such violence upon myself.

I picked up the burgundy-striped waistcoat—one of my father's more sober patterns—and threaded my arms into it, buttoning it at the front and tightening the lacing at the back. Next, the well-fitted tail jacket. I shrugged my shoulders into it, wishing, for a precarious and uncomfortable moment as it gathered across my back and refused to slip into place, that Weatherly had stayed to help. A few wriggles and heaves of my shoulders got it over the line. I thrust my knitted purse into the side pocket. It had been one that Julia had made for our father and barely contained the forty guineas I had drawn. It was a great deal of money, but then I had no idea what a brothel would charge for such a soul-destroying commodity.

Finally, I donned my beaver hat and picked up my gloves.

One last look in the mirror showed a travel-worn but reasonably fashionable mid-aged gentleman who plainly needed a new valet who could tie a cravat.

I took a deep breath. Time for Mr. Anderson to go to supper.

Men did not glide, Weatherly had told me in the carriage, nor did they hold their arms close to their bodies. I must abandon my feminine neatness and expand into the space around me. A purposeful stride, a swing to the arms, my chin up and chest out.

It all felt a little out of control as I walked across the busy reception area of the inn to the public dining room. Yet no one marked my strutting progress; I was but one more gentleman making his way to his evening meal.

I stopped momentarily at the inn's entrance to watch the passing pedestrians along High Street, the encroaching twilight softening their forms into silhouettes. Fashionable young men sauntered alone or in pairs, elegant women strolled upon the arm of a companion, and townsfolk hurried politely at the edge of the footpaths. One young girl—a maid from the inn taking a moment of respite like myself—stood in the shadow of the kitchen annex. In the short time I watched, she was in some way encroached upon by every man who passed: a comment, a gaze held too long, or in one instance a threatening step toward her and a laugh as she drew back.

It occurred to me that I could count on one hand the times I had walked alone outside the Duffield estate. In public I was with Julia and a maid or a footman. Never without company or, perhaps more to the point, protection. Men impinged upon women without thought; another male right in a world of male rights. Most would say they were God-given rights, but now that God was not my inevitable answer, I found I had many more questions.

The maid retreated into the inn, and so did I.

At the dining room doorway, the smell of roasting pork and buttery pastry sent an aching imperative to my stomach. The Plow dining room was famous in the area—according to Mr. Bickham—and had recently been refurbished at great expense. Indeed, it was a handsome space: large dimensions, a pleasingly high ceiling with handsome moldings around the three chandeliers, and walls papered with a fashionable botanical print upon eggshell blue. Servingmen—smartly dressed in white aprons—darted about the close-set tables, almost all of which were full of men talking, drinking, and helping themselves to bowls and plates of steaming food. Here and there a woman sat among them, the gaudy brightness of her clothes or the volume of her laughter marking her as demimonde.

Could I really step into such a male domain?

Bickham greeted me with a harried bob, raising his voice above the bass rumble of conversation. "Mr. Anderson, at present we have no single table, but if you do not wish to wait, you are very welcome to sit at the long table. The Tewkesbury Races have brought more people than we expected."

I followed the flourish of his hand to view the long communal table set in the center of the room. It sported benches instead of chairs along each side, and eight gentlemen currently populated it: six in one group and two in the other, all of them cheek by jowl. There was just enough space at the near end for another pair of men, or a single diner, like myself.

I had thought to dine alone to minimize the danger of discovery. As it stood, however, Weatherly would probably return with the address of our goal soon, and I was ravenous.

"Certainly," I said.

He took my hat and gloves and handed them to the waiting cloakroom footman. "May I introduce your nearest dining companions, sir?"

"You may."

I followed Bickham as he wove through the tables and nodded a greeting here and there. As we reached the long table, the two gentlemen nearest the end glanced our way, the remains of their meal before them.

"Mr. Anderson, may I present Mr. Sands and Mr. Gerrint."

They both stood, with difficulty, in front of their bench seats, and returned my bow with some deference. Bickham had rightly marked me as their senior in age and rank; I was a good ten years older, and while my father's clothes were a little out of fashion, their exceptional quality cried *gentleman of means*. My new companions wore more fashionable clothes—their shirt points higher and their waistcoats shorter—but the colors were conservative and the cuts only adequate without the fit of a master tailor. The garb of lawyers, perhaps, or men of business. Lady Augusta would never have accepted such an introduction, but Mr. Anderson was pleased to do so.

Bickham crooked a finger to a passing server as I took my seat beside Mr. Sands. The bench was hard under my thighs; no shifts or petticoats to cushion my seat tonight.

"We have an excellent roasted pork, sir, and a ragout of venison. A pigeon pasty too. The fish is trout, baked, with butter, and new potatoes."

"I can recommend the pork and venison," Sands said, indicating his clean plate.

"I will take that recommendation, then," I said and leaned back to allow the server to place plate, cutlery, and a large white napkin before me.

"And sides, sir, with a cider to go with it all?" Bickham asked.

I had never drunk cider—it was not a lady's drink—but why not? A nod completed my order. Bickham bustled off to fulfill it.

"'Tis a tight fit, hey?" Sands said and slid along the bench a little to give me more room. I planted my legs a little wider apart—a scandalous shift, but so much more comfortable for the set of my tailbone upon the wood.

"Are you just come to Cheltenham, Mr. Anderson?" Gerrint asked.

"Arrived a few hours ago," I said.

"Devilishly crowded," Mr. Sands offered.

I stiffened at the profanity—no, too prudish. "Devilishly so," I managed. Apparently, Mr. Anderson was a vulgarian too.

"It's Lord Byron, you know," Sands said.

"I beg your pardon?"

"He's come to stay, and women have actually followed him here. When he walks down the street, there's a whole gaggle of them behind him."

"It's true, I've seen it," Gerrint interpolated. "Makes you sick."

"Mind you, the word is that Lady Melbourne is orchestrating a match between him and her niece, the Milbanke girl," Sands added. "I hear it's to distract Byron from Lady Caroline Lamb, Lady Melbourne's daughter-in-law. She's gone a bit mad over Byron, you know."

I did know—I had seen them at one of Lady Melbourne's routs and witnessed William Lamb's silent humiliation—but I had not expected men to gossip about it in such a way. A juicy scandal, it seemed, was owned by all.

"Lamb should beat her and lock her away. She's making a public fool of him," Gerrint said, looking at me and Sands for our agreement. "She's not even trying to be discreet."

The dishes of food and my mug of cider arrived and were placed before me, interrupting the conversation. A lucky circumstance, since my acting skills were probably not good enough to hide my true opinion of Gerrint's suggestion.

I made a show of picking up my napkin and leaning over the meat plate to inhale the smell of crisp pork fat, stalling further talk.

I was halfway to laying the cloth across my lap when I realized only women set their napkin in such a way. I snatched it back up. Had anyone noticed? No one looked my way; it seemed not. I tucked the edge of the white linen into the top of my waistcoat and picked up my cutlery. A spear of my knife caught two slices of thick pork. I deposited them onto my plate, then scooped up a large spoonful of ragout and green beans.

But first, a mouthful of cider.

Holy star! I coughed down the pungent mix of bruised apple and throat-burning alcohol. No wonder it was not offered to ladies.

"I believe someone is calling you," Gerrint said, nodding toward the doorway.

"Calling *me*?" Then I heard it, rising above the clamor in the room.

"Anderson!"

Weatherly would not call me in a such a manner. I turned in my seat and scanned the busy room, catching sight of a familiar set of broad shoulders and tilt of head. Good God—Lord Evan, weaving his way through the crowded tables.

I turned back, clutching my cutlery. Heat rose through my body; he would see me in men's garb. I placed my knife and fork on the plate, using the moment to gather myself. By the time I stood, Lord Evan was upon us.

27

What was he doing here?

His body held the stiff fatigue of a full day in the saddle and he was dressed for riding: buff leather breeches, top boots, and dark green riding coat, all besmirched by road dust but not out of keeping with the dining room company. Had he ridden all the way from Reading?

He bowed and offered a packet.

"Anderson. I have brought a note from your sister."

Of course; he must have met up with Julia on the road—how else could he have known my whereabouts and pseudonym, and secured her note?

I felt the curious eyes of Sands and Gerrint upon us. Clearly, I had to do more than gape at the man. Hurriedly, I returned his bow.

"Mr. Hargate, well met." I forced a smile onto my face. He gave a tiny nod; at least I had used the right name. I took the note. "Thank you."

"May I join you?" He nodded to my table companions in general acknowledgment. "I've not yet dined."

"Of course." I recollected my manners. "Allow me to introduce Mr. Sands and Mr. Gerrint. This is my friend Mr. Hargate."

Courtesies were duly exchanged. Lord Evan took the bench opposite me.

I opened Julia's note: *I am waiting at the York Inn. He arrived in London just as I was leaving and would not be put off. J.*

I looked up from the missive. Lord Evan watched me, expression guarded. If he had gone to London before coming here, he must have left Reading only hours after Thomas had given him my message. A swift change of heart, and an extraordinarily long ride. He did, indeed, look fatigued and perhaps a little thinner than when I had last seen him. Yet, even with the exhaustion, his gray eyes held the warmth of a smile.

I refolded the note and slipped it into my jacket pocket. Such a tumult coursed through me—joy and relief, but also anger at the crushing betrayal I had needlessly felt—and I could not show any of it.

"I had not expected to see you in Cheltenham. I thought you had other business." I picked up my knife and fork and sawed through the pork, somewhat violently.

"I decided I would come, after all." He leaned back as plate, cutlery, and napkin were laid before him by the server, then said to the man, "I'll have what Mr. Anderson is having. A meal fit for a hungry man."

Very funny. I chewed the mouthful. I'm sure it was tender and full of flavor, but it may as well have been wood.

Mr. Sands, hearing the break in our conversation, said amiably, "We are to the billiard rooms. Two streets back." He jerked a thumb over his shoulder to indicate the direction. "If you fancy a game, come by. We could stand a wager to spice things up."

"That is kind of you," Lord Evan said. "But Mr. Anderson and I have other plans."

Since I had just stated I had not expected him, it was plain we did not have plans. The other two men exchanged glances again; for all the bonhomie in Lord Evan's voice there was also a clear note of *you are intruding* and, together with his size and an almost imperceptible tilt of his chin, the message was received. Sands and Gerrint drew back. It was a male exchange I rarely saw—this was men's society and it did not show itself in drawing rooms or assemblies.

Sands and Gerrint rose and with murmured farewells stepped over the benches, leaving Lord Evan and me with a little more privacy to talk.

He leaned forward, his tone for my hearing only. "Mr. Anderson, is it?" He eyed my countenance. "Very nicely done, and the manner too. I like your hair that way."

"It is vulgar to comment upon another's appearance," I said, ignoring the treacherous skip of delight at his approval.

"It is awfully high in the instep to point that out," he countered.

I glared at the deserved riposte but said, "You came with Julia?"

"I did. She told me the plan and, frankly, you are both raving mad. You cannot do this alone."

"I tried to enlist help but was refused." I intended to sound aloof but all I heard was prim offense.

"I gave you my reasons in my return note."

"Yet you are here. So, why did you come?"

The server arrived with Lord Evan's dishes, forcing us back from our close conference. On the man's departure, Lord Evan busied himself with tucking his napkin, yet I caught his soft answer. "I was worried for you."

I had been in the process of lifting a forkful to my mouth but stopped midway. He had come on my account despite the possibility of arrest.

For me.

I pressed my lips together, trying to contain my smile. I knew I was staring at him in a manner that was well beyond propriety, particularly between two men, but he did not look away either. He lifted his shoulder in a minuscule shrug as if to say, *What else could I do?*

The moment was broken as the six men at the other end of the table rose and left, leaving us the only diners seated along its length. For now, we were able to speak freely.

"But nothing has changed, has it?" I said softly. "You are still in danger by being here." I glanced around the crowded room. Maybe someone here, now, could recognize the Reading highwayman and call the watch.

"Perhaps not so much in Cheltenham, but in London, yes." He made his own survey of the room, then leaned closer. "I have not told you the whole story. Perhaps I should have. The truth is I did not complete my sentence. I had my ticket of leave that allowed me to work in the colony . . . and then I stowed away on a ship. Luckily the captain was shorthanded so he took me on as crew and did not put me off at the first port. So, here I am."

It took a second for the awful import of his words to sink in; not only was he a highwayman, he was an escaped convict. "Good God, do they know you have absconded?"

"I am assuming so, thus my caution," he said with a glimmer of a smile. "Still, I had to come back to England."

"Because of your sister?"

He frowned. "How exactly do you know about my sister?" He closed his eyes for a second. "Ah, Bertie. I had thought he would keep his mouth shut."

"No, it was not like that. He did not give up the information willy-nilly. And he gave no particulars, insisting that it was your situation to impart." I leaned forward hopefully. Would he, indeed, finally impart it? Was Mrs. Ellis-Brant's gossip true?

"I do admire your keen curiosity and determination."

He was deflecting the subject, but I was not going to be put off. "But if your sister is in need of help, maybe I can be of service."

"My dear, it is none of your business and I will not make it so." He met my eye for a grave moment, then addressed his meat, carving a large piece.

I sat back, disconcerted by the sudden inflexibility in his voice.

"So why have you been talking to Bertie about me?" he asked and ate a forkful of pork. On dispatch of the mouthful, he added, "Would it by chance be about the duel?"

"It was," I admitted. "But I believe I have found something."

"And what would that be?"

"There may have been a short time when Sanderson, his second, and the doctor would not have been viewed from the dueling ground. Perhaps something occurred then."

He shook his head. "I appreciate your enthusiasm, but it does not matter. I have served the sentence"—he paused and gave a wry smile—"well, almost served the sentence. The damage is done. Besides, by absconding, I have become a fugitive. A new crime which could send me back to New South Wales, if I am lucky, or more likely they'd hang me." It was said blithely, but I saw the shadow within it.

"But if the original crime was not committed by you, surely then your escape would not be a crime."

"I do not share your faith in our courts." He met my eyes, no guard upon the wretchedness in his expression. "Has it not occurred to you that, although I never intended to kill Sanderson, I actually may have done so?"

"Are you that bad a swordsman?" I asked roundly.

He drew back. "I beg your pardon?"

"Both Bertie and your brother assured me that you are one of the best swordsmen they know and would never have made such a clumsy error."

"My brother?"

Ah, I had not meant to mention Lord Deele. "I met him recently at a ball."

"Met or maneuvered?" He raised his brows at my shrug of admission. "How was he?"

"He seems well. Are you aware his marchioness is enceinte?"

"I am."

"He does not like Bertie, does he? Thinks he should go straight to hell."

"Charles was headed for the clergy before he inherited the title, and I assure you he would have been well suited to the living. He is very pious. In fact, he is so firmly set in his faith that he cannot tolerate any other way of existing." He cut a slice of potato, intent upon his food.

"Like your sister's way of existing?" I asked softly.

He looked up from his plate. "You are persistent." He shook his head, refusing to answer my question. Or perhaps denying that his sister was, indeed, like Bertie. The idea was, after all, based on Mrs. Ellis-Brant's gossip, and that held every possibility of being a pack of lies. "All I will say is my brother's narrow idea of Christianity seems to bring more suffering into the world than relief."

From his tone, Lord Evan did not agree with his brother's idea of faith. Of course, that did not mean he had forsaken his own belief in God, yet maybe he would understand my own struggle. Did I dare voice it? I looked down at my plate, forming the words in my mind. *I no longer believe in God.* I had never said them out loud. To deny God was a criminal act—not often prosecuted, but an accusation could still ruin a life. Only last year a young poet by the name of Shelley had been expelled from Oxford for espousing atheist views. But, more importantly, what if my confession created a gulf between Lord Evan and myself? What if it quelled the warmth in his eyes and replaced it with alarm or disgust?

In the periphery of my vision, a bustling figure came into focus. Mr. Bickham, approaching our table at some speed.

I cleared my throat, swallowing the dangerous words.

Bickham stopped beside me, his customary generous smile replaced by a tight curve over clamped teeth. His eyes darted to the tables near us, patently checking that the other diners would not overhear. Good Lord, had he somehow realized my true sex?

"What is it, Bickham?" I managed.

He bent to my ear, his breath warm and beery sour. "Mr. Anderson, your valet has come to some kind of grief. He is in the old stables. You may need to summon a doctor."

28

Lord Evan and I followed one of the inn's stableboys across the rear courtyard.

The boy lit our way with a lamp, its light swinging across the worn cobbles and catching the liquid eye of a lone horse standing tethered in one of the stalls. As we headed into the darker recesses of the yard, the smell of roasted pork and spilled ale from the inn gave way to the earthier odor of dung and straw, and the more stomach-turning stench of the tavern's nearby soil pit.

"Your man's in the last stable," the boy said, looking back over his thin shoulder. "Mr. Bickham said to put him there; didn't want him inside. 'E's awful beat up."

My mind conjured blood, bone, death. I quickened my pace, shoe heels loud upon the stones. Had Weatherly been attacked for his skin color? He had suffered two such cowardly assaults in London. Or was it to do with his mission to find the brothel?

"Is he insensible?" Lord Evan asked.

"'E's groaning a lot," the boy said cheerfully.

Conscious, then—that was good, wasn't it? I caught Lord Evan's eye. He gave a nod of reassurance. And oddly, I was reassured.

The boy stopped in front of the end stable, both half doors closed. "In there," he said.

"Thank you." I held out my hand. "I'll take the lamp now. You may go."

He sniffed and eyed me with some expectancy. Ah, a payment. But I had no small coin.

Lord Evan dug into his jacket pocket and withdrew a penny. "Here, lad. And for that I'll want a pail of water and some clean rags too. You can leave them outside the stable door."

"Yes, sir. Thank you." The boy pocketed the coin and passed me the lamp—fueled by a wick stuck in a greasy blob of tallow—then headed back toward the tavern.

I held up the lamp and reached for the stable door.

"Wait," Lord Evan said softly, his outstretched arm halting me. "Weatherly?" he called, then pulled the top stable door ajar and stood back—a man who had previously found danger behind closed doors.

A pained grunt issued from within. Lord Evan raised his brows at me for confirmation. I nodded—it was Weatherly's voice within the pain. Still standing back, Lord Evan pulled both doors open.

His caution was contagious. I lifted the lamp and we both leaned in.

The flickering light illuminated the whole of the small stable. Weatherly lay on the straw-covered stone floor, propped against the far wall. Blood oozed from a cut above his right eye and his jaw and mouth were so swollen that his breathing huffed in small pants. His breeches were streaked with filth and his jacket had been ripped apart at the shoulder line. He squinted up at us, one arm in an awkward hitch and cradled by the other.

"Dear God, Weatherly, what happened?" A few steps took me to his side, the lamp highlighting more injuries to his dear face; the white of his right eye had turned bloodred, the skin around it double its normal size.

"Thought I saw a chance to get her. The bull and his men stopped me." His words were thick through the swelling.

"The bull?" I crouched beside him, trying to ascertain the extent of his injuries.

"The whoremaster," Lord Evan said. "Why on earth did you go in alone, man? They could have killed you."

"I saw Marie-Jean. Had to try," Weatherly said. His bleary eyes found mine. "Sorry."

I laid my hand on his arm: I would have gone in alone, too, if I'd seen the girl. "How is she?"

"Just a glimpse, but . . ." Weatherly wet his damaged lips, his eyes closing for a moment as he drew breath. "They've beaten her."

I fought back the burning rise of bile, unable to get another word past the fury in my throat.

"Found a door in the basement, through the scullery," Weatherly added. "Leads to a back lane for the soil man."

"Another way out, hey?" Lord Evan said. "Which brothel is it?"

"On Winchcombe Street. Number 22. I planted a facer on one of them. Knocked him out, but there was at least two others and the bull."

"Good work." Lord Evan crouched in front of Weatherly, examining his face. "Do you have pain when you breathe? Did they kick you in the ribs?"

"Repeatedly. With enthusiasm," Weatherly said with some of his old dryness.

Lord Evan gave a low harrumph; half sympathy, half diagnosis. It seemed he knew something about such injuries.

"The good news is that your lips are not blue so your lungs are probably not punctured, but I'd say you've got a broken rib or two," he said. "Not much we can do for them; they'll have to heal on their own. May I look at your arm?"

On Weatherly's grunt of permission, Lord Evan slowly felt along flesh and bone beneath the wrecked jacket sleeve. Weatherly hissed as the probing fingers reached his shoulder.

Lord Evan sat back on his heels. "Arm's not broken, but your shoulder is dislocated. We'll have to put it back before it becomes too swollen to shift."

"We?" I said. "Do you know how to do it?"

"I was assigned to the prison surgeon for five years and he left all the dislocations and floggings up to me. I did two or three dislocations a week." He looked up at me, a rueful quirk of his lips acknowledging my obvious horror. "A lot of fights and men trying to get out of restraints."

Good God, I could not even imagine how he survived such a place.

He settled on his knees and wiped his hands down his coat. "Do you wish to go ahead?" he asked Weatherly.

"Merciful heaven, yes. Please put it back," Weatherly murmured.

"It is going to hurt like the devil, but it will be quick. I want you to lie on your back and extend your injured arm out to the side."

Slowly, Weatherly sat up and swung his legs out, then lowered himself flat onto the filthy floor. In agonizing increments, he dragged his arm into position through the dirt and straw, leaving a dusty arc of swept stone.

Lord Evan suddenly straightened and glanced back at the open stable door. "Ah yes, thank you. You can leave that and go," he called.

I peered into the gloom and saw the silhouette of the stableboy. He had brought the water and rags and stood watching from the shadows. I had not even heard him approach.

"Can I watch?" he asked. Little ghoul.

"No," Lord Evan said. "Get along or Mr. Bickham will hear about it."

The boy placed the pail and rags on the ground and, with one last look at our fascinating tableau, disappeared from sight.

Lord Evan stood and crossed to the stable door. Although the boy had departed, he took no chances. No wonder he had managed to make his way back to England and elude capture.

"He's gone. Mr. Anderson, will you please go around to Weatherly's other shoulder?"

Still crouched, I shuffled around into position, a maneuver that would have been impossible in skirts.

"Now, hold down his uninjured shoulder so that we get good leverage."

Both Weatherly and I looked up at him. A lady did not lay hands upon her butler; it would be a breach of all that was proper. Still, we were in extremis and I could not bear to see Weatherly in so much pain.

"I do not think the usual rules apply anymore, my friend. We are in this together."

He lifted his head from the floor at the word *friend*. "Are you sure, my lady?" he whispered.

"I am not scandalized by such democratic behavior if you are not."

His swollen mouth lifted at one corner and he slumped back upon the stone and straw. "Let's get it over and done with, then."

I braced myself on my knees and grasped the firm round of his shoulder through his jacket. To my astonishment, Lord Evan sat on the straw-scattered floor and positioned himself at right angles to us, legs outstretched. He placed one booted foot against Weatherly's torso.

"I am not on an injured rib, am I?" he asked.

"Not at all, sir."

"If we are successful, you will hear and feel a clunk as the shoulder relocates. Ready?"

That, apparently, was my cue too. I pressed my weight on Weatherly's good shoulder—muscle and sinew tense under my palms—as Lord Evan locked his hands around Weatherly's wrist and pulled slowly on his arm, leaning back for traction. Weatherly's breath stuttered in pain. Lord Evan leaned back farther, frowning in concentration as he manipulated the limb. The shoulder under my hands lifted. I pressed harder, forcing it down. Suddenly, Weatherly gasped and we all heard a soft pop.

"There! It is in," Lord Evan said.

"Oh, well done," I said warmly.

"You can let go now," Lord Evan said to me. I sat back as he withdrew his foot and released the man's wrist. "Rest for a while, Weatherly. If you get up too quickly it might slide out of its socket again."

Weatherly explored the miracle with tentative fingers. "The pain is all but gone. Thank you, sir."

Lord Evan stood. "Well, it will be sore for a while yet. You will need to wear a sling." He offered me his hand. "May I assist you?"

Indeed he could; I did not fancy clambering up like a newborn foal. I took his hand and pushed myself upward. He caught my momentum and pulled me easily onto my feet, the impetus swinging me a step too close. For an awkward moment, we stood almost chest to chest, and then I stepped back.

"Thank you." I ducked, busily brushing straw off my breeches to cover the flush of heat in my face.

"We need a change of plan," he said.

I stopped my vigorous brushing. "In what way?"

"You must not enter that brothel. It is too dangerous."

"What? Are you proposing to go in by yourself, find the girl, and bring her out without any help at all?"

He crossed his arms. "That is exactly what I propose. A bawdy house owned by an abbess is one thing, but this place is run by cutthroats."

An abbess? Ah—no doubt criminal cant for a female whore keeper. Certainly, I had to admit the violence unsettled me—from Weatherly's injuries, the men who had inflicted them were brutal and without conscience. Yet that was exactly why I had to go into that terrible place. Those same men had the keeping of a child.

"I asked for your assistance, Lord Evan, not your supervision," I said crisply. "I would be glad of your help, but I am going into that bawdy house to rescue Marie-Jean."

I met his eyes defiantly—ready for the fight—but found admiration, not combat.

"I had to try," he said, the admiration turning to a glint of amusement, "but I rather thought it was a lost cause. I know from Thornecrest that you are not easily dissuaded."

"Quite right." I gave a last brush down of my breeches to hide the pleasure of being so understood.

Lord Evan crossed to the doorway and picked up the bucket and rags and placed them next to Weatherly. "Best clean up before you join Lady Julia." He took up a position at the door, clearly on watch.

"Allow me to help, Weatherly," I said.

"You do not need to do that, my la—" He stopped. "That is far too democratic."

"Weatherly, this is not the time to have a fit of missishness. Let me help you clean up. Please."

With a reluctant tilt of his head, he acquiesced. I dunked one of the rags into the bucket and wrung it out, the freezing water sending an ache through my fingers. Likely water from a deep well, so at least it had a chance of being clean. I wiped the blood from Weatherly's forehead, scrutinizing the wound. A split above his eyebrow.

"It is not too deep," I reported, and dunked the rag back into the bucket. The water darkened with blood.

"I should go back to the brothel with you," Weatherly said, squinting as I wiped again. "Act as a diversion. If they see me again, they will come after me and you will have time to find Marie-Jean and get her out."

Lord Evan turned from his watch. "A brave thought, Weatherly, but if you are caught, you may not survive another beating."

"Lord Evan is right, Weatherly. You have played your part—we know for certain that Marie-Jean is in the house and we have a possible escape route." I looked up at Lord Evan. "Now it is our turn."

I saw the answering gleam in his eye. "Renegade," he said softly.

Since this was no time to smile, I bent back to dabbing Weatherly's forehead.

29

Julia leaned forward in the carriage seat, her tired face only inches from my own.

"No. I will not allow you to put yourself in such danger!" The exhaled force of her vehemence made me blink. "Look at what they have done to Weatherly. Look!"

Obediently, I looked. Weatherly sat propped against a pyramid of cushions on the bench seat next to me with his eyes closed, asleep. Exhaustion and pain had finally claimed him. The yellow firelight from the York Inn's outside torches flickered across his face, accentuating every cut and swelling.

"You must not go into that place, Gus. Leave it to Lord Evan."

Outside the carriage window, Lord Evan's head turned at the mention of his name.

"Hargate," I corrected and earned a sisterly glare. "Julia, one man can no longer do this alone. It needs at least two if we are to succeed."

I drew back but she followed my retreat, leaning across the center well to grasp my forearm so tightly that I could feel her fingernails through my jacket.

"You are not a man, Gussie. Let Lord . . . let Hargate find someone else. Please!"

"I am here because we could not find anyone else. Weatherly

saw the girl in the house, my dear. They are already mistreating her. We do not have time to enlist another man of the ton we can trust."

She shook her head, but by the stricken look in her eyes she knew I was right. "Even so. The danger, the horrid violence . . ." She released my arm. "You could be hurt—"

"I am with Hargate. I will not be alone. Take the carriage to Albion Street. We will come through the soil alley behind the brothel. And then we will be gone from this place." I took her hand. "You know it must be done."

"I know, I know." She turned and raised her voice a little, aiming her words through the window. "I also know that Hargate best bring you back, unharmed, or he will answer to me!"

Lord Evan's head tilted in acknowledgment.

"There, see—he will," I said.

"Do not take any stupid risks," Julia cautioned. "And if it is too dangerous, quit the attempt and we will think of another plan." She kissed my cheek, giving a fraught laugh as she hit my side-whiskers. "Is that understood?"

I gave her hand a squeeze. "Understood."

I opened the carriage door and climbed down the step.

"Are we ready?" Lord Evan asked. He shut the door and nodded to Julia, who watched us from the window. She returned the nod, her lips all but disappeared into a tight line of apprehension.

"We are." I turned and addressed John Driver up in his seat, wrapped in his summer greatcoat against the cool evening. "You know the address and what must be done, John?"

"I do, my—" He paused. "I mean, sir. The horses are fresh and we can make a first change at Burford."

"Good man."

John twisted in his seat and looked through the small window at his back that allowed a narrow view within the coach. "May I ask, will Mr. Weatherly recover?"

"He will."

John nodded. "He'd be the last to begrudge what happened. Not when there's a soul at stake. But don't worry, if those ding boys come our way, they'll have to get past me and Hades." He bent and patted the large blunderbuss holstered beside the driver's seat. Its name, he had once told me, came from the fact that it blasted the hell out of anything in its path. My father had always allowed any staff who had their letters to borrow books from his library. John, it transpired, favored the Greek myths.

"We'll give them what for and a bit more," he added.

"I can vouch for that," Lord Evan said dryly.

"Aye, sir." John eyed him beadily. "Although I'm glad, now, that me and Hades didn't plump you."

"As I am," Lord Evan murmured.

"Let us hope it will not come to using Hades," I said, raising my hand in farewell.

John looked down at us from his high seat, his lean, sun-weathered face set into grim lines. "Forgive me for speaking out, but we'll be taking a valuable commodity from them—that's how they'll see it. An' greed don't give up easy."

On that ominous pronouncement, Lord Evan and I walked toward High Street. Almost immediately I began to fall behind, my stride too short, too ladylike. A skip and hop caught me up to Lord Evan's side. I lengthened my gait until we walked in unison. Two men striding across the stone flags with purpose.

"Your sister is not well, is she?" Lord Evan said.

"You can tell?" Of course he could tell; he had assisted a prison physician for years. I had also just broken my sister's confidence again. I bit my lip; Lord Evan invited too much confidence. Still, he did have medical knowledge. "She has been ill for some time now and last night she fainted. We fear it is a . . . a malady that has afflicted other women in our family."

"I am sorry to hear it," he said softly. The set of his shoulders seemed rather too consolatory.

"Her doctor says she is not getting any worse," I said quickly.

He looked over his shoulder at the carriage. "Forgive me, but to my eye she looks worse since the last time we met."

I turned to look back as well. John Driver still watched us from his perch. Seeing our attention, he patted Hades in its holster.

"Your driver is a cheerful fellow," Lord Evan said. "Still, he has a point. If we don't get away clean, it is going to be a nasty fight." He stopped our progress at the entrance of the inn's courtyard. "Your sister is right too. You must not take unnecessary risks. If I tell you to run, you must go immediately and not look back. With or without the girl."

I crossed my arms. Here was something I could at least be certain about. "I thought we had been through this. I will not run and leave you or Marie-Jean."

He waited until a young man in a smeared smock pushed a cart full of coal past us, then said, "It is one thing to snatch a child from danger, but another to face the kind of violence that these men inflict. You must swear on God's name that you will leave when I say or I will go no further."

I hesitated. On God's name?

"Swear it," he said.

By the mulish set of his jaw, he was adamant. But then, so was I.

"All right. I swear on God's name," I said, which more or less satisfied both our positions.

Number 22 Winchcombe Street was a handsome terrace with a fine portico supported by fluted columns and a balcony on the first floor. It was set on the end of a stretch of eight such houses that curved ever so slightly like the Nash-designed crescents in Bath. To my eye, it looked to be recently built, like much of Cheltenham—the town had increased rapidly in size to meet the needs of the fashionables who now flocked to it every August. And by the position of this house of ill repute, that plainly meant *every* fashionable need.

The soil alley ran behind the terrace, with one entrance—the end where Julia and the carriage would wait—emerging onto Albion Street and the other onto Fairview Road.

All the windows of the house were lit, from basement to attic, but curtains shielded the ground floor from curious eyes. Lord Evan had outlined our plan on the walk over: first, locate the whoremaster and the ruffians at his command; second, disable or distract as many of those men as possible; third, find Marie-Jean and escape through the kitchens to the waiting carriage.

The second and third steps were, apparently, interchangeable depending upon the number of ruffians and, most importantly, our run of luck. A rather unsettling admission.

We approached the portico steps. A large man in fustian breeches and a drab coat lounged against one of the front fluted columns. He had the square, oversized look of a pugilist who fought heavy.

"The bull?" I asked softly.

"No, I'd say one of his bruisers," Lord Evan returned under his breath.

"One at the door," I counted.

"Better than two. Ready to play the gull?"

Since every part of me jumped with nerves, the role would not stretch my acting skills in any way.

Neither I nor Lord Evan was armed; for my part, I had promised Julia I would not take a gun, and Lord Evan had, it transpired, sold his pistol to retrieve his horse from his former partner in crime. Still, I wished I had slipped one of my father's dueling pistols into my jacket pocket.

Lord Evan threw his arm around my shoulders. Even his hoaxing embrace caught my breath. "This is it, Anderson," he said, slurring his words as we stopped at the bottom of the steps. "I told you it was bang up to the mark."

I made a show of peering up at the front door. "So it is. Shall we?"

"We shall!" Lord Evan took my arm and we lurched up the steps. "Hello, my fine fellow. We hear this is the place for quality quim."

Good God, I had never heard *quim* said out loud before. I turned my gasp into a cough.

The bruiser's assessing gaze took in two slightly foxed older men who were plainly good pickings. He straightened and, with a bow, opened the door.

"Indeed, it is. Come in, gentlemen."

And, with that, we were inside the house.

I had entered a brothel before to retrieve my father's body, but that had been in a London rookery and the house had been a sordid, sorry place with peeling walls and damp carpets. This establishment could have housed a duke.

We were met by a maid—fully dressed, much to my relief—who took our hats and gloves and placed them upon a gilt-edged bureau already housing a good number of such personal items. With a curtsy, she led the way across the marble hallway. Three paintings adorned the walls in gold rococo frames; rather florid depictions of classical myths. Leda and the Swan, Europa and the Bull, Antiope and the Satyr. Of course, all myths of seduction. Or, depending on one's perspective, rape.

The air was overly warm, with a heavy perfume that held a hint of cloves and an odd musky smoke that clogged the back of my throat. It did not help that my mouth was so dry that I had no spit to swallow.

The maid stopped at a doorway—the murmur of conversation rising above a softly played harp—and curtsied again.

"The salon," she announced and stood aside for us to enter.

I barely noted the opulence of the room or the six or so men lounging in armchairs or upon the sofa, drinking wine and laughing. All I could see were the young women, barely covered in sheer silks, slowly parading past them. One girl, her pale body draped in green with gold silk leaves in her red hair, was surely no more than fourteen. I remembered the Covent Garden book I had found in my father's study, and the ages of the women listed within. This girl might have been here for years already.

"You seem to have taken a liking to our Diana," a low, pleasant voice said, breaking my horrified thrall.

A woman stood before us dressed in a garnet silk gown with a spray of red feathers in her dark hair and a calculated smile. I guessed her to be my own age, but with the colors of youth painted on cheeks and mouth.

She curtsied and wet her lips with the tip of a catlike pink tongue. "A fine choice. She has a flair for the Italian pleasures. I am Mrs. Dillard. Welcome to the Temple of Hera."

"I am Lennox and this is Anderson," Lord Evan offered with a small bow.

Lennox? Another alias.

I hurriedly made my own bow.

"Actually, Mr. Anderson is looking for something more specialized," Lord Evan added.

"Flogging, is it?" Her gloved hand made a flourish toward a woman swathed in blue silk standing near the white marble fireplace, with strong shoulders and the ruddy complexion of country life. "We have Deidra, an expert."

Lord Evan made an appreciative sound, but a shift of his weight directed my attention farther along to the doorway that led to the adjoining room. A heavy, tow-haired man in a well-fitted linen coat leaned nonchalantly against the doorjamb: broad shouldered, mean eyed, with a firm-jawed countenance that might have been called good-looking if it had held any warmth at all. He watched the parading women with a proprietorial air, then flicked a snuff-stained finger at the girl in green.

It was as if he had raised his hand to strike; she flinched, tucked in her chin, and hurried to one of the men sprawled upon the long velvet sofa. With a smile, she pulled the silk away from her breasts and draped it playfully across his face, although her eyes were fixed upon the tow-haired man.

I glanced at Lord Evan—*the bull?*—and saw the answer in the fleeting compression of his lips and martial light in his eyes.

"At the moment Deidra can offer green nettles alongside the usual birch," Mrs. Dillard said. "It is coming to the end of their season, but we still have enough for a good session. We also cater to sartorial whims if you prefer women's garb or clergy."

"Mr. Anderson's requirements are even more specialized than that," Lord Evan said. "He is here for a cure. The virgin kind."

Her arched eyebrows rose. "Ah, now, that cure is very specialized indeed. And very expensive. Still, it is possible that we may be able to fill that prescription." She smiled gently at her own joke. "Does your friend have the coin for such a cure?" Her voice flattened into the marketplace. "A pony."

Good God, twenty-five pounds; a footman's yearly wage. I touched the knitted purse in my pocket. I had not thought I would need over half of the forty guineas I had brought. John Driver had been right; this vile practice was lucrative.

She looked over at me, a tilt of her head questioning my financial resolve. I nodded, not trusting myself to form words. It was difficult enough to keep a buyer's expression upon my face.

"He will want to see the cure before he commits," Lord Evan said.

She looked across at the bull, a lift of her chin catching his attention. He pushed himself from the doorjamb with heavy grace and made his way across the room.

"Mr. Holland, this is Mr. Anderson," she said. "He wants a cure. A special cure."

Holland stood a good four inches over me and an inch too close. His gray-eyed gaze was flat and unblinking. It took all my resolve not to step back.

"Show us your blunt, then."

I pulled the purse from my jacket. With stiff-jointed fingers, I slowly worked open the drawstring top.

Mrs. Dillard peered inside, her little tongue flicking out again. "Guineas, Mr. Holland. He's more than *well equipped*."

"Yellow boys, hey?" Holland said. "The price has gone up. Forty."

"Your woman here said a pony," Lord Evan said, his voice rising. "One pony! That was the price offered!"

The volume of his protest stopped the conversation within the room. Even the half-clad girl seated at the harp ceased playing. Lord Evan rocked forward on his toes.

Dear God, what was he doing?

Holland stretched his neck to one side then the other, like a pugilist preparing for a fight. "Well, it's forty now," he said, his voice loud in the sudden silence.

Mrs. Dillard's eyes darted from the bull to Lord Evan, and she leaned ever so slightly back.

At the corner of my eye, another man in fustian breeches and red waistcoat—this one short and squat but still threatening—appeared at the hallway door. Ah, now I understood—another of the house's ruffians flushed out from cover. Two so far, and the Bull. The odds were getting worse.

"Thirty guineas," Lord Evan said.

"Forty." Holland's smile showed two long canine teeth. "If you don't like it, your friend can go and get his cure somewhere else."

"Forty is acceptable, Lennox," I said quickly, my voice a little too high and breathy. "I'll pay forty."

"There, we have a deal," Mrs. Dillard said promptly. "Don't we, Mr. Holland? Forty yellow boys."

Holland sniffed. "Aye, a deal."

The drama was over. The men in the room turned their attention back to the girls and the wine, the conversational buzz and music rising once more.

"That only gives you one hour, mind," Holland added.

Mrs. Dillard stepped forward again. The smiling hostess. "What about you, Mr. Lennox? What do you fancy?"

"I will see what is on offer here," Lord Evan said. For a fleeting moment he met my eyes: *Step three. Get the girl.*

I gave the barest of nods. Yet step two still had to be managed, and I would be leaving him alone to deal with at least three men, all of them fighting above his weight.

"Of course. Take your time," Mrs. Dillard said. She crooked a finger at me. "Mr. Anderson, follow me."

30

I followed Mrs. Dillard along the corridor toward the back of the house. Her gown was of good-quality silk, but a button had gone near the lace-trimmed neckline and the show of petticoat through the gap was dark with grime. Only the outward show of gentility. How did she get here? It was no doubt a sorry tale, but any fellow feeling within me died at the thought of the child she and Holland had stolen.

She looked over her shoulder, the glance almost coquettish. I gritted my teeth into a smile.

"You are a quiet one, Mr. Anderson." When I did not respond, she added, "I'll bring the girl to you. She'll have had a draft so she'll be good as gold, but if she plays up, a slap or two should bring her into line. Or if you prefer, we can tie her down."

"That won't be necessary." Too hurried. I took a breath and added in a more measured tone, "Nor is there any need to drug her. I would prefer you did not."

"As you wish. But if she is more trouble than you want, just call and one of my men will bind her." We stopped at a closed door. "Would you like some wine while you wait? We have a good French burgundy."

Liquor was tempting—for courage—but I needed a clear head. "No, thank you."

She opened the door and stood aside. I stepped into what would have been a small library or study in a genteel home, but here had been transformed into a bedchamber. At least five gilt candelabra—positioned on the hearth mantel and a dark-wood side bureau—lit the room. The soft light fell upon a large iron bed with four posts, the top two with leather straps looped around them. A long mirror stood opposite it, the entire bed reflected in its glass.

Good God. I averted my eyes.

A fire burned in the grate, and with the window closed, the air in the room verged on hot. A damp tickle of sweat had already gathered under my arms—no doubt nerves as much as the heat—and the gum under my side-whiskers itched again.

"I will return with the girl, Mr. Anderson. Make yourself at home. There is a banyan in the clothes press if you would prefer," Mrs. Dillard said and closed the door.

That explained the heat: to accommodate a lack of clothes. My shoulders lifted under a crawl of disgust. I hoped Mrs. Dillard would keep her word and not force a draft upon Marie-Jean. A drugged child would be even more difficult to smuggle out of the house.

I walked over to the sash window—possibly our escape route?—and pulled back the red velvet curtain. The view looked out upon Fairview Road and the shadowy frontage of a carriage house. Farther along, a line of house windows. A hard push of my thumb upon the window snib shifted it open. I hooked my fingers under the wooden pane and lifted, but the window did not budge. I tried again with more force, but no, it was stuck. Or maybe . . . I ran my fingertip along the wood on the right side and came up against a hard nub of metal. Ah yes, nailed down.

To stop people getting in? Or out?

Either way, the only way to exit was through the door. I twitched the heavy velvet back into place.

It was all very well and good to find Marie-Jean, but how did Lord Evan propose to disable Holland and his bruisers? I could only imagine it would be injurious to himself. The thought pushed me across the room in search of something I could use as a weapon.

I opened the door of the small cupboard beside the bed and found a chamber pot. Half-full. I hurriedly closed the door upon the old-piss smell. Perhaps the mahogany clothes press set against the wall would offer something.

The top drawer caught upon its runner, jamming halfway open with something rolling and clunking within. I bent and peered inside; small clamps of some kind. On what part of the body . . . ?

I rammed the drawer shut with the heel of my hand, then pulled open the one below. Far less alarming: a folded red damask banyan, what looked like a clergyman's cassock, and a selection of women's gowns.

I picked up the cassock and let the heavy black serge drop to its full length. A stink rose from its folds: dried sweat. Even in my apostasy, finding such a garment seemed outrageous. I hurriedly folded it in half and dropped it back into the drawer beside the pile of women's gowns.

The top gown looked to be of surprisingly good-quality blue linen. I gathered it up and shook out its folds. A generous cut with the drawstring ties longer than usual. Probably to accommodate wider shoulders and bigger girths. Did some men really wish to wear a gown while engaged in . . . well, in whatever?

Who was I to talk, in my false whiskers and men's garb?

A knock made me jump. I stuffed the gown back into the press and pushed the drawer closed with my thigh.

"Yes?"

The door opened. Mrs. Dillard dragged a young girl by her arm into the room.

Finally, Marie-Jean.

The child wore only a thin white shift, short enough that her bare knees and shins showed. Her curly brown hair had been pulled back and confined by a dirty white riband, a travesty of innocent girlhood.

"Do as Mr. Anderson tells you and you'll get a currant bun after. All right?" Mrs. Dillard said.

The girl nodded, her large eyes fixed upon me. She was gangly—all legs and thin arms—and her face was rigid with terror, but I saw no evidence of the violence reported by Weatherly. Had he been mistaken?

Mrs. Dillard looked across at me. "Payment now, please, Mr. Anderson."

"Oh, of course." I dug into my pocket and found the purse.

Mrs. Dillard's little pink tongue flicked out again as I loosened the drawstring and counted out the forty guineas into a blue cloth she held out. "Thank you, Mr. Anderson."

Marie-Jean stared at the floor. Her ringlets were wet, the ends making a damp pattern upon the grubby shift. She had been washed, or at least doused in water.

Mrs. Dillard drew the corners of the cloth up together and twisted them to make a pouch, the clink of the coins loud in the tense silence. She gave a small nod and smile—business transacted—then pushed Marie-Jean farther into the room.

"Now, keep in mind what I said, Mr. Anderson—just call if you need anything. Your hour starts now." With that she closed the door.

The girl flinched at the click of the latch. I pushed the empty purse back into my pocket, listening as Mrs. Dillard's footsteps retreated.

Finally, all was quiet. We were alone.

I held up my hands, palms out. "Hello, Marie-Jean," I said softly. "Do not be afraid. Miss Finchley has sent me to take you home. You are going to be safe."

The girl stepped back, her bare heels bumping against the closed door as she pressed herself against the wood.

"I'm not Marie-Jean," she said.

31

The girl who was not Marie-Jean and I stared at each other.

"What?" I dropped my hands.

"I'm Lizbeth. Marie-Jean is downstairs, in the locked room," she whispered.

There were two girls?

Then an even more terrible thought dawned. "Lizbeth, how many of you are in that room?"

She eyed me anxiously, then slowly tucked her thumb into her palm and held up her hand.

Four fingers.

Dear God. I pressed my hand over my mouth. Four girls, stolen to be used by grown men. The vileness of it rose into my throat, choking me. But no time to give in to emotion; I had to think clearly.

But four girls. Four!

There was no question; we had to get them all out. Yet I did not even know where they were in the house. And how was I to get word to Lord Evan that we were rescuing four girls, not just one? It changed everything.

Could I pay one of the maids to give him a note? I looked around the room. No pen or paper, and even if I did have them, I had no coin left. Besides, could I really trust that it would get to him? I saw no path that would not arouse suspicion or lose the advantage of my hour of unsupervised time.

Besides, right now, I had to deal with the frightened girl in front of me.

I knelt on one knee—so as not to loom over her—and smiled in as calm a way as I could manage. "Lizbeth, my friend and I want to take the four of you away from here to be with Miss Finchley. Has Marie-Jean told you about Miss Finchley?"

Lizbeth nodded. "She said she was her teacher, and kind."

"She is. And I want you and the others to be safe with her."

Lizbeth's face creased into a breathy sob. "But I want to go home. I want my ma and pa."

"You have a mother and father?" Lud, I had assumed these fiends had been stealing orphans. Lizbeth's parents must be beside themselves. "Then we will return you to your ma and pa," I said hurriedly.

She nodded, wiping her wet eyes with the backs of her hands. At least now the wretched fear in them had been replaced with hope.

"Lizbeth, can you take me to the locked room? Do you know the way?"

She cast a look at the closed door, her shoulders hunching. "They don't let the men like you go downstairs. What if the missus sees us, or one of Mr. Holland's men?"

Damn, it would be too risky to try to sneak around without being seen. The place was abuzz upstairs and no doubt downstairs as well. How was I to get to the other children? Who would not be noticed in the bowels of a brothel?

A rather mad notion popped into my mind. Did I dare? I looked across at the clothes press. For all the risk, there was a satisfying sense of symmetry to the idea.

"Lizbeth. Do you know how to act? Do you ever pretend to be something you are not?"

She fixed me with a slightly admonishing eye. "That's lying. My ma said not to lie."

Lizbeth's ma was clearly a careful parent. Would I frighten the girl even more if I showed her my masquerade? I did not want her to scream when I peeled off part of my face. Then again, even if she did scream, it would probably not turn a hair in this vile house.

"It is not lying if it is a theatrical, or if it is in a good cause. Right now *I* am pretending. I am not really a man; I am a lady pretending to be a man. Watch." I carefully pulled my right side-whisker away from my cheek and held it out. "See? It is a wig glued to my face."

"Oh!" She stared at the dangling side-whisker. "Pretending, like the traveling players."

"That's right. Good girl." I pulled the other side-whisker off. "I have been pretending to be a man so I could come inside to help you and the other girls, but now I am going to become a woman again."

Lizbeth's mouth shifted to one side as she considered my words. "So you can go downstairs," she said. "So you can pretend to be one of them."

The girl was quick.

"Exactly. I am going to become a maid and we will not be out of the ordinary. Come, help me change."

It did not take me long to wriggle out of my father's jacket and remove his cravat, waistcoat, and breeches. I kept his shirt, hose, and shoes. I donned the blue round gown over the shirt, and with a bit of folding and smoothing, the white linen created a good enough modest chemisette and the appearance of long sleeves. A tug and tie upon the gown's ribbon drawstrings at neckline and bust drew it into the right shape. I tied it into a bow at the front, then turned for Lizbeth to tie the bust drawstring at the back.

She pulled upon the ribbons to tighten the fit, then tied them, her little knuckles poking into my back as she made the bows. "There," she said. "I do this for Ma sometimes."

"Well done."

I gathered up my father's discarded clothes, dumped them in the press, and shut the lid. It felt wrong to leave them behind. Still, my father would have likely laughed himself into a fit at the irony of their new home.

I stepped in front of the mirror to survey the effect. Rather good, except the gown was a bit baggy and short on my long frame and my hair was too manly. The dress length did not matter much; many servants wore their gowns above their ankles for practicality.

The hair, however, was a problem. I brushed it back in the way Monsieur Pierre had shown me, but it did not improve the situation—no maid would have such a fashionable cut. I needed a cap.

I spun around, looking for an answer. Aha. The cravat; somewhat grayed and decidedly limp. Perfect. Back at the mirror, I wound the muslin around my head and tucked in the edges. Voilà! A work turban.

"What do you think? Will I pass as one of the maids here?"

Lizbeth peered into the reflection, her lip caught in her teeth. "You look right." She hesitated and I nodded encouragingly. "But they don't talk so nice as you or walk so proud."

"Yes, good points. Thank you. Now, if someone stops us, I am going to pretend that I am returning you to the room. All you have to do is look scared. Can you do that?"

"Yes," Lizbeth whispered.

Yes, indeed. No acting required.

I patted her shoulder. "You are very brave. Once we have freed the other girls, we will go out through the back, along the soil alley. My sister has a carriage on the street waiting for us."

Lizbeth considered the plan solemnly. "There are a lot of bad people here. How are we all going to go out the back with no one noticing?

A good question. To which I had no clear answer. "Leave that to me and my friend."

An inadequate response—we both knew it—but she nodded.

"Ready?" I asked, my hand upon the door handle.

"Wait." She touched my arm, and then I heard it too. Someone walking past, along the corridor. Lizbeth tilted her head, listening, then gave another nod.

I carefully opened the door a small way and peered through the gap.

The corridor was empty, the music and sound of voices from the front salon softened into a hum by distance and walls. A muffled slapping sound and obscene groans issued from farther along the corridor. I opened the door all the way and we stepped out.

To our right, the salon and Lord Evan. Dear God I wished I could get a message to him. Or better, have him by my side.

Lizbeth's small hand slipped into mine.

"Servants' stairs are this way," she whispered and pulled me in the opposite direction.

32

The rear staircase was tucked in beside a narrow servery room that now held shelves stacked with washed linen. The ten or so bare wooden steps down to the basement showed scuffed wear, and two of the risers were stained with an ominous red. Blood? I pushed away the gruesome thought. I did not need to add Gothic imaginings to my sense of foreboding.

I peered down the staircase, listening. A woman's voice, harsh and high, screeched, "Idiot! I said put it on the hob!" A clash of coppers followed—no doubt some unfortunate scrambling to do her bidding.

"That's the cook," Lizbeth whispered behind me. "She brings us food. It's awful."

"How long have you been here?"

Lizbeth shook her head. "I don't know. Days and days."

Not taken at the same time as Marie-Jean, then. They must abduct girls all the time. Another gruesome thought. Still, it was no use standing at the top of the stairs condemning them. I took Lizbeth's hand again.

"Remember, I am returning you to the room, so hang your head."

She nodded. Her hand was damp within mine, her clasp so tight that the edge of her nail squeezed into the flesh of my forefinger. I did not loosen her grip—we both needed the contact.

Slowly we descended, each step down quickening my heartbeat. Someone passed the top of the staircase and we both stopped, frozen, waiting for the challenge, but it did not come. Lizbeth's breath released in a soft hiss of relief as I gripped the wooden banister to steady myself. We resumed our slow creep down the steps.

Finally, we made the dimly lit basement corridor. The staircase ended in an alcove beside a still room—its purpose clear from the gleam of jars and bottles through the doorway. Opposite, a butler's pantry that now served as a wine cellar. The smoky air smelled of boiled meat and animal fat—no doubt the yellow tallow candles set in the iron sconces—and underneath it all, a rancid scent of stale rose perfume.

I peered out around the alcove wall. Farther back along the corridor, a well-lit doorway showed the edge of a solid table with benches on either side. A servants' hall. No way of knowing if anyone sat in there, but it was their working hours, so hopefully not. And at the very end of the corridor was the sound of more clashing. The kitchens and scullery. Our way out.

At the opposite end of the corridor, I made out a door with windowpanes that would probably lead to a front basement courtyard. Brighter light spilled out from a room on either side of it; usually the butler's bedchamber and the housekeeper's parlor. Occupied? Again, no way of knowing.

A tug upon my hand drew me toward the kitchens. "This way," Lizbeth whispered.

We stepped into the corridor.

"Who are you?" The voice came from the servants' hall.

I wrenched Lizbeth behind me. A man emerged from the doorway, wearing the same fustian breeches and red waistcoat as the other men above.

"What you doing?" he added. "Ain't she just gone up?"

I smiled. "*Bonsoir.* You startled me. I am Celestine. Madame Dillard has hired me to keep watch upon *les enfants*. The children. This one is finished, to be returned to *la chambre*. I mean the room. That is the right way to say it, yes?" I was perhaps overdoing the French accent, but it was better than trying to emulate the distinctive sounds of Gloucestershire.

He walked forward, eyeing me suspiciously. A very small ruffian, indeed, standing at no more than my sister's height and compensating with a cocky swagger. He had a red, swollen jaw; perhaps the lackey that Weatherly had knocked out.

"Émigré, hey?" He sucked on his front teeth. "Not a Boney supporter, are you?" He gave a wine-stained grin. "'Cause if you were I'd have to stick you."

"*Non, non.* I fled France."

He scrutinized me once again—as if any Bonaparte leanings might be inscribed upon my face—then looked down at Lizbeth. Her shoulders were hunched, gaze upon the floor. "That was quick."

I gave a small shrug, hopefully Gallic. "So, you are the one that Monsieur Holland puts in charge with all this downstairs, yes?" I said, waving my hand to take in the basement. "You are trusted with the guarding of *les enfants*."

He straightened under the blatant flattery. "Surely am. Founder, that's me. Come on, then."

I squeezed Lizbeth's hand. She returned the squeeze but kept her head down.

He led the way toward the kitchens. "I suppose this one will be shipped off to one of the other nugging-houses now she's breached," he said over his shoulder. "One less will make things easier."

So this was the fate of the stolen children: to be pressed into a life of prostitution. I could not find the words to answer, barely managing to nod.

We stopped outside a door opposite the servants' hall. Probably a storeroom. The key had been left in the lock and a tin candlestick stood upon a stained side table, the greasy tallow candle unlit.

"I shall put this one back and check on the others, yes?" I said. "You do not need to wait."

"Got to wait," Founder said. "Have to keep the door locked. Only Mrs. Dillard can take one of 'em out."

"Ah, of course," I said.

How was I to get four children past this man?

He turned the key, eyeing me all the while. "So, you're a Long old Meg. Must make getting a man hard, aye? That an' being a frog an' all." He grinned again. "Then again." He looked down at his groin.

I smiled back, hiding the impulse to punch him in the face. "*Très amusant.* I will knock when I wish to come out."

"Wait, you'll need this." He picked up the candlestick and took a step to the nearest sconce, lighting the thin tallow from the other in the iron holder. Clearly, they had left the children in the room with no light.

"There you go." He passed me the candle, turned the door handle, and opened the door.

As I had thought, the room had no light—from candle or even window—and a foul stench emanated from within. Another full chamber pot, by the ammoniac sting. The small light from the candle penetrated the gloom and I made out bare stone walls and two narrow cots. On the cot to the left, two tow-headed girls lay curled around each other. On the right, a dark-haired girl lay huddled by herself. All of them staring at me and blinking in the light.

"A right stink, hey?" Founder said.

"*Mon Dieu*, why is there no candle?"

He shrugged. "Mrs. Dillard don't want to waste good tallow on them. 'Sides, they might burn the place down."

Celestine, the collaborator, bit her tongue, although Augusta raged within.

"*Allons-y*," I said to Lizbeth, steering her forward.

We walked into the prison cell, the door shutting behind us.

33

I let go of Lizbeth's hand and lifted the candle. Not one of the girls moved, their stillness like a caught breath. I understood: to move was to be noticed.

"Which is Marie-Jean?" I asked, keeping my voice low. Just drawing in the air to speak made me want to gag.

Lizbeth pointed to the cot on the right.

The dark-haired girl upon the bed watched me approach with the blank stare of terror. I crouched down.

Weatherly had not been mistaken, after all; Marie-Jean had a bruised and swollen eye. For a hot, raging second I wanted to set Holland and Mrs. Dillard alight and watch them burn.

I closed my eyes, trying to stop the rise of fury. Such violent, unchristian thoughts. My sister would be horrified. Then again, she would also be horrified by this brutal treatment of children. She should be in place in Albion Street by now. So close and yet she and the carriage felt so far away.

I opened my eyes—some measure of calm restored—and smiled. "Hello, Marie-Jean. Miss Finchley has sent me to take you home." I turned and gathered the other two girls into the announcement. "All of you."

For a second, silence. Then Marie-Jean slowly sat up. She was small for her age, and her thin body, clad in a stained shift, trembled uncontrollably. "Miss Finchley?" she whispered, her little heart-shaped face alight with relief. She looked at the door.

"She is not here, my dear. She is still in London, but she has sent me and my sister to take you home."

The other two girls sat up, watching. One was about the same age as Marie-Jean, the other a little younger, perhaps.

I waved them over. "Come, quickly."

A plan—born of desperation—had begun to form in my mind. If the recent events at Thornecrest had taught me anything, it was that household items made excellent weapons. A Wedgwood vase had brought Sir Reginald down. I had one possibility in this god-forsaken room.

"What are your names?" I asked the other two girls as they clustered around me and Lizbeth. Both were dressed in the same sort of thin shift. Although it was the tail end of summer, the air in the room felt damp and cold, and they were all shivering.

The older of the two said, "I am Jessica, and this is Faith. She's my sister, but she don't talk."

Now that I knew they were related, it was easy to see the similarities in their wary posture, lank blond hair, and gaunt faces. Faith reached across and touched my hand: tiny freezing fingers, the nails raw from biting.

"Hello, Faith," I said. She nodded, her countenance as weary and gray as an old woman's.

"Now, listen carefully. My sister has a carriage waiting at the top of the soil alley." I pointed to the left, toward Albion Street. "When the door opens, you must run as fast as you can to the kitchens, out the backyard, and up the alley." I pointed to the left again, all four pairs of eyes following the jab of my finger. "Remember, that way. Don't stop until you get to the carriage that is waiting there. I will be following right behind. Do you understand?"

The girls nodded.

"What if we get caught?" Jessica asked. She had a wiry toughness about her that made me think that she had run before.

"Fight as hard as you can and I will come to help." Not the best plan, but it was all I had.

Jessica gave one sharp nod, her mouth set.

"Now, line up against the wall near the door and get ready to run out when I say. Understood?"

Again, they nodded.

Lizbeth took Marie-Jean's hand, helping her from the bed, and all four girls pressed themselves against the wall. I handed Jessica the candle, then crossed to the dark corner of the room to collect my chosen weapon.

Gingerly I picked up the full chamber pot. Heavy. The stinking contents slopped up against the side and over, wetting my fingers. I tucked in my chin to stop from gagging and carried it to the closed door.

"Snuff out the candle," I whispered.

Jessica raised the tallow. Her lips pursed and then we were plunged back into darkness.

Bracing myself, I called in Celestine's voice, "Founder. *Mon chér*. The candle has gone out. I need another!"

"Bloody hell." The door opened and Founder stood silhouetted against the hallway wall.

He stepped in. With all my strength I threw the contents of the chamber pot at him. The urine and feces hit him full in the face, splashing across the wall and corridor. He staggered into the door—slamming it against the wall—choking, his hands to his eyes. "Jesus Christ!'

"Run," I yelled.

The girls ran, ducking past the gagging, blinded man. I grabbed his soaking wet arm and wrenched him into the room, his weight swinging me off-balance. I skidded on feces and rammed into his chest as he flung his arm out blindly. His elbow hit me under the chin, snapping my head back. I gasped, the bone-jarring pain and ammoniac stench bringing tears to my eyes. His body was a blur between me and the door. Wildly, I swung the empty chamber pot at the shape of his head. It connected in a crumbling smash of cheap porcelain. He dropped to his knees, howling.

I ran into the hallway and slammed the door closed, my fingers fumbling against the slippery, wet key. It turned just as the weight of an enraged body hit the door on the other side.

"Bitch!" Founder screamed as I steadied myself against the hallway wall, blinking away wet, stinging pain.

A loud yell rose from the direction of the kitchens. A crash of crockery. The girls!

I ran toward the sound, my sight finally clear. As I passed a larder room, a chorus of high-pitched screams split the air, and then three of the girls burst out of the end doorway and came running toward me. Lizbeth, Marie-Jean, Faith. No Jessica. Had she escaped out the back?

A woman in an apron, her reddened face set into a snarl, barged out of the kitchens behind them.

Could we make the front courtyard?

I swung around, but a heavyset man had emerged from the housekeeper's parlor, blocking the front basement door.

"This way," I yelled to the girls, herding them along the corridor. Founder was still yelling and banging the storeroom door, the doorframe shaking under his frenzy. "Where's Jessica?"

"Gone," Lizbeth said, through sharp pants of fear. "Alley."

One free. Thank God. Had she found her way to Julia?

We reached the staircase, the woman—the cook—still in pursuit. "Rachel!" she yelled. Another woman emerged from the kitchens.

"Go!" I herded Faith and Lizbeth up the steps, but Marie-Jean had frozen into a crouch. "Marie-Jean! Get up!" She cringed back against the wall.

I grabbed her under the arms and swung her up against my hip just as the cook reached us. Marie-Jean was small, but she was still a weight. I staggered, unbalanced.

"Who the hell are you?" the cook yelled, spittle spraying.

All I had free were my feet. I braced and kicked. My foot connected with her kneecap with a sharp crack. She screamed and crumpled to the floor, but her kitchen colleague was approaching at speed.

I lurched-hopped back into balance and took the stairs, every tendon and muscle straining as I climbed with Marie-Jean clinging to me. Faith had made the top, but Lizbeth had stumbled halfway up and crashed against the balustrade.

I freed a hand and wrenched her up by the back of her shift. Her scrabbling weight dragged at my shoulder in a tearing pain. "Keep going!"

We reached the ground floor. The screaming and commotion had brought a curious half-clad man to the door of the back room. At the sight of us, he drew back, the door slamming shut.

"Hargate!" I bellowed, urging the girls along the corridor. "Hargate!"

Faith led the way as we ran toward the front door. Ahead, people came running out of the salon. Dear God, it was Holland and the squat bruiser. And Mrs. Dillard behind them.

All three blocked our way.

Behind them, the patrons and girls clustered at the salon doorway, watching.

It took Holland only a second to realize the situation. "Stop them!" he ordered.

He bent and pulled out a needle-thin knife from his boot. I lunged and grabbed Faith, stopping her headlong dash toward the blade. What now?

Over my shoulder, the heavyset man from the basement had made the top of the staircase and blocked the staircase and corridor.

"Girls!" I gathered Faith and Lizbeth against me, Marie-Jean still in my arms. Her short breaths fluttered hot against my neck. The other two girls pressed against my body.

We had nowhere to go.

34

Holland started toward us, the knife aimed at me. "Put down the squeaker, or I'll gut her."

"You are despicable," I hissed, backing up a step.

A figure barged through the ranks of people watching from the salon door. "Get out of my way!"

I knew that voice: Lord Evan.

He ran, swinging a candelabra. A flash of gilt and the heavy base caught the squat bruiser on the temple with a thud, dropping him like a sack of coal.

Holland spun around. "Jonas!" he yelled. "Get in here."

"Your man Jonas is down too," one of the onlookers yelled cheerfully. "As sweet a facer as ever I saw."

Standing over the other fallen ruffian, Lord Evan's attention switched to me. "Run! Now!" Then he took in the girls clinging to me. "Good God. Three?"

He lunged toward Holland, but Mrs. Dillard blocked his way. He raised the candelabra again. She shrank back.

"Graves!" Holland shouted. "Get in here!"

The front door slammed open and the bruiser from the portico stepped in, already bouncing upon his toes. He saw Lord Evan with candelabra raised and ran at him, fists swinging.

That was all I saw, for Holland turned back to me. The knife and his nasty smile filled my vision, his long canines giving his face a feral cast. The girls pressed harder against me, Marie-Jean's breathing holding a tiny sob within each pant.

"Mr. Anderson, I take it?" Holland said. He waved the knife from side to side, like a chiding finger. "I don't like being duped, especially not by an old bunter."

I had no idea what *old bunter* meant, but the cold fury in his eyes and the knife were threat enough.

"Girls, get behind me," I said, releasing my hold on Marie-Jean. She slid onto her feet. I grabbed her arm and steered her behind me, waving the other two girls next to her against the wall. "Stay back," I said.

"I say, that's not right," one of the men from the salon said. "Holding a knife on a woman."

"Don't get between a man and his whore," another said.

Whore? Then again, I was in a whorehouse.

"Help us!" I yelled at the onlookers, but no one moved, their faces avid for the fight.

I caught a glimpse of Lord Evan, locked in a struggle with the bruiser, both men pounding fists into the other's ribs. No possibility of help there.

Frantically I searched for a weapon or shield. Three canes had been laid beside hats on the side bureau, but they were too far away. Holland would have me before I reached them. Only one option, and a poor one at that.

I lunged and wrenched the painting of Leda and the Swan off the wall and ran at Holland. The corner of the gold frame caught him in the chest. A murmur of appreciation rose from the onlookers. Holland staggered back.

I rammed the long edge into him, aiming for his throat, but the weight slanted it down into his chest again. The momentum forced him back another step, but I had lost the element of surprise. He grabbed the frame on his side and thrust back at me. I braced and held firm, but only for a moment. His strength pressed it into my chest, the bruising force pushing me backward into the wall.

He wrenched the frame sideways. I hung grimly on to my side—the width of the painting was the only thing between me and the knife—but he yanked it again and again. My fingers cramped, my grip loosening. I gritted my teeth through the pain, but it was no good. He twisted the frame, bending my wrists too far over. I let go.

The frame arced and landed with a slap upon the floor. Holland charged. I ducked, but not fast enough. The blade ripped into the round of my right shoulder. I did not feel it go in, but I surely felt it come out. A stinging burn deep in my muscle that gathered itself into roaring agony. I gripped the wet, pulsing wound. Stabbed! I was stabbed. The comprehension made the pain even worse.

Marie-Jean screamed. It sounded oddly far away.

I stared down at the bright red blood welling up between my fingers and the wet stain spreading across my father's shirt. My body felt heavy, yet I knew I had to move again. Away from the blade, away from the girls. I had to draw him away.

I stumbled toward Lord Evan, bloodied palm sliding flat upon the wall. Lord Evan would know what to do. One step, two, then my legs buckled. I fell on my knees, against the wall.

Holland loomed above me, the knife in his hand glistening with my blood. I had to move, but my body was locked in pain. Holland raised the knife.

Yelling erupted near the salon, the onlookers pressing back.

"Get away from her!"

I blinked, my sight bleared with tears. So much fiery pain in my shoulder and I could not gather enough breath. But I knew that voice.

Julia.

She stood in the doorway, the long, heavy blunderbuss aimed at Holland, her face half-covered by a blue neckerchief. Like a highwayman.

"I said, step away or I will blow your head off," she yelled.

I giggled; my sister was a terrible shot. I pressed my hand over my mouth, tasting the metal salt of my blood. Mustn't giggle. I gulped for air again, the pain radiating into agony across my chest. No, only shallow breaths. I panted, the short gasps keeping me just above the wave of pain poised to engulf me again.

Holland stepped back, his hands raised. "You!"

"Yes, me." It was Weatherly's voice.

I squinted through the strange gray fog in the hallway. Hard to concentrate, my focus slipping and sliding away from my thoughts.

"Weatherly, get the children," my sister ordered. "Hargate, help Gus."

A figure appeared in front of me. I looked up. Ah, Lord Evan. Blood seeped from his nose and a cut above his right eye, but never had I seen a face so dear to me.

I smiled up at him through the fog. "Dearest Lord Evan. My one true love." I tried to stand, but the hallway lurched into a sickening spin.

"Whoa there!" He lunged and stopped my sideways pitch, propping me back against the wall. "You have lost a lot of blood." Gently he pried my hand from the wound. "Let me see."

A tug upon my shirt pulled back the torn edge.

I clung to his hand. "Am I dying?"

"No, you are not," he said firmly. "Nothing essential has been hit."

He slid his hand around my waist, lifting me onto my feet. A liberty, but it seemed a good idea to lean into the solid support of his body. He pressed his palm hard against my bare shoulder. The pain of it speared through my whole body. I gasped, then an absurd panting giggle rose again. Bare shoulder! What would Julia say?

"Can you walk?" he asked.

I nodded, although it felt like wading through mud. Too much effort. Besides, I had something important to say . . . if I could form the words.

"Girls. Four of them," I finally murmured against his neck, the words woolly in my parched mouth. He smelled rather good: lemony, with a tang of metal. Or perhaps that was all the blood. "One got out."

The hallway seesawed around me. I slid downward, my momentum halted by two strong arms, then everything pitched and rolled again as Lord Evan swung me up against his chest. Like a bride. Ha!

"All the girls are out," he said, his voice rumbling against my temple.

Faces, staring at us, agape. Mostly men. We had not been introduced: impertinent jackanapes. Then cooler air. We were outside, on the moonlit street. For an excruciating second, everything focused: a thousand pinpoints of agony in my shoulder, Lord Evan's arms holding me close, Weatherly and the four girls at the carriage. And Julia with the blunderbuss aimed at the house, walking backward at our side.

Julia. My darling Julia.

"She's not a very good shot," I whispered.

I felt Lord Evan laugh against my hair.

And then he faded and I was falling into soft, dark silence.

35

I woke in the carriage, propped in the bodkin corner upon cushions. Dawn light showed a number of faces peering at me. By the grinding judder of the wheels and the lurching sway of the cabin, we were traveling at a decent speed.

I drew a deep stuttering breath, smelling the rich fruity tang of brandy. My feet were cold; somehow I had lost my shoes.

"She's awake," the girl opposite me announced.

Who was she? Then the gist of the past few hours rushed back upon me, along with the burning pain in my shoulder. Her name was Lizbeth, and I had been stabbed.

Dear God, I had been stabbed!

I scrunched my eyes closed, then opened them wide, seeking some clarity of mind and vision. But no, I could not remember much, apart from running with the four girls and the knife. Everything else was a blur.

"Are we all safe?" I asked. Except it did not come out as words, more as a dry, crackling groan.

"Everyone is safe, my dear," Julia said, clearly still able to understand me. She sat beside me, holding my left hand. I tried to lift my right, but the pain was too great. "We have passed Botley Hill," she added.

Botley Hill? That was less than forty miles from London. I had been insensible for most of the journey back.

I cleared my throat, finding saliva and my voice. "We got them out!" I squeezed her hand, my grip absurdly weak. "You were magnificent!"

"I was terrified, Gus," she said. "I thought you were dying."

"Me too," I said, ignoring the anger in her voice; I did not have the energy to answer it. "And then you arrived with Hades." I managed a wan smile. "I thought we were not going to use guns."

Her mouth tightened; too soon for teasing, it seemed. "When Jessica told me the circumstances within the house, it was the only way I could see to get you out. Even then, the cur who stabbed you came after us. John had to discharge Hades in the middle of Cheltenham to make him desist!"

The dawn light through the tree canopy illuminated the cabin in short flickers of pink light that caught the deep furrows in her face. "I thought I had lost you, Gus. You were in such pain." She took a wavering breath. "So much blood."

I squinted down at the burning ache. Still in a lot of pain, but the blood had been cleaned up. A thick wad of cloth had been expertly bound around my shoulder. The smell of brandy emanated from it. Someone had cleaned my wound with liquor—no doubt the work of Lord Evan. The favor returned.

"Here, have some lemonade." Julia passed me a clay tumbler.

"You brought lemonade to a rescue?"

"Of course not. I secured it from the last posting inn."

I flexed my cold toes. "What happened to my shoes?"

She wrinkled her nose. "They were covered in excrement so I threw them away. And your hose too."

How did my feet get covered in excrement? I could not remember.

She pushed my hand toward my mouth. "Finish the tumbler, now. Lord Evan says you are lucky—the knife missed all that was important—but you must drink as much as possible to restore the blood you have lost."

I sipped at the tart drink, welcoming the sting of the cool liquid against my parched throat. Where *was* Lord Evan?

Weatherly lay propped in the far corner, his eyes closed, his injured arm cradled in the other. On the seat lined up beside him, the four girls: Marie-Jean, leaning against him; Faith and Jessica, holding hands; and Lizbeth, folded into the corner across from me with a half-eaten pasty upon her lap. All wrapped in blankets and plainly exhausted. But no Lord Evan. Had he already left us? Surely he would not leave without saying good-bye.

"Lord Evan is on the driver's seat with John, in charge of Hades," Julia said, seeing the question upon my face. "He wants to escort us back into London." She gently squeezed my hand. "Do you need some laudanum? I have some in my medical box."

Even that squeeze sent shooting pain through me. A dose of laudanum would be welcome. But I could not slip back into insensibility. Not yet.

"Julia, Lord Evan cannot come into London with us," I said, lowering my voice. "He did not serve his sentence. He absconded to help his sister. It is likely he already has a bounty upon his head. If he is caught, he may face the gallows."

"Absconded? Oh dear." Julia chewed on her lip. "He does not want to leave your side, Gus. He has said as much."

I could not help the leap of my heart at that avowal. Even so, he had to be dissuaded. A task that only I could do. Yet, I did not even have the strength to reach up to knock upon the window.

"Stop the carriage, Julia. I must speak to him."

"You are going to send him away?" I heard an odd note of relief in her voice. Not, I think, for Lord Evan's sake.

"It is not his fault, you know," I said. "I decided to retrieve all four girls. Surely you understand I could do nothing else? The fact that I got stabbed is just unfortunate."

Julia turned her face away. "Unfortunate? That is certainly one way to describe it!" She drew a breath through pinched nostrils. "Of course I understand you had to save the girls. I applaud it," she said, sounding very much as if she did not applaud it. "Still, when you are in Lord Evan's company you are too reckless. You become another person."

"That is unfair. I have always been reckless."

Although perhaps she had a point; I did feel strong and smart and a great deal bolder when I was with him. All admirable qualities in a man but adding up to recklessness in a woman. Yet, I rather liked the person I was in his company.

She waved away my protest. "We will talk about it later. For now, you must make him leave, but do not exert yourself too much or you will start bleeding again."

She knocked hard upon the small window behind us. Almost immediately, I heard John Driver call out to the horses, their gaits slowing as he pulled them up. The carriage eased into a standstill next to a field populated by a flock of sheep, their heads popping up at the unexpected arrival beside their stone wall.

"Girls, we will have a short time for the necessaries," Julia announced. "Do not venture too far from the coach."

The carriage rocked slightly as someone alighted from the driver's seat. The field-side door opened and Lord Evan peered into the cabin, face gaunt—by my reckoning he had been awake for thirty-six hours now. His nose was a little swollen and the split skin above his eye had still not closed.

"Is everything as it should be?"

The query was general, but his attention had fixed upon me, his head to one side in a diagnostic tilt. "You are awake, Lady Augusta. I am glad to see it."

"Yes. Awake." I smiled, absurdly glad to see him too. "Are you well?"

"Nothing too life-threatening." He smiled back, a heart-stopping mix of roguery and reassurance.

"My sister wishes to speak to you," Julia said crisply into the moment. "Come, girls. Out we go. Bring your blankets, but do not let them drag upon the grass."

Lord Evan handed Julia down and then the girls, one by one. Every rocking descent from the carriage sent a sharp pain through my shoulder. I bit back my groans; they would only upset Julia.

As Faith passed, she smiled and touched my hand again—a warm butterfly brush of sympathy. I felt an absurd rise of tears; just for that smile, it was worth it.

Finally, Weatherly stood, bending stiffly to accommodate his height, his arm held gingerly across his chest.

"How are you, Weatherly?" I asked.

"Better than you," he said bluntly, eyeing my wad of bandaging. "Forgive me for listening to your conversation—I could not help it—but Lady Julia is right. I am grateful that we've retrieved Marie-Jean and the other girls. But it is one thing to do good works. It is another entirely for a lady of your connections to be stabbed in a brothel."

I watched him slowly descend the step to the verge, eschewing Lord Evan's offered hand. I could have snipped back at him that my pedigree did not elevate me so high—after all, my father had died in a brothel. But I had neither the energy nor the desire to spar with him.

Outside, the sheep had come to the fence, much to the delight of Marie-Jean and Lizbeth, who stood upon a hillock and offered pieces of pasty to one of the curious flock. Jessica and Faith hung back, suspicious of the creatures.

I sucked in a breath as the cabin rocked again under Lord Evan's weight. He stepped up and swung into the seat opposite.

"Your sister and butler are annoyed with me," he said as he leaned over and shut the door. "They believe I should have saved you from this injury, and of course they are right. You should not have even been in such a situation."

"I assure you they are more annoyed at me," I said. "This was all my idea."

He shook his head, clearly not conceding responsibility. "How is the shoulder? Painful, I would expect."

"It is," I admitted. "Did you clean and bind it?"

"I did. A small piece of your shirt had gone in with the thrust. It often happens but it had to come out quickly or the wound could go bad. Considering Holland had a stiletto, the cut is not too deep."

"Stiletto?"

"An Italian blade—one of the thinnest around. Often used for assassination. It goes deep and leaves very little opening. You are very lucky he struck where he did—no organs or arteries. I have given your sister the name of a young doctor—Edinburgh trained—who has experience with such wounds. He is very discreet."

"Thank you."

He nodded.

The silence lengthened between us: not entirely comfortable. He rubbed his chin, the scrape of the few days of stubble audible in the silence. Although the current fashion was for clean-shaven men, I rather liked the look upon him. Gentleman-pirate.

"Your sister said you had something to say to me?" His hand smoothed the back of his cropped hair. "Was it about the hallway? Believe me, I know you were under great duress."

I frowned, trying to remember the hallway. All I could see in my mind was the knife coming at me. I pushed the terrifying image away. "I am sorry, I cannot remember anything about the hallway."

"Ah." He sat back. "If you cannot remember, then it is of no consequence."

"No, tell me, please."

"It is of no consequence." A flick of his hand waved aside the subject. "What is it you wish to say?"

I watched him for a moment longer—had I said something awful in the hallway?—but his expression had shifted into polite inquiry. A neat turn of the tables; it would be churlish now to press him upon the matter.

"I wish to say . . . no, I want to insist that you do not come into London with us. It is too dangerous. What if someone recognizes you?"

He crossed his arms. "There is some risk, I suppose, but it is not as if every second person will know me. I wish to see you all home safely and I want to be certain that you recover properly."

A worthy wish, and one that I desperately wanted, too, but it was not in his best interest.

"It does not need to be every second person, Lord Evan. It just needs to be one person who is looking for you. And they will be, won't they?" I tried to lean forward to drive home my question, but the pain brought me up short. I settled for a stern frown. "You are an escaped prisoner. No doubt they will already have a bounty upon your head."

It was a guess, but it stood to reason: he had been free long enough for a letter to make its way from the penal colony.

He conceded the point with a reluctant squint of one eye. "It seems so. I have heard report that a thieftaker has been asking about me."

"See, you cannot risk it! You have a duty to your own safety and to your sister. You must stay free to help her. You must stay free."

"It appears we both have a duty to our sisters—" He stopped and rubbed his forehead as if scrubbing away what he was about to say. "You are right—I must consider Hester. I will escort you to Maidenhead and then we will part ways."

"Good. I am glad you are seeing sense."

I had won, but the victory felt hollow. And *part ways* seemed unresolved. Surely we would see each other again?

"I will write, though," I added. "And if you need any help with your sister's situation, please call upon us. And there is the matter of the duel too. I may have more information."

"You must heal first," he said. "And then we will see where we are."

Not quite the answer I wished to hear.

He leaned across to the carriage door and opened it, then sketched a bow in his seat. "I will say my farewell now."

"Good-bye," I said, nodding my own courtesy. He was going back to the driver's seat already? It seemed we were destined to take our leave of each other at carriage doors.

He ducked and descended the step, leaving me alone in the carriage.

"Promise me you will stay safe," I called.

He turned, as I had wanted him to, and smiled. Yet his usual roguish gleam had gone. "Only if you promise to do the same."

Lord Evan left us at Maidenhead. Pain stopped me again from leaning forward in my seat, and so I could not watch him walk around the corner into the town center. I hoped he still saw my wave and smile. Hoped he turned back to see them. I could not bring myself to ask Julia if he did. She looked too relieved by his departure.

I slept from Maidenhead into Hanover Square, waking only when John Driver pulled up the horses. The carriage window curtains had all been pulled across except the one at which Julia sat. We were in the mews, behind our house. Samuel and Miss Finchley stood in the stable courtyard, the latter in a red cloak and upon her toes trying to see within the carriage. Opposite me, Weatherly peered out, his face softening. Not, I am sure, at the sight of Samuel.

"I told John Driver to take us directly to the mews," Julia said. "The whole of the square does not need to know our business."

Samuel opened the carriage door with a bow. "My ladies, a situation has arisen."

"Wait, Samuel," Julia said. She waved Miss Finchley closer. "We have Marie-Jean."

The apprehension in Miss Finchley's face eased into a radiant smile. "Oh, my ladies, thank you." She bobbed into a curtsy. "God bless you."

"There is more," Julia said, another wave bringing Miss Finchley up to the door. "Literally more. The fiends had taken three other girls as well. This is Lizbeth, Jessica, and Faith."

Miss Finchley, admirable young woman that she was, overcame her shock in a second and smiled a welcome.

"Hello, girls, you are safe now, thanks to Lady Augusta and Lady Julia."

"And Mr. Weatherly," I said. I knew our modest butler would, without doubt, fail to report his part of the adventure. "It was his heroic actions that gave us the information we needed to escape."

Weatherly eyed me balefully from the opposite seat, but I was unrepentant.

Miss Finchley smiled up at him, her admiration shifting into concern. "You are hurt, sir."

"It has already been put right," he said gruffly. "But it was my honor to be of service."

"Lizbeth was taken from her parents and must be returned," Julia added, blithely ignoring the undercurrent between Weatherly and Miss Finchley. Or perhaps she did not sense it. "However, Jessica and Faith are in need of a home. Would you and your sister be willing to take them into your school? Lady Augusta and I would be pleased to assist with their upkeep alongside Mr. Weatherly's contribution."

"Of course," Miss Finchley said, bobbing another curtsy. "They are very welcome. You are so kind to support our endeavor."

Behind her, our footman was kneading his gloved hands together and looking back at the house.

"Samuel, what is it?" I asked.

"There is a man waiting in the morning room, my ladies, who will not leave. He barged in an hour ago and says he is from Bow Street and will see you, come what may. He says his name is Mr. Michael Kent."

I drew in a sharp breath, the shock radiating through my shoulder. A Bow Street Runner, here?

The Runners had once been little more than corrupt thieftakers. Now they had the authority to investigate crimes and arrest wrongdoers on behalf of the Home Office; the closest thing the English could come to stomaching the French idea of a "police" force.

There could be only one reason for such a creature to visit us.

I pressed my fingers into my forehead, trying to contain the tumult of thoughts and dread. I had not thought they would be so hard upon Lord Evan's trail. Thank God he had not escorted us into London.

"We cannot possibly see anyone now," Julia said. "Lady Augusta is injured. Tell this Bow Street man to leave. He must return another time."

"I have tried to do so, my lady, many times, but he refuses to go. Thomas says he is known as Kent the Gent, famous for his persistence. He does not give up, ever."

"I will eject him," Weatherly said, rising.

"No, you must not get into a scuffle with a Runner, Weatherly." I waved him back into his seat. "Samuel, did you tell him we were away from home?"

"No, my lady, just that you were not available."

"Good man. Weatherly, stay in the coach and take Miss Finchley and the girls back to her school. Julia, you and I will return to the house through the scullery and go upstairs to change. If Mr. Kent wishes to wait, then that is what he will do until we are ready to receive him. We cannot refuse him—he has the authority of the Bow Street Office—but we do not have to play the game his way."

"It is about Lord Evan, isn't it?" Julia said.

"Without a doubt."

"Already. Dear God help us." Julia crossed herself.

I closed my eyes, trying to conjure the strength to stand and face this new enemy. Mr. Kent might have the authority to investigate, but he was not the only one seeking information.

I had three questions that only he could answer: how much did he know about our connection to Lord Evan, how had he learned of it, and how close was he to running down his quarry?

36

Upstairs on the side bureau, a letter waited for me. A hand I did not recognize. I took it with me into my bedchamber and, with some difficulty, broke the wafer and spread it upon my writing slant as Tully prepared fresh bandaging for my wound.

It was a reply from Colonel Drysan, retired. A brief missive that agreed to a meeting, at my convenience. I could almost feel the curiosity within the crisply written words. Although our meeting would have to wait until I was somewhat recovered, at least here was progress.

Tully deftly redressed my wound and I changed into my loosest-fitting morning gown, her bandaging hidden by my lace capelet. I had thought the piece a bad purchase—far too matronly—but now it was coming into its own. I just hoped the wound did not start bleeding again and soak through the high frilled neck of the gown.

All in all, it was just on an hour before I followed Julia down the stairs to the ground floor to meet Mr. Kent. I kept my grip tight on the banister; occasionally the world swayed alarmingly, and if my sister saw me so debilitated, she would call a halt to this interview, come what may. I had to see this man and discover what he knew.

"What are we to say?" Julia whispered over her shoulder. She had changed, too: her favorite morning gown in pale blue cambric with intricately pointed lace at throat and sleeve. An abundance of lace always made my sister feel confident.

"As little as possible, I would think," I said.

Our father had once told me that if you wish to discombobulate an opponent, make him wait. Mr. Kent had certainly waited, but if he had such a persistent nature, perhaps waiting held no discomfort for him. Whereas, it had definitely unnerved me.

At the morning room door, Julia peered at me more closely. "Are you sure you are up to this? You look ghastly."

"I am well enough. Besides, we should not put him off any longer."

I nodded to Samuel and he opened the door, bowing as Julia and I entered.

"Bring tea, please," I said as I passed him. I was still parched despite the barley water and broth that Cook had sent up alongside my new dressings.

The Runner stood with his back to us, studying our Lawrence portrait with intense concentration. This rearview afforded us a vision of a large physique, closely curled dark hair, and a jacket admirably cut and molded to his broad shoulders.

"Mr. Kent, I presume? From Bow Street?"

He turned. Good God, it was the man from Hyde Park: he had been watching us, after all. And now he stood in our morning room, just as self-assured and well turned out as before; long pantaloons strapped under his polished shoes, a pale blue waistcoat, and a well-tied cravat in the difficult mathematical style. One would almost think him a gentleman.

"I am Lady Augusta Colebrook and this is my sister, Lady Julia," I added.

He made a perfectly acceptable bow. "Good afternoon. I appreciate you seeing me at such short notice." Said without any inflection, but I suspected it dripped with irony. He glanced back at the portrait. “Am I correct in thinking this is by Mr. Lawrence? It has his early style upon it.”

Julia and I were both silent for a moment; neither of us had anticipated a discussion of art.

“You are correct. That is well recognized,” Julia finally said, plainly impressed by his knowledge since Mr. Lawrence did not sign his paintings.

To be frank, so was I. A man of Kent’s station and profession would, I imagine, not usually follow art, let alone be able to recognize our current master.

Julia tilted her head, considering the painting. “It does indeed have all the markings of his earlier style. We sat for Mr. Lawrence a long time ago when we were presented at court, so of course the likeness is no longer—”

“Not at all. The likeness is astonishing,” Mr. Kent interrupted with warm gallantry. “Mr. Lawrence has the ability to capture his subjects’ essence, I think, and here I see two young women of extraordinary character and spirit.”

Julia sent him a sideways glance from beneath her lashes. “Mr. Lawrence is indeed known for such perceptions.”

Mr. Kent gave a soft, appreciative laugh. He had a somewhat crooked smile that matched the rugged slant of his once-broken nose and held a lot of appeal. Julia smiled back, her rare dimples making a show.

Lud, I knew that look upon my sister’s face; he had found her passion for art and now she was well on the way to being charmed. Not only that; he had laughed at her wit. And her reply? As close to flirting as my sister came.

I cleared my throat and indicated the chaise longue. “In what way can we help you, Mr. Kent?”

He crossed to the offered seat—the slight limp I had noticed at the park in evidence—and sat with a flick of his coattails upon the edge of the green velvet. Julia and I each took an armchair.

I caught my sister's gaze as I turned to sit: *What are you doing?*

She gave me innocent eyes. Perhaps she did not realize she had flirted with him. Since Robert's death she had barely acknowledged any unrelated men beyond the usual courtesies, let alone bantered with them. That was more my style.

It was a relief to settle into the armchair. My shoulder throbbed incessantly, and any misjudged movement sent sharp pain into my neck and across my chest. I knew I held my arm in an awkward position, bent and frozen in place. Had he noticed? I clasped my hands together in an attempt to hide my immobility, holding back a hiss of pain. Why had I sent Samuel for tea? I would not be able to pick up the cup without showing my disability.

"I believe you are acquainted with Lord Cholton," Mr. Kent said. It was not a question.

"We are acquainted with a good number of England's nobility," I said. Swords drawn: *En garde.*

"But Lord Cholton is a particular friend," he pressed.

"He is a long-standing friend," I conceded. So, Mr. Kent either knew of Bertie's contact with Lord Evan or had made the connection between the two men and now looked for confirmation.

"You saw him recently, I believe, at Hyde Park."

Julia drew in an audible breath. She had finally recognized him. "You were watching us at the gate," she said. "I recall you now."

"You do?" He gave a self-deprecating smile. Far too craggily attractive. "I had not thought myself so memorable."

"In that you are incorrect, Mr. Kent," Julia said. "You must, I think, stand out wherever you go."

"Clearly to my advantage, this time," he countered.

Good Lord: both of them were at it.

"It must be a drawback in your line of work," I said.

He observed me for a long moment, his astute gaze flicking down to the awkward position of my arm. "I do not hide what I do, Lady Augusta. I am an agent for the Home Office and in particular the Bow Street magistrate."

"A Runner," I said.

An almost imperceptible pinch of irritation crossed his face. "A vulgar nickname. We are agents."

Ah, a sore point. "So, what does a Runner want with us, Mr. Kent? Surely not to confirm that we are friends with Lord Cholton?"

"As Lady Julia noted, I was at Hyde Park at the same time you met Lord Cholton. I observed you visiting the Ring. May I ask what you were doing there with him?"

"Certainly. We were visiting the Ring," I said.

He smiled, this time not so charmingly. "You seemed to be enacting something."

"What do you mean?" Julia asked.

"I observed Lord Cholton prone on the grass and you, Lady Augusta, seemed to be taking note of distances."

Too astute, by half.

I wet my lips. "Lord Cholton felt unwell and so he took his rest under the tree for a few minutes."

"I see." From his tone, what he actually saw was me lying through my teeth.

A knock upon the door broke the tense moment.

"Come," I called, perhaps a little too urgently.

The door opened to admit Samuel, carrying the tea things and a plate of almond macaroons. He set the tray down on the small table between us and Mr. Kent with a sharp, loud clack upon the Italian marble. Then, with a bow, took up his position near the door. It was oddly reassuring to have him in the room again.

"Tea, Mr. Kent?" Julia asked.

"Thank you."

Julia elegantly poured, offered the milk, which was declined, and passed the cup and saucer to him. The entire operation was achieved with both of them watching each other as if I did not exist.

"Augusta, tea?" Julia asked.

"Thank you, no," I said, swallowing against the dry ache of my throat.

As Julia poured her own tea, Mr. Kent helped himself to a macaroon with apparent pleasure. The smell of fragrant tea and nutty sugar brought a wash of longing to my mouth. I averted my eyes from the tray.

On completion of his macaroon, Mr. Kent sat back. "Delicious. Your cook is to be commended." He looked across at Julia. "Do you know Lord Evan Belford?"

A surprise attack, and most effective, for we both stared at him in silence.

"Oh yes," Julia finally said. My breath locked in my throat. "Well, I mean we *knew* him," she added. "It must be at least twenty years ago since we saw him, before the horrid duel. Do you remember, Augusta?"

She threw the conversational ball to me, with an added silent comment: *He is clever; watch out.*

"Indeed," I said, answering both of her remarks. "We only knew him in passing, but it was a great scandal at the time. Why do you ask, Mr. Kent?"

He leaned forward, as if drawing us into a confidence. "Lord

Evan Belford has absconded from his incarceration in New South Wales and is now back in London. He is a convicted murderer, Lady Augusta, a desperate man who we believe is now engaged in highway robbery. He has a bounty upon his head and he will be found and brought back to justice and the gallows. Very soon."

Gallows.

"I do not see what this has to do with us," I managed.

"Lord Cholton was friends with him prior to his transportation," Mr. Kent said. "We suspect he may be in contact with him now. Of course, it is a common-law crime to assist an absconded prisoner in any way. Perhaps Lord Cholton is not aware of that?"

"I cannot speak for Lord Cholton," I said. "Perhaps you should speak to him yourself."

A disingenuous suggestion: Bertie had kept Lord Evan's secret so far, but I did not think he could handle the likes of Mr. Kent. Surely by now Bertie would have left London with the majority of our acquaintances. Dear Lord, I hoped he had left.

"I have been informed that Lord Cholton has gone to his seat up north."

"Of course he has," I said, hiding my relief in disdain. "We are entering the hunting season and it is coming up to quarter day. Besides, he must attend the assizes court." A not-so-subtle reminder that Bertie was a magistrate.

"I see. But you stay in London?"

"We do," Julia said a little too brightly. "For our brother's wedding and a move to Grosvenor Square."

"Yet you traveled back from someplace this morning. I saw your coach pass the house. Where have you been?"

Good God, he observed everything. I looked at Julia and she looked back at me, both of us blank. I had to say something.

"We were visiting a friend who is ill. Perhaps on her death bed. Near Botley Hill." I internally winced at the excess of information. I should have just refused to answer.

"I see."

He knew: not exactly, of course, but he knew we were somehow involved with Lord Evan. Time to end this interview, before we gave away anything more.

"We have calls to make, Mr. Kent. Is that all of your questions?"

"It is. For now."

"Samuel, please show Mr. Kent out."

Our footman opened the door.

Mr. Kent rose from his seat and bowed, his eyes meeting Julia's as he straightened. "It has been a pleasure to meet you in person and in Mr. Lawrence's fine art. If you do see Lord Cholton, please remind him that aiding Lord Evan is a punishable offense."

"Of course," Julia murmured.

"I would not wish to see him in trouble," he added.

On that oblique warning, Mr. Kent departed the room.

37

We waited, listening as Samuel returned Mr. Kent's hat and the front door opened and closed. Julia rose from her chair and crossed to the window. She stood to one side, hidden by the swagged curtain, and watched the street.

"Well, he is dangerous," I said, leaning forward painfully to pick up the teapot in my left hand. I urgently needed tea. "Thank goodness Lord Evan is well away from London."

"Definitely dangerous but also rather charming, too, in his own way," Julia said.

"It was obvious you thought so."

"Antagonizing the man is hardly going to help us or Lord Evan, is it? Better to be sweet."

I stared at her; my twin could still surprise me.

Julia returned to observing the street. "It will probably not be of much help, but if Mr. Kent is sympathetic to us it might hold us in good stead. For all his bonhomie, I would say he is a very resolute man."

"Surely he would not dare charge us with aiding Lord Evan."

"I think this man might dare a great deal."

I shakily poured tea into a clean cup and placed the teapot back upon the tray, almost dropping it the last few inches. The interview had taken more of a toll than anticipated. I did not bother with milk but picked up the cup and took a large mouthful, letting the bitter warmth wash down my dry fear.

"I must get word to Lord Evan today," I said.

"You cannot."

"I know you are understandably wary but—"

"No, it is not that." She pointed in the direction of the church. "Mr. Kent is still here, talking to a man who I think has been set to watch us."

"What?" I placed the cup back upon the table and rocked forward, ignoring the sharp shooting complaint of my shoulder as I hauled myself to my feet.

"Stay away from the window," Julia warned.

I backtracked to the mantel and followed the wall to stand at her side. Sure enough, Mr. Kent stood at the corner of the square's central garden in conversation with a wiry, rougher-looking man wearing a cap. They both looked in the direction of our house, the man in the cap nodding assent to Mr. Kent's instructions.

"Lud," I whispered. "You think they would follow a messenger, then?"

"Yes."

"But I must get word to him."

She laid her hand upon my uninjured arm, consolatory but adamant. "Lord Evan already knows there is a bounty upon his head, Gus. There is not much more you can add, really, is there? I think any contact at present would be dangerous, especially for him. Besides, he has evaded them so far."

"I could visit Charlotte and send a messenger from her house."

"You can barely stand, my dear. Besides, what makes you think you would not be followed and your message intercepted? I do not think you could live with yourself if you were the cause of Lord Evan's arrest."

She made a good case for not sending a message, but it still felt as if I was abandoning him.

An equipage approached, the pair of bays in the traps nicely matched and the chaise a little old-fashioned but well kept. It pulled up outside our door. A footman in neat drab climbed nimbly down from the seat beside the driver and opened the cabin door.

"Is this for us?" Julia asked. "Are we expecting someone?"

A woman emerged—small and aged, but sprightly with it—and I realized what day it was and who had arrived.

"Oh dear God, it is Madame d'Arblay. I invited her to call upon us. Remember?"

Julia rapidly retreated from the window and stood behind her armchair. "We cannot see her," she whispered, as if Madame could hear us through the walls. "You are almost dead upon your feet as it is."

"She has come specifically on my invitation and as a great favor," I whispered back. "It would be unforgivable to send her away." Time to tell my sister the truth. "I asked her to come to speak to you, particularly."

"Me? About what?"

We heard the front door open, and the murmur of voices as Madame gave her credentials to Samuel.

"Charlotte told me that Madame had her breast removed by surgery to save her life," I said rapidly. "I wanted you to hear about another possibility—"

Julia's cheeks flushed bright red. "You told Charlotte? You told Madame d'Arblay, a complete stranger?"

"And Lord Evan," I admitted.

Julia slammed her hand down upon the back of the chair. "Lord Evan! Did you tell the whole damn world?"

I winced at the *damn*; Julia never used such vulgar words. "Charlotte guessed, and—"

A knock upon the door stopped me. I glanced at Julia: *We cannot send her away now.*

Julia's mouth thinned, her eyes bright with fury: *No, we cannot.*

She drew a deep breath, then turned and said with forced calm. "Come in."

The door opened. "Madame d'Arblay," Samuel announced.

Madame entered the room and curtsied. She still wore her pelisse—a refined affair in pin-tucked burgundy silk and pearled buttons—but had been divested of her bonnet and carried her gloves. A short visit, then, as good manners demanded.

We returned the honor, although Julia's back was rigid. It took a lot to rouse my sister into fury. I had thought she might be angry, but this was incandescent.

"Welcome, Madame," I said. "Please, come, have a seat." I sought my sister's gaze, but she pointedly kept her eyes upon our guest.

"Thank you. It is a great honor to be invited," Madame said.

"Samuel, clear the tray and bring fresh tea, please," Julia said.

To the untutored ear, her voice sounded sweet and musical, but I heard the snap of teeth within it. Apparently, so did Samuel; his shoulders hunched and he started to gather the used tea things with alacrity.

An elegant gesture from my sister directed Madame to the chaise longue. "You must forgive our cramped quarters at present, Madame. We are moving to another accommodation."

"Ah yes, I know the chaos such shifts bring, both in body and mind," Madame said in her gentle way as we took our seats. Had she noticed something awry in Julia's manner too? I would not be surprised; Fanny Burney was noted for her understanding of human nature. "Do you go far?"

"Not at all," I interposed. "Just to Grosvenor Square."

"A most elegant address," Madame murmured, her countenance

set into sweet inquiry. I imagined such a pleasant expression had served her well in the royal court when she had been the queen's Keeper of the Robes.

I glanced at Julia. She sat in the armchair next to me, unnaturally still.

A silence descended.

No use paddling in the shallows.

"I heard that you have not been well lately, Madame," I said, plunging in, "but have thankfully made a full recovery due to a surgical procedure."

At the corner of my eye, Julia's hands clenched in her lap.

"It is true. I was most fortunate to have the care of the best surgeons in France." She glanced at Julia. "But perhaps it is not a subject that all wish to talk about."

"I would not wish to keep you from speaking, Madame d'Arblay," Julia said, her voice clipped. "Especially since my sister seems set upon me listening to your experience. Please go ahead. Do not spare any detail."

At that moment, Samuel arrived with the tea tray and an array of fancy iced cakes. A welcome breathing space for all.

Madame accepted a cup of tea and a cake. I refused both; my arm ached so savagely that I did not dare even move in my seat in case I cried out.

"You were saying, Madame?" I prompted.

With a nod, she placed her cup back upon its saucer and seemed to settle into the chaise longue a little more; the storyteller ready to begin her tale.

"About August, two years ago, I began to be annoyed by a small pain in my breast, which grew from week to week. It was heavy rather than acute, but I did not feel uneasy about it."

Julia made a soft sound of accord; the description clearly held some familiarity. Madame heard it, too, for she tilted her head in sympathetic alliance. Julia, however, did not acknowledge it.

Madame continued, "My husband pressed me to see a surgeon and so we summoned Dr. Jouart. Yet, despite his care, I grew worse. It was now that I began to perceive a real danger. I consulted a celebrated surgeon—Monsieur Dubois—and it became apparent that a small operation would be necessary to avert evil consequences."

"Were you afraid?" I asked.

"Indeed. My dread was so great that I consulted another eminent surgeon, Dr. Larrey, who offered a course of action that did not involve surgery. I made some progress with him, but then three dreadful circumstances combined to set me back: the death of the beloved Princess Amelia, the illness of her venerated father, the king, and, the principal of these evils, the sudden death of my dear friend's husband, Mr. Lock. These terrible losses changed me so much for the worse that it was decided that it must be surgery after all."

"Your grief worsened your condition?" Julia asked. She laid her hand upon her own breast. Was she thinking of Robert?

"My grief and my fear, to an alarming degree; it was the effect of deep emotion upon the body. In fact, during the formal consultation to receive my consent to the operation, Monsieur Ribe, the anatomist, charged me to cry! He said to withhold or restrain myself might have seriously bad consequences." She shook her head. "As you can imagine, that did not reassure me.

"And so, with sentence thus passed, I was in hourly expectation of a summons to execution. However, three weeks passed, until one morning—the last of September 1811—a letter was delivered to me. It was from Dr. Larrey to say that the surgeons would be with me at ten o'clock. Even so, it was not until three o'clock that four carriages arrived outside my door. Almost immediately,

Monsieur Moreau, one of my physicians, entered my room and gave me a wine cordial, then went to the salon. I rang for my maid and nurses, but before I could speak to them, my room was suddenly full of seven men in black: Dr. Larrey, Monsieur Dubois, Monsieur Moreau, Dr. Aument, Dr. Ribe, and two pupils.

"Monsieur Dubois ordered a bedstead to be brought into the middle of the room and two old mattresses and an old sheet. I began to tremble violently at the preparations and stood suspended for a moment; should I escape? I looked at the door, the windows—I felt desperate—but it was only for a moment and my reason took command again.

"I was asked to take off my long robe de chambre—which I had meant to retain—and Monsieur Dubois placed me upon the mattress. He spread a cambric handkerchief upon my face. It was transparent, however, and I saw the glitter of polished steel. I closed my eyes. I did not want to see the terrible incision. But a silence most profound ensued. It lasted for several minutes. I could only imagine they were taking their orders by signs and making their examination. I did not breathe. Finally, Dr. Larrey said in a voice of solemn melancholy, 'Who will hold me this breast?'

"No one answered, at least not verbally, but this roused me for I feared they imagined the whole breast infected—feared it too justly—for through the cambric, I saw the hand of Monsieur Dubois held up. His forefinger first traced a straight line from the top to the bottom of the breast, secondly a cross, and thirdly a circle, intimating that the whole was to be taken off.

"Alarmed, I sat up, threw off my veil. 'I will, Monsieur,' I said and held my hand under my breast. I explained the nature of my sufferings, which all sprang from one point. They listened attentively but in utter silence, and then Monsieur Dubois once again placed me back upon the bedstead and spread the veil back over my face. How vain my representation, for immediately I saw the fatal finger describe the cross and the circle again. I felt hopeless then, and desperate. I closed my eyes, wholly resigned."

"Were you awake the entire operation?" I asked, appalled.

"I was awake and adhered to my resolution of resignation despite my terror and the torturing pain. However, I believe I fainted twice during the dressing of the wound; at least, I have two total chasms of memory that stop me tying together what passed. And I warn you that what I describe next is most distressing. It stayed with me so vividly that for months I could not speak of the terrible business—could not think of it—without going through it again." She looked across at Julia. "Are you sure you wish me to go on?"

I could see why she asked; my sister's complexion had paled ashen white and her lower lip was caught between her teeth.

"Perhaps we have heard enough," I said.

"No, we will hear the whole of it. That is, if you are able, Madame," Julia said, turning her shoulder slightly away from me.

"I am." Madame took a fortifying sip of tea, then replaced the cup upon its saucer, the pause increasing the suspense. She pressed her hand to her burgundy bodice, a mirror of my sister's pose. "The dreadful steel was plunged into my breast—cutting through veins—arteries—flesh—nerves. I began a scream that lasted unintermittingly during the whole time of the incision, and I marvel that it does not still ring in my ears, so excruciating was the agony. When the wound was made, and the steel withdrawn, the pain seemed undiminished, for the air that rushed into those delicate parts felt like a mass of tiny, sharp, forked poniards that were tearing at the edge of the wound."

For a second, I was back in the brothel hallway, Holland above me wrenching the stiletto from my shoulder, the pain just as Madame described: a mass of tiny, forked daggers tearing at my flesh.

Madame's voice brought me back to the morning room. "When again I felt the instrument describing a curve—cutting against the grain, if I may say so—the flesh resisted so forcibly that the doctor tired and he was forced to change from his right hand to his left. Then, indeed, I thought I must have expired. I attempted to open my eyes—but they felt hermetically shut. For the second time, the instrument was withdrawn. I thought the operation was over. But no, the terrible cutting began again, this time to separate the bottom of my breast from the upper parts to which it adhered. Yet again all was not over; Dr. Larrey was but resting his hand. And, oh heaven! I felt the knife rackling against the breastbone—scraping it! I was in utterly speechless torture.

"I heard the voice of Dr. Larrey, asking everyone present if anything more remained to be done, or if they thought the operation complete. The general voice was yes, but the forefinger of Dubois pointed—I literally felt it elevated over the wound although I saw nothing and he touched nothing, so sensitive was the spot. And again began the scraping. And then Dr. Moreau thought he discerned a peccant atom, and still and still Dubois demanded atom after atom."

She drew a deep breath and released it, her eyes closing for a moment. It was difficult to hear her story, but not, it seemed, as difficult as telling it.

"Overall, the operation and the dressing lasted twenty minutes, and when all was done my strength was so totally annihilated that I had to be carried to my bed. My nurse told me that my face was utterly colorless. As I was being moved, I opened my eyes and saw my good Dr. Larrey, almost as pale as myself, his face streaked with blood and his expression one of grief, apprehension, and almost horror. I cannot think of it with impunity."

Madame pressed her fingers into her forehead and rubbed, as if massaging away the memory.

"But it has ended happily," I said. "You are here and well."

"Indeed, I am well. In the end, I was convinced that danger hovered about me and only an operation could save me from its jaws. And it did. At present I am following Dr. Larrey's preventative wisdom: prescriptions and diet and so forth." She smiled. "I call it my Larrey system."

Julia sat back. "A most dramatic cure, Madame. I am sincerely glad it succeeded."

Madame inclined her head in thanks. "Is there anything else you wish to know, Lady Julia?"

"No, Madame. Your descriptions were very vivid. Very clear."

"The truth is always best, is it not?" Madame said soberly.

Julia glanced at me, the line of her mouth unyielding. "It is."

38

Julia stood at the window again, watching Madame's departure. Neither of us had said anything since our guest left the room. We were suspended in an awful, heavy silence: a communication in itself.

I closed my eyes for a second, gathering the last of my strength. A terrible weakness washed through me on throbbing waves of pain and fatigue. I needed to lie down, to sleep, yet I could not leave my sister's wordless fury to fester behind me.

"Charlotte guessed what was wrong," I finally said: a lance upon the abscess.

Julia continued to stare out the window.

I tried again. "I thought that perhaps speaking to someone who had faced the worst might be . . . useful."

She turned at that, her face white. "Why would you think that hearing such a horrific experience would be useful? Why did you not tell me that was the purpose of her visit? You had plenty of opportunity to do so." She paced across the room and came to a stand behind the chaise longue, clutching its carved edge. "I will tell you why: because you knew I would not wish to hear about such barbarity. You betrayed my trust and you decided you knew better than me about my own illness."

With effort, I sat forward, panting through the pain of the movement. "I do not think that. But I cannot place my trust in one doctor who just gives you pills and elixirs that seem to do as much harm as good. Did you hear how many doctors attended Madame?"

"I would never allow men to cut into my body. Into my most intimate areas." She opened her arms wide, looking down upon herself. "This body is God's work and it is his to heal or take unto himself. I have faith in God's plan for me, Gus, and so should you."

"I cannot." I paused—ready to divert the subject—but no, as Madame had said, the truth was always best. "I do not have faith, Julia. Not anymore. I must place my faith in this world, not in the hope of the next. I know your condition is not close to needing a surgical cure, but if it came to it, why would you accept death when there is possibility of saving your life?"

She stared at me. "You have lost your faith?" She crossed to me, dropping to her knees. "Oh, my dear Gus, my poor, dear Gus. Surely it is just the pain and fatigue talking."

"It is not the pain and fatigue, Julia. This has been a long time coming. I could not bear to see you die the same way as mother and Aunt Elizabeth. That is not the work of a merciful god. I no longer feel the holy affections. At all."

She sat back upon her heels. "Ah, now I understand. Now I see the reason for this self-appointed mission." She took my hand, her skin dry against my damp palm. "You cannot save everyone, Gus. It is God who saves us."

"I can save some people," I said stubbornly.

"But look at what price. Abandonment of grace and God's joy, broken promises, subterfuge, ever-increasing risk. You were nearly killed last night, and Weatherly is sorely injured. Not only that, it has placed us all in danger from the Home Office, especially Lord Evan. What about next time? Will there be more risk? More danger? Will someone have to die?"

I had no answer. Or perhaps I did, and knew it was not what she wanted to hear. The stabbing had frightened me to my core as well, but I still wanted to help people. I still wanted to be more than this world allowed me to be, just a spinster past her prime.

My twin watched me, reading my intractability with a sigh. "This compulsion has become too dangerous. You wished me to listen to Madame d'Arblay's experience and I did. Now it is *your* turn to listen. She said her illness was exacerbated by grief and apprehension. Well, this adventuring brings me too much apprehension. Too much grief. You say you want to save me, then here is the way: I want to return to our quiet lives before we took up this mad mission. I want you to cut ties with Lord Evan. I want you to stop this foolish investigation into his past. Please, stop it all, for my sake. For your sake. And, yes, for Lord Evan's sake, for you place him in mortal danger by dragging him into these wild adventures."

Tears stung my eyes. "I thought you were with me. I thought you understood."

"I did, but not anymore. The cost is too great, Gus. What if that knife had stabbed you three inches lower? I lost Robert to a senseless accident. I cannot lose you to foolhardy heroics. Promise me you will end all this. Promise me you will let Lord Evan be."

Every fiber within me fought against her words, but I knew she was right. To save my sister and to save Lord Evan, I had to stop. I had to let go of the bold, reckless Augusta, and I had to let go of the man who saw that renegade woman within me.

"Promise me, please," Julia insisted.

I had to let go.

"I promise," I said and slumped back in the chair, barely able to breathe through the pain of my wound. And the new pain in my heart.

Upstairs in my bedchamber again, I walked over to my desk. Colonel Drysan's reply sat, still open, upon my writing slant. I picked up the letter and closed my hand, crumpling the paper into a ball. Time to stop it all. I had promised.

Hours later, I woke in my bed, jarred from a pain-ridden doze that had only skimmed the surface of sleep. The afternoon sun slanted through the gap in the curtains across the damask cover; a shaft of light in the shape of a sword. My eyes still felt tear swollen, my mouth dry and tasting of old tea. Yet, bright in my mind, a picture of the brothel hallway: Lord Evan standing above me as I crouched against the wall, my blood-wet hand clasped to my shoulder. And then my voice, full of relief and hazy joy.

My dearest Lord Evan. My one true love.

A dream?

No, a memory.

I had called him my one true love. And, heaven help me, for all its mawkish sentiment I had meant it.

Case 3

The Madness of Women

39

I scrunched my numb toes in my boots as our carriage ground its way along the gravel driveway of Duffield House. We had pushed on past the last posting house in order to arrive in time for dinner, and one of my feet had gone to sleep. Opposite me in the bodkin seat, Julia yawned, the fatigue of the day's travel leaching her face of color.

It had been three weeks since we had rescued Marie-Jean and her companions from the brothel. Lizbeth had been returned to her grateful parents, and Jessica and Faith were safe in Miss Finchley's school alongside Marie-Jean. Julia had written to the magistrates in Cheltenham about the brothel, but neither of us had much hope of it being closed.

It had also been three weeks since the Bow Street Runner, Mr. Kent, had made his unwanted entrance into our lives. A resolute man, Julia had called him and, indeed, his persistent surveillance of us had curtailed our activities. Even so, a few days after our return from Cheltenham, I decided we must write to Lord Evan to warn him about this new threat. It was the only conscionable thing to do, I argued, and Julia reluctantly agreed.

As it happened, my sister ended up writing the letter; my injury would not allow me to hold a pen. It was a curter message than the one I had envisioned—only a few lines that informed Lord Evan of Mr. Kent's interest in us and advised him to stay away in both person and letter. With Julia as my scribe, I could not compose the letter I truly wished to write. I had promised her I would cut Lord Evan from our lives—for his sake as much as hers—and so my real letter could only be inscribed upon my heart, written and rewritten during the long wakeful nights of my convalescence.

My dearest Lord Evan. My one true love.

We gave the curt letter to Charlotte—on her farewell visit before she left London for her estate—and she agreed to post it to Bertie Helden with the direction for him to then dispatch it to Lord Evan. An elaborate route designed to avoid the Bow Street Runner's interest. It seemed to have worked, for we had not heard from Lord Evan since our good-bye at Maidenhead. Part of me was relieved he had taken heed of our warning and was safe. And the other part? It kept writing that real letter, over and over again.

Julia suddenly sat up straight, her hand upon the carriage window. "I do not believe it. The old oak is gone," she said.

I leaned over to look, my shoulder sending a warning jab of pain. Three weeks of healing had brought back mobility, but the knife wound still spiked when I moved too quickly.

The thick line of trees on the east rise of the park had a new gap ripped open in its center, marring the leafy prospect. Our dear old oak, gone. The tree had served as our childhood retreat from tepid baths, drawing lessons, various singing masters, and our little brother. Had Duffy truly cut down the ancient tree? It had been Father's favorite part of the Capability Brown landscape he had commissioned. Unsettling to think it no longer stood sentinel.

"It was old, I suppose," Julia added.

"That is no reason to cut it down."

"Perhaps it was diseased."

I made no answer, but my sister could, as usual, read my mind.

"It is his estate now, Gus," she said warningly. "And it is no wonder he is keen to make his mark upon it; he loves it just as much as we do, and Father never took any notice of his ideas. Some of them were good, too—you know they were. Besides, we are here to celebrate his wedding, not rail against his improvements."

"Improvements." I snorted.

"Promise me you will be pleasant. You have been irascible this whole last week."

I felt my fury rise, always so close to the surface these days. "I have made as many promises as I mean to, Julia. Let us leave it at that."

"No need to bite my head off. I only want everyone to get along."

Little chance of that, but I did not voice it.

She sat back as we drove between the walled formal garden and the maze. Two gardeners stopped trimming the maze hedge to doff their caps. Beyond them, I glimpsed the preparations for the tenants' wedding feast in the "meadow"—a grassy area reserved for such local celebrations—with workmen setting up beer tents and spits.

I turned my attention to the first glimpse of Duffield House: its crenelated clock tower rising above the maze hedges. Always my favorite view. Then we veered right into the gravel forecourt and the glory of Duffield House opened up before us.

Its foundations had been built in medieval times, but a later forebear who clearly had a whimsical nature had made additions in the English baroque style. The entrance—guarded by classical stone columns adorned with somewhat louche naked figures—extended into the fairy-tale-like castle frontage and the clock tower. On either side of the entrance, a rounded-arch arcade extended to the east and west wings to create the cloisters, a covered walkway that had been our hoop-rolling path, skipping racetrack, and, now, our sedate walking promenade. The side wings—a massive three stories each—jutted forward, creating the forecourt, their corners rising into extravagant openwork parapets, the stone decorations cut into scrolling flowers around the family crest.

Although Julia and I had been living in London for twenty years now, it still felt like coming home. We returned every September to ride the hunt—at least, I rode while Julia watched—as well as every Christmas for a month or so until the roads let us pass again. As it stood, however, there would be no riding for me this visit; my shoulder was still not strong enough. My poor Leonardo—no doubt underexercised and champing at the bit for a good run.

"I am thinking of bringing my hunter back with us," I said, to ease the tension between us. "There is more room in the mews at the back of Grosvenor Square than at Hanover. I can ride him on the tan."

"Won't you find that restrictive? You cannot go above a trot."

I made a noncommittal sound. Certainly, Hyde Park had a galloping restriction during the day. However, at dawn, London grooms were allowed to gallop their charges on the tan for an hour or so, and I knew that some genteel riders joined in the fun. Not many women, mind you, but that would not deter me.

"I'm sure I will manage," I said. Julia did not need to know my plan. Careering down the tan on an eighteen-hand hunter would definitely not fit into her idea of our return to a safe life.

Julia gave a small shrug. "As you wish."

The carriage pulled up at the front entrance, the second coach bringing up the rear with Weatherly—brought to assist the estate staff during the wedding celebrations—and our maids, Tully and Leonard, in charge of the rest of the luggage.

Pullam and Mrs. Longworth, the housekeeper, stood waiting at the bottom of the stone steps. The coach rocked as Samuel, our footman, descended from his jump seat and opened the carriage door.

"Good afternoon, Lady Augusta," Pullam said as I took Samuel's hand and found the carriage step. For once I needed his assistance; the journey had stiffened my joints.

"How are you?" I inquired. "How are the wedding preparations?"

"All in hand, my lady." He turned to bow to my sister as she alighted. "Good afternoon, Lady Julia. His lordship is currently finalizing the chapel arrangements with Miss Woolcroft and Sir Henry Woolcroft and will welcome you and Lady Augusta in the drawing room before dinner."

"Good. I would welcome a rest," Julia said.

"I need a walk," I said, turning toward the stable. An offering of a few apples to Leonardo would work out the aches in my legs and back. I looked back. "If there is anything urgent you need to speak to me about, Mrs. Longworth, I'll be in my room in about twenty minutes."

The housekeeper hurriedly stepped forward, her hands clasped tightly at the front of her neatly pleated bodice. "Lady Augusta, there has been a change in the room arrangements. You are in the Yellow Room, and Lady Julia, you are in the Flower Room."

"The Flower Room?" Julia echoed. "But that is—" She stopped.

In the East Tower, as was the Yellow Room. The guest wing.

"His lordship has redecorated the apartments for the new mistress in the West Tower," Pullam said without expression. "Your former rooms are part of that conversion."

Our former rooms in the family wing; the rooms we had lived and laughed and cried in for much of our lives. All our memories and belongings swept aside.

We were guests in our own home.

"I see," I bit out, clamping down upon a bright flare of anger.

Longworth and Pullam were not the ones who should feel its heat. “Still defending his improvements?” I said in an undertone to Julia as I passed.

“It is his right,” Julia said, but I heard the hurt in her voice.

“I am in the Yellow Room,” I said pointedly to Tully, who had just alighted from the second carriage. I stripped off my gloves and handed them to her. “In the *guest* wing.”

I headed toward the stables, digging my heels into the gravel driveway and finding some relief in the heavy, grinding stride. I had to admit that Pullam’s description of Miss Woolcroft as the new mistress of Duffield House had also stung. As firstborn sister, I had been mistress of the house since our mother died. Of course, when Duffy married Miss Woolcroft in a few days, she would be countess and mistress, yet it seemed I had already been replaced.

I walked more quickly, passing through the stone arch that led into the stable courtyard and the comforting smell of hay and horse dung. These changes to our lives were inevitable—I knew that—but Duffy always found the worst way of dealing with us. Julia would say it was just thoughtlessness, but I was not so forgiving. In fact, I would wager that Duffy had put a great deal of thought into his “improvements.”

I stopped at the apple bin and opened the lid. Almost full with a good selection of new apples from the orchards. I chose one with a fair amount of green—Leonardo liked a good crunch—and lifted it to my nose. The fresh perfume brought a wash of saliva and reminded me I had not eaten much of the meal supplied at our midday stop. Leonardo would not begrudge me a bite. I sank my teeth into the fruit, the tart juice washing away the sour ash of my anger. I headed to the stalls, still chewing.

Behind me, John Driver was slowly turning the chaise in the forecourt, ready to bring it into the yard to unhitch the tired team.

Two of the grooms stood waiting outside the tack room: old Jim and Peter, both small and wiry, almost like a young and old version of the same man. They doffed their caps and bobbed their heads as I approached.

"Jim, how are you? How is your wife?" I inquired. Old Jim had taught me to ride as a girl. He had been a youngish man back then but had been both patient and kind to Julia and me as we learned the art of riding sidesaddle.

"Very well, milady. How do ye do?" Old Jim said. No smile. His demeanor was usually dour, but he was grim, even for him.

"I am well, thank you." I looked along the line of stables with their fronts open to the yard and held up the apple. "Where is Leonardo? Has he moved stalls?"

Peter looked sideways at his elder.

"Ah." Old Jim rubbed at his mouth. "I thought you knew, milady. His lordship sold Leonardo a good month ago to Mr. Solson."

I rocked back on my heels as if he had struck me. "What? No, that cannot be right." I looked along the stalls again. "Where is he?"

"He's gone, milady, to Mr. Solson of Billingsworth Hall, past the next village," Old Jim said. "I thought he rode a bit 'eavy for Leonardo, but his lordship wouldn't have it."

"Are you saying Lord Duffield sold my horse?"

"Aye, milady," Old Jim said, eyeing me.

I drew in a shaking breath. My Leonardo—the horse my father had given me. Duffy had stood right next to me when Father had told me Leonardo was mine. Yet he had sold him, without a word. A month ago. Good God, he had sat in our drawing room and looked me in the eye and said nothing. The perfidy of it finally blazed through my numb shock. For a second, I could see nothing, all air and sight gone, only blind, burning rage.

"Peter, go fetch Lady Julia," I heard Old Jim say.

I fought for breath, the two men coming back into focus. "No!" Peter stopped a few steps away and looked back, shoulders hunched. "That won't be necessary," I managed.

I spun on my heel, toward the chapel.

Not even my twin sister, with all her sway upon me and her desperate desire for harmony, would silence me this time.

40

My journey from the stables across the forecourt was fueled by a silent litany of fury—*how dare he sell my horse, how dare he put us in the guest wing, how dare he cut down the oak*. Every step I took built my rage until my head pounded and hot tears stung my eyes.

"My lady, are you quite well?" I heard Weatherly say as I passed the luggage coach, still being unloaded.

I waved his query away, unable to form words past my blazing fury. I marched past the East Tower toward the chapel. It stood a good two hundred yards from the main house, a leftover from the house's medieval beginnings. I still clutched Leonardo's apple as I marched up to the Gothic oak doors, its undelivered weight anchoring me to my outrage. I rammed the heel of my free hand into the right door and pushed my way in, the pain through my arm barely registering.

I paused, adjusting to the dim light. The cool air held the earthy scent of old stone and the bruised perfume of spent roses. Before me, eight rows of wooden pews stood on either side of a wide central aisle, and at the far end of it, four people clustered before the altar in conversation. Duffy in his fashionable country ensemble, Miss Woolcroft sporting a much befeathered bonnet, her father in comfortable tweed, and the vicar, a black-clad twig of a man. All of them turned at my entrance.

"Ah, Augusta," Duffy said. "You are here. How was your journey?"

I strode down the aisle. "You sold my horse. Without even a damn by-your-leave, Duffy. You had no right!"

Miss Woolcroft gasped at my profanity, her feathers bobbing in agitation. Her father stepped in front of her, his ruddy face shocked. I had a momentary pang—I liked Sir Henry—but this was family business and he was not yet family.

The vicar—an ineffectual young man at the best of times—hurried forward, flapping his hands at me as if herding a wasp out the door.

"This is God's house, Lady Augusta. Please, your language."

I ignored him, all my focus upon my brother. Duffy had straightened, a strange light in his brown eyes. Perhaps I was seeing through my fury, but that light seemed oddly jubilant.

"You did it on purpose." I knew I was right.

"This is not the place or time, Augusta," he said. "You are making a spectacle of yourself. I cannot imagine what Sir Henry and Miss Woolcroft must think of you. Go outside. I will be with you when I am finished here."

"No, you will answer me now. Leonardo was mine. What you have done is tantamount to theft!"

It was perhaps a wild accusation, but he was not going to dismiss me in such a condescending manner. Even my pigheaded brother could not ignore a charge of horse theft.

He gave me a hard stare, then turned to Sir Henry and Miss Woolcroft and bowed. "If you will excuse me." He nodded to the vicar. "Please continue. I will return when my sister has calmed down."

He turned on his heel. "Outside," he hissed as he marched past me toward the double doors.

I followed him down the aisle, resisting the urge to throw the apple at his supercilious head. He pulled open the door and, with a sarcastic bow, ushered me out onto the cobbled courtyard.

The door clanged shut behind us. Duffy turned on me, his fair skin blotched red with his own fury. "Do not ever do that again, Augusta. You embarrass me and you embarrass yourself with these unhinged hysterics."

I drew myself up so that I stood well over him. "Hysterics? This is not hysterics, brother. This is me demanding to know why you have sold my horse."

"It was not your horse, Augusta. It was mine."

"What do you mean? You were there when Father gave him to me."

"I have no recollection of that." He sliced his hand through the air. "None. Besides, even if that were the case, Father did not transfer ownership to you in the records."

I stared at him, disconcerted by his denial. But no, I had not imagined him being there nor Father giving me the horse. "You were standing right beside me when Father said I was the only one who could handle Leonardo, so I must have him as my own. He said it was an early birthday present."

Duffy's eyes narrowed. "Oh yes, the favorite child. The best rider, the best hunter. You think too much of yourself, sister. Father always raised you too high. But he is not here anymore to pander to your vanity. You are just a woman—an old woman at that—and I am Lord Duffield. If I choose to sell a horse in my stables, I will."

I leaned back from the venom in his voice. "You sold him to spite me? Are you that childish?"

"I am not the childish one. You slighted Harriet at the ball for no good reason, you bought a house to spite me, you throw Father's words at me all the time—" He broke off, then drew a long breath through his thin nose, nostrils pinched. "Frankly, you are here only because I am obliged to have you at my wedding and because Julia would not have come if you did not. Be thankful that you are still welcome—now that I am marrying Harriet, you no longer have any position in this house other than as my guest. Remember, besides Julia, we are your only family, Augusta. You should watch yourself. You should behave with more propriety and gratitude."

"Gratitude? For what should I be grateful, brother?" I said through my teeth.

"That I have put up with your conceit for so long; your ridiculous belief, instilled by Father, that your opinions hold as much worth as a man's. No one wants to hear you, Augusta. No one wants to see an old maid thrust herself forward—it is embarrassing to watch."

He turned and hauled open the chapel door. At the end of the dimly lit aisle, three faces had turned toward us, listening.

"Rule your behavior, Augusta, or I will be forced to rule it for you. And do not deceive yourself, I will do so if I am forced."

He walked back into the chapel, the heavy door clunking shut.

41

"I thought I would find you here."

The late afternoon breeze snatched at Julia's words. I turned from my vantage: the gap where the old oak had once stood. Only a stump remained now, level with the ground and faintly smelling of sap. Julia crossed the last few yards of grass, still in her carriage gown, a shawl folded over her arm.

"There is a chill coming down in the air." She held out the shawl. Her favorite sea-green paisley.

I was still holding Leonardo's apple, the flesh browned now around my bite, my hand damp and sticky.

"Old Jim," Julia said, answering the unvoiced question on my face. "He told Weatherly about Leonardo, and Weatherly told me."

"Ah." I felt an absurd rise of tears. "Duffy should not have sold him."

Julia shook out the shawl and placed it around my shoulders. She arranged it around my back, then stepped closer and folded me into a quick hug. "No. But we will speak to Mr. Solson and arrange to buy Leonardo back."

"You do not know what Duffy said to me." I drew my arm back and hurled the apple across the grass, my shoulder twinging at the force. The fruit arced against the clouded sky, bounced, then rolled down the gentle incline. "He felt obliged to invite me here. Obliged!

He says I have too high an opinion of myself, that Father raised me too high. That I am just an old woman and my opinions are not wanted. That I am an embarrassment." I stopped, gulping for breath. "Am I, Julia? Are people laughing at me behind my back?" I felt the possibility rise through me, a rush of hot humiliation.

"Absolutely not," Julia said. She took my hand, her touch, as usual, bringing comfort. "You are well respected. Brummell is your friend, for goodness' sakes—he listens to your counsel, and you know he cares not a fig for most people. And Charlotte, too; she does not suffer fools. Do not let Duffy rile you."

"I think he hates me. Truly hates me."

"No, I'm sure he does not." Julia looked out over the vista and sighed. "He is just jealous. We all knew you were Father's favorite growing up. Duffy was always away at school and you had Father to yourself. It affected Duffy greatly. And it still does, although Father is no longer with us."

Jealous? It was conceivable, I suppose. Father had favored my company over Duffy's. I shot her a glance. "What about you? I never thought how my closeness to Father would affect you. I am sorry."

She waved away my contrition. "No, no, I am different to Duffy. I was always a little . . . intimidated by Father. Happy not to be noticed. Of course, he loved us all, but he admired you—your boldness and self-possession. Father could not admire someone as mild as myself—a follower—just as he could not admire Duffy's need for reassurance or his resentments. But you see, I had you. I've always had you. Duffy had no one."

I squeezed her hand: *You will always have me.*

She squeezed back: *I know.*

"I cannot sit down to dinner with Duffy and the Woolcrofts. Not tonight." I drew in a breath. "He wants me to make myself small and silent—demands it, if I am to have any rights to this place and our family—and I am too furious to do that."

"He will see it as a further snub."

"I know, but if I sit at that table, it will end in a quarrel. I know it."

Julia released my hand. "Take a tray in your room, then. I will tell them you have the migraine, and we can all start afresh tomorrow. All you have to do is not rise to his bait. Be above it all. It is only for a few days."

A few days? There, my sister was wrong. Duffy would be judging me even more now, ready to rule my behavior if it did not meet his expectations of a deferential spinster sister.

I looked out across the grassy field, which eased into a small wood of birch trees and bushes. I knew that beyond that small stand was a deep pond—always cold and a wonderful place to dip hot feet in summer—and then beyond that were the grazing fields and a copse of beautiful ash. This estate was part of me. It would be unbearable to be banned from its beauties or its people, who had been part of my life since birth.

"I will try," I said, ignoring the hard knot that tightened my innards. "I will try."

The next morning, in the small, bare dressing room that adjoined the yellow guest room, Tully clasped my coral beads around my neck. Her cool fingertips upon my nape lifted my shoulders into a shiver. The dressing room did not have its own hearth. If I was of a mind to make a list, I would add that to Duffy's petty payback.

"I am sorry, my lady." Tully rubbed her hands together. "It is brisk this morning. Would you like a shawl?"

"No, the morning room will be warm enough."

I had taken a tray in my room the previous evening and, for all my emotional turmoil, had slept heavily and without dreams. Now I could delay no longer. I had to face my first trial: breakfast with Duffy.

"I saw Miss Leonard in the corridor," Tully ventured as she re-pinned a curl into place.

I raised my brows; permission to share the gossip.

"Sir Henry and Miss Woolcroft have arrived from the dower house to take breakfast."

"Ah." I met Tully's eyes in the mirror. "Unusual."

"Ordered with Cook last night," Tully added.

"I see."

Duffy was going to have his moment of public censure, come what may. I had promised Julia I would ignore his barbs and rise above it all, but I knew my own fury had not abated; the knowledge that my horse was in someone else's stable—someone riding too heavy for him—sat like a burning coal in my innards. Not to mention what Duffy had said to me.

My entrance into the bright morning room was met with a bow from Sir Henry, who rose from his seat, and a nod from Miss Woolcroft and Julia. Duffy neither rose nor nodded but stared at his plate of cold beef with his arms crossed and a scowl upon his face.

I curtsied to Sir Henry and took my seat beside Julia. She smiled up at me with a warning in her eyes: *Duffy is still angry.* A rather redundant warning.

Cook had done an excellent job at such short notice: fresh brioche, seed cake, toast, sliced cold beef, glazed ham, two cheeses, and a whole salmon, all served upon the new fine white service with the family crest that Duffy had ordered for his bride. A pity the thought of eating any of it made me bilious.

Pullam arrived at my elbow with the silver mail salver and offered the letter upon it. The direction to me was written in Charlotte's hand. She must have guessed we had already arrived at Duffield. I picked it up, my heartbeat quickening. Had she received something from Lord Evan? The packet felt enticingly thick and heavy.

"Has this just arrived?" I asked.

"Yes, my lady, by messenger," Pullam said.

"Who is it from?" Julia asked.

"Charlotte. I will read it later." I placed it on the table beside me, although every part of me wanted to tear it open to see if another letter was enclosed. Julia eyed it with misgiving; she, too, knew what it might contain.

One of the footmen brought the coffee pot and filled my cup. I took a mouthful of the hot, dark brew, savoring the deep bitter taste.

"I hope you are feeling better this morning, Lady Augusta," Miss Woolcroft said, pausing in the buttering of a piece of toast. "You were missed last night. You always bring such vivacity to a party."

It was said with sweet courtesy, and yet . . . was that a snide note I heard? Perhaps I was placing my own ambivalent feelings about the girl upon her innocent words.

"I am quite well this morning, thank you, Miss Woolcroft. I'm sure it was just the shock of so many improvements to Duffield House."

Miss Woolcroft popped a small square of bread into her mouth, watching me. I suspect she had missed my own note of hostility. Duffy, however, shifted in his chair: he had certainly heard it. Julia stared down at her plate and I felt her foot press against mine. I glanced at her sideways.

Do not rise to the bait.

Easy for her to say.

"Indeed, Lady Augusta. Change can be most disordering," Sir Henry said kindly. "May I cut you a piece of seed cake?"

"Yes, please." I passed him my plate. It would give me a reason to look at the plate and not at anyone around the table.

Sir Henry picked up the knife and began to cut. Conversation, it seemed, was not going to flow this morning. Duffy continued to glare at his plate of beef, Miss Woolcroft chewed another tiny square of bread, and Julia sipped at her tea. The only sound was the clack of the knife upon the plate as Sir Henry positioned the generous slice of cake, then passed it back to me.

"Thank you, Sir Henry."

"Augusta, I believe you owe Sir Henry and Miss Woolcroft an apology for that disgusting display in the chapel," Duffy said abruptly. He sat straighter. "And me, too, for that matter."

Ah, so here it was—the public and humiliating apology. Yet even thinking about saying the words made my throat close in fury. Under the table, Julia pressed her foot harder against my own. I stared down at the seed cake.

"Gussie," Julia whispered. She compressed her lips: *Just do it. Be the better person.*

"Augusta!" Duffy's voice had a new harsh tone. "Did you hear me? You need to apologize!"

"Lord Duffield, truly it is not required," Sir Henry said quickly.

"If Duffield says an apology is required, Father, then it is," Miss Woolcroft said smoothly. "Besides, she defiled God's house with indecent language." She turned her blue gaze upon me, clearly waiting for me to make amends to God and my brother.

Sir Henry looked across at his daughter, aghast. "Harriet, it is not for you to demand an apology from Lady Augusta."

"In a few days, I will be Countess Duffield, Father. I am sure

Lady Augusta does not wish our new sisterhood to be tainted by ill feeling or blasphemy."

From that comment, I rather thought our new sisterhood was already tainted.

Beside me, Julia stiffened. "I think the regrettable incident should just be forgotten. Let us all start anew."

"You cannot play the diplomat this time, Julia," Duffy said. "You are always trying to smooth over Augusta's ungoverned outbursts."

Ungoverned outbursts? Did he mean my righteous anger?

"You cannot smooth it over this time," he continued. "She has offended my betrothed and her father. Augusta, apologize!"

"I rather think it is you who must apologize, Duffy," Julia said crisply. "You knew very well that Father had given Leonardo to Augusta, and yet you sold him anyway."

"So you are siding with her as you always do," Duffy snapped. "You never side with me."

"I am siding with the truth," Julia snapped back.

I stared at my sister. She hardly ever raised her voice, and especially not to Duffy. Why this sudden abandonment of compromise? It heartened me, but the last thing I wanted to do was to drive a wedge between her and our brother. And, somehow, for all its prosaic staging in a quiet morning breakfast room, this confrontation felt dangerously as if it could be irretrievable.

"Julia, it is quite all right," I said, laying my hand upon her arm. I faced my brother and his betrothed, both of whom sat with their heads tilted in judgment. It was, perhaps, a better match than I had initially thought. "Duffy, Miss Woolcroft, Sir Henry, I apologize for any offense I have caused."

"That does not seem sincere to me," Miss Woolcroft said. "What do you think, Duffield?"

Julia drew in a sharp breath.

"Harriet! What on earth—" Sir Henry said.

"If you excuse me, I will retire," I said, interrupting Sir Henry's shock. I picked up Charlotte's letter and stood, one of the footmen hurriedly stepping forward to pull back my chair.

"No, Gussie, you do not need to leave," Julia said. She was the most fired up I had ever seen.

"I think I do, my dear." I was a breath away from another *ungoverned outburst* and a blink away from furious tears. I had to leave: I would not give Duffy or Miss Woolcroft the satisfaction of seeing me so discomposed or baiting me back into a quarrel.

I nodded to my sister and Sir Henry and, with only a small tremble in my legs, walked out of the room.

42

In the entrance hall, I hitched my skirts and took the grand staircase two steps at a time—as I used to in my youth—then doubled back along the corridor to the long gallery on the first floor. The vigorous and indecorous climb worked some of my anger from my muscles, but I still felt bilious from stifling my rage. Madame d'Arblay had told us that suppressing one's emotions caused illness. If that were the case, I should be flat upon my back and half-dead.

I had thought I had come to terms with Duffy's jealousy, but the heat of his vengeance still shocked me. And clearly Miss Woolcroft now felt secure enough within her impending rank to voice her own judgment. Duffy had finally found his ally in life. A good thing I did not rely upon them for my livelihood. If I had been a spinster without means and dependent upon their goodwill, how desperate my life would be. As it stood, I did not wish to stay here. But I could not leave. Propriety and familial expectation demanded that I remain for the wedding. Besides, it would distress Julia and place her in an untenable position.

From now on I had to withdraw from the battlefield. A depressing thought.

The gallery was, of course, empty. It ran the length of the cloisters below: a long corridor at least two coaches wide that had provided wet-weather refuge in our childhoods and a place for me to escape in my youth. The outside wall was all windows, the inside wall decorated with paintings—portraits of forebears mainly, and one particularly good Grand Canal by Canaletto. The Venice view usually made me stop and dream—the far water horizon promising so much—but this morning I had a letter to read. I headed to the far window seat, the view overlooking the east-wing side of the forecourt and a glimpse of the dense green hedge maze. The inset wooden bench seat had always been mine, a place to read and think and make sense of the world.

I sat on the hard wood and turned the letter over to the seal, the Davenport coat of arms pressed into the red wax. I cracked it open with my thumb and unfolded the packet. I could not stop a sob of relief when I saw the slim second packet enclosed with my name in Lord Evan's hand. I brushed my fingertips across his bold handwriting. But first, Charlotte's missive.

Davenport Hall,

15th September 1812

My dear Augusta,

Herein is a letter I received by messenger from you-know-who, with the instruction to forward it to you as soon as possible. On calculation, I decided you must already be at Duffield House for the wedding, and so I have sent it forthwith, hoping I am right. Take care, my friend, and know that I am at the ready if you require my services.

Your friend always,
Charlotte, Countess Davenport

Darling Charlotte. I placed her letter on the seat and turned my attention to Lord Evan's packet. My fingers were not quite steady as I broke the wafer that sealed it.

The Duke's Head
King's Lynn

12th September 1812

Dear Lady Augusta,

I hope this letter finds you much recovered.

Although I know you warned me against contacting you, I find I am in need of your urgent assistance; not on my own behalf, but on behalf of my sister, Hester. She is in a situation that threatens her well-being and perhaps even her life—charged with attacking two men, and incarcerated in a mental asylum called Bothwell House, reserved for women of her station near King's Lynn. An opportunity has arisen which offers the possibility of extracting her from the place, but it requires a married couple to take on the madhouse positions of Porter and Matron. My first, and only, thought went to you, my dear Renegade. The task requires an adventurous spirit, courage, and resourcefulness, all of which you have in abundance. Your sister's help, too, would be welcomed, for I know that together you are a formidable force.

Please, if it can be done safely, come to the Duke's Head in Lynn as soon as you can. Dress plainly and use the name Allen, for our roles are people of the working orders. I will wait here until the 18th of September, but after that date this opportunity to rescue my sister will be squandered and I must withdraw and find another way to free her from her torment.

I remain your friend always,
Lord Evan Belford

I lifted my eyes from the letter and looked out upon the view of the empty gravel expanse of the forecourt. Good God, his sister had been incarcerated in a madhouse—I could think of nothing more horrifying. I had read about the conditions and regimes in some of the asylums, and the descriptions of their brutality had made me feel ill. Had she really attacked two men? There must have been mitigating circumstances and the punishment did not really fit the crime; surely more a matter for the magistrate than the mad doctor. Did Lord Deele know that his sister had been incarcerated? One must assume he did, and either could not or would not help. No wonder Lord Evan had risked his life to return to England.

I scanned the letter again, finding the date until which he could wait. The eighteenth was but two days away. The day of the wedding. All of my being wanted to answer his call for help, but I had promised my sister that I was done with adventuring. Done with Lord Evan.

And yet, he was asking for my help. Our help. It would not have been an easy decision for him—he had said time and time again that he did not want to drag me or Julia down into his criminal life. And Julia had made me promise to let him go. And to let the renegade Gus go.

But he had twice answered my call for assistance. Could I really ignore his plea?

The impossibility of both leaving and staying hunched me over his words. Did I have to choose between my sister and my love?

I heard a footfall along the corridor as familiar to me as my own heartbeat.

Julia.

I settled myself more firmly into the window seat as she entered the gallery. She saw me and quickened her pace. I had not marked it at the breakfast table, but she wore her lavender morning gown; back to the soft colors of mourning.

"Here I am," she said.

"There you are," I responded. An old childhood greeting.

"I went to the library first. I thought you might be in your spot there, but of course you came here." She picked up Charlotte's letter—her gaze skimming the signature—and passed it back to me. "Well, that was awful," she said, settling beside me on the bench seat. "Miss Woolcroft has certainly got the bit between her teeth."

"Thank you for standing up for me."

"I am sorry it took so long." She eyed Lord Evan's letter in my hand. "Is that one from him?"

I nodded and passed it over.

As Julia read, I smoothed out Charlotte's letter, bracing myself for the inevitable. My sister would, rightly, remind me of my promise and the importance of the wedding and the duty of family. And for all my heart-driven impulse to go to Lord Evan, I would have to agree.

Midway through the letter, Julia gasped and looked up. "Incarcerated in a madhouse? Do you really think she could be mad?"

"I do not know. But even if she is, Lord Evan says her well-being and life are threatened and so she must be rescued from the place."

"I cannot imagine what the poor woman is enduring."

I nodded mutely. She returned to the letter. As she came to

Lord Evan's request, her mouth twitched sideways, a sympathetic grimace that I knew meant she recognized my dilemma. She looked up at the end, a knit between her brows.

"It is all right," I said. "I will not go."

She sighed and folded the letter. "Do you know what I realized during breakfast?"

"That Miss Woolcroft is a cow?"

She laughed. "Yes, but also something far more important. I realized Duffy wants to force you into his idea of what a woman our age should be: hardly seen and definitely not heard." She bit her lip. "And, to my shame, I realize that I have been doing the same. I'm sorry, Gus, can you forgive me? When you were hurt, I became so frightened, but now I know I must not hold you back. You must go to Lord Evan and help poor Lady Hester. It is your calling to go out into the world and right such wrongs."

"You think I should go?" My heart quickened at the thought of seeing Lord Evan: a hard drumming of joy. Yet my sister's blessing on the enterprise—as important as it was—did not change anything. "What about the wedding? What about your health? I could not bear to bring you down further. Besides, I cannot just leave; Duffy would never forgive me and he will take it out on you."

"You leave Duffy to me. And as for my health, that is between me and God." She raised her chin, knowing my thoughts on that belief. "I will brook no argument on that score."

"So you will not come and help?" For all my excitement, I felt suddenly bereft.

"I will stay for the wedding—one of us must, for propriety's sake—and then I will come." She smiled. "My calling, it seems, is to follow my adventurous sister. As it always has been since we were children."

"With a blunderbuss," I said.

She snorted. "That is a new addition."

I put my arm around her and hugged her to me. "Thank you."

Her arm tightened around me for a moment, then she released me and unfolded Lord Evan's letter. "Now, let us plan your escape."

43

If I was to reach Lynn—or King's Lynn, as it was also called—in time to meet Lord Evan, I would have to leave Duffield House the following day. After much discussion in our little nook, Julia and I decided we must enlist Tully, Weatherly, and John Driver to aid my departure.

Tully was in charge of organizing an appropriate outfit and traveling box for a woman about to become a matron in a private madhouse. Weatherly was in charge of ordering the landau and John Driver to be ready—on the pretext of Julia and me making a call to a neighbor—and once again switching his role to footman for our real journey to Ely and the inn where the mail chaise collected its passengers.

That night, after a meal with just Julia and me at the table—Duffy had pointedly gone alone to dine with the Woolcrofts at the dower house—I lay awake considering our plan from every angle. There could be no escaping the fact that I would be leaving a mess behind me. Quitting Duffield House and absenting myself from my only brother's wedding was an unforgivable act, and I could not help but feel guilty for the pain I was about to cause. Or perhaps, more accurately, the blow to my brother's pride and his overkeen sense of propriety. Whatever the case, I did not look forward to facing him in the morning knowing I was about to step beyond the bounds of all that was sacred to him.

As it happened, Duffy did not make an appearance at breakfast either. Perhaps intentionally, although by Pullam's report he had been called to mediate a problem with one of the tenants. On that intelligence, Julia and I hastily quit the table and made our way to our rooms: me to dress in my new guise and Julia to don her outerwear. We had, at most, an hour to make an unseen departure.

It did not take long for me to complete my transformation.

I tucked my fob watch upon its neck chain under the collar of my chemisette and turned to view myself in the mirror. Tully had refashioned one of my old gowns, stored here at Duffield House, by reducing its full back to a more practical proportion and stripping it of its expensive lace. In the reflection, I saw a tall, neat woman with hair confined in a plain linen cap and wearing a well-fitted but somewhat outmoded green dress with a white cotton chemisette modestly filling its scoop décolletage. A respectable and dependable woman who worked hard for her livelihood.

Good morning, Mrs. Allen.

I stifled a smile at the name. Yet, beyond that amusement, a multitude of questions teemed in my mind. Would I be able to act my role? Could we rescue Lady Hester? Should I tell Lord Evan that I remembered what I had said in the brothel hallway? If I did tell him, what if he did not feel the same way? Then again, what if he did feel the same way? And what about acting as husband and wife? What if there was only one bed in our quarters? Would we share it? Did I want to share it?

I looked away from the reflection of my flushed face.

"You have another gown for work and one for best, my lady, as well as an apron, linen for a week, a nightgown, and indoor shoes.

Any more and it would look suspicious," Tully said, closing a small studded box. It was the kind that all servants used to keep their belongings. Tully had found it abandoned in the attics: the last possession of a poor maid who had died of an influenza. "I have also put in the balm for your shoulder. Remember to rub it in if it pains you."

"I will," I said, although applying balm seemed a rather prosaic pastime on a rescue mission.

"I've packed some bread and cheese in your basket." She lightly touched its handle. "And I think it might be best if you take my cloak, my lady." She picked up the scarlet garment and passed it to me. "It is the style among us and will fit with your masquerade. Yours is too fine."

"Good idea. Thank you." I shook out her cloak and twirled it around my shoulders. The red worsted was thick—made to repel rain—and tied at the throat with a thick grosgrain ribbon. I had seen many country women wearing them, and even a few daughters of the gentry.

"What should I do when you are gone, my lady?" Tully asked.

A good question. "You had best collect all my belongings here and get them ready to take back to London. We will sort them when I return. And say your good-byes, Tully. I doubt we will be returning to Duffield House soon. Once the wedding is over, Lady Julia will have further orders."

Tully curtsied. "Yes, my lady, and good luck. I hope your reunion is wonder—" She stopped, her face reddening at the near overstep. "I beg your pardon."

Ever the romantic.

I smiled. "I do too."

Weatherly arrived to inform me that the landau and Lady Julia were waiting and to collect my box. I followed him down the grand staircase carrying my basket, with Tully's red cloak and my plain blue gown hidden for the carriage ride beneath the voluminous folds of my own fine velvet cloak. I could not hide my humble unadorned straw bonnet, but I did not usually wear a lot of flowers or feathers so it would not be noted as odd.

Weatherly stopped at the bottom of the staircase and walked to either side of it to check that we were alone in the spacious entrance hallway. It appeared we were, for he said, "My lady, may I make a suggestion?"

"Of course, Weatherly."

"Allow me to take the stage with you. Not as a companion; we would pretend to be strangers. You have never taken the mail before and it is not a place for a gentlewoman. Nor is a port town like Lynn. I would see you to safety." He gave a wry smile. "Well, at least into Lord Evan's protection."

From his tone, that was no protection at all, but I let it pass.

"Ah, but I am not a gentlewoman, Weatherly. I am Mrs. Allen, on her way to a new position as matron. It is more important that you are here. I want you to make sure Lady Julia has an ally when I am noticed missing and that she is safe when she travels to joins us."

"I can do both. Your absence can be hidden until tomorrow."

True, but while my reasons about Julia's safety were sincere, I also had to admit the last thing I wanted was my butler with me at the moment I reunited with Lord Evan.

"No, I will go alone," I said.

Julia was already waiting in the carriage. Weatherly handed me up and I settled into the seat beside her, stowing my basket at my feet.

"So, what do you think?" I asked, parting the cloak to show her my ensemble beneath. "Do I look the part?"

"Authentic," Julia said. "Walk on," she called to John Driver. He clicked his tongue and with a flick of the reins urged the bay pair into a walk.

As the landau's wheels rumbled across the gravel, I took one last look at Duffield House. At its beloved arched cloister, the elegant east and west wings, and the tall clock tower that was the first part of the house that came into view as one drove up the driveway. The sight of its crenelated top had always meant I had come home. Not anymore. This was Duffy's home, and the home of the new countess, and after the wedding tomorrow, I doubted I would be welcome.

"It will not be forever," Julia said, reading my expression. We passed the dense green hedges of the maze. "Here, you have forgotten one thing in your ensemble." She passed me a small jewelry box covered in blue sharkskin and bearing the name Rundle and Bridge.

I opened it. Inside sat an Irish gold love ring with a crowned heart between two hands. I knew the ring—Robert had given it to my sister as a token of their love upon their betrothal.

"Oh, Julia. I cannot."

"You must have a wedding ring if you are to be a wife, even a false wife, and the claddagh ring is sometimes used for vows."

"Are you sure? I know it is special to you."

"You are more special," Julia said firmly, although she kept her eyes upon the ring. "And I think Robert would support your endeavor to save Lady Hester."

I slipped the claddagh band onto my left ring finger, the finger that had a direct link to the heart. Or at least that was what the Romantics said. As a girl, I had never longed for marriage like some of my friends. And Julia, too, once she had met Robert. Yet the sight of the ring on my finger conjured Lord Evan's face. In truth, I could see myself married to him, and happily too; the most impossible union I could ever choose. A disgraced peer, a convict on the run, a thief.

"You are thinking of Lord Evan," Julia said.

"Am I mooncalfing again?"

"A little. You do realize it has been but three months since you met him, and hardly any time of that has seen you together."

"True," I conceded, "but every time we have been together he has shown me his worth. How often do other women see their men in the kinds of dire situations that we have been in? How often do they see them time and time again act with honor and compassion under the worst circumstances?"

It was Julia's turn to concede the point. "You love him—that is plain. But it is also plain that this liaison is impossible. Forgive me for being the voice of doom, but it is astonishing that he has still evaded capture."

"I know."

"Just be careful with your heart, Gus."

She took my hand—the one wearing the ring—and held it tightly as we passed the Duffield House gates and turned onto the road to Bedford.

"Robert had the ring blessed, so it will bring you God's protection too." She cast a sideways glance at me. "That probably means nothing to you now, but I know it will keep you safe."

I nodded. If it gave her any ease of mind, that was meaning enough for me.

In the village of Duffield, just fifteen minutes into our journey, the local publican, Mr. Turrbridge, hurried out of his tavern to the side of the road and hailed the landau. John Driver looked back for instructions.

"Should we stop?" Julia asked me.

I nodded. I had met Mr. Turrbridge many times at the assizes with Father. Although a genial man, Mr. Turrbridge was neither frivolous nor a time waster. Something of import must have made him come out to wave us down.

We drew up beside him. He bowed, the top of his bald pate pale and freckled.

"Good morn to you, Lady Augusta, Lady Julia," he greeted us. "Thank you for stopping."

"Good morning, Mr. Turrbridge," I said. "You look concerned. Is something amiss?"

He rubbed his palms together. "I am not sure, my lady. But I wanted to alert you in case . . ." He lifted his shoulders. "Perhaps I am being overly cautious, but a man, a stranger, was here asking about you and Lady Julia." His gaze traveled to my sister, then back to me. "I just didna like the look of the fellow."

Good God, had Mr. Kent, the Runner, followed us down here? I glanced at Julia and saw the same alarm.

"Was he a good-looking, strongly built man of about six foot with dark hair?" Julia asked. "Well dressed, like a gentleman?"

"And a crooked nose, once broken?" I added.

Mr. Turrbridge considered the description. "He was a big one, for sure, but sandy haired with red side-whiskers, and his nose didna look like it had been broken. Weren't well dressed, neither."

I looked again at Julia. Not Mr. Kent, then. Nor was it my second, more hopeful guess: Lord Evan. So, who was it?

Julia leaned forward. "You say he was asking about us?"

"Wanted to know when you had arrived at Duffield and who came with you. Too nosy by half. I didna tell him anything."

"Thank you, Mr. Turrbridge," I said. "If he comes again, see if you can find out his name for us."

He bowed again. "That I will, my lady."

"Drive on," Julia said. We both settled back in the seat.

"I do not like the sound of that," I said when we were out of earshot of Mr. Turrbridge. "Could it be one of Mr. Kent's men?"

"Could be," Julia said. "Although I never saw someone like that outside the house."

"Neither did I. At least we have a description of him. We must keep watch, especially when you come to meet us."

Julia nodded. "I will."

I looked back at Weatherly, seated on the groom's seat behind us, and raised my brows: *Keep a very close watch.* He nodded too.

44

A quarter of the way into my journey to King's Lynn on the mail coach, I regretted refusing Weatherly's protective presence.

I had managed to secure an inside seat, but so had four other people in a space designed for three. I was jammed between the window on one side and a man who reeked of unwashed crevices on the other, who insisted, even after a firm request to move, on pressing his thigh against mine and surreptitiously cupping his privates. At least that was what I thought he was doing—I kept my eyes directed anyplace but him. I pushed my basket against his leg, hoping to force him back an inch.

My efforts were watched by an amply proportioned woman of my own age wearing a squirrel-trimmed version of Tully's red cloak. She herself sat crammed against two men conversing loudly about pig prices but had staked out her seating space with a well-placed package. After I attempted another jab of my basket, she leaned across the straw-covered footwell and said over the rattle of wheels and clash of tack, "Don't worry, my dear. At our age, it is a compliment."

"I see no compliment," I said.

She observed Mr. Odorous again, then said dryly, "I see your point. Where are you going? All the way to Lynn?"

"Yes, to meet my husband," I said, raising my voice. Perhaps if Mr. Odorous knew I was a wife, he would desist.

"Ah, your husband," she echoed just as loudly, impish collaboration in her face. "A brawny man, I'm sure, to match your own height?"

I nodded vigorously. Mr. Odorous had still not moved his thigh, so I added, "Indeed, he is to be the new porter at Bothwell House and I am to be matron."

Even as I said it, I knew it was a mistake. *Never offer more than you should*, my father always said—and he had debated in Parliament. I had given away too much.

The woman drew back, all impish lightness gone from her face. Still, Mr. Odorous's thigh shifted from my own. I sent him a cold look, at once relieved and annoyed that only the conjuring of a porter husband forced him to stop.

The woman observed me for a sober moment, then said, "You are to be matron at the madhouse?"

"Yes," I said shortly. No more information from me. But she leaned forward again, this time with urgency in her voice. "Forgive me for meddling, dearie, but I must tell you that Bothwell House is a bad place. My husband and I run the Duke's Head at Lynn, and we've had people passing through who have been released, or in one case run away. That place breaks people. There is even talk that women are dying too often. You would do well to rethink your plans."

"I thank you, but we are set upon it," I said, and looked out of the window at the passing countryside to end the conversation.

We arrived at the Duke's Head in King's Lynn almost upon two o'clock, according to my fob watch. As the horses and coach clattered into the cobbled forecourt, I saw Lord Evan standing at the front entrance and could not stop my sudden smile. Pure mooncalf, Julia would say.

"Ah, your husband is awaiting you," my collaborator said. "I can tell from your face." She cocked her head as the coach drew up to the hotel's handsome frontage, painted a fashionable powder blue. "And I can see why you are smiling, dearie." She turned to Mr. Odorous. "You better hope this lady is of a forgiving nature."

He glared at her, but I felt him slide a little farther away from me on the seat.

"King's Lynn," the coachman hollered. "The Duke's Head."

At that moment, Lord Evan spotted me, his smile so full of relief and warmth that I felt my heart leap into a hard beat.

My collaborator sighed gustily. "To be waited upon with such enthusiasm," she said.

One of the inn's footmen opened the carriage door. "Finally," she said, eyeing him beadily. "Thought we were going to be stabled with the horses."

"Not a stall big enough for you, Mrs. Cullers," the footman said.

"You're a cheeky jackanapes, Billy Pierce," she said comfortably and handed him her package. "Help me down, then, and this lady too."

Billy obediently handed Mrs. Cullers down. I passed him my box from under the seat, gathered up my basket, then reached to take his offered hand.

"Allow me," Lord Evan said, stepping up to the coach door.

"Who are you, then?" Billy said, defending his position.

"It is all right, Billy," Mrs. Cullers said. "'E's her husband."

"Oh, right you are." Billy touched his forehead and drew back.

I took Lord Evan's hand, meeting his eye. Oh, how I had missed these moments of amused collusion.

"You came," he said, for my ears only as I stepped, somewhat stiffly, down to the cobbles.

I breathed in the sea air, such a relief after being shut up in the sweaty cabin. He did not release my hand as we made room for Mr.

Odorous to descend. But then, I did not pull it away. We stood, hand in hand, and it felt as if every nerve in my body was centered in that grasp.

"You asked. Of course I came," I said softly. "We were at Duffield House for my brother's wedding tomorrow." He raised his brows at that admission, but I shrugged. "He sold my hunter without telling me, and we nearly came to blows. I suspect I won't be overly missed."

"He sold Leonardo?" Lord Evan said, aghast. "That is a cur's trick."

He remembered my horse's name. "To a neighbor who rides too heavy for him," I said, unable to keep the bitterness from my voice. "My sister stays for the nuptials but follows straight after. She says she will bring the blunderbuss."

He snorted. "I believe it. And the Runner? Did he follow you to Duffield House?"

"No. At least I think not. But someone else has been asking about us in the village." I gave him the man's description. "Do you know him?"

Lord Evan shook his head, frowning. "Perhaps another Runner? Or worse, a thieftaker."

I'd had the same thought. Dear God, two men after him. How many more? I cast a searching look around the forecourt, just in case, but no one was paying us particular attention.

"Missus, don't forget your box," Billy called to me, hoisting it up.

Lord Evan nodded to him, then brought my hand to his lips and pressed a light kiss upon my gloved fingers before releasing me. A flush warmed my cheeks. Was he just playing his role as devoted husband, or was that truly for me?

"I am very glad you are here, wife," he said, then turned to receive my luggage.

"Lordy be," Mrs. Cullers said behind me. I turned to see her fanning herself theatrically. She smiled, casting a knowing look at Lord Evan.

"Thank you for your help," I said. "I am Mrs. Allen."

"Mrs. Cullers," she said, giving a stern eye to Mr. Odorous as he made a hasty exit from the forecourt. "When do you make your way to Bothwell? Will you stay the night? I'm sure we can find you a room."

Lord Evan shot a glance at me: *She knows?* I pressed my lips together: *A mistake, sorry.* "Thank you, no," he said. "I have a cart hired to take us anon."

I smiled my thanks and nodded my farewell to the good lady as Lord Evan led the way into the inn.

"We are going to Bothwell House now?" I asked.

"More or less, but there is someone you must meet before we leave." He looked over his shoulder, expression grim. "She has the full story and it is best you hear it from her."

"Who is it?"

"I will let her explain," he said.

The dining hour was in full swing in the public room of the Duke's Head. Lord Evan led me through the crowded tables, the smell of roasting beef and savory pudding setting up a nag within my innards. Tully's bread and cheese had been a long time ago. Unlike at the Plow Inn at fashionable Cheltenham—where I had dined as Mr. Anderson—a few respectable women sat at the tables with their male kin, their dress marking them as wives and daughters of trade. Lynn was a busy market and fishing town and, incidentally, the birthplace of Madame d'Arblay, so it held some claim to cosmopolitan sensibilities.

We headed toward the dining boxes set along the far wall, which provided some privacy among the hustle of waiters and patrons. A young woman, clad in a quality teal pelisse and tastefully trimmed cottage bonnet, sat in the last one by herself. She looked up as we approached, her pale face built on fine, long lines with a particularly determined jaw. Despite the fact that she was taking a risk sitting alone in a hotel dining room—so vulnerable to harassment or being mistaken for a woman of ill repute—she had a strong air of self-possession.

"Allow me to introduce Miss Elizabeth Grant," Lord Evan said to me, stowing my box under the table. "Miss Grant, this is Mrs. Allen."

Miss Grant nodded in greeting. Brown eyes—keenly aware—assessed me.

"Good evening," I said and, with as much grace as I could muster, slid into the bench seat opposite.

Lord Evan sat beside me, his body close to mine but without touching. I fancied I could feel his warmth, but perhaps that was the rise of heat across my own skin.

"Miss Grant is Lady Hester's—my sister's—friend," Lord Evan said, placing an emphasis on the last word. "Two years ago, they were living together in Wales when my brother tricked Hester into meeting him, whereupon he took her to Bothwell House, one of the few private madhouses that takes only women of good family. Deele committed her indefinitely. She has been incarcerated there ever since, and Miss Grant has been waiting here for a chance to deliver her from her imprisonment."

Lord Deele had committed his own sister? This must be why Bertie had written to Lord Evan.

"Committed for what reason?" I asked, although I had a fair idea, having met Deele. I glanced at Lord Evan. "Your letter to me said she was charged with attacking two men. But surely that cannot be true."

"No, it is true," Miss Grant said. "She attacked Lord Deele and one of his footmen. But I am certain she did so only to free herself from being forcibly taken."

"My sister would not have gone quietly," Lord Evan said. "She always stood up to our brother, even as a child."

And that would have played into Deele's hands. How easy it would be for him—her guardian—to name her violence as madness rather than desperation. Who would gainsay a marquess?

"Hester is not mad, Mrs. Allen. She is as sane as you and I," Miss Grant said. "I believe she was committed because she refused to marry the man her brother insisted upon and instead ran away with me." She stared at me, a challenge on her face. "I love her and she loves me."

So Emelia Ellis-Brant had been right about the first part of this unhappy story: Miss Grant and Lady Hester were, indeed, of Anne Lister's ilk and had run away together. Emelia had not known, however, that Lord Deele had then deceived his sister and incarcerated her in a madhouse. Hester's choice would have disgusted him, as he had been disgusted by dear Bertie, and he would be convinced she was set on a path to hell. Yet it still shocked me to my core that he would abandon his sane sister in a madhouse. A despicable, unforgiveable act.

"You must love Lady Hester a great deal to have stood here as sentinel for two years," I said.

Miss Grant gave a brusque nod.

It was indeed a testament to her regard. Could I stand so staunchly alone for years in my love for Lord Evan? Was that the fate ahead of me? I looked at him, lost for a moment in the bold contours of forehead, nose, and chin and the shift of expression as he listened to Miss Grant. Then I realized I had missed some part of an explanation.

". . . I tried to get inside to see her, but Lord Deele has left instructions for no visitors other than himself or Lady Deele. I set up quite a hue and cry about that, but to no avail. And of course, the keeper of the asylum, a vile man by the name of Horace Judd, knew my face from these encounters, which dashed any idea of me taking a position within the asylum to attempt a rescue. Prior to her abduction, Hester had introduced me to Lord Cholton, with the intelligence that he was . . . like us. So, I visited him and he proposed writing to you in the hope that you would come. I took a cottage here in Lynn so I could be near her while I—while we—waited." She looked down at the scuffed table, running her finger into a deep scratch. "I do not even know what state she is in, or even if—" She stopped, unable to voice that final terror. Beside me, Lord Evan shifted in his seat as if shaking off the idea that Hester could be dead. "She is the dearest, most wonderful person," Miss Grant added. "Full of life and mischief and wit. I cannot bear to think . . ."

"Has Lord Deele or Lady Deele ever come to visit?" I asked, trying to divert the conversation from such a melancholy direction.

"No. Not once in two years," she said.

"But is she not of age?" I asked. I had limited knowledge of the "mad laws," but last year I had attended a lecture by Mr. Samuel Tuke, a Quaker, who—in line with the religion's mission of social reform—advocated for more humane treatment of the insane instead of shackles and violent interferences. I was sure I'd heard him say that one could not incarcerate a sane person of age against their will.

"Our father extended her guardianship to age thirty-five. She is now thirty and under the guardianship of the incumbent Lord Deele," Lord Evan said.

Which should be you, I thought, but I did not voice it. He would, without a doubt, be agonizingly aware of how his situation affected his sister.

"The private madhouses like Bothwell are a law unto themselves,"

Miss Grant said. "And there is so much corruption among the officials that inspect them. I have written to many people about it, but who will listen to a spinster woman with no family connection to the committed lady? Especially when that lady is the sister of Lord Deele, who committed her in the first place."

Her expression held such frustration and fear that I reached over and took her hand. "We are here now. And we will soon know how things stand."

She looked down at our clasped hands—how long had it been since she had been touched?—then clung to my fingers. "Thank you. I cannot express how grateful I am that you are here."

"My sister will be coming soon too," I said. "Lady Julia Colebrook. She knows the situation. Well, at least she knows where we are going and what we propose to do. Make yourself known to her when she arrives and tell her everything."

Miss Grant released my hand. "I will. Thank you."

A figure approached. Billy, the footman.

"Mr. Allen, Joseph is here with the cart," he said.

"Thank you." Lord Evan nodded to Miss Grant. "We must go now. We will get word to you once we understand the situation."

He extracted his long self from the booth and retrieved my box, hoisting it onto his shoulder. I gathered my skirts, slid along the seat, and, with one last reassuring press upon Miss Grant's hand, followed him through the tables.

At the dining room doorway, a familiar figure bustled toward me from the servery and called, "Mrs. Allen, do wait!" It was Mrs. Cullers, carrying a parcel wrapped in a white cloth.

Lord Evan was already out the door and halfway across the busy foyer, but I stopped for her and smiled courteously.

"I have packed some food for you and your husband since you do not have time for a meal," she said.

I took the offered parcel. It had quite a heft to it. "Thank you, that is very kind. Do we owe you . . . ?"

"No. It is a gift, dearie." She leaned closer, her voice low. "My husband and I go to Bothwell every Friday to deliver beer and spirits. If you ever need anything . . ."

"I am not sure what you mean," I said carefully. I did not trust this interest in us.

She shook her head. "It is none of my business, I know, but—" She glanced back at the solitary figure of Miss Grant, still seated in the booth. "I know that story: it's hard to keep your business quiet in a town like this. Now, I'm not saying I agree with the way she and her *lady friend* live, because I don't, but neither do I agree with dumping a woman who ain't mad in a place like Bothwell." She turned her attention back to me. "Seeing you and her, it don't take an Oxford don to put two and two together. I'm just saying, every Friday."

On that she nodded and left me standing in the middle of the busy foyer with the parcel of food and an uneasy thought: if Mrs. Cullers could so easily see our intention, who else might put two and two together?

45

Lord Evan had hired a dog cart, driven by an elderly man by the name of Joseph and pulled by an equally elderly horse called Jasper. We set off once Lord Evan had paid his shot, our luggage stowed in the dog box and Lord Evan and I settled on the backward-facing seat behind the driver. In answer to Lord Evan's query of our traveling time, Joseph had shouted over his shoulder, "'Bout an hour if Jasper stay bright all the way."

Jasper, it seemed, felt very bright, for we clipped along at a good rate. The roads beyond Lynn, however, were in poor condition, and Lord Evan and I found ourselves jolted together over and over again on the cramped bench. Finally, we both had to brace ourselves with feet apart, our thighs touching. It occurred to me that, unlike my experience on the post, this male leg against my own did not offend me. Quite the opposite, in fact, with every nerve in my body keenly aware of the firm length of thigh against my own.

I wanted to tell him I had remembered my words in the brothel, that I had meant them, but the clank and grind of the old cart upon the road was so loud that any conversation had to be yelled, as much to Joseph as to Lord Evan. Not an ideal way to declare one's love.

Indeed, after a few failed attempts at more desultory conversation, we did not try to talk at all. Instead, we ate the generous wedges of pork pie provided by Mrs. Cullers and watched the country road pass by—bordered by slender poplars, tall grasses, and the flat expanse of reclaimed farmlands—our legs touching and occasionally his hand finding mine upon the seat.

"Bothwell," Joseph finally bellowed.

We both turned to look.

Ahead a redbrick wall ran along the roadside, at least six feet high and stretching into the distance, the blank expanse of it only interrupted by the curve of an entrance. We continued until a tall wrought iron gate came into view—topped by rather sharp-looking spikes—with a small porter's lodge set at its side.

Joseph drew up and twisted around in his seat. "I can't take you up to the house. Mr. Judd only allows food and drink deliveries."

"We have to walk up?" Lord Evan said.

"Aye."

A few minutes later we were standing on the side of the road with our luggage at our feet, watching Joseph and Jasper rattle off back toward Lynn.

Lord Evan turned and surveyed the gates.

"Whatever happens now, I want to thank you," he said. "There are very few women who would do this. Who would even be able to do this."

He smiled but I could tell his focus was already fully upon the task before us. As it should be—his sister's life was at stake. My revelation would have to wait.

He rang the porter bell. We waited at least a minute, and then a young ginger-haired man, who had surely heard our arrival in the cart, finally slouched out.

"Aye?"

"We are Mr. and Mrs. Allen. Mr. Judd is expecting us," Lord Evan said.

"Aye."

He unlocked the smaller side gate and stood back to allow us to enter. Lord Evan swung my trunk back up onto his shoulder. I picked up his portmanteau. Something within it clunked heavily, but I decided to ignore it.

"I can take that too," Lord Evan said.

I waved away his hand. "No, I can manage. I am no fainting lady," I said pointedly. He was treating me as Lady Augusta, not Mrs. Allen.

He gave a nod. Message received.

"Follow the drive," Slouch said, a jerk of his head pointing the way along the driveway. I smelled a strong reek of beer as I passed him. "Mr. Judd's been expecting you for two days, so he's in a right mood," he added helpfully.

The drive was a handsome packed-dirt approach with a line of oak trees on either side, just touched with autumn hues, and well-cut lawns beyond them. Ahead, a glimpse of red brick through the trees promised a house at least as large as a gentleman's hunting lodge.

"Well kept," I said, passing the portmanteau to my other hand. Its weight seemed to be increasing. "I'm surprised. Mrs. Cullers said the place was a misery."

"It is probably all show for visitors and new arrivals," Lord Evan said. "The plan is to find Hester as quickly as possible and leave."

I swung the portmanteau a little higher between us. "Is that why you have a pistol in here?"

"Lesson learned."

"I must say, your plan is simple to the point of naïve," I drawled.

He smiled at the echo of his own words at Thornecrest, as I knew he would. "True, but in all seriousness, I have no idea what state Hester is in. We will have to work out a plan once we know how things stand."

"You had best tell me what a matron does, or they will see through me in a second."

"You are in charge of the women inmates, the staff, and the day-to-day running of the asylum. Like a housekeeper. I am the porter, so I oversee all the comings and goings and administration."

Well, I had managed Duffield House and our London home for years, so I could probably manage an insane asylum. "How did you get the positions? Surely there was someone here already?"

He smiled, a hint of devil in it. "Miss Grant and I hired a solicitor to write to the incumbent porter and his wife about an inheritance that had to be claimed in London by this week. We put money together for the prize—a sizable amount—and sent them enough blunt to pay for the post chaise too. I then wrote to Judd inquiring about positions, and here we are, ready for action. Albeit without a plan."

He gestured with his free hand as Bothwell House came into full view. The red brick glimpsed through the trees had emerged as a large two-story manor house. An unusually tall oriel window—made up of three panes set in stone moldings—protruded from the first floor above the front portico and was bracketed in place by three huge carved corbels shaped like scrolls. On each side of this handsome bay window were three double-sashed windows on both ground and first floors, with gabled attic windows set into the slanted roof. Such an extravagance of glass; the window tax would be exorbitant.

Beside the house stood a small outbuilding, most probably the original stables, with room for six horses at most, but the high-set window in view was barred. The first sign that the gracious manor was not quite as it seemed.

"That is our modus operandi—making it up as we go along," I said, hoping to reassure him. And, in truth, myself as well. "We are making quite a habit of it."

He turned from observing the house, his expression grave. "This is the last time, dear renegade," he said gently. "Once Hester is safe, I am leaving England."

"Leaving?" I kept walking beside him, but it felt as if an abyss had opened up and every step took me closer to its edge.

"I came back to help Hester. I am not sure how we are to achieve her safety yet—not with Deele still as her guardian—but once she is free and able to live her life as she wishes with Miss Grant, I must go. Even if I had a reason to stay"—it was said with a sidelong glance—"England is too dangerous for me now, and it is too dangerous for anyone to be around me."

He meant it was too dangerous for me to be around him. Still, I did not care. More to the point, did he mean I might be a reason to stay? What if I declared my love as I had planned? Would that make him stay? Possibly, probably, but then he would end up hanged, because of me. No, no, I could not put him in such danger. He had to leave.

"Where will you go? You cannot go to the Continent. The war." Good God, he was not going to fight, was he?

"No, I am not for soldiering," he said. Did I see a moment of disappointment in his dear eyes that I did not fight for him to stay? "Maybe Jamaica."

Not the war, then, but a sea journey just as full of danger. I wet my lips and managed, "A long way."

Perhaps I could go with him? A new life, together. For a second, I saw a flash of us looking out on a lusher, hotter landscape, hand in hand, happy. But that would mean leaving Julia. I could not abandon my sister. My twin. Perhaps she could come with us? She said her calling was to follow me. But no, she was too ill and I could not drag her from her home and her doctor and all that was safe and loved into a life of danger and desperation.

He had to leave, and I had to let him go. Not by the will of others, this time, but by my own. I felt as if I had lived a hundred years of agony and yet we had walked only a few yards into the forecourt.

"Do you hear that?" Lord Evan said, coming to a halt, his body tense.

I stopped beside him. With the crunch of underfoot gravel gone, I heard it too.

Wailing. The low, melancholy sound sent a prickle across my nape.

Just as the keen rose into a bone-chilling shriek, a young woman appeared around the corner of the house and hurried toward us. A maid, by the look of her plain blue dimity dress and linen cap

"Mr. and Mrs. Allen?" she asked, bobbing a curtsy. At our nods she continued in a breathy rush. "Mr. Judd had me waitin' for you. Come this way, please. I'll take you to him."

"What is your name?" Lord Evan asked.

"I'm Tilda, Mr. Allen." Her gown was a size too big on her thin frame and stained, but her face was clean and her smile—missing one front tooth—genuine. "I'm senior maid."

I had, by habit, turned to climb the steps to the front door, my mind still upon the prospect of Lord Evan leaving. At the corner of my eye, I saw Tilda's head jerk in surprise. Of course, the front entrance was not for the likes of Mrs. Allen. Fool. I stopped and coughed, correcting my trajectory. A timely reminder to keep my mind wholly upon the masquerade and not the heartache that threatened to consume me.

Tilda took us around the corner of the house, past the stable. The girl did not seem to hear the moaning and shrieks that emitted from the building.

"Who's in there, dearie?" I asked, mimicking Mrs. Cullers's speech: a good fit for a matron.

"That's the incurables and paupers," she said. "The others are in the house."

Lord Evan looked at me, the same horrified question in his eyes as in mine: was Hester in there?

"Can we see inside?" Lord Evan asked nonchalantly, but his hold upon the box had tightened into a white-knuckled grip.

"I don't have keys, sir. Besides, Mr. Judd wants to see you. We daren't keep him waitin'."

Lord Evan motioned for us to continue; clearly he, too, had heard the genuine fear in Tilda's voice. It seemed Mr. Judd's word was law.

We turned the corner of the house into a small cobbled courtyard bounded by three redbrick outbuildings. A glimpse through the doorway of the first showed two sweaty women at work washing linen over steaming troughs.

"Laundry," Tilda said, rather unnecessarily. "An' that's the bathhouse and behind it the treatment rooms," she added. Her eyes slid away from the smaller buildings. The front building—the bathhouse—had both a normal door and an iron-barred gate.

I looked back as we headed toward the house. The single window was barred too. Not a bathhouse for the staff, then, but for the inmates. In Mr. Tuke's lecture, he had described a treatment used extensively in madhouses: the cold-water bath. Hours sitting in freezing water, and sometimes with it poured ceaselessly upon the head. He had pronounced it a cruel and useless treatment and advocated warm baths instead to calm the disordered mind. I lifted my shoulders, trying to shrug away a shiver of apprehension.

46

We entered the house proper, straight into a busy kitchen. The cook—a woman with hunched shoulders and a deeply etched frown—looked up from dressing a fowl. Beside her, two young, flushed-faced kitchen maids continued to cut potatoes, sneaking looks at us as they worked.

"Mrs. Carroll, this is Mr. and Mrs. Allen, the new matron and porter," Tilda said.

Mrs. Carroll and the two girls bobbed curtsies.

"Glad yer here at last," Mrs. Carroll said, wiping her hands on her filthy apron. "Will you be takin' your dinner in your parlor, like t'others before? Or in the servants' hall?"

"In the parlor, please," Lord Evan said.

We were, I supposed, the equivalent of senior servants and so would naturally take the privilege of dining in our own rooms. Frankly, I was relieved; less interaction meant less chance of my masquerade slipping into discovery.

Mrs. Carroll gave an abrupt nod, then looked directly at me. "You look strong enough," she said somewhat cryptically. The two kitchen maids shifted, glancing at each other.

Strong enough for what? Before I could decide whether Mrs. Allen would ask such a question, the moment was overtaken by Tilda's urgency.

"Mr. Judd is waiting for them," she said to the cook, motioning us onward.

She led us out of the kitchen into a dim corridor, lit only by two tapers set in sconces, past an empty servants' hall to a plain wooden servants' staircase.

"Mr. Judd's study and bedchamber is up there." She pointed in the direction of the front of the house as we climbed the steps. "Your lodgings are at t'other end of the house. You can leave your things on the way."

We arrived in another long, dimly lit hallway. A sudden eruption of screaming—from the floor above, it seemed—stopped both Lord Evan and myself. We looked up. It sounded as if murder was in progress.

"That's just Miss Drummond," Tilda said. "She always has a scream about now."

She led us left, to a set of two doorways at the end of the corridor. Beyond them was a back door that stood open, a walled garden visible beyond.

"That's the patients' garden when Mr. Judd lets 'em go out. This is your parlor and bedchamber. That second door don't open—that's your bedchamber. It's got a dresser set against it." She opened the first door. "Put your things in there and I'll take you to Mr. Judd."

The parlor inside was a small but neat room with a bluebell-print wallpaper, two shabby but well-stuffed armchairs before a hearth, and a scuffed and scratched round table that could accommodate four, at a pinch. Another doorway showed the adjoining bedchamber, and the obvious fact that it contained only one marital bed.

"Fires are lit at five in the evening. Hot water at six in the mornin', if that suits, and breakfast at seven. We eat dinner at one, usually, and supper at nine."

"Thank you," Lord Evan said, placing my box on the ground. I stowed his portmanteau beside it, not daring to look at the bedchamber again.

"Are there many ladies of quality here at present?" he asked as he removed his coat. The strain in his voice was palpable, at least to me.

"Oh yes. We got about six. The rest are respectable ladies, too, and a few paupers from the county."

I glanced at Lord Evan. Not specific enough.

I took off my bonnet and placed it on a serviceable side bureau. "Any noble ladies?" I asked, feigning mild interest.

"A marquess's sister and a viscount's daughter. Not that you'd ever know it now."

Dear heaven, what did that mean?

Beside me, Lord Evan stiffened, his attention swinging from Tilda to his portmanteau. From the fierce fix of his eyes, he was a second away from wrenching the firearm from the bag and storming his way to his sister. No plan, no idea where she was, and every chance of being stopped and restrained by the attendants.

I grabbed the back of his arm and dug in my nails. It was enough to pull him from his mad intent. He drew a breath, passing his hand over his face.

"Are you all right, Mr. Allen?" Tilda asked. "You came over all pale-like."

"He is quite well," I said. "We have just not eaten in a while. All the traveling, you see."

"I'll ask Mrs. Carroll to have something waiting for you here." She bobbed a curtsy and stepped back out into the corridor, a very clear prompt for us to follow her to Mr. Judd.

Tilda knocked on Mr. Judd's door.

"Come," a gruff voice called.

She opened the door and stood back, her cheerful manner replaced by tense attention.

I followed Lord Evan into the study, hearing the soft click of the door as Tilda closed it behind us.

All we needed to do now was to convince Mr. Judd that we were Mr. and Mrs. Allen—porter and matron by trade—and claim our right to see the inmates.

Judd sat at his desk, perusing a ledger, and did not look up as we entered. Nor did he acknowledge us as we stood in front of the desk, like two recalcitrant children.

Lord Evan glanced at me, a flick of one brow echoing my own thought: *A ploy to intimidate us.* Mr. Judd was clearly a man who enjoyed power.

The room was opulent in comparison to what I had so far seen of the house. The walls were paneled halfway up in oak and then papered in a handsome burgundy-and-cream stripe to the ceiling. The rug under our feet was thick and almost new, and the desk we stood before was a mahogany Chesterfield—I had seen it in the innovative catalog Mr. Chesterfield had created to order his designs. The desktop was neat, with only the ledger and a handsome silver pen, inkpot, and sander arranged in a neat line.

Finally, Judd sat back in his desk chair and considered us, his head tilted to one side. Older than I'd expected—at least fifty—but with an animal vitality that showed itself in the constant rubbing of his thumb across his fingers and a keen, almost predatory look within his small, red-rimmed eyes. I felt them flick over my body from head to toe and then heard a small sniff of dismissal.

"Well now, Mr. Allen, I thought you would be here two days past," he said to Lord Evan with an insincere smile that flashed yellowed teeth.

It seemed we were, indeed, to be chastised children.

"It was my fault, Mr. Judd. I was delayed in my travel," I said.

His gaze returned to me. "I was not speaking to you, Mrs. Allen." He turned his body in the chair toward Lord Evan. "Do you often let your wife speak for you, Mr. Allen?"

"No, sir. She forgets herself sometimes." He dropped his voice into a savage hiss. "Keep your tongue still, woman. No one wants to hear from you."

Even though I knew Lord Evan was playing his role, the echo of my brother's words hunched my shoulders.

"You will not be paid for those days missed," Judd said, chin jutting belligerently. "I'll start your year from today."

Lord Evan ducked his head. "Yes, sir."

"Bothwell House runs as I want it to, and I expect you to learn its ways quickly." Judd tapped a leather-bound book. "This is the ledger of inmates: we have twenty-two at present. It also notes the regimes ordered by Dr. Horby. He comes once a fortnight unless there is some urgent matter."

We both stared at the ledger in Judd's stubby hands; here was the information we craved.

"I will read it to you once, Mrs. Allen," Judd continued. "I hope your memory is good, because I do not want you to be bothering me for the information again."

For a moment I was perplexed. "Am I not allowed to read the ledger, sir?" I asked.

"Read it?" He scoffed. "Are you telling me you can read?"

"Yes, sir." A small devil prompted me to add, "And tally."

His eyes narrowed. "How could you come by such an education?"

A good question and one for which I did not have an answer. Swift retribution for my hubris.

Luckily Lord Evan was thinking more quickly. "My wife was a lady's maid before we married, sir."

I glanced at him, glad in this instance for a man to speak for me. He was, I could see, trying to avoid staring at the ledger.

"Well, you are not in a grand house now, Mrs. Allen, are you? Quite the opposite—a madhouse," he said with a curious giggle that more befitted a girl than a grown man. I managed to smile at the poor witticism. "I cannot abide a woman who thinks she is above her station." He observed me sourly. "There are a lot of medical instructions in here. I doubt you will be able to understand them by yourself."

A man who fully subscribed to the popular philosophy that women did not have the minds for education, even when presented with evidence to the contrary. Moreover, he seemed the type who would refuse anything a woman suggested simply because it came from a female mind. Which way to step to get that ledger? I decided on meek and obsequious.

"You are no doubt right, sir." I left it at that, exercising even more restraint than I had with Duffy.

He grunted and turned the book on its edge. "I will give this to you, then, for you to peruse. Mark those sections you do not understand." He picked up a set of at least ten keys on a long leather thong and handed them to me. "These allow you to enter all inmate rooms and are to be kept upon your person at all times."

He looked over to the door and called, "Tilda."

She must have been waiting directly outside, for the door opened and she curtsied.

"Show Mrs. Allen the inmates. Take Geoffrey with you." He turned to me. "He is one of our basketmen. You will have four at your bidding and four maids."

"Should I not go too?" Lord Evan asked quickly.

Judd frowned. "I do not know what your duties were in your last position, Mr. Allen, but here the porter does not deal with the inmates. We have a delivery of liquor tomorrow. You will come with me and learn the procedures."

I curtsied to Judd, risking a last look at Lord Evan.

The message was clear in his face: *Find her.*

47

A basketman, it transpired, was a very large man who controlled the inmates, moved them about the asylum, and hauled supplies in and out of the rooms.

Geoffrey seemed to take up most of the width of the hallway. He stood at my height but with formidably broad shoulders, a barrel chest, and heavy dark brows set above humorless eyes. His demeanor was one of resentment, and I had a sense that his large and grimy hands would not be overly respectful when touching an inmate. If I was a woman incarcerated in this place, I would be very afraid of Geoffrey.

He waited, one leg jiggling with impatience, in the hallway alongside Tilda for my instructions while I opened the ledger and flicked through the pages. I tried to steady my hand and slow my breathing as I searched for Hester's name. Some pages had been cut out—the stubs of paper still in evidence—and a few had a line through them with a date of release.

"I would like to begin with the noblewomen," I said, stalling for time. "They are kept in here, is that correct?"

"We call 'em the housers," Tilda said with a nod. "Them and the rich ones whose family have paid for the better rooms."

Names flashed past at the top of the pages: Kelly, Barnard,

Stamford, Callister. Ah. There it was: Lady Hester Belford. She was here. She was alive.

I ran my finger down the neatly written page, reading rapidly. Fits of anger. Violence. Refusal to eat. Melancholic mutism and Imm. What was *Imm*? And the remedies: cold baths, force-feeding, leeching, cupping, and something called caustic blistering. Dear God.

"This one first," I said, tapping the page. At least my voice did not tremble. "Lady Hester."

"She's in with Lady Roberta," Tilda said, leading the way to the servants' staircase at the back of the house.

Geoffrey fell in behind me and I had the uncomfortable sensation of someone a little too close and staring at my nape as we climbed the steps.

I glanced down at the page again. *Imm*—what did that mean?

The staircase took us up into a long hallway that mirrored the one below but was brighter from the afternoon light coming through the tall oriel window that I had seen from the outside. Like my own bay window at Duffield House, this one also had a box seat built in that followed its curve beyond the wall line. The air held a strong smell of boiled cabbage and old piss. I counted at least four doorways ahead, the house doors replaced by sturdier cell doors with small inspection hatches set at eye height.

Tilda led the way toward the front of the house. "They used to be bedrooms and dressing rooms," she said, waving a hand at one pair of cell doors set close together. "But they were walled off to fit more housers in. They pay more, you see."

As we approached the oriel window, I saw two figures outside in the forecourt. Mr. Judd and Lord Evan, in disagreement, it seemed, from the agitated waving of Judd's arms in the direction of the stables.

"This is Lady Hester's room." Tilda stopped at the last doorway on our left.

I had carried on a few steps to the window to see what was happening below and leaned over, my knees pressed against the bench seat. The top was hinged, like my Duffield House seat, for storage underneath. A place, perhaps, to conceal any tools of escape we might need.

The first-story height gave me a good view of Judd's balding pate and Lord Evan's thick dark hair. Whatever had excited Judd now seemed to be concluded, for he waved Lord Evan onward, the gesture an irritated flick of his hand. I suspected Lord Evan had asked about the stable inmates.

"Mrs. Allen?" Tilda prompted. I turned. "They are all locked," she added, looking at me expectantly.

Ah, the keys. I found the end of the leather thong around my neck and gathered up the keys in a jangling chime. "Which one?" I held them up. "Is there a way to tell?"

Tilda pointed to four keys on a small secondary leather loop. "Those are for up here. The others are outside. And the long one by itself is the skeleton key for the shackles."

Shackles. Good God.

After two tries, the third key on the upstairs loop was the right one. I turned it in the lock and opened the door.

The smell was the first thing I registered: an overwhelming stench of piss and feces, just like the prison room in the brothel. There was no covering upon the window, and the late afternoon light showed two beds with a figure in each, flat on their backs. The woman farthest from me lifted her head from the mattress, her head shaved. Hester?

"You better stay outside," Tilda said, stepping into Geoffrey's path. "You know how Lady Roberta gets round men." At my look of inquiry, she added, "She gets screamy."

"I don't do what you say, Tilda Wilson," Geoffrey said, his tone as nasty as the expression on his face.

"But you'll do what I say," I said firmly. "Wait outside. I will call you if we need you."

For a second I thought he was going to disobey—his mouth bunching into tight rebellion—but I drew myself up into full Lady Augusta. He stepped back. Sometimes my height and barely concealed fury were an advantage.

With one last breath of reasonably clear air, I entered the room, Tilda close behind me. I heard the door shut, but I was transfixed at the sight before me. Both women were lying in their own soil, their filthy nightgowns bunched around their nethers so that their pale legs—marred by bruises and sores—were visible. Their ankles were shackled to the end bedposts, the skin red-raw from lacerations.

The shaved-head woman whimpered at our intrusion; the other stared fixedly at the ceiling in a way that I instinctively knew was wrong. I clenched my hands, trying to control the visceral horror that made me want to run from the room. A matron would have seen this over and over—she would not want to cry with pity.

"Who is who?" I asked, my tone cold and brusque. It was the only way I could force my way past the horror lodged in my throat.

Tilda pointed to the alert woman. "That is Lady Roberta. The other is Lady Hester. She don't move much."

Imm. Dear God, Hester was *immobile.* How were we going to get her out if she could not walk?

I went to Lady Roberta first, for I could not escape the desperation in the woman's dark eyes. "Hello, Lady Roberta," I said.

She observed me for a startled moment, then struggled up onto her elbows. "Hello," she replied, her voice hoarse. Her manner did not seem mad at all.

"I am Mrs. Allen, the new matron. We will get you clean again."

Lady Roberta fell back upon the filthy mattress. She watched me, her eyes wary, as I crossed to the other bed and squatted down beside it.

Lady Hester Belford was emaciated. All the bones in her face were pronounced, the proud Belford nose overlarge against hollowed cheeks and sunken temples. I leaned closer and listened. At least her breathing was smooth, no dangerous rattle. I touched her hand—freezing cold, the skin dry. Neither she nor Lady Roberta had any covering for warmth or comfort. I twitched the filthy nightgown down over her thighs. Her ankles had a wide band of raw skin circling them from the shackles, a band of scabs showing a once higher placement of the irons. I gathered up her bone-thin fingers and held her hand.

"Lady Hester," I said. "Lady Hester, can you hear me?"

No response, not even a flicker of eyelids fringed with dark lashes the same deep brown as her roughly cropped hair. She was in some kind of deep fugue.

I looked across at Tilda, trying to control my fury. "Are they shackled all the time to the bed?"

"Mr. Judd says they have to be 'cept for a few hours if one of the basketmen can be spared to watch 'em. If they can move, that is, poor souls," Tilda said, looking with pity at Lady Hester. "We change the bedding and wash 'em every second day."

"And they have no way of relieving themselves except in the bed?" It was this outrage, perhaps, that infuriated me the most. To make a woman soil herself every day and lie in it. "Are they all kept like this?"

She drew back at my tone, hands bunched against her chest.

"Yes, ma'am. All fourteen housers. Well, 'cept for the one—" She stopped.

"Except for the one, what?"

She looked over her shoulder at the closed door and dropped her voice into a whisper. "Mr. Judd has his favorites now and again. Miss Tollbrook is in the next room. We keep her clean and she's shackled on a chain."

"I see." I felt my gorge rise. Poor Miss Tollbrook. "What about those in the stables?"

"Them got no one paying their way, so Mr. Judd just leaves 'em there. They get food once a day, or at least most days, and Mary and I try and get in there once or twice a month to clean it out, truly, but he don't like us wasting our time."

I pressed my fingers against my eyes, trying to comprehend such treatment of fellow human beings. No, I could not, it was inconceivable. However, I had the will and the position to make things better. And, by all that was merciful, we would start immediately. I was matron, after all.

I drew up the keys, sorting through them until I came to one—longer and shaped more smoothly—than the others. "Is this for the irons?"

Tilda peered at it, then nodded.

"Firstly, I want the rooms in the house to be cleaned, the women washed—with warm water, not cold—and the linens changed."

"Today?" Tilda asked, wide-eyed.

"Yes, today. And, secondly, I want you to show me the stables."

I knelt beside Hester's feet and slid the key into the shackle lock. I tried to turn it, but it was stiff—clogged, no doubt, by blood and skin. After two more hard turns, it gave way with a dull click. I opened the cruel restraint, then gently pulled them free from her lacerated ankles.

"Mr. Judd ain't gonna like that," Tilda whispered.

Mr. Judd was lucky that it was I who had found Hester, and not Lord Evan. Otherwise he might have found himself at the end of a pistol barrel. A just response to such cruelty, perhaps, but one that would not help Hester's, or indeed Lord Evan's, cause.

48

Tilda and I dispatched the other maids and basketmen to their cleaning duties, chivvying those who had anticipated a more indolent late afternoon and evening. Once all was in motion, Tilda led the way to the stables, the daylight already slanting low and lengthening our shadows across the gravel. My fob watch told me it was close to five p.m.—we only had an hour or so before sunset.

"Who is in there?" I asked, opening the ledger. "How many?"

"Eight. I don't know all their names," Tilda confessed, ducking her head. "There's a Penelope. She's been 'ere at Bothwell the longest and can be a bit violent. And Black Sally, poor soul. And Anna, too, she's a Friend, she says, you know from that society."

"A Friend. Do you mean a Quaker?"

"That's right."

How did a Quaker end up in such a place? The Society of Friends were known to take particular care of their distressed members, especially after the dreadful death of Mrs. Mills in the York asylum, twenty or so years ago.

"Let us look inside, then, and see who is who." No use looking at the ledger yet. I placed it on a barrel beside the stable door and sorted through the keys.

Tilda pointed to the correct one. "You should stand back," she said as I inserted the key into the lock.

I opened one side of the large double doors, but I was not ready for what was inside. The wall of ammoniac air that hit my face sent me into a paroxysm of coughing and gagging, my eyes watering into a painful blear. I staggered back a step.

"Best to let the place air out a bit 'fore we go in," Tilda said.

"There is no wailing, like before," I managed. Were they all dead?

Tilda wiped her own streaming eyes on her sleeve. "Not when we open the door. They think they're gonna be fed and if they set up a fuss sometimes the basketmen don't give it to 'em."

Inside, some light came through the two barred windows set opposite each other. I made out heaps of straw alongside each wall with figures curled in them and, at the far end, a stall that had been left intact. A series of wooden planks had been laid on the front pitching floor in a zigzagging path, like those on muddy streets. I dragged the door open wider, holding my breath, and saw why: the floor was ankle deep in excrement.

I did not want to step into the place, but it had to be done. For the sake of the women inside. I picked up my skirts and stepped gingerly onto the first wooden plank. It sank a little into the stinking filth but did not slip. Keeping my breaths shallow, I trod along the narrow wood and headed into the dim, cool building.

The first inmate—a Black woman—was half-naked, only a ragged towel gown around her nethers. As my streaming eyes adjusted to the gloom, I saw her face. Good God, she was old, the hand, shielding her eyes from the influx of light from the doorway, wizened and clawlike. Her whole body was covered in excrement, from head to foot. At my attention she burrowed farther into the stinking mound of straw that was clearly her bed, the shift of her leg slapping a chain in the muck. I followed its crusted length to a ring in the stable wall.

I looked to the next filthy half-naked woman—an even older white woman—a few yards away. Another ring, another chain. They were all chained to the wall.

I turned and took three stumbling steps out again, the plank sinking deeper under my haste. I just made it to the corner of the stable before I heaved. Sour bile and vomit hit the gravel. I heaved again, all my horror and pity and disgust wracking my body.

Finally, I stopped vomiting, my chest aching from the deep retching and the fury that burned my innards.

"Oh no, Mr. Judd is comin'," I heard Tilda say behind me.

I turned to see the man stalking across the forecourt, every step sending a spray of gravel. "Mrs. Allen, what are you doing?" he yelled, face ballooning with rage. "I did not authorize this!"

I spat my mouth free of vomit and straightened to meet him. This time there would be no obsequious woman. No *yes, sir, no, sir.* Even so, I had to tread carefully. I had to get those women out of that foul place.

"Mr. Judd," I said and crossed the yard or so between us, planting myself in the gravel in front of him. He stepped back, clearly unused to a furious five-foot-nine woman looming over him. "The conditions in that stable are deplorable. Horses are kept better than these women. You should be ashamed."

He stared at me, taken aback by the attack. Still, he wore that male armor made of God-given superiority and quickly rallied. "They are paupers and they are mad." He thrust his face an inch from mine. "They are lucky to get a meal and a roof over their head."

Lucky? For a second, his red, blotchy face blurred with my rage. I drew in a breath, the cool evening air stinging my retch-raw throat and chest. These women were not even human to him. This man would not be moved by pity or shame. He had neither. I had to find another route. Something that would threaten him and the lucrative fiefdom he had created for himself.

A wild idea sprang forward. Most of the newspapers were currently reporting upon the appalling conditions at many of the madhouses and the criminal abuses by the keepers. A gamble, but I had to take it.

"That may be so," I said through my teeth, "but I happen to know that Bothwell House is scheduled to be inspected next month. Not by the local inspectors but by those in the reform movement. You will lose your license if they see the current state of this place."

"What?" Judd eyed me, ready to dismiss such a claim, but I had found a chink in that armor. "How could you know that?"

A rapid crunch of gravel turned us both. Lord Evan, striding toward us.

"My wife has a cousin who works for the county clerk," he said, coming to stand beside me. A united front. "Let her do her work, Mr. Judd, and you will retain your license."

"We will just not show them the stables."

"That did not work at Carter House in Bristol," I said, clawing up the name of a failed asylum from the recesses of my memory. "The inspectors demanded to see all areas and the asylum was closed, the keeper imprisoned."

Judd's jaw shifted. How he hated to be beholden to a woman. "Is that true?" he asked Lord Evan.

"It is, sir."

"Do just enough to get us through, then," Judd said, with a dismissive lift of his chin at the stables. "I do not want to spend an unnecessary penny on them."

He turned and walked up the front steps of the house. With

one last look at us, he opened the front door and disappeared inside, slamming it behind him.

"Have you found Hester?" Lord Evan asked in a low voice. "She is not in there, is she?" He stared into the dark, stinking stable.

"No, she is in the house. She's alive," I whispered.

Not the whole truth, but I doubted a loving brother would be able to contain his reaction to what I was about to say. I took his arm and led him farther away, out of Tilda's earshot.

"What is it?" he asked as we walked. "Something bad. I can see it in your face."

"Hester is in a fugue. I could not reach her and she has not eaten for some time. She is very weak."

"They have starved her?" Lord Evan's hands clenched, his body shifting forward into battle readiness. He turned with intent toward the front door, through which Judd had retreated.

"No!" I clasped his fists, pushing them down. "You must not confront him. Not yet. Too many lives are at stake."

He stared unseeingly at me, lost in his rage.

I leaned close to his face, filling his vision. "Lord Evan! Not yet. You will ruin everything. Listen to me!"

I saw the shift in his eyes—a return to sanity. He drew in a shaking breath. "Not yet," he ground out. "But he must pay." He looked at the windows above us. "I must go to see her now!"

"No, I beg you to wait for that too," I said. "Her roommate, Lady Roberta, does not abide men. We must go together so I can calm her in your presence."

And we must go together because what he would see would shatter him. I could not imagine seeing Julia in such a state. He must not go alone to see Hester.

"I will not wait any longer. It has been twenty years since she has had a brother she can rely upon. That is long enough."

"Please, do this for me," I pleaded. "Do it for the other women here. We will go to Hester as soon as possible."

He closed his eyes, clearly caught between rage, guilt, and reason. And this time I did not know which way he would step.

"I will wait," he finally said.

49

It was dusk by the time we had unshackled the eight old women inside the stables and helped them out onto the grass beside the building. I spoke to the woman they called Black Sally, her true name Sally Bright, who had been committed by a clergyman after she violently fought off his advances. And the Quaker woman, Anne; she hardly remembered how she had come to this place, only that she had woken up from a fit of some kind to find herself incarcerated and with no one willing to listen.

Up on the portico, Mr. Judd watched the proceedings with arms crossed—the king observing his kingdom. Did he hear the whimpers of these women, frightened by sudden change, or their sobs of pain when they stood upon limbs so unused to carrying their weight?

I retrieved the last woman from the stable. She had been chained inside a stall right at the very back and clung to my arm with a hearteningly strong grip as I slowly led her across the slippery planks to fresh air and the makeshift washing area.

I eased the emaciated woman down onto the grass to wait for one of the maids. Like the other women, she wore only a decrepit towel gown stiff with filth that barely covered her bony body. Old white scars—some in perfect circles, some long straight lines—showed through the dirt. A map of failed madhouse cures.

"By my count, we should be almost done," Tilda said, passing me a damp cloth to wipe my own hands and arms.

"Yes, this is the last one," I said. "She was right at the very back."

Tilda looked down at the woman on the grass. "That is Penelope. Be careful, she don't look like it, but she can plant a good facer. She broke one of Geoffrey's teeth, you know. Mary is almost free; she can clean her."

She raised her hand to catch the attention of one of the maids across the grass who was wringing out her cloth over a bucket, her nose wrinkled in disgust. Indeed, the stench of excrement was still strong. The women really needed baths, but that would be a task for tomorrow.

"Ah, she does not see me," Tilda said. "Wait, I'll get her."

As Tilda went to fetch Mary, I took a moment to wipe myself free of the muck and catch my own breath. The next challenge was to find enough space for the women to sleep in the house. Lord Evan was overseeing that rearrangement of beds within the larger rooms—a task I hoped would direct the energy of his fury.

I wiped my hands on the rag. The old woman on the grass looked up at me, blinking large blue eyes within a skeletal face framed by lank hair. She seemed peaceable enough, no imminent violence in her demeanor. I stopped wiping. Something seemed oddly familiar within that devastated countenance.

She suddenly smiled, a stretch of dry, cracked lips across rotten teeth.

"Lady Augusta." Although seated, she ducked as if curtsying. "'Pon my soul, it is you! 'Tis a sad crush tonight, is it not?" She peered around at the silhouetted figures of the other women upon the grass and the attendants beside them. "Where is your sister? Is Lady Julia dancing already?"

That voice, thin and whispery, cast me back twenty years into the ballrooms of my youth. I stared at the old woman before me, her shriveled features shifting in my mind to a younger face. Merciful heaven, surely not.

"Miss Wardrup?" I crouched beside her. "Are you Penelope Wardrup?"

She smiled again. "Yes? What is it?"

I pressed my hand to my chest, unable to take a full breath. Was this truly Penelope Wardrup, the girl who had been presented at court with Julia and me? Who had stabbed her brother twenty years ago? We had all thought she had been sent to India to marry a Company man. Instead, she had been sent to Bothwell House to be locked away forever. Twenty years buried in this forsaken place.

"I do not have many dances tonight," she said. I saw her eyes fix upon Judd standing on the portico. She shrank back. "Careful, Lady Augusta, he is a Dark Walk." She grabbed my forearm in that strong grip, her eyes finding mine. "He is a Dark Walk. You must warn your sister too."

I looked over at Mr. Judd. A Dark Walk: our girlish code for a dangerous man. A man who would take advantage at every opportunity. An apt description.

I pressed her hand. "I understand. He is a Dark Walk."

"He took my babies," she whispered.

Babies? The word brought a crawl across my scalp. How could she have babies? She was unmarried and secured in a madhouse.

"What do you mean?" I swallowed, my mouth bone-dry. "You have borne babies?"

"Two." Her grip tightened, her voice dropping into a hiss. "Do not tell. You must not tell."

"I will not," I said.

"Promise." That grip, so tight. So desperate. "Promise upon God."

"I promise." I closed my eyes for a second, trying to push past a lifetime of rigid courtesy—of preached judgment—to ask the unaskable. "Whose babies, Miss Wardrup? Who fathered them?"

"Oliver, but no one knows." She held her forefinger to her cracked lips. "Shh. Him . . ." She nodded toward Mr. Judd. "He said I was pretty."

Oliver? But Mr. Judd's name was Horace. Oh, now I remembered. My gut lurched, tightening into sick certainty. Oliver was her brother. The one she had stabbed.

I drew a shaking breath. "Oliver, your brother? And Mr. Judd?"

She nodded, raising her forefinger to her lips again.

"Do you know where the babies are?"

She raised her head, her chin lifting toward a stand of seven or so oak trees at the border of the asylum's land. "First 'twas a monster, he said. And t'other still."

I followed her gaze to the trees. "They are there?"

"He showed me."

Dead. Rest their souls. And buried so near her in the stables. A constant torment to her poor mind.

I looked across at Judd standing on the portico. Yes, he would be capable of such cruelty. Then again, perhaps none of it was true. A delusion from a mad mind.

I looked down at the hand clasped around my wrist. At the blue eyes that still held a remnant of the young girl, and the truth of loss. No, this was no delusion.

A figure approached: one of the maids with a bucket of fresh water. "Shall I wash her now, Mrs. Allen?" she asked.

"Yes, please do. And her name is Miss Wardrup."

I gently disengaged Penelope's cold fingers from my arm and stood, looking over at the stand of oaks. The soft purples of dusk had darkened into the inks of evening. The trees stood outlined against the night sky, silent and still. Too late now to search for the terrible truth.

Tomorrow, then.

Tomorrow, I would search for Penelope's babies.

50

Lord Evan and I stood outside Hester's room, listening to the sounds of the slumbering house. Cries and murmurs and the occasional snore. It was near midnight, an hour since we had finally settled the eight old women into beds and calmed the rest of the inmates. Everyone who had toiled to rescue the stable women, from the youngest kitchen maid to Lord Evan and myself, was exhausted. Yet he and I had one more thing to do before we could rest.

"Hold the candle up," I whispered.

He lifted the cheap taper in its iron holder. In the small glow, I found the lock and slid in the key.

"I'll go in first and speak to Lady Roberta." The last thing we needed was the poor woman to start screaming at the sight of a man and wake the house again. I had read the notes about her in the ledger: melancholia. She had been here for a year and the list of "medical interventions" had been brutal reading.

"Be swift," he whispered. Although he stood a few inches from me, I could feel the tension in his body.

I took the taper from him and gave a reassuring smile. What he was about to see would break his heart and I could do nothing about it. And that broke my heart.

Inside, the soft light from the moon cast the two beds and their inhabitants into gray shapes. During the reorganization of the rooms,

I had purposely kept Lady Hester and Lady Roberta by themselves. In deference to their rank, I had said, but in truth it had been for this moment.

At my entrance and the intrusion of candlelight, Lady Roberta sat up upon her bed. Lady Hester, in the first bed, did not move, of course, but I saw that her poor ankles were no longer shackled and her bedding and nightgown were clean. The chamber pot I had insisted upon stood in the far corner.

As I approached, Lady Roberta drew her legs under her body, watching me.

"Lady Roberta. How are you?"

She looked down at the clean linen. "Thank you. I am much restored. I hear that you have done the same for everyone else. Even the poor souls in the stables."

An entirely lucid response.

"Yes." I sat on the end of the bed and patted the clean sheets. "As you see, I keep my word. I am here to tell you that a man is about to enter the room." Her hand clenched into the bedclothes. "You have my word he is no threat to you. He is my husband and Lady Hester's brother. He wishes only to see her. I will stay with you throughout. Do you think you can contain your fear?"

"My fear is only of Mr. Judd and the basketmen," she whispered. She tilted her head, the candlelight deepening the shadows of exhaustion and ill use under her eyes. "If your husband is Lady Hester's brother, Mrs. Allen, then surely he is a nobleman, and you a noblewoman."

Yes, entirely lucid.

"That is a long story," I said. "For now, we are Mr. and Mrs. Allen. May I bring him in?"

She looked over at her inanimate room companion. "She could

not get over the betrayal of her brother. The way he tricked her and brought her here."

"That was Lord Deele. This is a different brother," I said swiftly. Very different.

Lady Roberta nodded. "Yes. She spoke of her other brother. Perhaps he will help. She has not always been like this. Just the last month or so. She stopped eating."

By the light of the taper I crossed to the door and opened it, stepping aside for Lord Evan to enter.

He stood for a second upon the threshold, taking in the bare room and the faint smell of excrement still within it.

"The first bed," I whispered, although I was sure he needed no direction.

He stepped in. I peered up the corridor to see if our activity had roused anyone—no movement, just soft darkness and the mutterings of troubled sleep. I closed the door.

When I turned, Lord Evan had kneeled beside Hester's bed and taken her hand. He pressed a kiss upon the limp palm.

"Hester," he said. "Dear girl, it is Evan. I am back."

Her face remained still, the only movement the slight shift of her chest up and down in breath. Was she too far gone?

Lord Evan bent closer until his forehead was an inch from hers, their profiles in the candlelight so alike; that strong Belford nose and stubborn chin. He brought her hand up and laid it upon his chest, perhaps hoping that the beat of his heart might reach her own.

"Hessie?"

I walked over to them, holding up the taper. On the other bed, Lady Roberta watched with the same intensity as I did.

"It is Evan," he said. "Try, Hessie. Please, try."

Nothing. Her face remained as still and blank as a marble statue.

"Hold her," Lady Roberta said, swinging her feet to the ground, the lacerations from the shackles dark rings around her ankles. She stood, somewhat shakily, and shuffled over to me. "We are touched only with indifference or violence here. Hold her with love."

Lord Evan looked up at me. I nodded. It was worth trying.

He sat upon the bed and with infinite tenderness gathered up his sister in his arms, cradling her against his chest.

"We are here to take you home, Hester," Lord Evan said. "We will take you back to Elizabeth. She is waiting for you. Elizabeth is waiting for you."

I touched the claddagh ring upon my finger. Given to Julia with love. And blessed, Julia had said. If bare, wordless hope was a prayer, then I prayed, as much for Lord Evan as for Hester.

Perhaps it was the name of her beloved, or perhaps it was Lord Evan's hold, but her eyelids fluttered. She opened her eyes. Dulled and unfocused. For a second, she looked unseeing into his face. I leaned forward—was she too damaged?

"Evan?" she said, her voice whispery thin.

"Hester. Thank God." He pulled her against his chest in a close embrace. Such joy in his voice. Such relief.

He looked up at me, seeking me out to share the moment, and that made me smile almost as much as my joy in Hester's return to her wits.

"We are here to take you home," Lord Evan said again.

"You are here to rescue her," Lady Roberta said, beside me, her voice strangely flat.

"Yes."

She grabbed my arm, the sudden action wrenching me off-balance so that I nearly dropped the candlestick in my other hand. The taper flame stuttered, our shadows shivering across the walls.

"Take me with you, please," she pleaded. "When you go, everything will return to what it was. He does not allow any visitors. We are abandoned. Please do not leave me here."

Her grasp was so tight, so painful, that in reflex I tried to pull free.

She collapsed onto her knees, her face raised in supplication. "I beg you, please. I can help. I will do anything. Please."

Lord Evan half rose, as if to help, but he was still holding Hester. I shook my head—I felt no threat. Besides, what she said was true. When we left, all the cruelty and indignity would return. I had not thought beyond rectifying what was immediately before me, but this was not a wife rescued from a murderous husband, or four children retrieved from an unlawful abduction. This was an asylum full of women, committed by law, some of them incarcerated for more than twenty years. I could not rescue one and leave all the others to endure Judd's rule. But how to save them all? It seemed an impossible task.

"Lady Roberta, we will take you with us. Please, stand up. You do not need to beg."

"We will?" Lord Evan said.

"I think we must," I said.

Lady Roberta looked up at me, the hope within her eyes clenching my heart. "Your word. Give me your word."

"You have my word," I said. "When we go—and it will be soon—we will take you with us."

51

Back in our rooms, Lord Evan stood by the parlor table, staring down at the cold pasty and congealed gravy and potatoes that were the remains of our supper. Tilda had brought us the meal in between the arrangement of inmates, but we had barely had a chance to eat any of it.

He broke off a piece of the pastry, studied it, then put it back upon the plate. "I am too tired to eat," he said.

"I am as well." I looked across at the corner of the bed in view through the doorway. For all my exhaustion, I felt an unsettling buzz through my body. "We need to sleep. Tomorrow promises to be as difficult as today."

He turned his head, following the direction of my gaze. "You take the bed. I will sleep on the floor. I am used to it."

An excellent and honorable solution, yet I found myself saying, "Surely it will look suspicious when the maid comes in to make the fire. To see you upon the floor."

"We will have had a marital disagreement," he said lightly.

I shook my head. "I do not want to have a marital disagreement."

He looked at the bed again. "What do you want?" Such a direct question. And said with such gentle intensity.

I looked across at the face that was now so beloved, at the broadness of shoulder and muscular length of arm and thigh, at the natural grace and enduring strength built by hard labor. What did I want? Strangely, not the carnal act, although certainly my body had awakened to that idea; but this was not the time or place for such beginnings. We were both exhausted. But, more importantly, he was leaving, and I must—as Julia had implored—protect my heart. No, I just wanted the small intimacy of lying side by side in the dark. To hear his breathing match my own. Something to remember.

"To be together, that is all."

He smiled. "That, I can provide." He gave a courtly bow, the graceful honor a silent promise. I was safe. But I knew that, anyway.

The bedchamber was a sparsely decorated room: white walls, a window with a thin curtain, the bed, and two small, roughly made tables at each side. A small cross hung above the wooden bedhead. An ironic addition, for surely any god had abandoned Bothwell House.

"Which side would you prefer?" Lord Evan asked from behind me.

Merciful heaven, I had no idea. I usually slept star style in the middle.

I cleared my throat. "The right." When in doubt, make a decision. Any decision.

I placed the taper down upon the right-side table, careful not to be seen watching him as he moved to the other side. Had I noticed before how smoothly and silently he walked? No excess movement, no ungainly arms, no clatter of bootheels upon the bare wooden boards.

A thick patched velvet overlay covered the bed. I pulled it back. The sheets, in the taper light, were a great deal grayer than I would have liked. I touched the slubbed linen, rough and cold. "A little damp, I think."

"Upon the cover, then," he said.

I sat on the lumpy mattress and unlaced my boots. On the other side, Lord Evan worked off his own boots. An oddly domestic moment.

Feet free, I considered my stays. No, that would mean my dress and chemise off, a number of steps too far. I swung my feet up onto the bed and, twisting around, shook out the meager pillow. Something to do as I accustomed myself to his presence.

Lord Evan took off his waistcoat, deftly threw it upon the chair set against the wall, then swung his own stockinged feet up onto the bed.

We both lay down at the same time, the synchronicity making me huff a nervous laugh.

He looked across at me, smiling. Our hands were an inch from each other. As if by silent agreement, we both moved until our little fingers touched, like they had in the dog cart. I drew a breath—how could such contentment and agitation burst through me at once? I glanced sidelong at him, not quite able to look him in the eye.

"Are you comfortable?" he asked.

If comfortable meant every nerve in my body alight with the sense of him beside me, then yes, I was comfortable.

"I know we were to come in here, find Hester, and leave," I said slowly, "but I could not leave these women in such a state. I had to at least clean them. Give them some dignity."

"I understand. Did you know he does not allow anyone to visit, on the pretext that it would disturb recovery? And the caustic blistering. Dear God. I have seen a lot of brutality in my life, Lady Augusta, but this place is . . ." He gave a small shake of his head.

"Augusta," I said.

He turned his head on the pillow, a furrow between his brows.

"Please, call me Augusta. Or even just Gus." My heart beat absurdly hard. Only Julia called me Gus. Would he think me vulgar for offering such familiarity?

"Ah." His mouth turned up at the corner. "Then you must call me Evan."

I smiled. *Evan.*

"As I said, I do understand," he said, returning to business, "but I want to get Hester out of here tomorrow. I cannot bear to think of her up there now, behind a locked door. So debilitated and at the mercy of these interventions."

"It is hard, I know, but she has hope now." I hesitated, wondering how to say the next. "I do not think tomorrow is possible, Evan." Using his bare name felt both precious and awkward. "She cannot walk by herself and we do not have the transportation for her until Julia gets here."

"I will take her," he said. "Steal a horse and ride out."

I turned my head to look him in the eye. "Where to? It would have to be on the run with you since you are an escaped convict and she an escapee from a madhouse. She would not survive it. Hester needs careful medical attention and rest. She must be taken out of here legitimately, or at least with the appearance of legitimacy."

He looked up at the ceiling, the muscles in his jaw clenching. I knew my reasoning went against every brotherly feeling in his body. A sigh finally acknowledged the truth of it.

"Do you have a plan?" He rolled his head upon his pillow to look across at me—dark hair askew—and smiled wryly. "Of course you have a plan."

"Your brother has mandated that only he and his wife can visit Hester. I doubt very much that Judd would know what Lady Deele looks like. I will send a note to Julia and tell her to come as Lady Deele."

He considered the idea. "That could work. As porter, it is up to me who gets in and out, and in this case a visitor will be allowed. When is she due in Lynn?"

"The day after tomorrow. I will send a letter back with Mrs. Cullers, the publican's wife. She comes tomorrow with her husband to deliver the liquor."

"Can she be trusted?"

"She does not like this place and offered help if I ever needed it. I think we must trust her. Will you secure me some paper and ink?"

"Of course. There are plenty in the porter's office."

I rolled onto my side, crooked my elbow, and propped my head against my hand. The gravity of what I had to say next required a more upright world. "You heard me promise Lady Roberta that we would take her?"

He rolled onto his side, mirroring my position. "I did. While I agree with the sentiment, it is going to be difficult."

"I am not going to leave until I find a way to improve the lot of all the women in here."

He frowned. "Is that even possible?"

"I do not know, but I must try. I think Judd has stepped well over the line between medical interventions and murder."

Briefly, I told him about my encounter with Penelope Wardrup.

"If what Miss Wardrup says is true," I concluded, "then Judd could be removed. The county cannot allow a murderer to run a madhouse. I am going to the oak trees at dawn to search for her babies. Will you help?"

"Of course. You know I will always help you."

He looked at me with such intensity that, for a heart-pounding second, it seemed as if the space between us contracted. Nothing seen or heard but the curve of his mouth and the quickened rhythm of his breathing. Had I leaned forward? Had he? Then I heard his breath release, as if a decision had been made.

I blinked, the space between us unchanged. Or perhaps regained.

"If we are to be digging in the dirt at sunrise, then let us have a few hours' sleep," he said, but his voice was not quite as smooth as before. He settled down onto his back again.

Sleep? I doubted I would be able to do so now. Still, if I did manage to find my way to slumber, it would be hard to rise after so little rest. I swung my legs to the ground, rising enough from the bed to draw back the curtains. Hopefully the dawn light would wake us.

I blew out the taper and settled back upon the bed. For a second or two the room was pitch-dark; then my eyes adjusted. The crescent moon allowed enough light to shape the edges of the bed and tables into gray shadows and Evan's face into silvery contours. His eyes were already closed, his breathing regular. A man who had learned to embrace sleep whenever it was available.

I carefully lay back down and watched the rise and fall of his chest, the flicker of his eyelids, the easing of austere features into the softness of sleep. I committed to memory every shift and sigh, the sensation of his solid warmth so close to my body, and the comforting sound of his breath alongside mine until sleep overcame me too.

52

The dawn had almost brightened into misty morning by the time we reached the stand of oaks. A thick layer of leaves covered the ground, the vivid reds, golds, and browns coming to a soft, fiery glow in the daylight. Birds had begun to chirp and rustle among the branches above, the sound entirely too cheerful for the task ahead of us.

I rubbed my hands together, my fingertips aching in the cold autumn air. I had eschewed gloves and Tully's cloak in case they got in the way but now rued the decision.

Evan dug the shovel he had found in the gardener's shed into the ground and turned in a circle to observe the area. He'd had the sense to wear his coat and his hat. Mind you, a man's greatcoat was far more suited to digging than a woman's cloak.

"Where do we start?" he asked.

"If I were a man without principle trying to hide infanticide, where would I bury the evidence?" I asked, turning in a circle, too, dry leaves crackling under my feet. "But I cannot see an answer."

"Maybe I should just start digging. We will have to return before breakfast is brought and our absence is noted," Evan said.

It has been said that straight lines do not exist in nature. That such order is the realm of humankind. Perhaps it was that anomaly that caught my eye upon the trunk of one of the largest trees, set farthest from the house.

I walked over to the oak and crouched at its roots, breathing in the rich smell of morning-damp earth and crushed leaves beneath my boots. Carved deep into the reddish bark was the vertical line I had noted. I traced my forefinger down it, finding within the trunk's fissures the horizontal line that made the holy cross. From the weathered color of the carving, it was old.

"Here," I said. "Look."

Evan joined me, shovel in hand. "Well, someone had the decency to mark the grave," he said.

I touched the scarred wood again. "Decency or guilt?"

He shifted the shovel, pushing it into the ground. "What do you say? Here? Or a few more feet from the trunk?"

"Here," I said and shuffled back from the chosen site.

He began to dig. Shallow shovelfuls in case he hit something small and sacred. Five shovels down, we saw the first pale glimpse of bone.

Penelope had been telling the truth.

Evan stopped digging. We both crouched at the side of the grave and cleared the damp, cold dirt around the bone, pushing the earth up behind us.

A curve and then an eye socket. Not just a bone, a skull.

"Dear God," Evan said, looking up at me. "This is not a child's skull."

"No, I would wager it is a woman." Who was she? One of the missing pages in Judd's ledger? I looked around the autumn-dressed copse. "She is probably not the only one. Try there." I pointed to a spot a few feet beside the skull.

Two more digs produced only earth and fat worms. The third,

however, showed us the tiny hand bones of an infant. Curled as if holding a mother's finger. Tears sprang to my eyes. Born, only to die. No chance to live at all. Was that Judd's work? Or had nature tolled the bell? I looked across at Evan. He, too, had tears in his eyes.

"This is not a task for us," he said. "We must cover them up again and await a priest. May they rest in peace."

I stood and brushed the dirt from my hands as Evan refilled the spade and placed the earth carefully back upon the infant's bones. An idea had occurred to me as I had wept. A bold and desperate idea—built on a single encounter—but it might be a way to protect the women of Bothwell House.

I now had two letters to write.

The first letter lay on the parlor table beside the inkwell and sand, finished and affixed with a wafer. A brief missive directed to Lady Julia Colebrook with the instructions for our plan to remove Hester—and Lady Roberta—from Bothwell House, and a paragraph about my discovery of poor Penelope Wardrup.

The second letter had proved far more difficult to write, but it was finally done. I picked up the clay pot of sand and sprinkled it upon my signature—Lady Augusta Colebrook—and shook off the excess. A pity I did not have my seal for more gravitas. A wafer would have to do.

I folded the letter into a packet and wet the gummed side of the wafer, pressing it upon the open edges. There, signed, sealed, and carrying all my hope for helping the women with it. Now to wait for the arrival of Mrs. Cullers. Both plans hinged upon her agreement to deliver the letters for me.

I gathered my fob watch and checked the time. Almost nine o'clock. According to Tilda, that was the time to start the rounds.

I slipped the two letters into the front pocket of my apron and stood up from the parlor table and the remains of our breakfast. First, I must return the writing implements to Evan in the porter's office before my letter writing was noted by one of the attendants. Second, I would set Tilda to the task of feeding Lady Hester some soft bread soaked in milk. I trusted no one else to do it. And, finally, I would order all the basketmen to muck out the stables.

I smiled. That seemed a fair return for withholding food from the stables' women.

53

At midmorning, I stood in the storeroom beside the servants' hall and ran my fingers along stacks of brown paper parcels upon the shelves.

"What are these?" I asked Bertha, the maid in charge of stores.

"Them's the clothes and such the women arrived in. We wrap them and store them here until they get released or . . ."

"Die?" I finished.

She gave a quick nod. "Then Mr. Judd sells them to the clothes dealer."

"Does that happen often here?" I asked, keeping my voice casual.

Bertha shrugged. "Don't know."

Or, more likely, too scared to say.

I lifted a few of the packages, reading the labels. Three packages down I found one for Lady Hester Belford. Quite heavy.

A shout from the front of the house lifted my head from my inspection. "What is that? It is not one of the women," I said, trying to keep the anticipation from my voice.

Bertha cocked her head. "That'll be the liquor," she said, with an approving nod. "A good thing, too, since we are down to the last two kegs of small beer."

Mrs. Cullers had arrived. Finally. I pressed my hand against my apron pocket, feeling the reassuring resistance of paper.

"Start counting the blankets," I said, heading to the storeroom door. "I will be back."

I hurried down the dim corridor toward the kitchen and the clash of dinner pots. From my experience—albeit as the mistress of the house, not housekeeper—all foodstuffs would be delivered via the back courtyard.

I entered the kitchen, the reek of mutton boiling in huge pots turning my stomach. It reminded me, queasily, of the tanneries in Smithfield. The back door stood open, the Cullerses' cart, loaded with kegs and crates, visible through it. I caught sight of a portly well-dressed man—Mr. Cullers, I assumed—standing on the tray and rolling a keg onto Geoffrey's shoulders. Was Mrs. Cullers there too? I could not see a woman. All was lost if she had not come.

"Mrs. Allen!" the cook called over the clatter, wiping her hands upon her apron. "A word, please."

Reluctantly I turned to face Mrs. Carroll. Her hands were on her hips, her chin jutted forward. "Did you tell Tilda to take good bread and new milk up to one of the housers?"

"I did."

"What for? Them up there don't even taste it. The fresh is Mr. Judd's an' he won't like it wasted on 'em."

"What do you usually serve the women for their meals?"

"They get a midday dinner." She gestured to the pots of boiling meat. "Most times it's barley porridge with a bit of meat, an' hard biscuit or the old bread. Why?"

"The fresh bread and milk was for Lady Hester, who has emerged from a fugue," I said crisply. "She does not have the strength to chew upon such tough rations. Do you begrudge her nourishment?"

"It ain't me to begrudge nothing," Mrs. Carroll said. "It's Mr. Judd an' what he thinks. It's his orders you be goin' against."

"Then he can speak to me about it. As it is, I want her to have the same tonight. And indeed, every inmate to have twice-daily meals. Bread and milk for supper."

On that outrageous order, I turned and made for the door.

"You better get Mr. Judd's—"

I ignored her bellow and took the step down to the rear courtyard. Surely it stood to reason that only one meal a day—and that meager—would exacerbate a disordered mind rather than help it. In truth, all I could call upon was reason—I was no madhouse doctor or even a true matron. Moreover, I would be gone soon. Still, while I was here, I could at least try to improve the women's lot. I had not expected to feel such a sense of responsibility to madwomen, and frankly it was an uncomfortable burden. The plan had been to arrive, rescue Hester, and depart again. But what kind of person saw the degradation here and turned away from it? Not the kind of person I wished to be.

Outside, I searched the yard, my heart lifting. First, at the sight of Evan reading a bill of sale behind the cart. Then Mrs. Cullers in her squirrel-trimmed cloak and straw bonnet, watching the unloading of the kegs with a critical eye and a spectacularly ugly reticule knitted in the shape of a strawberry dangling from her arm. It was almost as atrocious as the pineapple I had knitted.

"Mrs. Cullers," I called. She turned and, upon seeing me, smiled. Yet the genial expression also held an unexpected element of urgency. Or was I projecting my own emotions upon her?

"Mrs. Allen," she said. "Well met, dearie. Do you have a minute?"

I did indeed. I slipped my hand into my apron pocket; one more reassuring check of the letters. As I reached her, she took my arm and firmly led me away from the cart toward the bathhouse, the strawberry reticule swinging frantically at the rapid pace. I looked back at Evan and saw the same wary surprise I felt: *Something is afoot.*

"I hear you and your husband are causing a stir here," she said softly, steering me around the corner of the bathhouse so that we stood out of sight.

"Where did you hear that?"

"Lester, on the gate. Lots of changes, he says. Such goings-on will be the talk of the town."

"Is that a problem?"

She looked around—clearly checking upon our solitude—her countenance set into sober lines. "Maybe. Someone has been asking around 'bout a big man with dark hair and a scar upon his cheek who may go by the name of Hargate or Belford. Reminded me of your man Allen here." She jerked her head back toward the cart and Evan.

I chewed my lip. "What did this someone look like?"

"A well-dressed fellow. Broke nose and dark curly hair cut short in the city way. Said his name was—"

"Kent," I whispered.

"Aye. You know him, then?"

Kent was in Lynn. How did he find his way so close to us?

I clutched her arm. "Did you tell him anything? Does he know where we are?"

She drew her mouth down and shook her head. "Me? I don't know anything. Nor does Mr. Cullers. Even for the shilling he offered. But we're not the only ones in town who saw your man at the hotel. Or you arrivin', for that matter." She drew back, eyeing me quizzically. "Are we bettin' on the wrong horse, here?"

I shook my head. "Definitely the right horse. Thank you for warning us." I pulled out the two letters. "Will you do something for me? For the women here? It is of the utmost importance."

She looked at the packets in my hand. "What is it you want done?"

"Lady Julia Colebrook will be coming to your hotel tonight or tomorrow. Please give her this note as soon as she arrives." I passed her the packet.

"A noblewoman?" She read Julia's name upon the front, her finger slowly following the letters. "Now, what would Mrs. Allen, matron, be doin' writing letters in such a fine hand, and to a lady, besides?"

"I cannot say. I'm sorry but I'm asking you to trust me. Please." I passed her the second packet. "This one needs to go by the first mail possible."

She squinted at the written direction. "Mr. Samuel Tuke, The Retreat, York." She looked up, brow furrowed. "He's that Quaker fellow, ain't he?"

"Yes, and the Retreat is the Quaker-run asylum. Please mail it, urgently."

"York, hey? That's going to cost him a good amount. They are mighty thrifty, them Quakers."

"I know, but if you are of a praying nature, Mrs. Cullers, then pray that Mr. Tuke pays the postage and reads my letter as soon as possible." I looked her in the eye to press home the importance of my final request. "And when you see Lady Julia, please tell her about Mr. Kent too. Will you do this for me? Am I betting on the right horse?"

"Nay," she said, and for a terrible second I thought she was rejecting my plea. Then she gave a huffing laugh and touched my arm in apology. "Sorry, dearie, just my little joke. Mr. Cullers is always saying I'm too corky for my own good."

She worked open the drawstrings of the strawberry reticule and dropped the letters inside. "Don't you worry, I'm the right horse, and I'll make sure your letters are sent."

Having longed for the arrival of Mrs. Cullers, now I could not wait until she and her husband departed. Finally, the supplies were unloaded and the couple waved good-bye, their cart rumbling across the rear-yard flags. As Mr. Cullers maneuvered his horse and vehicle around the corner, Mrs. Cullers looked back and held up her strawberry reticule, giving an exaggerated nod. The lady was clearly not one for subtlety. I looked around in case anyone had marked her odd behavior, but Geoffrey had lounged off to the kitchen, and inside the nearby laundry, the washerwomen were bent over their steaming vats, stirring their paddles. Evan and I were alone in the courtyard.

"Mrs. Cullers brought bad news," I said, pitching my voice low.

He turned to face me, shielding us from any curiosity from the laundry. "I gathered as much. Tell me."

"Mr. Kent is in Lynn. Mrs. Cullers described him and it could be no other. He knows your Hargate alias too."

He rubbed his forehead with the heel of his hand. "Damn. I had thought to have more time."

"You have to go. Now!" I whispered. "Kent will find his way here before long."

He gave a tiny shake of his head. "No. I have already thought on this and I cannot leave Hester."

"Do not be an idiot," I hissed. "If he comes, you will be taken."

He gave a crooked smile. "Says the woman who will not leave until she saves the entire asylum."

"Yes, but I do not have a Runner after me or a bounty upon my head."

"I am not about to leave you and Hester alone here with a foul man like Judd. The man is likely a murderer." He leaned closer, his hand upon my arm. "We will deal with Kent if he comes. Agreed?"

I knew the set of that Belford jaw—there would be no budging him. But then again, he was up against the Colebrook jaw.

Across the yard, Tilda emerged from the kitchen doorway. "Mrs. Allen, we have a problem with the new room arrangements," she called. "You need to come now, please."

"At the first sign of Kent, you go. Agreed?" I whispered.

He eyed me, his glint returning. "Stubborn woman." He gently grasped my arm: the pact sealed. "Agreed."

54

It is sometimes the smallest of things that rebuild dignity. Fingernails cut, hair brushed, clean clothes. That afternoon, Tilda, Mary, Bertha, and I worked our way around the inmates, providing such necessities. I wondered what Charlotte or Mr. Brummell would think if they saw me trimming the gnarled nails of Sally Bright or cutting knots from the matted hair of Quaker Anne.

As we worked, I observed the state of the women. Some were indeed disordered, but a good number were lucid and pitifully thankful for such attentions and release from their irons. I also took the opportunity to check the names in the ledger to see if any of the women listed were missing, perhaps consigned to the earth under the oak trees. All were accounted for, and I could only surmise that the missing pages in the ledger aligned with any absent women.

Twice Judd came barreling out of his study to countermand my orders—Miss Tollbrook was not to share a room, and only one blanket per inmate—but otherwise he returned to his customary indifference regarding the day-to-day running of the asylum. Judd was indeed a foul man. But he was also a man who did not want to lose his lucrative business, and Mr. and Mrs. Allen offered the way to retain it.

To any who observed, I was sure I seemed intent upon my supervisions and tasks, but in truth my mind was darting between hope and despair, going over our plan and estimating the time it should take Julia to get to Lynn, and my letter to York. She should arrive tomorrow, but perhaps Duffy had demanded she stay another day and she could not refuse. Or perhaps the roads were bad again. And it was more than possible the mail coach might lose a wheel, or Mr. Tuke might refuse the postage payment. On top of that, I was constantly listening for the commotion of another, less welcome arrival. Kent was no fool—he would at some point realize the connection between Mr. and Mrs. Allen and his quarry.

I endured another restless night, this time due to the same questions running through my mind rather than the proximity of the man sleeping soundly beside me. Evan seemed to be able to sleep through anything and then wake completely alert, a skill he said he had learned in the colony prison.

The next day, my morning duties seemed to drag endlessly. And still no Julia. The waiting dragged upon Evan, too, although he reported at our midday meal that he had found massive inconsistencies in the supply ledgers.

"Judd and our predecessors have made a tidy amount by falsifying the accounts," he said when Mary had served our food and departed the parlor. "Makes me wish Miss Grant and I had not, in fact, supplied the money for their so-called inheritance."

I looked down at the braised chicken leg on my plate. I had no appetite for it or the overboiled green beans that sat in the tureen before me. "The gateman knows that Julia may arrive, does he not?"

He paused in cutting his meat to nod patiently, for I had already asked the question twice through the course of the morning.

"All in hand. I have told Lester at the gate that Lady Deele will arrive today or tomorrow, and that no one else is to be admitted. It may slow Kent if he turns up."

I looked across at him, all my fear suddenly welling up. "Will it work? Can we do this?"

He reached across the table. I met his hand with my own in the center, our fingers curling into one another. "The only thing guaranteed is that something will happen, good or bad," he said soberly. "But we have our wits, our courage, the excellent support of your sister and Weatherly, and"—his eyes fixed upon his portmanteau under the bureau, the glint appearing again—"if all that fails, we have a loaded pistol."

I snorted and released his hand. "A speech to rival Nelson's." Yet I did feel reassured.

It was coming up to five o'clock in the afternoon when I heard coach wheels grinding over the driveway gravel. I was making my way along the first-floor corridor and the sound stopped me, my heart quickening into a hard beat.

Julia?

Or Kent?

I forced myself to walk, not run, to the oriel window, nodding to Bertha as I passed her coming up the stairs. I braced my hands on the cold stone windowsill and leaned over the bench seat. Directly below stood the gloriously familiar shape and blue-and-yellow colorings of our traveling coach. John sat in the driver seat with Hades in the long holster at his side, and Weatherly, in a footman's uniform, stood at the coach door. I breathed out, my relief misting the glass pane.

"Who is that, Mrs. Allen?" Bertha asked, suddenly beside me.

I flinched. "Sweet heaven, Bertha, you startled me." I drew back from the window.

"Sorry. I heard the coach." She rose on her toes for a better view. "Is it a visitor? I thought Mr. Judd said no one was allowed to visit no more."

"Perhaps he has changed his mind. Come now, back to work. Whoever it is has not come to see you."

I waved her away from the window but lingered long enough myself to see Julia, resplendent in buttercup yellow, take Weatherly's arm and step down from the carriage.

Enter, the false Lady Deele.

At least I hoped that was who had arrived. Had Mrs. Cullers delivered my letter as promised? Did Julia know the plan?

I hurried down the servants' staircase, Judd's agitation at the unexpected arrival penetrating even the thick walls of the house. I was sure I heard at least three vulgarities—one particularly forceful—that I had never heard before. As I took the final step down into the corridor, the string of obscenities changed into abuse aimed at poor Mary cowering in the front foyer beside him.

"Don't just stand there gawping like an idiot," Judd bawled. He and Mary stood well back from the door. "Go and get Mr. Allen."

Behind me, Evan climbed the last two steps up from the basement. Our eyes met and he gave a tiny nod: *Here we go.*

Indeed. I wiped my clammy hands on my apron and fell in behind him as he made his way to the front door.

"There you are," Judd said, seeing us approach. "God's blood, how did this happen? I made it clear that no visitors were to be allowed in."

Evan ducked his head, the picture of a bemused underling. "I don't know, Mr. Judd."

"You are the damn porter. I hold you responsible."

"Am I to be left standing out here all night like a ragman?" Julia's muffled voice said from behind the door. "My husband, Lord Deele, will hear of this outrage."

Judd looked wildly at the door. "Deele? Did she say Deele?"

"She did, Mr. Judd," I said helpfully. "It must be the Marchioness of Deele."

Rather extensive knowledge of the peerage for a matron, but Judd did not seem to notice. He pressed his hands against his forehead for a second. Was he truly considering not opening the door?

"Perhaps we should let her in," I said meekly.

He whirled around, lowering his voice into a whisper. "We get rid of her as soon as possible. Understood?"

Evan and I nodded vigorously. It was, after all, exactly what we had planned.

"All right, open the damn door," he hissed at Mary.

The girl wrenched open the front door.

"Finally," Julia said coldly and swept into the hallway, the dyed yellow tips of the ostrich feathers in her primrose bonnet bouncing with the irritated velocity of her entrance. She looked around, her nose elevated and slightly pinched with displeasure. Ha, I knew that expression: Julia was channeling the detestable and perpetually dissatisfied Mrs. Ellis-Brant.

Her eyes flicked across to me: *Is this what you had in mind?*

I pressed my lips together: *Exactly what I had in mind, dear-heart.*

"Welcome, Lady Deele," Judd said, stepping forward and making a creditable bow. "I am Mr. Judd, the keeper of Bothwell House. My apologies for the delay. Please come in."

"Judd, is it?" Julia said. He nodded and opened his mouth to add something, but she continued inexorably over him. "I have come to collect my sister-in-law, Lady Hester Belford. Here is my husband's letter." She motioned to Weatherly, who stepped across the threshold and bowed, handing Judd a packet sealed with red wax. "Bring her to me immediately. I wish to be on the return journey as soon as possible."

"My lady, we were not informed of your arrival," Judd said. "Lady Hester has not been discharged by our doct—"

"My good man, the Marquess of Deele placed his sister in this establishment and now he wishes to bring her home. That is the whole of it. Read his letter. It will all be made clear."

Judd broke the seal on the packet and unfolded the missive.

My twin looked directly at me. "You. What do you do in this establishment?"

I remembered to bob a curtsy. "I am Mrs. Allen, the matron, Lady Deele."

She waved a peremptory hand. "Well then, go fetch my sister-in-law."

At that order, Judd looked up from the letter, the full knowledge of Hester's physical condition in his startled eyes. My first impulse was to make him squirm a little longer. But no, the quicker we moved Hester—and Lady Roberta—into the carriage, the better.

"Lady Hester has lately refused to eat and so is quite weak, my lady," I said. "She will need to be carried."

"We tried to get her to eat, my lady," Judd said hurriedly. "Indeed, we were about to contact Lord Deele regarding her condition."

"Refusing to eat? I can believe it. Stupid, headstrong girl," Julia said. "Well then, Mrs.—" She clicked her tongue and turned back to me, eyebrows raised impatiently.

"Allen," I supplied, trying not to show my appreciation of her perfect Emelia Ellis-Brant.

"Yes, you and this man"—she gestured to Evan—"he looks sturdy enough. Bring Lady Hester down."

"Of course, my lady," I murmured.

Judd emerged from the letter again. "Before I can release Lady Hester, I will need the details of payment for the final account," he said. "Would you be so kind as to step into my office, Lady Deele?"

He clearly did not deal often with those of nobility, for no marchioness would discuss money. Or even be aware of its grubby existence.

Julia glanced at me—*what do I do?*—and I gave a tiny nod. We needed him busy.

"Of course," Julia said.

Judd jerked his chin at us, an order to get moving.

We were happy to oblige.

55

Evan and I did not speak until we were upstairs and outside Hester's room, well out of earshot.

"Your sister should go on the stage," he said as I sorted through the room keys. "Now comes the tricky part."

"Your scale of tricky is interesting," I said dryly. "See that bench seat under the window? I put clothes for Hester and Roberta inside."

He promptly crossed to the window, lifted the seat lid, and retrieved the two brown-paper-wrapped parcels within.

As I inserted the key into the lock, I heard the sound of gravel crunching underneath wheels. "Dear God, what is that?" I hissed.

Evan shut the seat and peered cautiously over the windowsill. "It is just John Driver turning the coach around."

I drew a steadying breath. "I thought it might be Kent."

"If Kent comes, it will be on horseback, not by carriage or gig."

"How could you know that?"

"He is ex-cavalry. Took a ball in the thigh on the Continent. Rides everywhere. Even has his old Elliott army saddle." He grinned at my unvoiced question. "It is not only Runners who have informants."

"Know thine enemy," I murmured.

I turned the key and opened the door. Inside, Lady Hester lay on her bed but had dragged herself up onto her elbow. Lady Roberta stood at the window, peering down at the forecourt. She turned at our entrance, thin face alight.

"Is it now?" she asked. "Is that carriage for us?"

"It is." I took the packages from Evan and ushered him back out the door. This next part was for women only. "Wait outside. We will not be long."

I closed the door. "Here," I gave Lady Roberta the parcel I had wrapped. "This is one of my gowns and a cap. Get dressed and then help me dress Lady Hester."

Even with my experience of dressing Caroline in her weakened state, the severity of Hester's debilitation made it ten times harder to get her into her clothes. I could feel the minutes ticking away as we removed her bedgown and maneuvered her lax limbs into her chemise. Every joint was visible and her starvation had made all her clothing two sizes too big. Lady Roberta and I managed to tighten the drawstring enough on the chemise and petticoat to make them fit, more or less, but the pretty sprig muslin gown she had once arrived in hung off her shoulders and gaped at the front.

"The . . . pelisse will . . . hide it," Hester managed to say, the effort closing her eyes for a second. Already exhausted from being dressed. Still, the prospect of escape had brought some color to her cheeks and lips.

"She is right. If she is wrapped in it, no one will see," Roberta said quickly and somewhat forcefully.

Clearly, nothing was going to stand in the way of her departure. Although she was not as thin as Hester, my gown still hung on her undernourished body. I hoped that, with the cap upon her shorn head, she would look like a maid from behind.

Together, we threaded Hester's bone-thin arms through the sleeves of the pink pelisse.

"My sister is playing the part of Lady Deele," I explained to

Hester as I buttoned the front. "Your brother will carry you down to the coach, and my man Weatherly will help you inside. You can trust him."

Hester gave a flicker of a smile. "I am glad"—she took a panting breath—"it is not really . . . my sister-in-law. She . . . hates me."

I knew the feeling.

"What about me?" Lady Roberta asked. "I cannot go downstairs."

"No, you are to come with me," I said. "We will go out the back and around the side of the house to the coach. You can run across and hide in it until Weatherly brings Lady Hester out."

I opened the door a crack and looked out. Evan stood beside the doorway, arms crossed, eyes intent on the corridor. The unyielding sentinel. Otherwise, the corridor was empty. He looked around—*ready?*—and I nodded, motioning him into the room.

"Evan!" Hester said, her voice reduced to a breathy whisper.

She managed to hold out her hand. He took it in his own and smiled at his sister. "Dear girl. Almost there."

He glanced at me, the apprehension raw within it. *So weak—can she do this?*

I gave a nod. She had her brother's courage.

Reassured, he turned to Lady Roberta and bowed. The courtesy straightened her back and she bobbed into a somewhat wobbly curtsy.

"Time to go?" Evan said to Hester. At her nod, he gathered her up into his arms, her head cradled against his shoulder.

"Remember not to smile so lovingly up into his face," I said. "That will give the game away."

Hester immediately frowned. "Better?" she whispered.

Evan smiled. "Much better. That's the sullen little girl I remember."

She gave a breathy huff of laughter.

I was the last to leave the room, locking it once again on our way out. All four of us made our way silently to the top of the main stairs.

"Good luck," I murmured to Evan.

"You too," he whispered.

I watched for a moment as he started down the steps carrying Hester's frail weight with heartbreaking ease, then turned to Lady Roberta. "Servants' stairs."

We crept past the cell rooms. I listened for any sounds of approach by maid or basketman from the back staircase but heard only someone singing a hymn within one of the rooms, and another inmate groaning. In truth, I was gambling on natural curiosity—the unaccustomed arrival of a noble visitor should have gathered a good number of the staff on the main staircase or in the corridor to view the spectacle, leaving us a clear path down to the ground floor and the back garden.

At the top of the back stairs, I held up my hand, halting Lady Roberta. Cautiously, I looked over the banister. Damn, my gamble had rebounded upon us. The two kitchen maids stood on the top steps peering around the wall at the proceedings farther down the corridor.

Wait, I mouthed to Lady Roberta. She nodded, pressing herself against the wall. She would not wait too long—the impulse to flee was in her widened eyes.

I straightened my back and marched down the steps. *Here comes Matron.* As I rounded the landing, the two girls heard my footsteps and whirled around, steam-reddened faces a picture of guilt.

"What are you doing here?" I demanded, reaching the bottom of the steps. "Go back to work."

The taller one bobbed a curtsy. "Mrs. Carroll said we could come and look, for a bit of fun, Mrs. Allen."

Clearly a lie: from what I knew of Mrs. Carroll, she had absolutely no concept of fun.

"I do not care what Mrs. Carroll said. Stop blocking the staircase." I shooed them with my hands.

Reluctantly they turned and took the steps to the basement, their downward treads thumping heavily on the bare boards in protest.

I looked up to see Lady Roberta peering over the banister from the floor above. I waved her down, then took a few seconds to check farther down the corridor. A much better outcome; a good number of the remaining staff had gathered at the main staircase: Tilda and Bertha with their hands over their mouths stifling giggles, Mary pushing away Geoffrey's wandering hands, and two of the other basketmen sneaking swigs shared from a brown bottle.

Lady Roberta paused on the bottom step. "Which way?" she whispered.

"To the back."

We passed the doors of the parlor and bedchamber that Evan and I had shared. I looked over my shoulder. Tilda had noticed us but turned her attention back to the study as Julia's voice peevishly, and loudly, asked, "For goodness' sakes, where is she? Why are your people taking so long?"

I increased my pace, ushering Lady Roberta out the back door and into the patients' unkempt walled garden.

The air outside had cooled. Overhead, darker clouds had gathered, blocking the autumnal afternoon sunlight—rain on its way. Lady Roberta stopped for a moment on the stone path, head craned back and eyes closed, breathing in the scent of long grass and white roses flowering their last. The path forked ahead: to the right, a small fountain with no water, and to the left, the iron gate that led to the side of the house and the larger gardens.

"Lady Roberta, this way. We must hurry," I said.

She opened her eyes, thrall broken. "I have not had fresh air for months. It is glorious." She looked back. "I hate this place. I hate it."

"Then, let us go," I said.

I took her hand, more to ensure she followed than from any sense of fellowship, and together we ran to the gate. It was, of course, locked. I gathered up my keys, finding the old iron one that matched. The lock turn was rusty and stiff, but finally it clicked. I thrust the gate open, wincing at the squeal of its hinges. I looked back, but no one came to the door to investigate.

We stepped out onto the side path that ran along the length of the house. Opposite us, a line of thick-trunked elms had dropped drifts of golden leaves like a carpet of guineas, the ground rising behind them into an uncut lawn. And tethered to one of the trees stood a black horse. Its legs were grayed by road dust, and the gun holster, strapped to its Elliott army saddle, was ominously empty.

Kent.

56

I pressed myself against the brick wall, dragging Lady Roberta beside me. The path ahead was empty. And behind too. I searched the tree line and the lawn behind it. No movement. Dear God, was he already in the house?

"Whose horse is that?" Lady Roberta hissed, looking around wildly.

"Kent. A Bow Street Runner. He is after Lord Evan."

What to do? What to do? My mind was blank.

"How can you be sure? Do you know his horse?" Lady Roberta asked.

No, I did not. She was quite right. I was assuming it was the Runner.

"Stay here," I said.

"What are you going to do?"

"I am going to see if it is Kent."

"Then I will come too."

"No. You must stay here."

She grabbed my forearm, thin jaw set. "I will not. You must not leave me."

I was her way out of this place, and she was not going to let me out of her sight. So be it. I did not have time to argue.

We crept along the brick wall of the house, bending double beneath the windows. Behind me, Lady Roberta's breath quickened from the unaccustomed exertion. Yet I could not slow down. Evan was in danger.

We arrived at the corner of the house. I held up a warning hand. She tucked herself behind me, panting.

I peered around the wall.

Our carriage stood in front of the stables, but John Driver was not in his seat or attending to the team of horses. Moreover, the lead horse had been tied to the railing outside the building. A dubious practice. Otherwise the forecourt was empty.

I drew back. Either John was standing on the other side of the carriage, or he had abandoned his team—something he would never do. Unless forced.

I wracked my memory: had Kent ever seen our town coach? Damn, I was sure he had mentioned seeing it when we arrived home from Cheltenham. And a Runner as observant as Kent would remember such details. He knew we were here.

I frowned. Something had seemed out of place. But what? I took another quick look around the corner. Ah, in the horse trough—the shape of a blunderbuss resting barrel first in the water, rendered useless. Kent must have surprised John, relieved him of Hades, and forced him inside.

"Well?" Lady Roberta whispered.

I drew back. "My guess is that Kent is inside."

"What are you going to do?"

I could barely think beyond the roar of fear in my head—if Kent arrested Evan, absconder and highwayman, it would be the gallows. For a second, it felt as if I lost touch with the ground—whirling soundless and airless inside my own terror.

"Mrs. Allen!"

Lady Roberta, her face an inch from my own. I gasped, pressing myself against the house wall, the cold, solid bricks anchoring me back to the world. I had to get Evan out. Had to stop Kent.

But how?

Perhaps a distraction. The coach and horses? No, we needed them.

"Mrs. Allen, should I get in the carriage?" Lady Roberta asked.

I looked at her intent face, every fiber of her being set upon escape. So many women waiting for escape. For freedom. An idea leaped forward. A mad idea, but the situation called for a woman's madness.

I caught up her hand and pulled her toward the garden gate. "We are going to the house."

She yanked against me. "No. What are you doing? I cannot go back inside. I cannot."

"This is the only way we—you—are going to get out." I hauled her another step, but she dragged on my hand, her slight weight still enough to slow me down. "Do you understand?"

She stood, teeth bared, poised to wrench herself free.

What was I doing? I released her hand. I could not force her to return to the house—there had been too much force in her life already.

"Please, Lady Roberta, I need your help."

She looked over her shoulder—at the forecourt, at escape. Then at Kent's horse watching us from the trees, ears flicking at our whispers.

"You cannot steal a Runner's horse," I said. "That is the gallows. Besides, you will not get far. Help me and I will get you out. I have given my word."

She turned back to me and drew a quivering breath. "What do you need me to do?"

I opened the back door and checked the hallway. Those clustered on the main staircase had moved along the corridor to be closer to the study door and a better view of the unfolding drama. I heard Julia's voice but could not make out her words. I made out her tone, though, and it was alarmed.

Then another voice. Commanding. Unyielding. Kent's.

I fought back the impulse to run down the hallway. Protect my sister. Confront Kent. Save Evan.

Not yet. I tightened my grip on the key to our rooms and motioned to Lady Roberta to follow me.

We walked swiftly along the wall to the parlor door. I unlocked it and gave the keys to Lady Roberta.

"These ones," I whispered, tapping the secondary loop.

She nodded and pressed the collection to her chest to curtail any jangling. I checked the onlookers ahead again. They were all facing away from us, and by the transfixed tension in their bodies and the gasps, the drama was building in Judd's study.

"Go," I mouthed.

I watched her head to the servants' stairs. Nothing else I could do but hope she followed my instructions.

I slipped inside the parlor and closed the door. At the side bureau, I crouched and pulled out Evan's portmanteau stored underneath. Inside, carefully stored and muzzle down, was the loaded pistol. I drew it out and with my other hand felt around inside the portmanteau for the leather powder horn. My fingers closed around the small bulbous shape. *Got it.*

I thumbed back the pan cap on the pistol, then flicked open the horn's silver lid. Plenty of black powder. I tapped it once over the tiny silver pan, my hand trembling so much that some of the powder missed and scattered upon the carpet. A dark sunburst of fear.

I steadied my hand. Another tap and the pan was full. A flex of thumb drew back the cap to cover it. There, loaded.

Could I really shoot Kent?

My attention fixed on the neatly made bed through the doorway. For a vivid, aching second I was lying beside Evan again, his warm hand touching mine, his face silvered and sleeping, every breath matching my own.

I stood and adjusted my grip on the pistol butt. I just hoped the ticking pad in the barrel still had enough lubrication and the powder behind it was dry enough to fire.

57

I opened the door and cautiously looked out. No one had moved outside the study—all attention was still fixed upon the open door. I eased out into the hallway, listening for any signs of movement upstairs. Nothing yet. Had Lady Roberta lost her nerve?

I considered the small group of people between me and the study door. The maids and three of the basketmen. My staff. But two days was not enough time to build loyalty—I could not rely upon them keeping quiet as I approached.

And so I walked up the hallway at a normal pace, gun held down at my side. No need to frighten them prematurely.

Tilda noticed me first. She stood at the back of the group and must have seen me in the periphery of her vision. She turned and, for an instant, her expression was one of guilt—caught loitering—then her gaze traveled down to my hand holding the pistol. I held my finger to my lips. She nodded but elbowed Bertha, who saw the gun and gasped, somewhat dramatically, clearly enjoying the thrilling situation. They both stood back, allowing me through.

A tap on the first basketman's arm—his name and his comrade's had not yet settled in my memory—caught his attention. Startled, he shifted to one side, taking his friend with him. Only Geoffrey now stood between me and Kent. A well-placed shoulder unbalanced him enough to allow me through the doorway.

It took a breathless second to orientate myself. Near the window, Kent stood with his pistol aimed only a few inches from Evan's head. Braced and motionless, Evan still cradled Hester, as tightly bound by her birdlike weight as if he wore shackles. She clung to him, eyes fixed upon the gun at her brother's head.

On the other side of the desk, Julia, John Driver—who had been shackled—and Weatherly watched, all of them in various stages of startled, immobile fury. And finally Judd, caught between Kent and my sister, still holding an itemized bill.

My eyes flicked past Julia, catching her plea: *No, Gus, don't!*

Too late. I cocked the pistol and swung the barrel at Kent. Not an entirely clear shot, but good enough. "Let him go," I said.

"Lady Augusta. We have been expecting your appearance," Kent said calmly.

"I don't understand," Judd whined beside him. "Lady Augusta?"

Kent drew an irritated breath. Clearly, he had tried to explain before. "Mr. Judd. The woman who calls herself Lady Deele is in fact Lady Julia Colebrook. The man holding the girl is not Mr. Allen but Lord Evan Belford, a wanted man. And our new arrival is Lady Julia's sister, Lady Augusta Colebrook. They are all involved in some mad scheme . . ." He cleared his throat, allowing a crooked smile. "My apologies, a bad pun. A scheme about which I am not particularly interested."

I braced my feet. "Let Lord Evan go."

"No," Kent said.

"I will shoot you," I said, and I think I meant it.

"Gus, put the gun down," Evan said, the warning palpable in his voice. "For Christ's sake, do not shoot a Runner."

"Gus?" Julia echoed, looking across at me. "When did that happen?"

"I have no compunction about shooting Lord Evan," Kent said.

His gun was indeed cocked. "The Crown will not quibble whether I bring him in dead or alive. And since my barrel is but two inches away from his head, he will surely be dead. Put down your gun."

I glared at Kent. "Lord Evan did not kill Sanderson in the duel twenty years ago. I am sure of it."

Kent gave a tiny shrug of one shoulder. "I don't care. He is wanted now for absconding, highway robbery, and horse theft."

"And fraud," Judd said. "They said they were Mr. and Mrs. Allen."

"I see you have arrived, Mr. Judd," Kent said dryly.

"Gus, put down the gun! Please," Evan said. "I cannot have you or Hester hurt on my account."

"On three, Lady Augusta, and then I shoot," Kent said. "One."

I felt my hand wobble. Did I believe him?

"God's blood, Kent, at least let me put my sister down," Evan pleaded.

"Two."

I saw Kent's body brace for the recoil.

Evan's eyes closed. Hester moaned, the sound guttural terror.

Damn.

"I am putting it down!" I said, releasing the cock. "See, I am putting it down." I crouched, placing the pistol on the carpet.

Behind me, a collective sigh of relief or maybe regret sounded from the onlookers.

A noise upstairs took everyone's eyes upward for a second. Were those footsteps?

"What was that?" Kent demanded.

Judd frowned. "Upstairs. Where the women are."

"The women?"

The sound gathered momentum. Moving, it seemed, along the hallway above.

"The women Mr. Judd has been abusing and killing," I said, standing again.

The commotion above had shifted down to the ground-floor corridor, shouts and shrieks joining the sound of fast footsteps down steps and along carpet.

I raised my voice. "You should be arresting Judd, not Lord Evan! We found bodies out there." I pointed toward the oak trees.

Kent, still standing with the gun at Evan's head, shifted to view the doorway. He did have a keen sense for oncoming trouble. "Killing women? Do you have proof?"

"She is talking nonsense," Judd said vehemently. "A fraudster. A liar—"

"We found the skeletons of women and infants buried in makeshift graves," I said over Judd's sputtering denial. "And the women can tell you, he and his men have assaulted them in the worst way!"

Lady Roberta had timed it well, after all. The hall and doorway suddenly filled with women in nightgowns, the protesting staff pushed away by the sheer number of inmates. Lady Roberta entered first, holding the hand of a very frightened Miss Tollbrook. Next, a determined Quaker Anne helping Penelope Wardrup, whose wizened features were twisted into righteous fury.

"She is speaking the truth," Lady Roberta yelled above the noise of emancipation. "Judd has forced himself on many of the women here. Him and the basketmen."

"True," Miss Tollbrook gasped, visibly shaking. "It is true."

Penelope's searing gaze fixed upon Judd. "My babies," she hissed. She pointed a bone-thin finger at him, and it was like a blazing sword of justice. "He killed my babies. Get away from Lady Julia, you fiend!"

She scooped up my pistol. Bracing herself, she cocked it with both hands and aimed at Judd, but the weight was too heavy. The barrel weaved from Judd to Kent and back again.

"Penelope, no!" Julia screamed.

The gun fired just as Judd lunged behind Kent.

The blast rang in my ears, the gunpowder smoke pluming through the room. I caught a lungful of acrid air and coughed, my vision blurred by stinging tears. Someone was hit. I heard the wet thump of the ball penetrating flesh and a body collapsing to the floor.

"Holy Mother of Christ!" Kent's voice.

I peered frantically through smoke and tears. Evan stood pressed against the wall, still clutching Hester to his chest. Thank God, not him.

Judd stood where Kent had been a minute before, staring at Penelope with eyes bulging in shock.

And Kent? I looked down. He was curled on his side on the ground, writhing in pain, one bloodied hand clutching his arm.

Dear God, Penelope had hit the Runner.

Before I could react, Penelope lunged forward toward Kent. No, toward his gun lying on the carpet.

"Stop her!" Judd screamed. "She's trying to kill me!"

I leaped to intercept Penelope but missed and staggered into the desk, the corner driving itself into my hip. The explosion of pain curled me over for a second.

Judd charged past Julia, circling around the desk. He rammed into Weatherly, shoving him into John Driver, who, with bound hands, could not catch himself. The two men crashed against the bookcase as Judd ran past me into the onlookers.

"Get out of my way," he yelled, fists and elbows battering a path through the crowd of inmates and staff.

Penelope was back on her feet, Kent's gun in hand. She ran to the door, the other women standing back to allow her, and the gun, to go after Judd.

I followed her into the hallway with one thought pounding through my mind—if she killed him she would hang.

Ahead, Judd was halfway up the main staircase. Penelope climbed a few steps behind, the gun pointed at his back, her aim weaving wildly.

"Penelope!" I yelled. "Do not kill him. You will have justice! I promise!"

She looked back but did not stop climbing the steps, fueled by a manic energy that burned in her eyes and bared her teeth.

Judd rounded the landing and pulled himself up by the banister. By the time I reached the bottom of the staircase and looked up, he had reached the first floor, Penelope only a step behind. She lunged for him, missed, and staggered across the corridor, blocking his way to the servants' steps.

I drove more power into my legs and took the steps two at a time, hauling myself around the landing. At the top I grabbed the carved newel-post, gasping for breath, my chest burning.

I looked down. Evan was halfway up the first flight. Tilda and Lady Roberta and a few other onlookers had reached the bottom of the staircase.

"Gus, wait!" Evan yelled.

No time to wait. Judd was already running toward the oriel window with Penelope close behind. What was he doing? The window was a dead end. Did he hope to barricade himself inside a cell? Most of the doors stood open, unlocked by Lady Roberta.

Pulling in a breath, I ran after Penelope.

Judd reached the end of the corridor. He grabbed the handle of Lady Roberta's cell and pushed. It did not budge. One of the few still locked. Of course, no one to release.

He rammed his shoulder against it. "No," he howled.

He spun around, facing Penelope. "You, stop! Right there. Stop!"

She did not stop.

He scrabbled backward, knees against the bench seat. She trod closer, relentless, the weaving gun aimed at him. He climbed up onto the bench seat, hands held out in front as if they could shield his body.

"Stop her!" he begged me. "Stop her!"

"Penelope, no!" I yelled.

She fired, the recoil pushing her back a step. I ducked at the explosion. Glass smashed and smoke billowed. I gasped and acrid air scorched my throat again. Through the plume of smoke, I saw Judd still standing on the bench, the window beside him smashed. The ball must have missed him by an inch.

"Ha!" Judd released a victorious breath. "Missed, you useless old bitch."

Penelope dropped the gun and looked back at me. Through the last wisps of smoke, our eyes locked—one terrible second that held twenty years of hell.

"No!" I screamed.

But Penelope was already running. She leaped onto Judd, arms wrapped around him, her momentum slamming them both through the remaining, jagged glass.

58

I heard the dull thudding slap of impact, the shriek of startled horses, and the crack and jangle of tack. I knew that sound: frightened horses plunging in their harness.

Evan ran up to me, catching me by the shoulders, spinning me against his chest. "Hurt? Are you hurt?"

"No," I managed.

Lady Roberta and Tilda ran past us to the window, crunching across the broken glass. They both peered over the windowsill. Lady Roberta spun around, eyes closed, head averted. Tilda drew back more slowly, hands pressed to her mouth.

Bad, then. The last brittle hope that Penelope had survived crumbled.

I heard John Driver's voice calling to his team, soothing them with the words that only horsemen knew. The thud and crack of tack stopped.

"I have to see," I said to Evan.

He took my hand, its solid warmth a comfort. "Are you sure?"

I nodded. I had failed to save Penelope, but I could at least be her witness.

Lady Roberta and Tilda made way for us. I drew a deep breath, then leaned over the sill. Below, Judd and Penelope lay sprawled upon the gravel a few yards apart, limbs akimbo, dark patches beneath their heads. Weatherly crouched beside them. He looked up, saw us, and shook his head.

I stepped away from the sight, my smoke-scorched throat clogged by guilt and sorrow.

Once the initial horror had worn off, Lord Evan took control of the mayhem. He ordered Weatherly to cover the bodies with sheets, told the maids and the last remaining basketman—the other three, it seemed, had run away—to gently return the inmates to their rooms, and asked Mrs. Carroll to continue with preparations for the evening meal, with extra rations. Tasks for everyone to focus upon rather than the grisly events. Only Bertha and one of the kitchen maids lingered in the hallway. Time to stop shaking and rally to my role as matron.

"Do you have something to do?" I asked them. My voice, at least, was steady. "Mr. Allen here has tasks if you do not."

Evan nodded. "I'm sure Mrs. Carroll could do with some help."

They curtsied and hurried down the hallway.

My sister's voice suddenly rang out from the study. "Stupid man, let Lord Evan help you! He has medical knowledge. Do you want to lose your arm?"

"I would rather not," Kent's voice said, clearly trying to force a jovial tone over pain. "But Lord Evan is hardly going to help me, is he?"

"My brother does not run away!" Hester said, her vehemence giving some strength to her wispy voice.

"I beg to differ, Lady Hester," Kent said. "I am sure he is in the next county by now."

Evan bent to my ear and whispered, "That appears to be my cue."

I smiled, but in truth I wished he had taken the opportunity to flee. From now on, it was even more dangerous for him to stay. Especially if the next part of the plan unfolded as I hoped it would.

"My sister wins that round," Evan said as we entered the study. "I am still here."

We both stared at Julia kneeling on the ground with Kent's head cradled in her lap, one hand pressing the hem of her yellow gown against his arm, the silk wet with blood. Not a view I had been expecting. Weatherly stood behind her, clearly ensuring my sister's safety. Not that Kent looked capable of anything more than lying on the ground, bleeding.

"See," Lady Hester said, but the vehement strength in her voice was gone. She sat propped in Judd's chair, the day's events leaching her of any color, with Lady Roberta—watchful and just as pale—at her side. They must leave soon, too, while they had the chance.

Kent attempted to lift his head. "Then you are a fool," he said, panting. "Lord Evan Belford, I arrest you—"

"Do stay still, Mr. Kent," Julia said, curtailing his spiel by pressing him back into her lap. "Lord Evan, I fear Mr. Kent is losing rather too much blood. You must help him."

"Are you serious?" Evan asked. "Why would I help him? He is trying to hang me."

"I do not want his help," Kent said.

"What you want is neither here nor there," Julia said, looking sternly down at him. He glared at her but subsided. She looked up at Lord Evan, chin lifted into severe admonishment. "I thought better of you than this. Do not disappoint your sister's belief in you. Or my sister's!"

When Julia used that tone of voice, I knew it was inevitable that both Lord Evan and Mr. Kent would eventually comply. They both put up some fight, but in the end, water, towels, and bandaging were fetched, a knife held over a flame, and brandy poured.

Both men were decidedly sullen throughout the entire operation—at least Kent was sullen for the time he was conscious—and the ball was dug out, the wound doused in brandy, and the arm splinted and bound tightly to stop further bleeding.

As Lord Evan washed the blood from his hands in a bowl of water, Mr. Kent finally returned to his senses.

"It is all done now," Julia said, crouching beside him. She offered him a sip of brandy. "The ball is out and Lord Evan says he got the shirt cloth, too, which he says can cause it to fester. The bone is broken, but it is a clean break."

"Thank you," Kent said, still a little dazed.

"Do not thank me," Julia said. "Thank Lord Evan, for he has surely saved your arm and probably your life."

And that, of course, was when I understood the genius of my sister, yet again. She had cornered Mr. Kent into a life debt. Or at least an arm debt.

"Thank you, Lord Evan," Kent said gruffly. "I owe you."

I shot her an admiring glance: *Well done.*

She inclined her head, acknowledging the laudation.

Now came the hardest part. For me, anyway. "If that is truly the case, Mr. Kent, then you will allow Lord Evan to borrow your horse."

"My horse?" Kent echoed.

Lord Evan, quick to understand, shook his head. "I am not leaving."

"You must." I took his hand, pressing home my plea. "While you can." I turned to gather Julia and Hester into the entreaty. "While you *all* can. Julia, you must take Lady Hester and Lady Roberta back to

London now. I am expecting the local magistrate to arrive tonight, along with Mr. Samuel Tuke, who I hope will take charge of this asylum. It would be disastrous if you are all still here."

"I will not leave you alone," Evan said. I felt his fingers close tightly around mine. This was the hardest part of the enterprise—sending him away. Most likely forevermore.

"Mr. Kent will be here with me," I said.

Kent, struggling to sit up, huffed in surprise. "I will?"

"You can hardly ride with that arm," I said. "We will stay here to stand witness to the crimes of Mr. Judd, abuser and murderer."

"What about the crimes of Lord Evan Belford, absconder and highwayman?" Kent demanded.

Julia patted his uninjured arm. "I am sure you would prefer to focus upon the murdering fiend you stopped, rather than the man you allowed to get away. Besides, you just said you owe Lord Evan a debt of honor."

"But—" Kent narrowed his eyes at my sister. "Diabolical woman," he said, but it was not an insult. "If I stay, it will be counted as payment in full."

"If that is what you wish," my sister said gravely, which further discomposed the Runner.

"You'll return my horse, too, Belford," he added forcefully. "His name is Caesar."

"Of course it is," Lord Evan said dryly. But he bowed. "Your horse will be returned to you in good order."

"Go, now, Evan," I said. "Leave, as you said you would. Go as far as you can. If you stay, all will be lost."

He drew my hand up to his mouth and kissed my fingers. I cupped his chin and drew him closer, rising upon my toes to meet him. Brazen, I knew, but I did not care. Our lips touched, softly at first, tentative—full of the truth we had dared not utter—and then with more heat, or perhaps more desperation. Our first, maybe our last, kiss.

"So, that's the way of it," I heard Kent say.

I pulled back and looked up into Evan's anguished eyes. A mirror of my own.

Indeed, that was the way of it, and would be forever.

59

GROSVENOR SQUARE, LONDON

ONE WEEK LATER

I closed *The Times* and folded it, looking out upon our new view of Grosvenor Square. Thankfully, no new arrests reported in the paper. Nor any articles about Jamaica. Every day, I scoured the pages. Firstly, to ensure Evan had not been detained, and secondly, for snippets of news about Jamaica. I knew the latter was foolish—it had only been a week since Bothwell House, and Evan had probably not even yet secured a passage to the West Indies. Moreover, it would be months before he reached Jamaica. Yet, reading about his destination helped ease the heavy ache in my heart for a moment or two. A link to him, albeit tenuous and distant.

The drawing room door opened to admit Julia, dressed in a handsome russet gown and with a smile upon her face.

"I think Hester will be able to sit up for a while today," she reported.

She cast an appraising look at the arrangement of the armchairs and sofa opposite the black marble fireplace: clearly still not to her liking. The placement of furniture in our new home was an ongoing enterprise. One that did not seem to be about to end anytime soon.

"Elizabeth is very happy. It was the best decision to bring them here," she added.

"Indeed. Cook is in her element making broths and jellies for the convalescent."

And also, I thought, for Julia—the madhouse adventure and the distraction of caring for Hester had lifted her melancholy, but I knew fatigue and pain still dogged her days.

The decision to bring both Hester and her—well, we had not quite settled on what to call Miss Elizabeth Grant—her *chère amie* to stay with us had been the last we had made before Julia left Bothwell House. It had been difficult to watch Julia leave, although not as hard as seeing Evan ride out of the gates, away from me to a new life so very far away. But I did not have much time to be despondent. Mr. Samuel Tuke and the local magistrate had arrived late that same night, a pleasingly prompt response to my letter, and one that also allowed Mr. Kent and me time to discuss the manner of our report. Although I felt that Penelope's death had been my fault, Mr. Kent made it quite clear that I was not to make mention of that, but to keep to the facts of Judd's perfidy. And so, upon the two men's arrival, we reported the terrible truth of Bothwell House.

As I had hoped, Mr. Tuke immediately proposed to take the place in hand. Mr. Kent then had a private conversation with the magistrate. I did not know what passed between the two men, but Penelope's and Judd's deaths were, it seemed, to be ruled as a murder and a suicide.

Despite Mr. Kent's—and my sister's—protestations, I knew I had failed Penelope. Every night, as I closed my eyes, I saw that last look upon her face before she ran at Judd. Julia said that I could not save everyone in the world, and to think of all the women at Bothwell House who now had some chance of dignity and comfort. True, but it was our failures that haunted us, was it not? And without the grace of a god, I must find my own way to forgiveness. At least I had been able to rescue Lady Roberta. She had found sanctuary with an aunt in Scotland and had written to invite us to visit at any time.

"I think we need to switch the positions of the sofa and armchairs," Julia said. "What do you think?"

I was spared the necessity of an opinion by a knock upon the door and the entrance of Weatherly, carrying the silver salver.

"A caller downstairs, my ladies," he said, an odd tone to his voice. He offered the salver to Julia.

"Early for a caller." She picked up the card and read the name, her top lip pressing hard upon the lower to stop a smile. "Yes, we are at home."

Weatherly bowed. "Almond macaroons?" he suggested.

Julia nodded and, with another bow, Weatherly departed.

I placed my newspaper upon the side table and tried to recall a visitor who particularly liked Cook's almond macaroons. "Who is it?" I asked.

Julia looked up from smoothing the lines of her gown. "Mr. Kent."

"Really?" I had not expected to see the Runner again. I eyed my sister, who had moved on from smoothing her gown to observing her reflection in the mirror above the mantel. "Whatever could he want?"

"I have no idea," she said, patting down an errant curl.

The door opened again.

"Mr. Kent, my ladies," Weatherly announced with only the slightest inflection in his voice. Our butler approved.

I stood to receive our unexpected visitor. I noted that his bow upon entrance was directed more to Julia than to myself. His arm was in a sling, but he wore his navy greatcoat over his shoulders—a well-cut example with a good number of capes—so he intended the visit to be short. A blow, no doubt, to Julia.

"Mr. Kent, do come in," my sister said, waving an elegant hand toward the maligned armchairs. I could not help but notice she had positioned herself under the Lawrence portrait.

"I thank you, but I cannot stay long," he said. "I have come to tell you that the case has been closed on Judd's murder and Miss Wardrup's sad demise."

"We had already heard," I said. "I suspect that we owe you a great deal in regard to that conclusion."

"Not at all," he demurred. "You might also be interested to know that I have Caesar back. Lord Evan is a man of his word."

"Yes," I said. "I know." I wet my lips. There was something I wished to ask—a question not quite the usual fare of a morning call. "Tell me, Mr. Kent, would you have shot Lord Evan if I had not put the pistol down?"

He tilted his head, his mouth crooking to one side. "I think I was more prepared to shoot Lord Evan than you were prepared to shoot me," he said.

A silence fell upon us. Mr. Kent and Julia looked at each other.

"Are you sure you cannot stay for tea?" Julia finally asked.

"No, I really must go. There is, however, one more thing I wished to say, and this will completely fulfill my debt to Lord Evan. It has come to my attention that a thieftaker is searching for him. A man who, even in my circles, is considered brutal. I suggest that if Lord Evan has not left the country, he should do so immediately."

"He is gone already," I said, my voice thickening. Just saying the words brought an ache to my throat.

Kent nodded, a sympathetic expression upon his face. "I am both glad and sorry to hear that, Lady Augusta."

When it came down to it, I rather liked Mr. Kent.

"Is the thieftaker you mention a sandy-haired man with red whiskers?" Julia asked. "If so, I think we have already come across him." She glanced at me: *The anonymous man asking after us at Duffield.*

"That sounds like him," Kent said. "His name is Mulholland and those he hunts are more likely to be brought in dead than alive." He cleared his throat. "Well, as I said, that fulfills my obligation to Lord Evan. I bid you farewell. I doubt that we will meet again."

He bowed and, with one last look at Julia, left the room. We both stood, listening to his footsteps descend the staircase.

"So, finis," I said as the front door closed.

"Not at all," Julia said. "He will be back."

"What makes you think that?"

She smiled. "Because he did not need to come this time."

An hour later, I was in the kitchen with Cook, discussing the provisions we needed to order for the convalescent, when Thomas appeared in the doorway that led to the kitchen courtyard.

"My lady," he said.

"Mind your cap, boy," Cook admonished.

Thomas pulled his cap off and ducked his head. "Sorry, my lady. John Driver said can ye come to the mews?"

"Is something wrong? Do not tell me Perseus is not improving."

Our lead carriage horse had bruised his right fetlock when the team had plunged in fright at the madhouse, and John Driver was applying all kinds of poultices.

I turned back to Cook. "Are you satisfied with what we have decided for the menus?"

"Aye, my lady. But John Driver best not think he can take my fresh milk and rosemary for that horse's leg again."

"I'll tell him," I said, following Thomas into the courtyard.

One of the many reasons Julia and I had chosen to buy in

Grosvenor Square had been the proximity of its mews, built behind the house. Thomas and I walked up the narrow, cobbled alley to the road that serviced our carriage house and stables. As we crested the small rise, the mews and John Driver came into view. He stood outside the row of stalls holding the bridle of a chestnut horse. No, not just any chestnut horse. Good God, he was holding Leonardo.

I picked up my skirts and ran across the road.

"Where did he come from, John?" I pressed myself against Leonardo's shoulder—breathing in his earthy horse smell—and ran my hand down his solid shoulder. "Is he sound? He looks in good condition."

As if in agreement, Leonardo shoved his muzzle into my hand, his soft lips searching for his rightful piece of apple.

"I've checked him, an' he's right as rain," John Driver said. "A bit underworked if anything. The boy who brought him said I was to give you this." He passed me a packet, sealed by a wafer.

I knew the writing, of course. Dear God, had Evan stolen Leonardo back for me?

I broke open the wafer and spread the pages.

24th September 1812

My darling G,

Do not be alarmed—I did not steal Leonardo. You will find his papers enclosed.

Now I must ask you to forgive me, dear Renegade, for I find I cannot run from England for warmer climes and the safety of distance. Too much holds me here. I know it is dangerous to stay, but I cannot leave Hester while she is still under the guardianship of our brother and her safety and happiness are not yet fully secured. Like you, I cannot abandon my sister. And, my love, I cannot leave you. I have always maintained that you should not delve into the circumstances of the duel twenty years ago. What good could it do? But now I ask you to delve as swiftly as possible. Somehow, I must clear my name: to protect Hester and, if you will have me, to stand beside you and make it up as we go along, forever.

Yours in every way,

E.

I folded the pages. Dangerous to stay? It was sheer madness, especially now that Mulholland was hunting him. Yet, beyond that fear was a joy so palpable that my hands shook. I would see him again. I did not know when, but we would be together once more.

"Are you quite all right, my lady?" John Driver asked, his brow furrowed.

I smiled—tasting the salt of tears—and rubbed Leonardo's nose. "Have him saddled an hour from now. And tell Thomas that we will be riding to Piccadilly. I wish to deliver a letter."

"Of course, my lady."

An hour should give me enough time to change into my riding habit and write an invitation to Colonel Drysan to call upon us.

And tomorrow morning, over tea and Cook's macaroons, I would ask the colonel to cast his mind back twenty years and give his account of the duel that killed his friend Sanderson and ruined the life and good name of the man I loved.

Author's Note

I have been entranced by the Regency era ever since my mother gave me my first Georgette Heyer novel when I was twelve. At that age, my fascination was with the era's glittering balls, silk gowns, and elegant etiquette. However, as I grew older and studied the history, I discovered just how exciting and important the period of the true Regency—1811 to 1820—was in terms of its political and social upheavals: a regent on the throne, a prime minister assassinated, and the Luddites breaking loom machines at the start of the Industrial Revolution, just to name a few of those upheavals. For me, the Regency is like the 1960s of the nineteenth century (but without the Beatles). As I have grown older, I have also noted that very few of the Regency heroines in the books I was reading were over the grand old age of twenty-eight. And so the Ill-Mannered Ladies were born: older, perhaps wiser, and ready to engage in the social and political world around them with a great deal of midlife attitude.

I have endeavored, as far as my research skills will allow, to make the Ill-Mannered Ladies and their world feel as historically authentic as possible. Following is a little more information about some of the real historical figures and situations that appear in the novel.

Fanny Burney (aka Madame d'Arblay) was a celebrated author, diarist, and playwright during the Georgian era, the same period in which Jane Austen wrote. Burney's debut novel, *Evelina*, was widely acclaimed and she achieved a great deal of fame in her long lifetime. She left us with an extensive collection of diaries and letters that give a fascinating glimpse of life as a woman writer in the eighteenth and nineteenth centuries, and of Georgian court life during her service as Queen Charlotte's Keeper of the Robes. Burney was one of the first women to ever write about the experience of a mastectomy, in her case performed without anesthetic. The description she gives of her breast cancer and surgery in *The Benevolent Society of Ill-Mannered Ladies* is taken from her letter to her sister Esther, written six months after the operation. It is an astonishing document, and the events of the actual operation depicted in my story are as she reported them. However, I have, for dramatic purposes, rearranged some sections and paraphrased to better suit a modern audience. The full transcript of the letter can be found on the British Library's website.

The heinous kidnapping and rape of young girls for the "virgin cure" did occur in the eighteenth and nineteenth centuries, and probably started much earlier, with documentation of it in the Renaissance. When I researched this distressing crime, to my horror I discovered that it is, in fact, still occurring to this day. It seems that in some ways humanity has not traveled very far in terms of ignorance, superstition, and crimes against children and women.

I based the appalling conditions and treatment of the women at Bothwell House on reports about the infamous York Asylum and Bedlam Hospital found in the excellent book *Bedlam* by Paul Chambers. While York and Bedlam were public hospitals, a large number of private madhouses, as they were called, were run as profitable businesses by people who often had no experience or interest in treating those living with mental illness. At this time, in the early 1800s, mental illness was seen as something that could be beaten, blistered, or leeched out of a person, and many of the "treatments" were little more than torture. The story of the women in the stables is based on a terrible case of thirteen elderly women kept every night in a small cell in York Asylum for years without amenities or anywhere to sleep and which was never cleaned out. The accumulation of feces had built up so high that the air grates were clogged. They were found more or less naked and covered from head to toe in their own waste by tenacious reformers, after being repeatedly hidden from inspectors.

Samuel Tuke is a real historical figure, and his book *Description of the Retreat*, written in 1813, provided an insight into the early asylum reform movement. He and his father founded the Retreat, an asylum initially for Quakers that became a model for a kinder and more humane treatment of people living with mental illness.

Acknowledgments

In the home corner: as ever, I thank my wonderful husband, Ron, for his unfailing support and equally unfailing roast chicken dinners. Thanks also to my dear friend Karen McKenzie and my parents, Doug and Charmaine Goodman. My dog, Buckley, is probably more hindrance than help (how many walkies do you really need in one day?) but, despite his furry demands, I love him and his company in my writing room.

In the professional corner: thanks to my brilliant agent, Jill Grinberg, and her team, who always have my back and loved Lady Gus and Lady Julia from the very start. Thanks also to the lovely Kate Seaver—I have so enjoyed our editing sessions—and the team at Berkley, including the talented cover designer Rita Frangie, Sveta Dorosheva, who created the stunning cover illustration, copyeditor extraordinaire Eileen G. Chetti, and proofreaders Lisa Davis and Isabella Pilotta Gois.

Two of the Ill-Mannered Ladies stories were submitted as part of my doctoral thesis, and so huge thanks to my advisory team, Professor Kim Wilkins and Dr. Bernadette Cochrane—I can now call myself Dr. Al.

I am also indebted to Nicola O'Shea, who is the trusted first editor of my work, and my friend Lindy Cameron, who asked for an "awesome" adventure story.

This book was written on the lands of the Bunurong People, and I wish to acknowledge them as Traditional Owners. I would also like to pay my respects to their Elders, past and present, and Aboriginal Elders of other communities.

The Benevolent Society of Ill-Mannered Ladies

ALISON GOODMAN

READERS GUIDE

Discussion Questions

1. Gus and Julia have a strong sisterly and twin bond and sometimes communicate without words. Have you ever experienced communicating without words to a close family member or friend? How important do you think body language and facial expression are when we communicate? Are you good at reading body language and facial expressions?

2. In the first case, "Till Death Us Do Part," Gus states, "Without civility there can only be chaos." Do you agree with Gus?

3. Gus and Julia are considered "on the shelf" at forty-two years old—their opinion does not seem to matter to some people nor are they seen to have anything to offer society. Do you think that kind of prejudice still exists?

4. The class system in nineteenth-century England was rigid with very little social mobility allowed. Do you think class systems operate in your world? If so, what are they and how do they operate?

5. While Gus's attraction to Lord Evan is not love at first sight, it does develop quickly. Do you think love at first sight exists? Have you ever experienced love at first sight (or a whirlwind romance)?

6. Fashion was an important part of a genteel Regency woman's life. In what ways do Gus's and Julia's choice of clothing and accessories help define their characters?

7. Coverture is the old English law that, on marriage, a woman's legal existence was merged into her husband's so that she had no legal identity of her own. All her possessions, her children, and even her body became the property of her husband. How have women's rights improved (or not improved) since those times?

8. Gus and Julia have a great deal of personal agency in the novel, and with great delight we witness them choosing to use this agency to help others. Do you think Regency women had this much agency? What factors then and now allow women the agency to live their lives as they wish?

9. Do you think Gus and Lord Evan are well suited? If so, how? What about Julia and Mr. Kent?

10. If a dating app existed in the Regency era, what would you name it?

Author Photo by Tania Jovanovic

Alison Goodman is a Melbourne-based author of historical and fantasy fiction. Her other novels include the Dark Days Club trilogy, an award-winning mix of Regency adventure and dark fantasy, and *Eon* and *Eona*, a *New York Times* bestselling fantasy duology published in twenty countries. Alison has recently completed her PhD, focusing on historical research and the Regency era, and can dance a mean English contra dance. She is fueled by coffee and roast potatoes and will travel a long way for a good scone.

CONNECT ONLINE

AlisonGoodman.com.au

AlisonGoodmanAuthor

AlisonGoodmanAuthorPage

Ready to find
your next great read?

Let us help.

Visit prh.com/nextread

Penguin
Random
House